9/87

FROM THE ASHES OF DEFEAT
THEY ROSE UP WITH HEARTS
OF DEFIANCE AND DESIRE

RIKI—Valiant in battle and as proud as the royal blood that ran in his veins, he was brave enough to defy the Pharaoh . . . but fate would test his courage in a deadlier arena—that of the heart.

MARA—Wife of Kamose, her early years as a street fighter hidden beneath fine cloth and glittering jewels, she would risk her life and her dreams for the passion of a lover's arms.

KAMOSE—Bastard son of the last Shepherd King, his obsession is to slay his father . . . but blood lust has turned this magnificent hero into a follower of a cult of cruelty and twisted desire.

MIRIAM—Beautiful daughter of the tribe of Levi, she dares to love an Egyptian with her whole heart, and her iron will is destined to become an instrument of her people's liberation.

SETH—Tempted by Babylonia's pleasures and wealth, this Child of the Lion discovers at last the secret of his birth . . . but may never finish the awesome journey back to his people and his fate.

SWORD OF GLORY

D0449920

Other Bantam Books by Peter Danielson
Ask your bookseller for the titles you have missed

CHILDREN OF THE LION
THE SHEPHERD KINGS
VENGEANCE OF THE LION
THE LION IN EGYPT
THE GOLDEN PHARAOH
LORD OF THE NILE
THE PROPHECY

Volume VIII

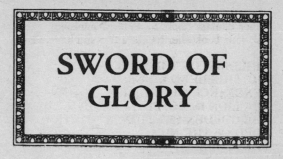

SWORD OF GLORY

PETER DANIELSON

Created by the producers of
**Wagons West, White Indian,
America 2040**, and **The Kent
Family Chronicles.**

Book Creations Inc., Canaan, NY · Lyle Kenyon Engel, Founder

BANTAM BOOKS
TORONTO · NEW YORK · LONDON · SYDNEY · AUCKLAND

SWORD OF GLORY

*A Bantam Book / published by arrangement with
Book Creations, Inc.*

Bantam edition / October 1987

*Produced by Book Creations, Inc.
Lyle Kenyon Engel, Founder*

*All rights reserved.
Copyright © 1987 by Book Creations, Inc.
Cover art copyright © 1987 by Bantam Books, Inc.
This book may not be reproduced in whole or in part, by
mimeograph or any other means, without permission.
For information address: Bantam Books, Inc.*

ISBN 0-553-26800-7

Published simultaneously in the United States and Canada

Bantam Books are published by Bantam Books, Inc. Its trademark, consisting of the words "Bantam Books" and the por-
trayal of a rooster, is Registered in U.S. Patent and Trademark
Office and in other countries. Marca Registrada. Bantam
Books, Inc., 666 Fifth Avenue, New York, New York 10103.

PRINTED IN THE UNITED STATES OF AMERICA

O   0 9 8 7 6 5 4 3 2 1

Cast of Characters
CHILDREN OF THE LION: Volume Eight
SWORD OF GLORY

Children of the Lion

Teti—First woman armorer of the clan
Seth—Teti's cousin; a genius on a quest
Tuya—Seth's mother
Sinuhe—Orphaned son of Teti's twin brother, Ketan
Neku-re—Teti's son

Foreigners living in Egypt's Black Lands

Apophis—King of the Hai invaders
Rasmik—Apophis's general

Freedom Fighters of Egypt's Red Lands

Kamose—King and Apophis's bastard son
Mara—Queen; Protector of the Habiru
Amram, Jochebed, Levi, Miriam—Habiru slaves
Isesi—Rebel leader; Miriam's lover
Baliniri—Vizier; Tuya's lover
Ah-Hotep—Baliniri's wife; former queen
Riki—Kamose's general; Teti's husband; Ah-Hotep's son
Amasis, Makare—Secret cult leaders
Tchabu—Seer

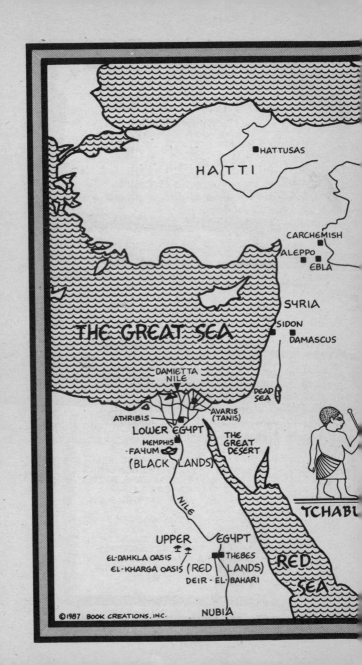

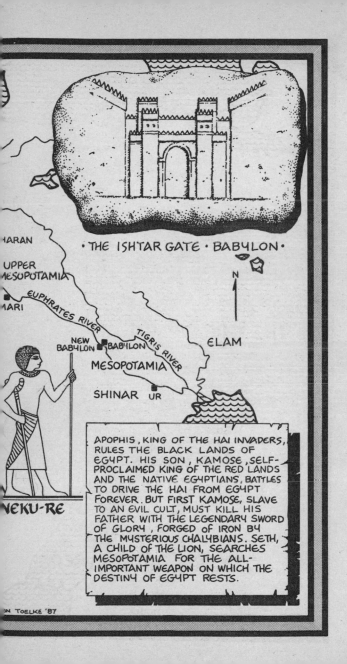

· THE ISHTAR GATE · BABYLON ·

HARAN

UPPER
MESOPOTAMIA

MARI

EUPHRATES RIVER

NEW
BABYLON BABYLON

TIGRIS RIVER

ELAM

MESOPOTAMIA

SHINAR UR

NEKU-RE

N

APOPHIS, KING OF THE HAI INVADERS,
RULES THE BLACK LANDS OF
EGYPT. HIS SON, KAMOSE, SELF-
PROCLAIMED KING OF THE RED LANDS
AND THE NATIVE EGYPTIANS, BATTLES
TO DRIVE THE HAI FROM EGYPT
FOREVER. BUT FIRST KAMOSE, SLAVE
TO AN EVIL CULT, MUST KILL HIS
FATHER WITH THE LEGENDARY SWORD
OF GLORY, FORGED OF IRON BY
THE MYSTERIOUS CHALYBIANS. SETH,
A CHILD OF THE LION, SEARCHES
MESOPOTAMIA FOR THE ALL-
IMPORTANT WEAPON ON WHICH THE
DESTINY OF EGYPT RESTS.

ON TOELKE '87

Prologue

The wind stirred the fronds of the tall palms and sighed softly in the night sky. The campfire had settled from a bright blaze to a flickering red glow in the cool of evening. Tall and gaunt, the elderly Teller of Tales had stood for many minutes looking at the small gathering at the remote oasis. He presented an imposing figure. His dark eyes were alert and piercing, and his long white hair and beard flowed over his robes.

The number of the faithful tonight was not many; numerous others had already pushed on for the next watering place and would now be making their way across the familiar track under the cold light of a baleful full moon.

He listened for a moment as the wind beat the waters of the small pond beside the fire. Then he stepped forward, and there was a great expectant intake of breath from the assembled listeners—then a sigh, then silence.

"In the name of God," he began, "the merciful, the benevolent . . ."

1

As the sharp old eyes scanned the group, a half smile, all-knowing and wise, played on his thin lips. "Hear now," he said, "the tales of the Children of the Lion, the men of no tribe, and of their ceaseless wanderings among the lands beside the Great Sea.

"You have heard how civil war came to the lands beside the Nile after the Hai Shepherd Kings invaded Egypt and how the sons of Jacob of Canaan suffered, in bondage to the usurper Apophis in the Egyptian delta. You have heard how Apophis sailed up the Nile to lay siege to mighty Thebes, only to be driven downriver when a new king of upper Egypt rose to challenge his power—Kamose, Apophis's natural son, who seers had prophesied would drive Apophis and the Hai invaders out of Egypt forever."

The heads nodded, and there was a murmur of recollection—which was abruptly silenced when the old man held up one bony, long-fingered hand.

"You have heard how the Children of the Lion involved themselves in the bitter fight to drive the Hai from Egypt. Ben-Hadad's son, Seth, wisest of the wise, set out for the far North, seeking the mysterious Chalybians, guardians of the secret of the making of true iron. The destiny of Egypt itself would hinge upon the success of Seth's great quest, for the seers had prophesied that Kamose could vanquish the Hai only with the legendary Sword of Glory, made of iron by a Child of the Lion."

Now his voice rose. "You have heard of Teti, the first woman to master the trade of the Children of the Lion, armorers since the earliest days. After the death of her lover, Netru, Teti withdrew to a desert oasis to raise an army of fierce warrior-women—half-Egyptian, half-Nubian—to guard the desert trade routes and prevent the Hai from attacking Thebes from the west.

"You have also learned how Riki of Thebes, once a child of the streets now turned general in Kamose's army, discovered the secret of his birth—the bastard get of Queen Ah-Hotep by the mighty soldier Baba of El-Kab. You have heard how Riki went to Teti's desert fortress and wooed and won her."

The faces leaned forward in the fading light as the wind rose and sang in the palms. The old man's voice took on power: "Now imagine a time three years hence, when many threads of destiny come together at last. The Egyptian insurgents under Kamose, king of the Red Lands, have fought their way into the domain of Apophis, king of the Black Lands, and now control Memphis, the Fayum, Lisht, and a full quarter of the delta from which they had been driven a generation earlier.

"In the far North Seth nears the magic moment when he will learn not only the secret of the smelting of iron but the secret of the Children of the Lion themselves!

"In the delta the sons of Jacob, in their darkest moment, learn of the impending birth of their own deliverer, who will lead them out of bondage!

"And, at the very edge of victory, Kamose's rebels will find their strength sapped by a great and subtle poison, which promises a worse defeat than Apophis could ever impose!"

There was a great groan of apprehension from the crowd. These were ominous words indeed, words they had no wish to hear.

But the old man's voice cut through the dark mood that lay aborning among them. His arms spread wide, and his voice changed to a tone of hope.

"But out of the darkness comes light!" he promised. "The blacker the night, the brighter the dawn! Hear me! Pure things will grow among noxious weeds! Weakness will breed strength! Forgotten purpose will be remembered, and goals once obscure will become crystal clear! From the ruins of a great land will come the weapon to cut the bonds that fetter the just and the righteous!

"Hear now of how that hope was born anew! Hear of how enlightenment came to the Children of the Lion! Hear now, my children, of the Sword of Glory, and how it came to be forged and brought home to the lands beside the mighty Nile."

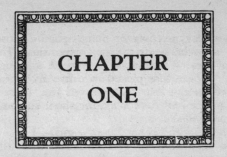

CHAPTER ONE

Upper Mesopotamia

I

The tavern, the largest in all of Mari, occupied the entire upper floor and the terraces of the most important commercial building in that ancient city. Latticed arbors shaded the outdoor terraces against the steady sun, which beat down even in late afternoon. In the distance one could hear the sounds of flutes and kitharas, of shawms and hand drums. Between the tables on the northern terrace, within earshot of Seth's corner table, a bored dancer, naked except for a cincher of faience beads and the twinkle of gold rings on fingers and toes, gyrated aimlessly to the beat of the drum, her belly undulating mechanically. From behind her came a roar of sudden male laughter and the sound of crockery falling and smashing.

"It's not even dusk yet," Seth's guest said, turning back to his own table. His eyes—dark brown, almost black, unreadable—caught Seth's and held them for a moment. "My apologies. My people are much given to the grape."

"No apology necessary," Seth replied. "Those drunkards we've been watching are my own companions. The big one is Anubis of Bast. When sober, he can lift a young bullock on his back. He was handpicked by a friend of mine to be my bodyguard on this trip. Let me tell you, there's no better man to have at your back in a tight place. The other . . ." He sighed and smiled.

"The one with his hand on the girl's—?"

"The very one. His name is Khet. To tell the truth, I find his presence on this expedition a trifle harder to explain. What can I say? He makes me laugh. I used to be such a terrible sobersides." He watched as the girl stopped dancing, turned, slapped Khet full across the face, and flounced away, ample buttocks quivering in indignation. He chuckled at the comic expression of surprise on Khet's moon face. "Now that I have finally learned to laugh, I'm reluctant to give it up. Before I had discovered frivolity, I was not fully human—I studied the habits of all the known animals of Egypt when I lived there. I never found anything that corresponded in any way to laughter."

The stranger's dark brow rose. "You're a man who observes life, then? And reflects upon it?"

Seth sat up and reached for the tall amphora on the table to pour wine. "Everything is observation and reflection," he said thoughtfully. "Or so it has been in my life until now. I think that, however belatedly, I am beginning to enter the sphere of action. Hence this present quest." He interrupted himself to lean over the terrace wall and look right and left down the street below. "I wonder what's keeping Criton," he said. "Well, never mind. Gudea, the caravan leader, directed me to you. He said, 'The man you want to see is Marduk-nasir.' Try as he might, he could not put a name to your line of work."

The dark-eyed man leaned back in his chair against the wall. One broad hand toyed idly with a strand of his thick black beard, which was cut in a style Seth had not otherwise seen in Mari. "Call me, if you like, a broker in information. No, please. Put your purse away. I sell nothing in this line. Let us say my money comes from an . . . important business I own. Information, I barter—your information for mine. Yes, you have probably come to the right man. If I do not know the information you seek, I may well know the man who does know it."

He allowed Seth to pour wine into his bowl, his eyes following a detachment of Mariite soldiers who had just entered by the northern stairs. "Thank you," he said, lifting the bowl. "Let me compliment you on your command of our tongue. I gather you're new to us, yet your accent is accurate, and your speech quite fluent. You take to it as though . . . *hmmm*. If I'm not being too personal, do I perhaps detect a smidgen of Shinarian blood, sir? That nose is worthy of a Babylonian."

Seth smiled. Already the man was getting information, easily, gracefully—and without giving up any so far himself! He laughed softly. "My earliest known ancestors came from there. Only my mother was Egyptian. My father's side came from Babylon, Haran, and Canaan. Have you ever heard—"

There was a commotion from across the terrace. Both men turned to look. There seemed to be an argument between Seth's drunken friends and the locals. Seth shrugged and started again. "Have you ever heard of a dynasty of armorers called the Children of the Lion?"

The reaction was instantaneous and startling. The dark eyes narrowed; there was the soft hiss of abruptly drawn breath. "Pardon me, sir," Marduk-nasir said. "You said 'Children of the Lion'?"

"You know of us, then? Belsunu of Babylon? Ahuni, his lost son who was raised by the armorer Zakir?" He smiled, seeing the recognition in the man's eyes.

"Do I know of you?" the man asked incredulously. "I was *raised* on those names. Ahuni armed the sons of Abraham so well that they turned away an invasion by the Four Kings. Kirta of Haran and his sons Shobai, the blind armorer, and little Hadad, the hero of the siege of Haran, are names every child of the northern lands knows. You are of this famous line?" There was the faintest touch of disbelief in his tone. "There was a mark the Children of the Lion all bore. . . ."

"Yes. I bear it." Seth's eyes darted to the northern corner of the terrace, where several men were now shouting at each other. He could see Khet, standing, weaving drunkenly, and waving his arms. "My mark is less distinct than some. The paw print of the lion is not so pronounced as that of my father, Ben-Hadad, but it is in the same place."

"Ben-Hadad? Then you're the grandson of the hero of—"

"Haran. Yes. My father was trained by Shobai. We both served, at different times, as advisers to Baliniri."

This caught Marduk-nasir just as he was lifting the bowl to his lips. He shot a sharp-eyed look at Seth and put the bowl down. "Baliniri of the siege of Mari? General under the great Hammurabi?"

"Yes," Seth confirmed, chuckling. He had to raise his voice a bit now over the shouting. "I thought that name would get a rise out of you. He's vizier of Upper Egypt now. Leader of the revolt against the Hai." Then the thought struck him that there was something foreign about Marduk-nasir, too. The accent, the style of hair and beard—he was not native to Mari. But where was he from?

"Go on, please," Marduk-nasir urged. "If you had any thought of impressing me, I must say you've succeeded. Tell me what you want and why you've come here."

Seth frowned at the scuffle that was going on across the terrace. Khet was being harassed by three big-boned Mariite soldiers, yet for some reason Anubis sat doing nothing. "Well," he said, "you've heard about the new king in Egypt? Kamose? The war against Kamose's father, Apophis, the Hai overlord of the delta?"

"Please enlighten me," Marduk-nasir requested, settling back in his chair.

"Kamose's army has retaken Memphis and the Fayum, the breadbasket of the southern lands, from Apophis, in spite of the fact that Apophis had fattened his army with thousands of mercenaries from all around the Great Sea. Also, for some unknown reason, King Nehsi of Nubia refused to send troops to aid Kamose's rebels. Kamose's armies have driven Apophis's front line far back into the delta itself."

"Kamose must be quite a warrior."

"Yes, but he also has good people behind him. Baliniri, on the home front as vizier, and Riki, Kamose's childhood friend, a mighty general taught his trade by Baliniri himself. Then there's Teti, my cousin, the first female ever to bear the birthmark of the Children of the Lion. She is married to Riki. Teti is the army's head armorer, and for the past three years I've been studying with her. I have some promise. We've got a good staff, all right."

"Lout! Oaf! Son of a dog!" The words came in the Mariite speech. Seth whirled to see a soldier draw his sword. Khet, standing before him, danced suddenly backward, only to fall into the hard hands of another Mariite soldier. Khet thrashed about, cursing. Behind them Seth could see Anubis slowly, almost sleepily, struggle to his feet.

Seth scowled. With a sigh he tried to continue. "It seems there was a prophecy, some time back, that Apophis would be killed and the Hai driven out of Egypt by his own son wielding an iron sword."

"An *iron* sword?" Marduk-nasir echoed. "But that's quite unlikely, isn't it? Everyone knows that the Hittites control the secret of the smelting of iron." There was something odd about his tone, although Seth could not say what it was. "The Hittites do not share this secret with anyone." He would have continued, but there were the clang of metal against metal and scattered curses. "Pardon me, my friend," he said to Seth. "There are six Mariite soldiers against two of your men. Hadn't you better—"

"Six to two. Not bad odds," Seth remarked, "when Anubis is in good form. Unfortunately he's had a bit to drink. But there! Did you see the way he handled that fellow?"

"Gods!" Marduk-nasir sputtered. "He bent a bronze sword double! It's hanging like a necklace around the neck of a Mari guardsman!"

"That's why Anubis was sent along," Seth explained calmly. "To continue, I learned something about iron and the Hai a while back. In the first place, it's not true that only the Hittites make iron. Kirta, my great-grandfather, was taught the procedure in the Greek isles. The Nubian armorer Karkara of Sado taught the skill to Teti, and she taught me. *I've* made iron," he said with pride. "I think my talents lie elsewhere, but I do know the process."

He looked hard into the eyes of Marduk-nasir, who suddenly realized what was in Seth's mind. Seth felt confident that he had come to the right man.

Seth hesitated. "The Hai," he explained slowly, keeping his voice down despite the din, "were once called the Shepherd Kings. They began their terrible migration from Hayastan, near Lake Van. They told the world they were forced to migrate because of a great drought. But there was no drought. They lied to us all." There was a loud crash off to his left, but he forced himself to keep his eyes locked with Marduk-nasir's. "The reason they left their homeland was—"

Marduk-nasir's hand snaked out, and the broad hand clutched Seth's forearm. "Please," he advised. "There are things best not spoken of where all ears can hear. You have learned something few men know." He ducked as a piece of crockery, thrown from some distance away, flew past his head. "Your comrades are fighting off-duty guardsmen over there. In a moment their row will attract the attention of the on-duty ones. We should not be here when that happens." He lifted one dark brow again and made a wry face.

"I agree," Seth said, standing. "Ah! Here's Criton coming. Meet me here when the crier calls the third hour, will you? Criton! Over here!" He clapped Marduk-nasir on the arm. "I'll tell you everything you want to know about the Egyptian situation." He turned to welcome the tall Greek coming toward them. "Criton! I think we're needed at the far end of the room!"

As the two moved away, Marduk-nasir hesitated at the top of the stairs, looking after them. Seth was tall but gave little impression of being a very physical person. He had the look and manner of a man of the mind—and a rich one at that, accustomed to having others do the hard labor for him. Yet the handshake he had given Marduk-nasir at their meeting had been powerful, with the hard, callused hand of a metalworker.

He thought, *Perhaps he's telling the truth about being a Child of the Lion.* Well, he would find out about that soon enough, and before letting out any secrets.

He focused on the tall Greek walking beside Seth as the two approached the brawlers. The curly-haired man Seth had called Criton was well-muscled, of aristocratic carriage, and looked like a man who could take care of himself, confident and reserved.

Yes! Why, just look at the way the Greek, his weapon still sheathed, disarmed the big Mariite soldier and, in one fluid motion, took him by the body armor and swung him around, ramming his head against the wall! And Seth: Who would have imagined the young man being able to handle a sword like that? He looked like a fencing instructor!

Marduk-nasir, with one foot still on the top stair, winced as the giant Anubis lifted two men by their body armor, his giant hands gripping the leather straps like threads, and slammed their heads together with a sickening crunch. As he did, the fat clown Khet, a drunken grin on his moon face, lowered his bullet head and barreled, crown first, into the belly of a towering Mariite guard, driving him back into the wall with a crash and knocking the breath out of him. Unsatisfied, the fat man picked up a half-full crock of wine and smashed it over his adversary's head, splashing the walls with wine. He touched a thoughtful finger to his fallen enemy's head, then brought it to his mouth and licked it. Then he shook his head, indicating his opinion of the wine.

Chuckling to himself, Marduk-nasir beat a hasty retreat. *The third hour*, he thought to himself. *At the same table.*

II

The altercation ended quickly. Seth, in a maneuver he had developed himself, disarmed his opponent with a deft flip of the hand. The sword spun across the room and harmlessly stuck, point down, in a tabletop. Seth feinted a stab at the soldier's gut but then stepped back to let the wide-eyed, frightened guardsman slip quickly to the staircase and disappear, leaving his weapon behind.

Seth shrugged, imagining the tongue-lashing the guardsman would get when he returned to the barracks unarmed. He turned and watched Criton, always the gentleman, help his fallen foe to his feet and knock the dust off the guardsman's soiled tunic.

"Are you all right? Very well, then. Off with you." He turned to Seth as the soldier moved away, holding his aching head. "How about you? Are you all in one piece?"

Seth smiled. "I'm fine. Look at our two serious drinkers."

Criton stood watching as the giant Anubis, who had one Mariite under his arm, his neck encircled by a mighty fist, swung at a second soldier and caught him over one eye. As the Mariite fell to his knees, groggy, the man under Anubis's arm struggled free and sank his teeth into the giant's thigh. Anubis bellowed in pain and cuffed the offender on the side of the head. The blow knocked the man over a table, upsetting a jar of wine.

Khet made a desperate dive and caught the jar before it spilled. His great round face broke into a comical grin as he tipped up the jar to drink. But the remaining two Mariites made for him, tackling him from behind. His feet knocked out from under him, Khet spluttered, spraying out the wine, and fell back atop one of the Mariites, knocking the breath out of him. The other man's grasp was torn loose by the fall, and he stumbled forward—right into the mighty hands of Anubis, who lifted him face-high and roared like a lion. The soldier fainted dead away.

Khet climbed to his feet and patted his round paunch. "There are occasions when it pays to be overweight." He looked down and saw the wine jar he had dropped, and the happy grin fell from his face. "Oh, no! That was the best wine we've had all day!" He paid no attention as the man he had fallen on escaped behind him. "Innkeeper! More wine!"

Only now did the proprietor poke a cautious face out from behind a half-open door. Behind him the dancer glowered at the four of them, her ripe beauty covered by a dark robe. "The damage!" the innkeeper moaned. "The damage to my—"

"To your reputation? Not to worry, my friend." Seth stepped forward, took the innkeeper by the arm, and spoke in low, reassuring tones. "Do you think we would stand by and allow these guardsmen to arrest you for selling wine made in another city and smuggled past the local monopoly without proper payment of customs?" He looked into the innkeeper's eye and knew he had scored a direct hit. "Fear not, my friend. Your secret is safe with us. And after our little encounter with these government lackeys, I doubt they'll have the guts to turn you in, as they have threatened to do."

"But—"

"There, now. Here's a little something for your trouble. And would you be so good as to share this"—there was the clink of a second group of coins—"with the musicians and the dancer? Tell them we consider them true artists, worthy of the custom of the kings." His smile was an unmistakable dismissal. He turned to his friends and beckoned them to follow.

"Can this be the same Seth?" Criton asked quizzically. "Your tongue drips oil. Are you quite sure you've no Greek blood in you?"

"Not a drop," Seth answered with a laugh, while Khet and Anubis stumped down the stairs behind the two of them. "Of course, as I told our new friend, Marduk-nasir, my earliest ancestors came from Shinar, and a Babylonian can talk a Greek out of his shadow when the moon's in the right phase."

"Outprattle, perhaps," the Greek said as they stepped out into the dusky streets and Khet and Anubis veered toward the well. "But outtalk? Never!" His tone carried an air of affectionate raillery. "Changing the subject, congratulations on that new parry of yours. I saw you put it to the test. I tried it myself, but it's not quite in my wrist yet."

Khet and Anubis stood by the well; as Seth and Criton watched, Anubis upended a full bucket of frigid water on the fat man, who let out a shrill howl. Seth grinned tolerantly, then said to Criton, "I made an appointment with Marduk-nasir for later this evening. That's why I tipped our innkeeper back there a bit more than he had coming."

"Then Marduk-nasir is worth further conversation?"

"I think he's our man. He's quite knowledgeable about things he has little right to know, and for some reason I don't think he's originally from Mari. I think he's from somewhere north of here."

Criton turned his curly head toward Seth. "Oh? North of here, you say? Perhaps—"

Seth shushed him with an upraised finger. "Possibly. I'll tell you when we're indoors again. Meanwhile, what did you learn?"

"Come along," Criton said. "That cold water looks good. It's been a long day, and this place is dusty." They took the bucket from Anubis's hands, and the Greek splashed his face.

"Well?" Seth asked.

"Ah, yes." The Greek sat down on the big flagstone ledge beside the well and dried his face on the hem of his tunic. "Well, we're passing through here at a time of some danger, it would appear. The king of Mari is a vassal of Samsi-ditana, as you know. All these cities along the trade route are. So far the great king has ruled with a light hand and is generally viewed as a benign leader."

"I wonder if the same applies closer to Babylon. We're a long way from Samsi-ditana's palace."

"Oh, the closer you get to Babylon, the greater the respect and love in which he's held. To hear the locals talk, it's a sane society with just laws and prosperity—no poverty or oppression." A touch of cynicism entered his tone. "As we all know, the gods seldom allow *that* sort of thing to go on for long. And sure enough, there's trouble brewing."

"Revolt?" Seth asked. "An uprising of the vassal kings?"

"Much worse than that," Criton said, scowling. "It's the Hittites. Their king feels that he has to show his valor by taking on the greatest kingdom in the northern world. He's marched on the western cities and has already taken Carchemish and Haran."

Seth's brows rose. "Taken two old Shepherd strongholds! That's news!"

"I have more news for you than that. There hasn't been a Hai overlord in either city in ten or twenty years. Hai domination up this way is largely a thing of the past. If Kamose can drive them north out of Egypt, Apophis will find few allies in Syria to take him in."

"Who is this Hittite king?"

"Mursilis. And he's a real bully, no doubt about it. The only reason he hasn't put Mari under siege already is that he came down with a fever, forcing a halt to the march just outside Haran."

"Has he declared war on Babylon?"

"Not openly. Carchemish and Haran, mind you, were free cities since the Hai moved out. Now they're Hittite vassals. As he is nursed back to health, Mursilis is thinking out strategy for the Babylonian campaign. My guess is that he'll use Mari as a test of Samsi-ditana's power and patience. If he takes the city and Samsi-ditana does nothing, he'll interpret this as a sign of weakness and press forward."

"Doesn't Samsi-ditana take the threat seriously? After all, we're talking about the Hittites."

"Yes. The only nation in the world with iron weaponry. Yet Samsi-ditana is used to situations in which no one challenges his authority. Thus he persists in acting as though Mursilis were some petty tyrant squatting atop a dunghill and squeaking about defiance. Well, it's not our affair. Our business lies elsewhere."

"No, but we'll have to change our route on the way back through this area if Mari's overrun by Hittites." He yawned and stretched. "I'm getting hungry. It might be time to shovel some food into our two brawlers over there, if only to absorb the wine they've taken in today." He glanced affectionately at their two companions in the middle of the little square. Khet stood on a large flat stone and examined a cut over his giant comrade's eye.

Criton frowned. "One of these days they're going to land
us in some real trouble."

"Yes," Seth agreed, "and they're going to fight our way
out of it, too." His tone became more thoughtful. "I've grown
very fond of them—and of you too. I've enjoyed the days of
our journey more than any time of my life. I never really had
friends before. I was always too withdrawn, reserved, an
intellectual loner. I never laughed—although I'm sure others
laughed at me from time to time because of my unworldli-
ness. I never told jokes or listened to them. I never . . ." His
voice trailed off, and there was a faraway look in his eyes.

"You were going to say," Criton suggested helpfully,
"that you've never fallen in love?"

"Well, now . . . I think I came close once, just before we
left. When was that? Gods! It must be the better part of three
years ago. I . . . I had a little affair with Aset. It was my first
experience with a woman—just as it was hers with a man—
and I'm afraid I bungled it. We quarreled, and I did not see
her again before I left."

"And now you regret this?" Criton asked.

"Sometimes. Now, don't you go looking down that long
Greek nose at me, you supercilious philosopher, you. Aset is
a marvelous girl, brave and likable. She is the sister of Isesi,
who's the leader of the secret resistance to the Hai in the
Egyptian delta, and she herself has done very valorous things
for the cause. She and I . . . well, we found ourselves at loose
ends and were thrown together, you might say. But just
then, I found myself unable to adjust to the idea of having to
consider another person's thoughts and feelings every time I
turned around. I must have seemed very self-centered." He
sighed. "And I'm sure I was. I've always lived this self-
involved life, locked inside the prison of this head of mine."

"Maybe you're just a late bloomer."

"Maybe. But there comes a time to grow, to expand, to
learn more of the world, to be committed. And this quest of
ours has done more for me in that direction than anything I
remember." The faraway look came into his eye again. "From
time to time I wonder how my friends are doing back in
Egypt; whether Kamose and Apophis have met in the field
yet, or whether my cousin, Teti, has given Riki a child. I
wonder how Mother's marriage to my old tutor Kedar is
working out."

He seemed about to continue in this reminiscent vein,

but something in the great Temple of Dagan, which towered over the row of dwellings that bordered the far side of the square, caught his eye. "Criton, look over there. The Mariites could give our Egyptian architects lessons. The more I look at the buildings here, the more I think that our people don't understand simple mud-brick construction at all. Look at the pattern the bricks make in the arches!"

Criton frowned. "I don't see—"

"There! The pendentives! Your people and mine would handle that section of the wall, where the arches come in, by introducing wooden beams. This, of course, adds to the danger of fire and leads to problems with rotting after the rains hit. These people don't have ready supplies of first-growth hardwood, so they have to make do with mud brick. But look what they do with it! They've conquered gravity, and with the simplest materials in the world! Notice how the pitch and stress have been changed. Why, if a man had the time, money, building materials, and the labor to work with this principle—"

Criton's expression, still visible in the dim light, showed his mild surprise. "How has it escaped my attention," he asked wryly, "that you're really an architect at heart?"

Seth laughed. "I have no idea what my area of specialization will be. But as a child I loved to play with blocks, making buildings and play cities."

"I see. And so now you're thinking of abandoning our quest for the elusive secret of the Chalybians—"

Instantly Seth's hand shot out and stopped Criton's lips. "Shhh!" he warned. "The walls have ears."

He removed his hand. Criton folded his arms over his big chest and looked at him, one brow raised. "All right," he whispered. "But that is why we've been wandering from city to city all this time, looking for people who can help us penetrate into a country that seems to be the most closely guarded secret in the world. We've been fluttering like timid little butterflies on the edges of this region for three years, and I keep wondering why we don't just take the plunge and—"

"*Nobody* ever enters the land of the"—Seth mouthed the word "*Chalybians*"—"and gets out alive. Their only trade is with the Hittites. Even diplomatic representatives from Samsi-ditana's imperial court are turned away. Mind you, these are people who were capable of driving over a million Hai from their lands."

As the light died, Criton looked into his friend's face searchingly. "If no one leaves their lands alive, what makes you think we're going to be the exceptions?"

III

The moon was large and full when Seth left his companions at their lodgings and made his way through the curving city streets to the inn where he was to meet Marduk-nasir. The cold white orb above had a malevolent look, and the light it cast on the warren of streets and alleys had a bizarre luminescent tinge, so the shadows were, if anything, a bit darker than usual and full of imagined horrors.

Seth had repeatedly pondered the apparent relation between the phases of the moon and human behavior. As a man whose whole life had been ruled by reason, he tended to reject many of the facile statements made by astrologers and soothsayers; yet there was no denying that when the moon was full, he was quite conscious of being in the domain of the irrational. He himself felt a little mad, a bit hysterical, and believed under the right combination of circumstances he could quite easily run amuck, disgrace himself, or commit a crime.

And what, he asked himself, did he feel on this particular evening? He knew that this was a night of destiny, when something strange and rare was going to happen to him. Various strands of fate might cross to lead him onto a new and radically different path, great things might be revealed to him, and his life would be irrevocably changed forever.

A chill wind raised goosebumps on the back of his neck. The evening's conversation with Marduk-nasir would, he felt, bring the end of his long quest, his entrée to the Chalybian homelands.

Only three years ago, he had learned that the Shepherd Kings, who had migrated south from Hayastan to settle in and eventually conquer the Egyptian delta, had been driven from their homeland by a mysterious race that lived between them and the Caucasus Mountains. This race, the Chalybes, had been greatly outnumbered by the Hai, but the Shepherds had run away in abject fear of the iron weapons borne by the Chalybians, whom they considered evil sorcerers.

Seth's inquiries had established also that the Hittites from Hatti, the only iron-wielding country in the world, had themselves never mastered the smelting of the black metal. The smiths who manned the forges of Hatti were instead members of a carefully guarded secret cult from Chalybes, who shared their secrets with nobody and only leased their services to the Hittites. They perceived themselves, or so Seth's informant said, as high priests of the religion of iron rather than as professionals who exchanged services for money. And their homeland was never successfully penetrated by anyone.

Now, after three years of searching in vain through Tyre, Damascus, Sidon, and other cities, he was getting closer to actually meeting and talking with one of these mysterious Chalybians—Marduk-nasir. A caravan leader named Gudea near the ruins of vanished Ebla had told Seth about a man in Mari who might have an answer to his questions. Gudea's trip had paid off so far: For the first time, Seth had found in Marduk-nasir a man who knew more about the Hai and Chalybians than Seth himself. Tonight he would learn just how much more.

Seth was convinced that the Hai would be driven out of Egypt only when Kamose, fulfilling the famous prophecy concerning him, confronted his father on the battlefield and killed him—with a Chalybian sword.

Chalybian iron was the only thing in the world guaranteed to arouse fear in the still-potent Hai warriors.

Suddenly his mood changed. *You're kidding yourself,* he thought. *The war back home may be over already, and Apophis may well be dead and Kamose ruling over Black Lands and Red Lands. You're in this for the adventure and because you believe that the Chalybians' secret is tied in with your own destiny. Chalybes is the crossroads where the choice you make will change your life forever.*

Drawing his cloak about him, he increased his pace, heart pounding, mind churning wildly.

Marduk-nasir was waiting for him at the same table in the western corner of the inn. But as Seth approached,

Marduk-nasir stood and motioned the young man closer. "Greetings," said the northerner. "I've reserved a private room where we can talk. Come with me, please." Seth's back stiffened. A trick, perhaps? He remained alert as he followed the dark-eyed man down a corridor to a room where Marduk-nasir barred the door behind them.

"This is more secure," he said, then pointed to chairs, a table, a modest offering of wine, bread, olives, and a cheese round with a long knife. "Food? Drink? No? Then we get down to business." He sat, unsmiling, and looked Seth steadily in the eye. "Forget telling me about Egypt. I have access to a network of spies that provides me with everything I need to know. You have not been in Egypt in three years; my spies were at the courts of Apophis and Kamose three weeks ago. I should hear from them shortly. Tell me instead about yourself."

Seth sat, wide-eyed, looking at him. "Me?" he said, caught short for a change. "I've told you. I'm the son of—"

"Show me the birthmark," Marduk-nasir demanded.

Seth stood, drew his garment aside, and showed the red blotch on his lower back, just above the kidney. "My father's mark was more distinct, as I told you. A lion's paw print—"

"I know what the mark of the Sons of the Lion—and, I gather, at least one Daughter as well—looks like, my young friend. And yes, I now accept the fact of your membership in the dynastic line of succession, if only for the sake of argument. Now tell me who you are. What kind of person are you? Why are you here? Why are you not still in Egypt, fighting the Hai? Tell me everything."

Seth blinked. But he recognized the tactic. "You put me at a disadvantage, keep me off balance. I used to do that to people," he said, sitting down again. "I was the son of a disappointed man. My father, Ben-Hadad, never recovered from having found out that my mother had had an affair with the vizier Baliniri." He watched the bearded man's dark brow shoot skyward. "He'd also been passed over in favor of my cousin when an armorer was needed for an important army expedition to Nubia. My father had been counting on that appointment, and it was more than he could take."

"How did this affect you?"

"My father treated me as if I'd been Baliniri's bastard. I became withdrawn, and for years people thought I was an idiot. But then Mother found a wonderful old teacher named Kedar, who took me as a pupil and declared that I was the

greatest genius he had ever encountered." He stated the fact
without vanity or embarrassment. "For all practical purposes
Kedar raised me, not my father."

"Go on." Marduk-nasir settled back against the wall and
studied Seth intently.

"By my teens I was sort of an absentminded philosopher
in the markets, answering anyone's questions about anything
but forgetting where he put his own sandals. If I hadn't been
born rich, I would probably have starved to death out of
sheer inattention."

"And some time back you changed? Because you do not
now seem unable to cope with life."

"It may have been the war, or . . . it's hard to say. There
comes a time when you're ready for a change, as if you'd
spent years in a cocoon and had metamorphosed into something totally different."

"This is true."

"I got involved. I brought my cousin back into the world:
She'd gone off into the desert to live a hermit's life, surrounded by a fierce band of loyal warrior-women trained by
Ebana, mother of King Nehsi of Nubia and founder of a
women's army called—"

"I know of the Black Wind," he interrupted. "My spies
were at the battle of El-Kab. I know your cousin lost her
valiant young lover, and Karkara comforted her. I later learned
he had offered to teach her the smelting of iron."

Seth found it was his turn to lean back against the wall in
the narrow room. His mind raced wildly.

Marduk-nasir smiled and continued. "Karkara taught Teti
how to make iron. She later taught you. But neither of you
has yet used this knowledge to strengthen Kamose's army.
Oh, you've made a few iron swords, to be sure. But you
haven't made weapons for the whole army. Why not?"

"I . . . don't know."

"And if you were to learn the secret of *perfect* iron—the
iron of the Chalybes, which is as much better than your own
product as yours is better than bronze—then what? Would
you then arm Kamose?" The words bit deep. "If you had so
dangerous a secret, what would stop you from using it to
build a position of power for yourself?"

"How can you know what is in my mind?" Seth said, his
brain reeling. "How can you know about Karkara? About

Teti? About me?" But then a single blinding thought came into his mind and left him gasping. "Karkara . . ."

"Yes," said Marduk-nasir.

"*Karkara* was your spy."

"Yes."

"Karkara was a—a Chalybian!"

"Yes, even though he led people to believe that he had been born in Nubian lands."

Seth shook his head, hoping to clear his mind. "I think I need a drink of wine." He poured himself a bowl and drained it. He offered it to his companion, who shook his head, and then poured for himself again. "Karkara taught the secret to Teti."

"He taught the first degree to Teti. There are other degrees."

"Teti—was she of the . . . the Chalybian . . . what do you call it? The cult?"

"No. She did not stay with it long enough. She was badly shaken up by the death of Netru, her lover. She went off into the desert with her education unfinished. Every man finds his level. And, apparently, every woman."

Seth drank again and wiped his mouth. "Marduk-nasir, can you tell me about my ancestors? Belsunu came from Babylon."

"Yes. He was raised by his mother. He did not know his father, who died when Belsunu was hardly more than a baby."

"He's the earliest one we know. There are legends about the sons of the First Man, and how one of them killed the other. The killer's name was Cain, and he was the first to work metal. When he murdered his brother in a fit of anger, a mark was put on him, which would keep all men from touching him. This was our family story about how we were always able to pass all borders to sell arms and the art of making arms."

"It makes a pretty story," Marduk-nasir said. "I have no idea if it is true."

"But anything you can tell me about my family would be gratefully received."

There was no answer for a time. Then Marduk-nasir leaned forward, poured himself a bowl of wine, and sipped it thoughtfully. "You have not asked how I know about the mark of Cain, know what it is supposed to look like, know enough to certify whether you are a Child of the Lion, as your mother claimed, or a get of Baliniri's."

Seth stared.

Marduk-nasir stood. He drew his garment aside, turned. Prominent on his back, over the kidney, was a perfect lion's paw.

Seth's gasp was audible.

"*You're* a Child of the Lion, yourself!" Seth sputtered. He was dizzy with the new knowledge. "You!"

Marduk-nasir sat back down. "That would be one way of putting it."

Seth continued to stare, openmouthed. "Is there another way to put it?"

"I am a Chalybian," Marduk-nasir said. "I am an adept of the thirtieth degree. As such I can initiate a beginner and at my discretion advance a pupil through the steps of the rituals and teach him up to the twenty-ninth degree. Forget your plan to enter Chalybes. There is no Chalybes. Or Chalybes is everywhere. The bulk of Chalybians cannot make iron and are adept at nothing. They simply want to be left alone. Only the Grand Lodge, which goes wherever a member goes, controls the mighty secret you seek. And you can enter the Grand Lodge only at the discretion of a brother member of a higher degree, and you can leave it only by death. But first you must prove some things about yourself." His voice softened. "You have proven them to my satisfaction. I will teach you."

Seth let out a befuddled sigh. "I can't get over it. You, a Child of the Lion!"

Marduk-nasir waited a beat. "You could say that," he agreed again. "Or you could say that you, my friend, are a Chalybian. As was Belsunu, whether he knew it or not. Welcome, my brother."

CHAPTER
TWO

The Nile Delta

I

The small group of Egyptian rebel soldiers sat in complete darkness. Low clouds hid the full moon now, and the only light came from the torches anchored well out into the Nile. There, along the long decks, they could see the foreign mercenaries eating, drinking, and making ready to bed down for the night.

"How many do you think there are?" asked Sem, one of the eldest insurgents.

Isesi, leader of the group, parted the reeds and made a quick guess. "Sixty on the first boat. No more than fifty on the Greek boat. The other . . . *hmmm*. Make the total a little under two hundred."

He smiled coldly. He could see his swimmers now, their dark heads barely visible above the water in the pools of light surrounding each vessel. Beside Isesi and Sem, the line of archers stood poised, arrows nocked, by a man with a closed lantern. He stood ready to open its metal side-flaps, to set fire to the gum-soaked brand that would in turn ignite each of the arrows before the archers let them fly.

"It looks too easy," Isesi said. "I shall have to go to the temple and do penance to the gods."

Sem smirked at Isesi's joke. It had been a long, hard struggle against the Hai usurpers.

"I'm glad to make fish bait of all of them," Isesi continued in a more natural, and vicious, tone. "Or, in the present case, crocodile food."

"I feel uneasy about our swimmers," Sem admitted. "You're sure that oil they put on their bodies will keep away the crocs?"

"That and the fact that they're coming from this bank. The crocs sun themselves and sleep on the far bank—the one closest to the boats. The crocodiles probably won't ever be aware of our boys. But when the foreigners jump overboard, they'll make for the bank nearest to their vessel—the bank with the crocodiles in the shallows."

"Ugh!" Sem shuddered involuntarily. "Some fate: drowning or being savaged by a crocodile."

"I know," Isesi said. "But we have to keep Apophis from getting help from these hired swords from across the Great Sea." His voice raised slightly when he saw that the swimmers had cut the anchor lines and were headed back toward shore. "There, now . . . let our boys get closer. We don't want anyone's arrow hitting one of our own men."

Sem, watching his friend, marveled at the change this war against the Hai had wrought in the gentle, retiring scholar Isesi. But war made the man or broke him. Many stout, large-muscled young dandies who had volunteered for the fight against the invaders had turned out to be cowards or weaklings, while the quiet ones like Isesi often turned out to be most deadly.

He glanced at Isesi's powerful upper body and arms, barely visible in the light from the boats, and remembered when he looked the timid, skinny scribe. Now there was an aroused leopard in his soul.

"Ready now," Isesi said through clenched teeth. "All right. Fire the arrows." The man with the lantern lighted his brand and moved down the line of archers and ignited each of the poised shafts. "Archers! At the ready. Aim . . . *fire!*"

Thirty fires rose above the Nile in looping, gentle arcs.

Downward the burning arrows sped, like shooting stars, onto the decks of the three boats!

Only a few of the shafts missed, and within moments a dozen fires burned. Hardest hit was the first boat; a native-built Egyptian craft made of papyrus reeds, it was quickly enveloped in flames. Beside it, the Greek ship's pitched deck was a wall of fire a moment later.

Howling with fear, the mercenaries leapt into the water and made for shore. But then came the first of the chilling, bloodcurdling screams as the reptiles on the banks made for the plentiful new food source.

Sem, on the far bank, winced. "I'm glad we can't see it."

Isesi's face was grim. "Group leader! Do you see any of them coming this way?"

The man on the end called back, "Yes, sir!"

"Don't let them reach shore! A bonus to the archer who hits one of them!"

"Right you are, sir!"

Across the river the screams rose in pitch, doubled in volume, and hung hauntingly in the night air.

The clouds had passed and the moon was high when Isesi and Sem dismissed the last of the irregulars. For a moment or two the two friends lingered, satisfied, at the crossroads. "It's been a productive evening," Sem commented.

"Productive?" Isesi said. "Try 'destructive,' my friend. What have we built?" He sighed. "It's necessary work, cutting off Apophis from as many sources of new strength as we can, but I don't feel terribly heroic. Do you?"

"Not especially." He put a hand on his friend's shoulder. "Don't dwell on it, Isesi. Go home and sleep the sleep of a man who's done a job well. Here, let me walk you home."

"No, no," Isesi said a bit too hastily; Sem shot a sharp glance at him but then shrugged away the quick suspicion. "I . . . I need to be alone, to finish plans for the attack on the supply caravan in the morning. Wake me early, will you? We'll talk then. Now, my friend, go in peace and safety."

When Sem was gone, Isesi hesitated for a moment, then set out at a brisk pace. The route was so familiar, he could have negotiated it with ease in pitch darkness; now, with the full moon having escaped the clouds, the path was simplicity itself.

His destination was a wretched gathering of hovels half a league upriver from the Nile's closest approach to Tanis. Here, in a hastily erected "village" of poorly constructed mud huts, Apophis's government had, a year before, resettled the greater bulk of the Canaanites: the family and retinue of Jacob, father of the longtime vizier to the Hai kings, Joseph.

The forced move to this paupers' town had been one of the greatest tragedies the delta had seen. The northerners—the Egyptians called them the Habiru—had arrived in great state and been welcomed to the court of the delta as a courtesy to Joseph, who had been in high favor with the Hai king. They had quickly invested in land, built stately homes, and become Egyptians in all but blood and name.

But then Joseph's fortunes had changed. One by one his rights and privileges had been taken away, and concerned for his family's safety, he had tried in vain to smuggle them out of Egypt. Caught in the act, Joseph had been put under a house arrest that had never been lifted.

In the three years that followed, Joseph's health had declined, as had the fortunes of his family. Their wealth, homes, and possessions stripped from them, they had even lost the means to feed themselves. Indigent and unemployed in a land that regarded them as foreign pariahs, they lived wretchedly as semislaves, chattels of the state, laboring in the back-breaking work of erecting new fortifications for the delta cities.

The patriarchs of the Habiru tribes—Levi, Reuben, Judah, and the rest—had been allowed for a time to live in the shadow of the walled estate that their brother Joseph still occupied under house arrest. Then they, with the younger generations, had been forcibly removed to the workers' villages.

The village near Tanis where Isesi was headed was assigned to the tribe of Levi. In the months since their relocation, Isesi's views about the Habiru had altered dramatically. When they had first arrived in Egypt, he had hated and resented them as privileged foreigners who, propped up by Joseph's influence, had lived in luxury while native-born Egyptians starved under the heavy hand of the Hai.

Now, however, the boys of privilege had become men without caste—hardly better than cattle or oxen, they were mere able-bodied drudges fit only to labor incessantly from dawn to dark raising tall battlements above the walls of Tanis, making the once-peaceful city a fortress protected by the characteristic sloping walls of a Hai stronghold.

It was obvious that in their first years here they had made the same mistake the Hai had made: growing lax in the observances of their own people, ceasing little by little to be true Canaanites as the Hai—once fierce nomadic warriors called Shepherd Kings—had ceased being true Hai. While losing their own identity as a nation, they had failed to become true Egyptians. Neither fish nor fowl, they had become contemptible to themselves and to the Egyptians.

But unlike the Hai, who had never regained their sense of national or tribal purpose, the Habiru had recently begun to recover their old integrity. Under the supervision of old Levi, Joseph's elder brother, they had begun to throw off the Egyptian customs they had adopted so enthusiastically upon their arrival and had begun a program to restore the old, monotheistic faith of their fathers. Adversity had begun to strengthen this almost-lost sense of purpose.

Isesi had come to pity, then admire them. And then, quite by chance, he had met Miriam. . . .

Passing the village one day, he had happened upon a Hai guardsman—evidently an overseer assigned to the village—forcing his attentions on a slim Habiru girl hardly out of her middle teens. Isesi had had no intention of stopping, not even to quarrel with a Hai overseer, but something in the girl's face and manner had caught his eye, and her cries for help had touched his heart. Almost without thinking he had intervened.

The Hai soldier could barely believe his eyes. A native-born Egyptian challenging a Hai warrior a head taller than himself! He had laughed heartily and prepared to dispatch the interloper—only to see Isesi, eyes blazing, draw his sword and, with insulting ease, outmatch him. Disarmed, the Hai soldier had died with a single stroke of Isesi's expert blade.

The girl had watched all this with horror but had not run away. Conquering her fear and loathing, she had helped Isesi dispose of the guardsman's body, burying him deep in the banks beside the Nile where the body would rot quickly and never be found.

He had admired her mettle. Then, the job done, he had had an opportunity to look at her closely for the first time— and had been dazzled by the native beauty that shone through her ragged clothing and mesmerized by the lovely olive-skinned face with the great brown eyes. He had asked her name. "Miriam," she had said proudly. "Daughter of Amram and Jochebed, of the tribe of Levi."

The memory tugged at his heart now as he approached the workers' village. Stopping in the darkness before a particular house, he pursed his lips and imitated the sound of a familiar night bird of the delta—once, twice, three times. Then he stepped back into the shadows of the Hai granary that towered over the neighboring fields, and waited.

In a moment the door of the little house opened. The interior was dark; everyone inside should have been asleep, for the dawn of a new and arduous day was not far off. But a slim figure slipped out into the night, and he ran to meet her. His heart beat fast as the full moon's light fell on the beloved face. Headlong she ran into his arms.

"Miriam," he said in a voice choked with love.

II

After the first moment of embrace she stepped back, holding onto his forearms and trying, in the unreliable light, to focus on his face. "Isesi," she said, "you're so tense. I'm almost afraid to ask what you've been doing."

"I'm almost afraid to tell you," he confessed. "But I suppose I have to. The Hai tried to sneak another draft of mercenaries past us. They failed."

"Ah," she said in a serious voice. "And your own people?"

"We didn't lose a man," he answered proudly. "We also destroyed their ships."

She did not say anything for a moment. "How strange it seems, after the way I've been raised, to rejoice at the news of anyone's death." The look on her face was serious, concerned, but her eyes were filled with love for him.

Then she smiled, although the underlying seriousness remained. "You know," she said, "my father would be pleased to hear about the evening's work, for all that he doesn't approve of Egyptians."

"I know," Isesi said, taking her hand and leading her to a

spot out of sight and earshot from her parents' hut. "Eventually we Egyptians and your people must make our peace. Whatever we may think about the matter. You remember I had to conquer some prejudices of my own," he added ruefully.

"I'm so happy you have, my darling," she said. "And really, Father isn't as obstinate as he sounds. It's just that we've had such a hard time of it."

"And there's no chance to reconcile the two groups," Isesi said bitterly. "My people for the most part feel as I did. We saw you as privileged foreigners living off the fat of the land while native-born Egyptians starved. We had no idea what was going to happen to you; we had no idea what sort of people you were, keeping to yourselves as you did."

She sat down on a low wall next to him. Their thighs touched. "We are clannish," she admitted. "Do you remember what I told you about our last visit to Egypt, generations ago? God had to put a curse on your king and blind him until he agreed to let us go." She sighed. "I have this terrible feeling it's going to take worse than that to get us free this time. I can't see that happening soon."

Isesi balled his fists. "If we could only win, once and for all," he said fervently. "If we could only drive the Hai out and put an Egyptian king on the throne of both the Red and the Black Lands!"

"You mean Kamose?" she asked.

"That's just the problem," Isesi said, shaking his head. "Kamose is half-Hai himself. If only he were to be succeeded by someone of pure Egyptian blood, someone whose credentials wouldn't be challenged by the nobility in the delta or the upriver barons!" He made a face. "Did I tell you the barons between Thebes and Nubia have never accepted Kamose? And Nubia has remained distant to him although they fought for him in the battle to save Thebes. They withdrew their ambassador last year."

"I hadn't heard that," she said. "What does that mean?"

"Maybe they found out something about him when he was upriver talking them into joining the fight."

She turned to look at him now. "He frightens me," she said. "He seems to hate *us* so. What could he possibly have against my people?"

"I don't know, but it has something to do with the years he spent in exile, after he escaped from the Children's Refuge. Rumor has it that he spent some time up north, in your country, but he never talks about it. Something must have happened to him there to embitter him so completely. You can't get him even to talk rationally about what he calls the 'accursed Habiru.' " He shook his head. "Of course, when I knew him, I felt much the same way about your people, so I can hardly look down my nose at him."

"Yes you can," she said in a voice full of affection. "You're a reasonable man—a scholar and a thinker. You're my Isesi." She reached up and kissed him lightly on the cheek. "My own sweet, dear man. Oh, if only I could tell Father about us!"

"You think that part of it is hopeless?"

"Not hopeless. We can't do it just now. Things have been terribly hard for him. Mother has to work so hard, and he blames himself and the Egyptians."

Isesi pounded an angry fist into his palm. "If we win, Kamose, whatever his feelings about your people, will owe me a lot. I've kept the fight going all this time here, under difficult conditions, with no weapons except what we could steal from the Hai we've killed. He couldn't have conducted his war the way he has without my friends and me. I ought to be able to lay down some sort of conditions."

Now a light seemed to come into his eyes, and his gestures became more animated. "Yes! I can become your protector! If I interpose myself between Kamose and the Habiru, he won't be able to say no to me. He couldn't possibly turn down a legitimate, humane request from a man who's been his right arm down here in the delta ever since he came back to Egypt!"

"Do you really think it would work?" she asked hopefully.

"Yes!" he said. "When he takes over here in the delta, he'll need some way to repay me for my services. If he doesn't, he'll lose respect and the army won't fight for him. He'll never get the support of the nobility or of the priesthood of Amon."

"But, Isesi, do you really think the priesthood will be anything but hostile to us, with our different religion and customs?"

"Why not? When Joseph was vizier, he had a fine working relationship with them. There was never any trouble, and they'll remember that. Even though his influence was increased because Joseph was married to the daughter of the high priest, they'll remember that he always dealt justly with their claims."

"I'm not so sure," she said. "Memories are short. And our whole experience of trying to get along with heath—I mean with people who worship many gods . . . well, it hasn't been good."

"We'll deal with all that when we've won and driven the Hai out of Egypt once and for all. And I think that won't be too much longer, Miriam! I can feel it, somehow!"

"Oh, Isesi, my darling! Maybe *then* . . . maybe when my father can see you at work, helping us, he'll give us his blessings."

"Miriam," he said, kissing the palms of her hands, "I don't want power or riches. I'd be satisfied with a quiet life with you by my side."

She drew his face down to kiss him lightly on the lips, then said, "I'd be so happy if I could just go home, home to Canaan."

He looked silently at her for a long moment. "You'd want to leave this country? Leave—" It was obvious what he had intended to say: "Leave *me*." But he could not force himself to say it. She touched his bare chest with one soft hand and reached up to caress his face with the other. "Isesi," she said, "I'm yours as long as we live. Wherever you go, I'll be beside you—all the way to the grave and beyond. The only way I'd ever leave you now would be if you stopped wanting me. If Father forbids our marriage, I'll be forced to leave him and go with you. But I want to see if I can reconcile the two of you. He has to learn what a wonderful person you are. He has to know."

With a great sigh he embraced her. "Oh, Miriam," he said between kisses. "I've never been so happy."

In the morning, Sem, rising early in the rebel camp and going in search of Isesi, found him sleeping deeply. Sem looked down and shook his head. *He pushes himself so hard,* he thought, and decided to let his friend sleep. He reached down and threw a light blanket over Isesi and walked away into the cool, clear dawn.

He looked up to see four of his men approaching, spears at the ready, guarding two strangers. He shot them a sharp glance. They had the pale skins of northerners—Canaanites or Syrians, if he was any judge.

"What's this?" he asked.

The senior guard spoke up, coming smartly to a halt and barking a quick order at his mates, who stood stiffly at attention. "We intercepted these two just after dawn."

He had no chance to finish. The taller and leaner of the two men spoke. "I am Amasis of Damascus," he said tersely. "My companion is Makare. We seek Kamose. It is my understanding that he is a leader of the fight against the foreign barbarians."

"Leader?" Sem echoed. "He's the rightful king of the Red Lands. By year's end he will be king of both lands, Red and Black. You have business with him?"

"We are blood brothers," Amasis answered. "We knew each other in the years after Kamose left Egypt as a boy. We traveled together, shared dangers, fought and bled for a variety of causes. He often spoke of returning to Egypt to reclaim an inheritance, but he spoke of no crown."

"Just because he didn't mention it doesn't mean he doesn't wear it," Sem said, thinking that the man reminded him of a hawk.

The stranger's eye was flinty, and his voice had the same cutting tone. "Perhaps the throne of Egypt was the inheritance of which he spoke. I put nothing beyond Kamose's power. He was obviously destined for great things. But even if this were not so, even if I had not known him, I would want to fight the Hai. They caused great suffering when they passed through the lands of the north. I had family in Ebla when the Shepherd Kings passed through. Ebla is no more."

"You wish to join our cause?" Sem asked, his eye settling the first time on the other man, Makare. For no reason he could name, Sem found himself disliking both of them. Makare was short, broad, squat, and immensely powerful, with arms the size of a strong man's thighs. He gave the immediate impression of brute power and ruthlessness.

Amasis's eye held its cold glare. "My friend Makare cannot wait to kill the Hai. I would like to see my old comrade first. There are matters of great importance to discuss and ways I can be helpful to your campaign." Seeing the question in Sem's eyes, he added, "Ways I can divulge only to Kamose."

"And it is your due to be blindly believed, then?" Sem could not keep the hostility out of his voice.

Now it was the heavyset Makare who spoke. His voice was a cavernously deep bass—the lowest, the most powerful Sem had ever heard—but had something of the chilling quality of Amasis's metallic baritone. "What proof do you need in order to believe us?" he asked. "Will killing Hai soldiers do it? How many do you wish us to kill? By when? Name the time, place, and means. There is no weapon I do not know, although my favorites are *these*." He held up hands the size of a full-grown baboon's—dirty, callused, their nails ragged. "We met a Hai patrol on the road here. All of them died quickly but one. After I had extracted from him the information I wanted, I pulled his head off."

Sem shuddered in spite of himself. "Dead will do," he said. "In pieces . . . that might not be necessary."

"Well? Tell us what you wish done. I want to begin killing Hai. Me, I *came* from Ebla. The Hai left not a man, woman, or child alive when they took the city."

Amasis smiled, and somehow his smile was even more deadly than his hawk-faced glare. "My friend here . . . I will not take him with me when I go to see Kamose—"

"*If* you are allowed to see him," Sem broke in.

"Makare will, if he is allowed, stay with the delta unit. He cannot forgive my old comrade Kamose for the half of his blood that is of Hai origin."

"I see," Sem said. "Well, you'll have to meet Isesi, our commander. Nothing happens here without his approval."

"Very well," Amasis said with a shrug. "We are at your disposal."

Sem turned to the commander of the guards. "See that they're fed and rested. Isesi will see them at noon."

III

In the fields Miriam, having finished the morning's labors, took some figs and olives out of her own ration and put them inside her robe to take to her father in the quarry. But at the entrance to that area she was stopped by a towering

Hai guard. "You," he said. "Where do you think you're going?"

"Please, sir," she said. "My father is Amram, of the tribe of Levi. I was going to take him something to eat."

"Give it to me, girl. I'll make sure he gets it." A sarcastic tone to his voice assured her that he was lying. She drew back. "Come on, now," he ordered. "Hand it over."

"Please. Let me take it to him. I also have a message for him." That wasn't quite true, but it was obvious the food would not be delivered to Amram unless by her hand.

"Come here, now. Why aren't you working?"

She stepped back, but not quickly enough. His heavy hand darted out and grasped her wrist. "Let me go!" she said. "You have no right!"

His grip tightened. "Now don't pull away, girl. I could cause all sorts of trouble for your parents and family."

She looked into his eyes, and what she saw there made her ill. She pulled, and when his grip stayed firm, she bent and sank her teeth into his wrist.

"Ow!" he bellowed, letting go. "You little vixen! I'll fix you. What did you say your father's name was?"

Miriam thought fast. "Imlah," she said. There was no such person. The last Canaanite to bear that name had died when she was a small child. "Please don't harm him." She backed away, all the way to a towering olive tree; then she turned and ran.

The runner awakened Isesi before the sun was high. He sat up, yawned, blinked, and swung his feet out of the hammock in which he had been sleeping since an hour before dawn. "Yes?" he asked in a still-sleepy voice.

"Sir," the runner said, panting, "I came as fast as I could. We got word that there'll be a convoy passing through in an hour or so, carrying food for the Hai troops at Tanis."

"Muster the troops!" Isesi ordered, instantly awake. "Call Sem! Wait—there he is. Sem! Over here!" Then he strapped on his sword belt. "Now tell us everything: where, when, and how many."

When the runner had done so, Sem said, "There's not a moment to lose. If they'll be passing through the olive orchard in an hour . . . hmmm. I can raise fifty men fairly quickly. That should be enough, I think. They can't spare too much of a guard these days, with the main army siphoning away so many men to fight Kamose down south." Then he thought of something. "Oh, by the way, Isesi. There's this pair of strangers who want to join us."

"Keep them under guard for now," Isesi ordered.

"One of them claims to be an old friend of Kamose's, from up north. Both look strong and fit. I'd say they are able to take care of themselves."

"You'll vouch for them, then?"

Sem hesitated. "Well, I'm not . . ." He paused again. "I'm probably just being overly cautious. I suppose they're all right. We could try them out in the present engagement."

"Right. You learn a lot about a man in a fight." Now, however, he lifted his head, and his eyes narrowed. "What's this? Miriam? What's she doing coming here? I didn't even know she knew where to find me." He turned away from them and watched the slim figure running toward him. He called back over his shoulder, "Muster the men, Sem. Bring the two strangers along. I'll be with you in a moment."

He moved out from under the latticed shelter and met the girl on the path under the tall palms. "Miriam!" He took her hands—and then noticed the welts on her wrist and forearm. "Miriam, how did you get those bruises?"

"Oh, Isesi, I didn't want to bother you, but . . . well, it's the guard at the quarry. I'm afraid that if he remembers Father's name—"

"The guard? The tall one?" He saw confirmation in her expression. "*He* did this to you? What else did he do?"

"Nothing, nothing. I can handle him. But like a fool I told him Father's name. I did my best to confuse him later, but if he remembers—"

"Go home and stay there until I tell you you can venture out again. I've got something important to do here that will take the better part of the afternoon, but I know when the guard gets off, and when he does, I'll be waiting for him. Don't worry."

"Don't do anything rash, Isesi. Please."

"I never do anything rash, my dear. Now go home."

"But—"

"Trust me. I'll take care of everything."

*　　*　　*

Levi, the elderly patriarch of Miriam's clan, had ridden the ten or so miles from Tanis to the outskirts of Avaris with increasing discomfort, calling down imprecations on the donkey's head but nonetheless giving thanks to his God that he did not, at his age, have to walk. Now, as he neared the lightly guarded compound where his younger brother Joseph lived under perpetual house arrest, he found he could no longer abide the animal's jouncing. He carefully dismounted and led the animal slowly to the main gate of Joseph's house.

The guard saluted and let him pass. By order of Apophis Joseph could have no visitors other than his brothers. Levi tied the donkey to a post and, his old bones aching, made his way up the stairs to the front door.

Joseph's wife, Asenath, opened the door for him. "Levi!" she said. "I'm so glad you could come. Quickly, please. He's been calling for you."

Levi stepped back and looked at her. She still had some of the beauty of her youth, when she had come to Joseph in an alliance arranged by her father, Petephres, high priest of Amon, for political purposes. "His heart?"

"I'm afraid so. He's already had the one attack. The physicians told us he might not survive the next one. Levi, I'm frightened. He looks like a ghost."

"Take me to him." Together the two hurried down the long hall to Joseph's room, where Levi's brother lay, his hands, like the claws of an old bird, on the coverlet. "Joseph," Levi said, "I came as quickly as I could."

But Joseph's head did not turn, and the eyes stared unblinkingly at the ceiling. For a moment Levi, his own heart beating too fast, thought his brother had died. But then the sunken eyes blinked. "Levi," the thin voice said. "Come here, please."

Asenath pulled up a chair next to her husband's bed, and Levi carefully sat down, favoring his aching back. "Joseph," he breathed. "I thought for a moment I'd lost you."

Now the head, prematurely white haired, turned toward Levi, and the deep-set eyes regarded him solemnly. "You will very shortly, I'm afraid, my brother." There was almost no wind in him; the words were hardly more than a whisper. "God has spoken to me in the night. He has told me my time is short."

"Joseph!"

"Please. I sent for you because you will inherit my status

as high priest of all the tribes when I pass on. I must speak to you of this."

Levi's mouth was drawn into a thin white line. He looked at his brother's ravaged face: Joseph was younger than he but looked much older. And now the reason for that came to Levi: *He's simply squeezed dry. All that he's suffered on our behalf, protecting us . . . it's used him up completely.* A great wave of sadness and regret swept through Levi, and he wanted to cry like a child. "Speak, Joseph," he said softly. "I hear."

"Levi," Joseph said, "the vision . . . God told me that unless our people return to His service, they are doomed."

"I know, I know," Levi said. "I am taking steps to bring them all back to the old customs and practices. Prayers, sacrifices . . ."

"Yes," Joseph whispered. "But it must not be perfunctory. All must believe. All must participate."

"Yes, yes."

Joseph's hand, weak, insubstantial, fell on his brother's weatherbeaten arm. "Levi. Remember this forever and teach it to all the tribes: God will not punish us forever for our folly of coming here and staying too long. But to be forgiven, we must return to being His servants, as our father was."

"Yes, Joseph."

"If we find our way to righteousness once more"— Joseph's voice was barely audible now—"He will send a man to save us. An emancipator."

"One of us, Joseph?"

"Yes. A man of your own tribe. He did not say when."

"I shall see to it." He smiled gently and patted the sick man's hand. "We have always thrived on adversity. It is in the days of riches and good health and prosperity that we get into trouble."

The dying man tried to smile. The weak fingers closed feebly around Levi's hand. "If I have your promise, I can die in peace. But . . . one act of self-indulgence. I ask nothing more."

"Name it, Joseph. Anything!"

"I would lie in the land of my fathers. I would be buried beside Jacob and Isaac and Abraham in the cave of Machpelah, near Hebron. Have me embalmed after the Egyptian fashion, as Father was. Then when this emancipator comes and takes the tribes back to the land God promised to Jacob—"

"Yes, Joseph. I understand."

Now Joseph looked him in the eye, and the commitment he found there satisfied him. He managed a thin smile. "Good," he said. "I leave our future in the best of hands. I can die contentedly."

Levi's own heart was suddenly pounding again. He began to understand that Joseph would, in a moment or two, be gone forever. Joseph, who had forgiven his brothers for their rash and thoughtless anger, which had led to his being sold as a slave in Egypt, and who had risen to a position eclipsing everyone in the great Egyptian delta but the kings he had served so well. Joseph, who had, in the days of the great hunger, brought his father and brothers out of drought-ravaged Canaan to live as rich men in luxury under his protection in Egypt—only to lose everything.

Why, when Joseph died, all their protection would be lost forever! And if their present lot was a difficult one, what would it be when Joseph was gone? A sinking feeling grabbed at his gut. They would be less than chattels! Slaves!

"Joseph . . ." he gasped in a sudden panic.

But the deep-set eyes were closed, and the drawn face was relaxed, peaceful.

Levi's own heart almost stopped. He leaned his face close to his brother's. He could not feel his brother's breath on his cheek.

"Joseph!" he said. And then, "Asenath! Come quickly!"

But however quickly she ran in from the next room, it was not fast enough. Joseph was gone.

Shaken, Levi sat alone in the great sitting room of his brother's house. Through the open door down the hall he could hear the voices of Joseph's wife and sons. He no longer shared their grief. The emotions that racked him now were quite different ones: pettier, more self-centered, and more cowardly.

He was, he admitted, frightened half to death. All his long life, there had always been someone to lean on, to ask the hard questions of, to seek advice from—first Jacob, then Joseph, who had effortlessly taken his father's place as patriarch of the clan despite his youth, assuming leadership over them even before Jacob's death.

Now? Now it was up to him, Levi! Was he up to it? Could he handle it?

IV

Now that his blood lust no longer ruled him, Isesi looked around at the scattered bodies, the cut throats and gutted corpses, and shuddered. Worse: When he looked down at himself and saw himself covered with the blood of the men he had killed, his gorge rose.

"There's a Hai herdsman over there who looks to have died of fright," Sem said, examining the man's clothing, which was clean and in one piece. "I'll strip him and bring you his tunic. But you better wash yourself off in the river before you put it on."

"Right," Isesi said, then turned to the under officer in charge of his unit. "Drive their supply wagons back to our camp," he ordered. "Wait until dusk and use the back road." He thought a moment. "Your garments look as bad as mine. Burn them." He smiled at the underofficer's wide-eyed look. "Don't be a prude," he teased. "The girls of the camp have seen you naked before. And nobody is going to laugh at you when you come into camp leading wagons bearing enough food to feed us all for a month."

"Yes, sir!" the soldier responded with an embarrassed smile.

Isesi turned back to Sem just as his friend approached, bearing the clean tunic. "Thank you," he said, moving toward the water and beckoning Sem to follow.

"What's going on?" Sem asked.

Isesi did not answer for a moment, watching the two new men. Amasis and Makare had been the bloodthirstiest of all, each butchering half a dozen Hai. The heavyset one had been particularly savage, desecrating corpses. Isesi frowned. "Did you see them in action?"

Sem nodded.

"And what did you think?"

"They are reliable in anything that involves killing."

"Yes. I don't like them, but we need everyone we can

get. The men seemed willing to listen to the heavy one when he spoke. Makare."

"Are you thinking of promoting him?"

Isesi shrugged. "He says he wants to stay with us. And we lost a couple of underofficers last week. No time to train anyone new."

Sem thought about it but did not comment. "The other one," he said. "Are you going to send him ahead to Kamose?"

"I don't know," Isesi replied. "Come, let's wash off. I have to do something on the way back, and I don't want to attract attention."

"I saw your girl in camp. What's her name? Miriam?"

"You know very well what her name is." They set out through the underbrush toward a sluggish arm of the Nile.

"She's a Canaanite. . . ."

"Yes. Who would have imagined that when it came my time to fall? . . . But while getting to know her, I've got to know them a bit. Not directly, of course, but through her. And they're really not all that bad. There's a thing or two to admire about them."

"Is this the same Isesi?" Sem asked. "You have always wanted the Canaanites' blood."

"I know. I was a real fire-breather when we started. But the more actual killing I do"—he held up one bloody hand and looked at it—"the less bloodthirsty I become. Actually, there may be a trifle more before nightfall."

"Do you want me to come along?" They had reached the water's edge, and Sem pulled off his tunic and poised, middle-aged and spindle-shanked, ready to dive in.

"No, no," Isesi said, stepping out of his bloody garment and discarding it on the ground beside the clean one. "It's rather private." Without another word he dived into the river, came up spitting water, and swam back to the shallows to stand and wash the dried blood off his arms and chest. He watched Sem standing knee-deep in the water and thought, *He's getting too old for fighting. I'll have to think up other work for him.* "There's an overseer at the quarry who's been stepping out of line."

"The quarry where the girl's father works?"

"The same." He looked down, satisfied that he was clean, and walked out of the water. "Today he put his filthy hand on—" He sighed, dried himself, and bent to pick up the sword belt he had laid down. But then he thought better of it. "I can't walk through the village carrying this. Lend me your dagger, will you?"

"Take it. You're going against him with only a short sword?"

"It's my best weapon. I haven't developed the wrist for the big sword. Don't worry." He looked up at the setting sun. "I'd better get on the way."

"What do you want me to do about Amasis and Makare?"

"Tell them to bed down. I'll make a decision in a day or so about Amasis going to Kamose. Meanwhile they're free to roam the camp. They've earned that much."

The last sentence, however, had an odd dying fall, and Sem looked sharply at him. "But?"

Isesi looked thoughtful. "There's something about them," he said, frowning. "Particularly Amasis. I'd like to study him a bit more before I let him go to see Kamose."

"Right," Sem said. "I'll keep my eyes open."

Amram had come home bone-tired, bent with fatigue. But now he stood tall and angry. "Those bruises," he said, examining his daughter's arm. "They came from him?"

"Yes, Father. But please don't do anything. It's nothing."

"Nothing? That dog of a Hai dares to put a hand on a daughter of Israel? This is not to be tolerated!" He looked at the dying sun in the west. "He'll be off duty in a few minutes. I've got to move fast. I know which road he takes home. I'll wait for him."

"No, Father!"

"Inside, girl!"

"Please—"

"Go!" The word cut like a lash. Miriam backed away from him, her eyes on his angry face. Then he turned and stalked away, armed only with his old shepherd's staff.

A moment or so after he had disappeared down the road, though, she saw a runner coming from the household of Levi, patriarch of her tribe. Disobeying her father's orders, she stepped out to meet the messenger.

"I have a message for your father," the runner said. "Is he here?"

She started to say no, but thought better of it. Amram might need an alibi, and this man could help provide her with one. "Yes," she answered, "but he's indisposed. I can take the message."

"Very well. Tell him Joseph is dead." He turned and went away as briskly as he had come.

Miriam stared after him. Joseph! Dead! Their only hope! Their only protector!

Unless Isesi . . .

Amram's heavy, hard-callused hand tightened on the stout staff by his side, and he lengthened his stride. The red rage in him had subsided, to be replaced by a more appropriate emotion—a cold and impersonal anger, which a man with a mission might well control.

The staff was a comforting presence. It was a very famous piece of wood within his clan, said to be the staff the patriarch Jacob had brought back with him from Haran so many years before. Fashioned from a hardwood shaft Jacob had cut down in the forests of the North, it had been a deadly weapon in that patriarch's capable hands. This was the traditional weapon of his people; Jacob's people had always been masters of the staff. Jacob himself had once killed a lion with one, and his brother, Esau, a mighty fighter, was famous for having been able to fracture every bone in an enemy's body without breaking the skin. And Esau had taught his twin, and Jacob had insisted that all of his descendants master the weapon.

There was still a glow in the sky up ahead, and now, down the road, in the lingering light, Amram could see a man coming toward him. His hand tightened on the staff, and his eyes narrowed. He felt the blood rush to his extremities as the hot rage boiled up in him once more.

But up ahead the man stopped, facing Amram and blocking his path.

Amram stopped and peered at him in the dim light. This person looked shorter than the guard. Amram turned the staff in his hand until he could put both hands side by side on its thick stock.

"You are Amram, of the tribe of Levi?"

"Who wishes to know?" he demanded.

The other's face remained impossible to read, with the only light source, weak and fading, behind him. "A friend."

"What friends does the tribe of Levi have in this accursed land?" Amram hissed. "Step aside. I have urgent business."

"I know your business, sir. The man tried to lay hands on a child of your blood. A girl named Miriam."

"How do you know this?" Amram asked.

"Never mind how I know," the voice calmly replied. "And as for what friends your clan may have . . . let's say there are people here who have hated the Hai longer than you have had reason to. And to such people, any excuse to cut a Shepherd throat is good enough." A chill slid down Amram's spine from the response.

"I wish to cut no throats," Amram denied. "The knife is not our weapon—"

"I know. But it is mine. And if you continue down this road, you will be disappointed, for the man you seek is not to be found."

Amram tightened his grip on the staff. "Indeed? And where is he?"

The man before him blew out a long sigh. "I gave him to the Nile. The Hai will have to find a new guard in the morning. The old one's bones are decorating the guts of a crocodile."

Amram snorted. "An Egyptian tells me this? An Egyptian robs me of my revenge?"

"I'm sorry about that," the slow reasonable voice said. "But if he'd died at your hands, the usual reprisals would have taken place. For the one Hai guard killed, two of your own people would have died. But before I fed him to the river, I removed his Hai tunic and left it pinned to a crossroads post with the knife I used to kill him. Also pinned to the post is a message of defiance from the Brotherhood of Shai."

"Ah! The resistance against the Hai! Joseph told us about you."

"Good. Now you know who your friends are. Go in peace. We will take responsibility for the guard's murder, and rightly so. The Hai will strike against us. Our spies inside their camp will tell us where and when they plan to strike. We will be waiting—in ambush. So you see, this evening's work will benefit us further."

Amram's hands relaxed a bit on his weapon. "But why do a thing like this? For foreigners, who share none of your customs? Who worship none of your gods?"

The man before him seemed to hesitate, as if trying to think out precisely the right answer. "All enemies of the Hai are potential friends, as long as a single Shepherd King befouls the soil of your land or mine, my friend. I have had my eye on this man who dared to lay a hand on your daughter. This is not his first offense against decency." There was a low, humorless chuckle before his next words. "It was, however, his last. He will bother her and you no more."

With that the figure, barely visible now as the last afterglow of the evening sun died, bowed from the waist and turned to go. But then he turned back and said, "Go in peace, Amram of the tribe of Levi. . . ."

"Wait!" Amram said. "I am in your debt. Who are you?"

The man paused. "I have confessed to murder before you. Better you should hear no name."

"But—"

The voice came from a man walking away and talking over his shoulder, his voice faint now. "Go home, my friend. Go in peace."

Amram stared after him, heart pounding. There were the most violently mixed emotions in his head. One of them was hope, which he had not felt since the terrible day long ago when, attempting to escape from Egypt, his people had been turned back at the border by Apophis's guards.

"Go with God," he said softly to the darkness.

V

En route to his own lodgings, Isesi spotted a light glowing inside Sem's tent, so he turned his steps in that direction. As he neared the pool of warm light, he could hear voices inside. Ducking to enter, he stepped within. "Ani! Tchabu!" he said. "Good to see you! And how are my friends Kamose and Riki?"

The man called Ani bowed low. "Kamose sends his greetings, and a scroll, before Sem on the table, written by his scribes, with detailed information on the campaign and a list of questions for you."

"Riki send also greeting," Tchabu added. Isesi smiled,

looking down at the tiny, twisted figure of the seer. The hunchback had not gone the whole way with Ani to Memphis but had tagged along from Bast, taking advantage of the armed guard that had accompanied Kamose's runner. "Riki come to meet us at Bast."

"Ah! And is our Riki a father yet?"

"No, no," the little man said. "Riki very worry. First child. Mind much disturb."

"I'm sure he has no idea how normal that is," Sem said knowingly. "I fretted terribly over my first." He turned to Isesi now. "Your . . . uh . . . business? . . ."

Isesi nodded. "Completed. He'll trouble the Habiru no more. I met Amram on the way and warned him off. A good man, perhaps an ally in time to come. His people have no arms but shepherd's staffs, but they're famous for what they can do with them."

"We'll need every friend we can find as the final push begins," Sem said. "Now, Isesi, come look at this letter from Kamose. In it he says—"

But he stopped dead. The eyes of all three men were on Tchabu, who suddenly underwent some sort of convulsion. The seer's face was fixed in an expression of extreme fright, and it was covered with sweat. He wrung his misshapen hands. His eyes rolled back up in his head. "Bad, bad," he warned in an agitated voice. "Very bad. Much danger . . ."

"Grab him!" Sem ordered. Isesi, however, was already at the little man's side; he took Tchabu's hands in his and held them. In past attacks Tchabu had been known to flail about wildly with arms and legs and had once knocked over a large urn and hurt himself.

But this time the spasm that had shaken him lasted no more than that first moment. His body shook violently once; then he slipped off into a trancelike sleep. Isesi laid Tchabu's body down very gently and put a pillow under his head. "There," he said. "You never know beforehand whether or not he'll remember this when he wakens."

"Good heavens!" Ani said. "Is he mad?"

"No," Isesi answered. "He has these spells and sometimes can see into the future. Occasionally he can look into a man's mind and read there what the man is unwilling to say. We've tried him in interrogations of prisoners, and sometimes it works. The trouble is, he has no control over when his gift is going to work." He looked at Sem. "He was talking about Riki and his fears over Teti's pregnancy just before it happened. You don't suppose—"

"It could be. I'll keep an eye on him while he's here. Perhaps there's some danger we know nothing about from the Hai camps hereabouts. Or it might have something to do with the fact that you came here fresh from killing a man in anger."

"That could be it," Isesi admitted grimly, the memory of his own rage still upon him. "Tchabu is sensitive to such things. Ani, could you stay with him while I prepare my response to Kamose's message?"

"Be glad to," the runner said. "I rather enjoy the little fellow's company. He has a unique perspective on things. Gods! Imagine being able to see into the future!"

"More of a curse than a blessing, I'd say. Now, what did you have to say to me about this scroll of Kamose's?"

Amram's wife was waiting up for him. "Jochebed," he said, "you won't believe what happened."

"Shhh!" she whispered. "Come over here, away from Miriam's wall. She'll hear you through it. I sent her to bed early."

"Jochebed, I met this man—an Egyptian—and . . ." He told the whole story in a rush, holding her hands. "An Egyptian! Can you imagine? Could I have been wrong about them?"

Her dark eyes were on his. "Not about most of them," she said. "I wonder if this could be the same man. . . ."

"What man?"

"I've seen him looking at us through the trees from time to time, as though he were watching over us. And . . . well, baskets of food have been left outside our house."

"Did you get a glimpse of him?"

"I never saw him clearly."

"I'll bet it's he. But wait! He said he was with the rebels against the Hai. The Brotherhood of something. *Hmmm.* Has Miriam seen him? Do you think she knows anything about this?"

But when the two of them tiptoed into the girl's darkened room, she lay in a pool of moonlight, sleeping sweetly—or appearing to, at any rate. On silent feet they stole back out of the room to stand and stare at each other. Suddenly Jochebed stepped forward and threw her arms around her husband, hugging him close, face buried in his chest.

"Watch your step there," Ani warned, holding out a hand to steady the little hunchback. "There was a big jutting root there. You could have taken a nasty fall."

Tchabu stopped in the path. "Ani," he said in that odd croak of a voice of his. "Danger not to Tchabu. Danger to all men. Danger to Isesi." His face froze.

For a split second Ani thought Tchabu was going to have another convulsion. But this time he remained in control of himself, although there was a grave expression on his face in the flickering light of the torch that Ani held high above their heads.

"Danger to *you*, Ani," the seer continued. "*Great* danger to you."

"How? Who?"

"Tchabu not know. But be watchful. Need eye in back of head. Danger very close. Bad thing. Very large bad thing. Tchabu no see clear. But Tchabu very much fear."

Amasis held his hand over Makare's mouth until the seer and the runner had passed. "It was the dwarf. Someone was telling me about him at dinner. He has the real gift of prophecy, but apparently no control over it. When it is working, he can read men's minds or look into the future. He's very dangerous to us just now."

"Well," Makare said, holding up one huge hand and flexing it, "he *could* have an accident."

"Not a bad idea, but don't rush it. We just got here. No one must ever suspect us of having anything to do with it."

"You are speaking to a member of the Assassins' Guild. I can cut his head off and make it look as though he'd done it to himself by accident."

"Forgive me," Amasis said sarcastically, "for harboring the smallest doubt. But it will always pay to remind ourselves not only of the dangers but the high stakes. This time we're playing for a kingdom, the greatest in all the world. And our dear brother in the great truth has apparently already laid the groundwork."

Makare's genuflection at the very mention of the cult to

which they both belonged was perfunctory. "You act as though all we had to do was walk into this place and take over."

"I feel that we have ahead of us a greater triumph than any man has ever brought to the Great One before"—here not one but two perfunctory signs against evil—"and that by this time next year, my friend . . ."

They both knew what was in his mind. Amasis sat down again and warmed his feet before the glowing coals. After a moment Makare joined him. "I take it you're going ahead with the trip to Memphis," the heavyset man said.

"Yes. People around here speak of Kamose as though he were some sort of demigod. There's a prophecy that names him as the promised deliverer from the Hai, for whom the Egyptians have been waiting."

"A lot of mindless drivel."

"You and I know that. But if *they* don't, all the better. When they declare him lord of Two Lands, king and emperor of all Egypt, they'll be putting on the throne a man—"

"Who is ours," the heavyset man finished. "Ours, heart and soul, ours forever. Unless, of course, he's forgotten." He poked the coals with a green stick, and flames flared for a moment.

"He bears the brand. But if, despite this, he has forgotten, I have ways of reminding him."

"The brand. I'd forgotten that."

"Yes. He went that far. It's under his hairline, where none can see. A good thing too—when we were on the galleys together, after that unfortunate incident in Sidon, we worked side by side, as naked as eggs. If the brand had been anywhere else, someone would have spotted it, and you know what the Sidonians thought of us back in that benighted age."

"Bah," Makare said sourly. "Ancient history."

"That may be, but they were against us, and now we're very strong there. You can't get much stronger than to bring a king over to your side."

The two looked at each other. "A king," Makare said thoughtfully.

Miriam sat up in her bed in the moonlight, hugging her knees. She knew that she would never be able to sleep a wink tonight. The incident with Isesi and her father was simply the most wonderful thing that had happened since she had met Isesi in the first place, and her heart was full of hope.

Imagine! He had not only met Father at last and made a good impression on him, he had saved Father's life as well. And, with that wonderful gift he had for communication— well, he *was* a scribe, after all—he had managed to let Father know that he was friendly toward the Habiru and was keeping an eye out for them.

And Mother would understand. She would eventually make the connection between the food baskets and the man in the road. What a dream come true it would be if the Egyptians and Habiru could get on together after the Hai had been driven away! Even if the Habiru were allowed to leave, it would be a smart military move for the new king in Egypt to make friends with the Habiru nation to his north, a nation that would make a good buffer against the mighty Hittites.

But she would choose to stay behind here with Isesi. Surely, after risking his life to save Father, after looking out for all of them the way he had been doing, Isesi would not be considered unclean, which was how Levi always spoke of the Egyptians. Surely there would be some special dispensation for anyone who had been so heroically friendly to their cause.

But just as surely as she had admitted this hopeful thought to her mind, reality destroyed it. After all, what had Levi said to his assembled clan last week? He had said that their present hard times were due to the righteous judgment of God against them for their impiety, their failure to keep the rituals and the sacrifices, their movement away from the path of holiness as it was established back in the days of Abraham. Levi had been especially harsh on those rash individuals in the community who had defiled themselves by marrying the "unclean."

She sighed. He had not said this too loudly, of course, because Joseph had been alive, and he had married an Egyptian, Asenath. Their two sons had been designated by Jacob as future patriarchs of newly appointed tribes of Israel.

But now Jacob and Joseph were dead. And Levi had promised to make the tribes more strict in their observances of the proper rituals and taboos—chief among them was the taboo against intermarriage.

How could her love for Isesi contend with so formidable an opposition as this? Was there no hope for them at all?

VI

"I'm not sure I like this," Sem admitted. "The two of us strolling down the main street of Tanis as big as you please, the day after—"

Isesi's finger across his own lips halted Sem's speech. "Fortune sometimes favors brazenness," he said with a smile, "if one has the good sense not to overdo it. The people in the city must have heard by now about . . . yesterday's activities. A guard missing! A shipment of food stolen!" His voice lowered to little more than a mutter as he said these things; then he went back to a more normal tone. "At any rate, it'll reassure the good citizens to see us here; otherwise they'd be worrying about whether any of us were casualties of the day's activities."

"You trust people more than I do." Sem's eyes went to right and left as they rounded a corner and turned into the Street of the Markets. "What's to stop someone from selling us out?"

"You haven't got your hand on the pulse of the city as I have," Isesi said. "It's finally beginning to get through to people that the Hai stand a very good chance of losing. Look, my friend. The last time our side could walk freely even in the southernmost districts of the delta, Baka was still alive. And where are we now? Thanks to Riki, Kamose, and a general weakening of the Hai, the battle lines are being drawn right before the walls of Athribis. If Athribis falls to us, Bast will fall. The next thing you know, Avaris itself will be under siege. The tide is slowly turning in our favor. Young people see this and are coming over to our side."

They were entering the first of the two markets on the street, and their voices were lost in the noise as six housewives fought over a niggardly shipment of onions at the greengrocer's stand. Isesi pushed his way past them, and the two emerged in the middle of the square.

Isesi looked around, perplexed. "This is odd. Where is Unamon the butcher? Here's his stand, but it hasn't been opened up today." Isesi turned to the grain merchant, stand-

ing next to the empty booth. "Pardon me, friend. I'm looking
for Unamon the butcher. Do you have any idea where he
might be?"

The grain merchant stepped back and made the sign
against evil. There was a great fear in his eyes. "How recently
have you seen him?" he asked cautiously.

"More than a month ago. But he's been working this
stand for as long as I can remember. Why? What's the
matter?"

The grain merchant turned his eyes away. His expression had the stiff formality of his voice when he said, "Nothing. I know nothing. Now pardon me, sir."

"Wait," Isesi said. "You've seen me here before. You
must know my face. I've been a friend of Unamon's ever
since I came to this region. Surely you can tell me what's
happened to him. Have the Hai taken him away? Gods, he
isn't dead, is he?"

The grain merchant shot him a shifty-eyed glance. "Don't
visit him," he warned. "That's very good advice, my friend.
And that's all I'm going to tell you. Good day, sir!"

Isesi and Sem exchanged puzzled glances. "Something's
wrong," Isesi said. "And look over there. The rug merchant's
stall—empty. The wheelwright's forge. The cooper's stall beside it. What's going on here?"

"I don't know. And I'll bet that we won't get much more
information from their neighbors than we did from Unamon's."
Sem frowned. "I don't like the looks of this at all. You don't
suppose the Hai have swept down and jailed them."

"What for? They paid the proper bribes." He put a hand
on Sem's arm. "Let's pay a visit to my old friend the butcher.
His house is not far from here."

Amram did not need to ask in the village the identity of
the man of the Brotherhood of Shai who had disposed of the
guardsman. Halfway through his description of Isesi, one of
his fellow workers said, "Why, everyone knows him. Where
have you been sleeping, my friend?"

"I keep to myself," Amram said. "I mind my own business. Give me the name."

The man looked around and satisfied himself that the
new guard was well out of earshot. "An Egyptian named

Isesi, an ex-scribe from near Avaris. He's even their leader. But don't spread the word. He's a hero to most of us."

"Huh," Amram said. "Ex-scribe, eh? That fits. He was shorter than a man you'd expect to see as a soldier, even in the irregulars. And he sounded intelligent." He closed his eyes for a moment and brought back Isesi's wiry, fine-trained young body as he had indistinctly seen it by the fading light of a setting sun. All the more odd that he should have been able to kill a Hai guard much larger than himself. "I'll keep the name to myself. Thanks for the confidence. I shan't betray it."

"You'd better not," his neighbor warned. "The man who betrays Isesi won't live long around here, and he won't die quickly or easily. All of us think a lot of him. You Habiru may not understand the depth of our feelings in these matters."

"Perhaps not," Amram said, looking him in the eye. "Not until now, anyhow. I'm just beginning to grasp a few things that have been beyond my understanding."

"Such as?"

"For one thing, that the first priority of all of us, Egyptian and Canaanite alike, is to get rid of the Hai. That until that happens, none of us can live any sort of decent life. Any man who's against the Hai is a friend of mine, whether or not he's of our faith."

"Now you're talking," his neighbor responded warmly.

The new guard saw them talking. "You! Get back to work! Or do you need the lash to convince you?"

Amram picked up his pickax. And he and his neighbor exchanged understanding glances as they turned back to their chores.

The door opened a crack. Behind it an eye appeared. "Go away," a voice inside warned. "You're not welcome here."

Isesi wedged a sandaled foot into the crack. "Please," he said. "Unamon is an old friend of mine. Could I only see him for a moment?"

"See him?" the voice sputtered. "He's dead, don't you understand? My brother's dead!"

Isesi blinked; his face hardened. "Dead?"

"He died a week ago. His body was burned a day later. Now go away, will you?"

"Burned?" Isesi said, shocked. "This nation believes in ceremonial burial, in ritual observances to insure safe passage to the Netherworld! If you burn a body, you—"

He stopped. He stared at Sem, then looked back at the eye behind the door. He waited a beat. Then, in a rush, he forced the door open.

Inside, Unamon's brother cowered, his dull eyes darting from Sem to Isesi and back again. His hands shook uncontrollably. His face was dotted with minute spots, some of which were bleeding. Others had already begun to turn black. Worse, the miserable wretch before them, shivering as if from extreme cold, was naked, unwashed, and stank of his own sweat. They could see the great buboes in his groin and armpit; one was oozing pus.

After a moment's shocked silence Isesi pulled Sem back, slammed the door, and reeled backward into the street.

"What was that?" Sem asked, aghast.

"Let's get out of here," Isesi urged. "Quickly, man! There's not a moment to lose! And don't tell anyone about what we just saw! If word gets out about this, we may have a panic on our hands!"

Sem was pulled hastily down the little street by the arm. He abandoned all attempts at conversation until he had been rushed all the way to the warehouse quarter, where none of the buildings had open doors or any windows.

"I don't know what got into you, Isesi," he said at last, puffing at the sudden exertion. "Maybe now you'd be good enough to explain."

Isesi just looked at him, not saying anything at all.

Finally it began to dawn on Sem. "But . . ." he began, then he let the thought die unspoken. "That's absurd. There's never been an outbreak of . . ." He frowned. "That sort of thing only happens up in the North. Never in Egypt. Everybody knows that. Why, in forty centuries of recorded history . . ."

Isesi stared at him.

"My uncle was apprenticed to a magus some years ago," Sem said. "He never finished the apprenticeship and graduated to journeyman status, to be sure, but he learned quite a bit before he was dismissed. The magus was from somewhere up along the Land of the Two Rivers. He told my uncle about an infestation that took place in Haran, back in the years before the Shepherds came."

Isesi's voice was flat and dull. "Yes, I've heard of it. An infestation that accompanied a great number of sightings of bats. Bats fed on the livestock on the hills around the city."

"Bats," Sem mused. "There *have* been reports. I paid them no mind."

He shuddered, looking into Isesi's eyes. There he saw confirmation of his own suspicions.

Plague! Plague had come to the Egyptian delta!

After work Amram sought out his grandfather, the patriarch of the clan. He bowed low before Levi and said, "Grandfather, my wife and child tell me there has been a message from you that Joseph is dead."

The old man remained seated and looked down at the dirt before their feet. On the sand he scratched meaningless symbols, then wiped them out. "This is correct," he said at last. "And I am much disturbed as to the portents of this for the future. Joseph was the last barrier that stood between us and the Hai." He sighed and made a single right-to-left slash with the stick across the patch of sand.

"That was what I was going to talk to you about."

The old man acted as though he had not spoken. "Joseph said that if we returned to the paths of righteousness, we would be sent a deliverer, an emancipator. A man, Amram, of our tribe, your blood and mine."

"Grandfather, that's all well and good, but that is the future you are talking about. I wanted to tell you that hopeful signs are beginning to make themselves known here and now. We are not as completely without friends as we thought. I have met an Egyptian, a leader of the resistance against the Hai—"

"Egyptians!" hissed the old man. "Heathen! Unclean! Our young have been fraternizing with them! Some of our sons and grandsons have ignored my wishes and have intermarried with the unbelievers!"

"Grandfather," Amram pressed on, "as a practical matter, we have to start looking for friends in this foreign land wherever we can find them."

"Friends?" said the old man, fixing him with blazing eyes. "Friends among these devil worshipers?" He threw up both wrinkled old hands, waving away the very thought as unthinkable blasphemy. "Amram! Amram! Look to your own house! Your own daughter has been seen speaking with an Egyptian! Speaking familiarly with him! No wonder God has forgotten us! No wonder we have fallen out of His favor!"

Amram stared openmouthed. He couldn't think of anything to say at all. *Miriam?* he thought. *My Miriam?*

VII

Sitting before the fire, Ani and Tchabu shared a light supper of cheese and olives, washed down with a hearty red wine of the delta. Tchabu was unnaturally quiet and had been so for the better part of the afternoon. From time to time Ani stole a glance at the little man, who sat bent over, his crooked limbs splayed awkwardly, his face an unreadable mask.

Finally Ani could stand it no more. "Tchabu," he ventured, "is something wrong? Aren't you feeling well?"

"Bad," the little man confirmed. "Much bad here." He turned his face toward Ani, and there was a hurt and stricken look in his eyes. "Bad thing. Bad people."

"Bad things I can understand," Ani said. "There's plague in the village. Several people have died. If, as Isesi tells me, you're sensitive to people's pain, that would certainly be enough to set you off."

"Plague bad," the little man agreed, looking morosely back to the fire. "But people more bad. Tchabu not like newcomers. Fierce men. Mean harm to me, you, all people in camp."

"You mean this Amasis fellow and the heavyset one. Well, I didn't take to either of them right off, either, but Isesi seems to think they can be useful. As a matter of fact, this evening he announced that he was sending Amasis on to Kamose. The other chap is apparently going to stay here."

Tchabu's head turned suddenly toward him. "Not send bad man to Kamose!" he cried out in a voice full of anguish. "Bad for Kamose! This man bad friend for him. Mean bad thing for all people, all Egyptian. Isesi *must* not do."

Then something new came into the little man's mind, and he drew back in fear, staring at his companion. "Ani, you must go," he warned in a changed voice charged with emotion. "You must go now. Very dangerous for you."

"But I have to wait for my message. Isesi is sending me back to Kamose with Amasis, with some communications for his army."

"Go, Ani. Go away now. Please, Ani."

Ani stared. What could have come over the little man?

A low fog had begun to steal in from the river, and there was a distinct chill in the night air. Isesi paused to pull a cloak over his shoulders before walking the perimeters of his camp, as he always did before retiring.

His mind was full of unrest. What a setback! He had thought things were looking up when he had had his conversation with Amram. The man had almost begun to warm to him, to admit for the first time that a man could be an Egyptian and not be an ogre. There had been hope in his heart for eventual understanding between the two of them. With that hope had come another hope, that he and Miriam could openly declare their love.

But now? At dusk Miriam, her face tear-stained from weeping, had come to tell him she had been ordered never to speak to him again.

"I tried to tell him, it was you who saved his life," she had said. "I tried to tell him that it was you who had been looking out for us all this time. But my great-grandfather ordered him to forbid my seeing you. Oh, Isesi, what are we going to do? If my people weren't suffering so terribly under the Hai oppression, I would just run away from home and come to you now. But I can't leave them when they need me. Mother and Father are barely getting by as it is."

"I understand," he had said. But of course he had not understood, not really. Suppressing his emotions, he had let her go back to her family, his own heart full of woe.

Now he sighed deeply. These Habiru! These stubborn foreigners, with their clannish ways! Why could they not see that with the Hai still in Egypt, all Apophis's enemies had to put aside their differences and pull together to get rid of that tyrant and his occupying army, which had made so many lives so miserable for so many years?

Perhaps if he himself went to talk to Levi . . .

But no. From what Miriam had said it was evident that

the old man, suddenly finding himself head of the clans, had already begun to harden into a position that allowed no negotiation.

Levi, he knew, had come to old age without ever being anything but a second in command, so now, as a leader, he had to be feeling insecure. People who felt that way were often the most stubborn of all.

Isesi now looked back at his own past and smiled ruefully. What a bigot he had been about the Habiru—about *all* foreigners in Egypt! Well, he had learned. Perhaps Levi could learn, too. Maybe he would have to.

He shivered and pulled his cloak more tightly around him. The fog was quite thick now; he could barely see from one guard post to the other. He would have to double the guard, to prevent intruders from slipping into the encampment under the cover of the blowing mist.

Ani went looking for Isesi, but the last of the fires had died, and the darkness and fog combined to make the search impossible. Even within the limited confines of the little encampment, Ani had managed to get himself thoroughly disoriented. In the dim moonlight that filtered through the fog he could not make out either the trail or the few landmarks he had depended upon earlier.

He stopped and cursed his own stupidity for not bringing a lighted torch. Perhaps he was being silly for going after Isesi anyway, he chided himself. The dwarf's premonitions could not always be reliable, and he would only make a fool of himself by communicating to Isesi the fears they had aroused in him. Now, if only he could find his way back to his own campfire—

Ahead, however, he suddenly heard a voice, singing low. He froze, listening. The voice was a deep and melodious bass, and the song was a hypnotic drone, full of aching sadness. He knew the voice, although he had never heard it singing. And he recognized the song, having heard it once in his youth, on a mission for the Egyptian government to Syria. It was a song of the dark cults of the Great Mother, which all men feared.

The Great Mother had many names. The oldest was Inanna and stemmed from ancient Ur and Eridu, cradles of all life. Her followers believed her to be the fountain from which all life, all reproduction, and all power sprang. Her story, savage and unrelenting, was the same in all lands, whether the name was Inanna or Ishtar or Cybele or Astarte or Aphrodite.

The singer's voice was almost tender:

> He is a tamarisk that in the garden has drunk no
>   water,
> Whose crown in the field has brought forth no
>   blossom.
> A willow that rejoices not by the watercourse,
> A willow whose roots are torn up.
> A herb that in the garden has drunk no
>   water . . ."

The voice sang in the language of the Syrians of the goddess's lament for her departed lover, the dead Dumusi—or Tammuz or Attis or Adonis. Every year he dies and goes to the Netherworld, to "the land from which there is no returning, to the house of darkness, where dust lies on door and bolt." Every year the goddess journeys in search of him to the Netherworld, and while she is gone, both men and beasts grow impotent and unable to reproduce their kind, and all life is threatened with extinction. This period is observed by the most horrible rituals, including human sacrifice, mass castration, and vivisection.

The cult believed that if the rituals were observed, then messengers of the great god Ea would be dispatched to the underworld to rescue the goddess from the terrible queen of the infernal regions. The goddess would be sprinkled with the water of life and reluctantly allowed to depart, bringing her revived lover, Dumusi, with her.

Dumusi would "hear" the lament twice: once when a youth, chosen as the "husband" of the goddess, was sacrificed by the cult just before midsummer, and then again when a second youth suffered Dumusi's final death—being torn to pieces by a priest of the cult while still alive, duplicating Dumusi's death by the bloody fangs of a wild boar.

Ani shivered violently in the foggy chill. What was the cult doing so far south, in a country where it had been banned for centuries on pain of death?

But of course! Amasis—and the sinister Makare, who

was doing the singing! Through these two the cult had spread to Egypt! They must be stopped!

"Very bad," a broken little voice beside Ani said, startling him. "Bad man. Tchabu much fear."

Ani turned in a panic. "Tchabu!" he whispered. "Go! Now!" He reached out in the darkness and shoved the little man from him. "Run!"

And as he did, he felt the knife in his back, just barely touching him, its razor-sharp point hardly breaking the skin. The silken voice of Amasis spoke. "Let him run. There is no place he can hide from us. But you—you stand where you are. Stand very still."

Ani craned his neck, trying to look back at the speaker. The knife bit deeper. "Hey," he said, trying to sound casual. "I was just looking for my tent. I got lost."

A face, square and black-bearded, loomed before him. It was Makare. His eyes were cold and mad, his mouth a red slit. Ani shuddered.

"You recognized my song," Makare said softly.

"No!"

"Dumusi dies a thousand times." Makare's frightful voice was almost a caress. "And a thousand thousands. In the month of Dumusi the parched earth is thirsty for the blood. No amount of blood, believer's or not, is enough to satisfy its thirst."

Ani, transfixed with terror, tried to cry out, but his voice broke and failed him. The unseen dagger in Makare's hand plunged into his body just below where the ribs met, ripping upward, tearing, savagely lifting him off the ground. The last sound he heard was Makare's low growl, a vicious, rumbling grunt like a wild boar's.

Little Tchabu writhed in the darkness, experiencing Ani's pain, feeling the life leave him. His whole body trembled with fear, and instead of running as Ani had told him to do, he remained rooted to the spot, not ten steps from the murderers. He could not see them, but he knew precisely where they were.

He had felt *their* emotions as well, and bore the agony of having witnessed the terrible scene of Ani's horrid death through their eyes. He struggled to master himself. In a moment they would come looking for him.

He had to run, as Ani had said, but where?

Kamose, he thought. *Kamose must be warned!* He had to make it to the camp of the Egyptians, to warn Kamose of the terrible danger. If these men were allowed to remain in Egypt . . .

He shuddered. The cult was a disease, one as virulent and dangerous as the plague that had suddenly appeared in Egypt. It would sweep across the whole land, infecting everyone.

It had already taken over much of Syria, he knew, and in the absence of the Habiru it had made great inroads in Canaan. Now it controlled much of the northern territories below the lands of the Hittites, west of the domain of Samsiditana of Babylon. Now it was ready to take over Egypt.

He could not let this happen. He had to escape upriver by whatever means, to reach Kamose at the head of his army and wise Baliniri in Thebes.

Tchabu agonized. His short legs could cover little ground, so his progress on foot would be too slow. Amasis would easily beat him to the Egyptian camp and discredit anything he might have to say. Amasis spoke the language of these people well, while he, Tchabu, could barely make himself understood. His only chance was to get there first and warn them of the terrible danger that had come to Egypt.

"You're out there, aren't you, little man?" Makare said. "And close by, too, I'll wager. Well, just stand still, and I'll come to find you."

Tchabu's heart was pounding wildly.

"Just stay right where you are," the voice said.

Closer! He could hear the soft footfalls now. A single shudder shook Tchabu's little body. He dived into the underbrush, stumbling through the palm scrub as fast as his tiny legs could carry him.

Behind him he could hear Amasis's voice: "What ho, the guard! Guard! Someone's been murdered! There's a spy among us! Help! Help!"

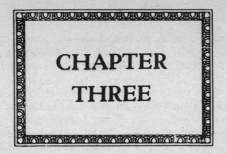

CHAPTER THREE

Before the Walls of Athribis

I

"Riki! Riki, sir, wake up!"

Riki came out of a troubled sleep, his hand already habitually reaching for the sword at his side. "What the—" His fingers closed on the handle of his weapon, and he would have struck at the intruder; but then reality broke through the web of illusion, half-dream, half-life, that had held him. In the flickering light of the only torch in his tent, he recognized his batman, Nibi, staring at him with frightened eyes, and his hand relaxed on the weapon.

"I'm sorry," Nibi said in his gently gravelly voice. "I wouldn't have waked you, sir, but the king gave me orders, sir. Personally."

Riki sat up and rubbed his eyes. "In the middle of the night?" He looked out at the darkness beyond the tent door. "How many hours before dawn?"

"Two, sir. His Majesty's runner woke me and told me to summon you now."

Riki stood, put on his loincloth, and searched with his toes for his sandals. Thus garbed, he buckled on his sword belt and only then returned his sword to its scabbard. "What does he want?"

"He didn't say," his manservant responded, "but rumors are already circulating among the watch. I think he's decided to hit them at dawn."

Riki yawned and made a moue. "They're ready to fall anyhow. I don't know why our men can't wait until morning to make an end of it." He yawned again and shook his head to clear it. "He does know Apophis has got away?"

"That should be evident to everyone, sir," Nibi answered. "It's common knowledge in the ranks, so I can't see how the king wouldn't know, too. Apophis got away under cover of that last counterattack the Hai tried, the one that seemed to have exhausted their will to fight."

Riki scratched his ribs and let out one last yawn. "Damn. Then why this call in the middle of the night? I don't get it, Nibi. There's a lot about the king that I don't understand these days. I'm sure it doesn't surprise you that Kamose and I haven't been getting along well lately."

"No, sir. That argument the two of you had before the walls of Memphis—"

Riki threw up his hands. "Sheer idiocy!"

"Please, sir. The night has a thousand ears."

Riki stared at him, then nodded slowly. "You're right. Thank you. I keep forgetting things aren't the same between him and me. Since he became king of the Red Lands, there's been a wall between us. There's a touch of his father's arrogance in him."

Nibi looked him in the eye, gulped, then took the plunge. "As of yours in you, sir."

There was a long silence. Riki's eyes bore into him. Nibi shivered but stood his ground. At last Riki let out a long breath. "I forget," he said. "You knew Baba of El-Kab. Better than I ever got a chance to know him."

"I served your father for ten years," Nibi said. "And I knew him for a proud and stubborn and insubordinate man. And, sir, if you'll pardon me—"

"Oh, go ahead and speak."

"Well, sir, I think that you test Kamose a great deal. If it weren't for your old friendship and the fact that you are of the real royal line of the Egyptian kings, with a better claim to the throne than Kamose"—here his voice lowered to a hoarse whisper—"I think he'd have had you hauled away in chains by now."

Riki held his frown for a long moment, then grinned. "Once more you remind me of why my father placed such trust in you," he said with rough affection. "It's hard to find a batman who will tell the truth when it needs telling."

"I'm glad you appreciate it, sir." Nibi placed his torch in the low receptacle in the middle of the tent floor, bent, and handed Riki his helmet. "Stronger even than the fact that Kamose knows about your mother, sir, is the fact that the line of troops know it."

"Fine," Riki said sourly. "Everyone in the army knows I'm a bastard."

"But son of the last queen of Egypt, sir, and of one of the greatest heroes the army ever had," Nibi added. "It's a wonderful story. You can't imagine how delighted the men were to find that your father had been the queen's lover, and that you and he were—"

"Enough," Riki broke in gruffly. "I imagine people calling me names out there."

"No, sir. Quite the opposite. If they're likely to call anyone names, it's—"

Now it was Riki's turn to put one finger over his lips. Nibi got the message instantly. The two exchanged glances. Then Riki said, "Come on. Let's go."

Outside were the faraway sounds of the garrison waking up and making ready for war. Riki strode impatiently through the long rows of tents, with Nibi limping gamely along after him. Nibi had been a troop leader under Baba in the old days but had sustained a severe leg wound that kept him from running after the foe. Baba, unwilling to discharge a good man, had pressed Nibi into service as his orderly, and Riki had inherited Nibi's services after Baba's death. Walking through the ranks, Riki cursed for the thousandth time the fate that had led him, after so many years of searching, to meet his father during the last battle the man ever fought. And how curious that destiny had made it the first battle in which he, Riki, had assumed command!

He had become a hero to the army that day, whereas

Baba had been a hero to his men for years. They would have died for him any day.

But perhaps it was not a fate to be cursed but one to give thanks for. Imagine: His own father had presided over his final fledging, over the battle in which he had come into his manhood once and for all! The man who had helped him come into his inheritance as a warrior and take command of the army had been the lost father he had searched for all his life!

He smiled warmly at the thought. *Fathers and sons.*

Now the other thought, the one he had been trying to avoid, tugged at his heart. It did not pay to think of one's loved ones in the middle of a battle; it tended to unman you, to make you overly cautious at precisely the time when you had to be bold and fearless. But . . .

Teti, he thought in spite of his best intentions. *Has she come to term yet? Am I a father at last? Do I have a son of my own? Teti . . .*

There was, of course, good reason for a warrior not to marry. If he started thinking of the cost or of what he would lose if he were to fall in battle, it would affect everything he did. And too often, these days, such things were on Riki's mind. A week ago he had hoped Athribis would fall quickly, so he could go back upriver to Thebes, to be with Teti when their first child was born. He missed her terribly.

But the Hai had held on doggedly, even when all hope was gone, even after Apophis had slipped away into the night like the coward he was and left his men to surrender or die. The fact that he, Riki, had been stuck here, unable to leave, had left him permanently out of sorts; he had had one argument after another with Kamose, Nibi, and even Elset, his finest general.

He frowned, thinking about it, and stepped up the pace, drawing away from Nibi as the lame orderly struggled vainly to keep up. There was a lot to fight with Kamose about these days, a side of his boyhood friend that he, Riki, did not know how to handle: He drove the men too hard. He had struck his orderly and fired a good officer over nothing at all.

And, worst of all, there was the way Kamose had handled the siege of Memphis. That had bordered on the unforgivable. When poor Memphis had first fallen to the Hai, there had been a terrible slaughter—the Hai had spent the night having their way with the helpless, unarmed women and children of the city.

When the Egyptians, under Kamose, had at last retaken the old capital from the Hai, they had understandably put the Hai defenders to the sword. But then Kamose had let his blood-crazed soldiers loose to rape and kill civilians just as the Hai invaders had done a generation ago! But this was Egyptians harming fellow Egyptians.

Riki's lip curled as he remembered the second fall of Memphis. He had received a blow to the head and had regained consciousness only after the walls were breached and the terrible cries of the civilians could be heard outside the city walls, where he had fallen. He had staggered inside, cursing, and had been appalled at what he had seen. He had ordered Kamose's no-quarter decree countermanded on the spot and had beaten one soldier insensible with the flat of his sword when he had caught the man raping a young girl.

There had been a blazer of an argument between him and Kamose then! And on that occasion he was sure that only the life debt owed him by Kamose had saved him. Now the debt was canceled; what would happen the next time they quarreled as bitterly as that?

Ah, Teti, he thought. *How I wish I were away from all this and home with you instead!*

Turning the corner and climbing the little hill toward Kamose's tent, which stood atop a rise for a better view of the surrounded city in the valley below them, he let his mind wander freely, and of course it went back to his wife. *Teti . . .*

He had never been in love before and had only a half-baked idea about what sort of woman would turn him into a lovesick fool: some tiny, delicate creature, soft-spoken and yieldingly feminine. But when lightning finally struck, he found himself in thrall to a tall, sun-browned, crop-haired goddess as tough, as hard, as tall as himself, and a little older . . . a woman with a strong forearm and hardened hands from years of journeyman work as a smith making weapons.

But it had been love at first sight, apparently as much for her as it had been for him. He had been sent on a secret mission deep into the desert, where she had withdrawn some years earlier to live an ascetic life with her band of warrior-women and the silent cheetahs with which they hunted. He had been ordered by Baliniri to bring Teti and her women into the war for the final showdown that would have meant the total defeat and destruction of the Egyptians if they had lost. Deep, deeper into the desert he had marched, and then, at the end of a string of oases, he had finally met her.

Shortly after their meeting she had suffered a seizure and had fallen to the ground as if she were dead. He had since learned that the attack had been brought on by the death of her twin brother, Ketan, whose mind she had to some extent shared. She had traveled with him into the Netherworld before returning. And in that magic moment before rejoining the living, she had seen into her own future and learned that she was to marry Riki.

So it had happened. They had been happier together than he could have ever imagined. She, who had loved before—a young soldier named Netru, who had died a hero at the battle of El-Kab years before—told him that even that earlier experience could not compare with what she now felt.

And, curse it, he had had to go back to war, leaving her just when she was coming to term with their first child!

He looked back. Nibi was struggling gamely with the steps, his bad leg obviously bothering him. Riki decided to wait. But as he stood, hands on hips, he heard rash, impatient footfalls behind him. He knew whose they were and did not turn.

"There you are!" said a harsh voice. "Where have you been? Get up here on the double!"

The steps went away. Riki, looking downhill, caught Nibi's eye. He raised one eyebrow and made a moue. Nibi blinked but said nothing, puffing awkwardly up to meet him, his perplexed expression evident by the light of the torches that stood to both sides of the path.

It was going to be quite a morning, Riki thought.

II

Coming into the command tent, he had almost made up his mind to let the affront pass. But when he straightened up and looked around, he saw Kamose alone. *Well*, he thought, *as good a time as any.* "Kamose," he said evenly, "I don't care how you talk when we're alone. I don't even care how you talk before my batman. But the troops down the hill could hear you abusing me, and for no reason—"

"No reason?" Kamose shot back in a tight, overbearing voice. "You took your time getting here, let me tell you! When I send orders down the hill, I expect an immediate response!" Riki caught the look in his eye, and there was something new there. "Damn you—"

"Here, now," Riki said, his tone more conciliatory. "What's wrong, old friend? Get up on the wrong side of the bed? Eat something last night that disagreed with you?"

At first the light words seemed to enrage the young king; then, after a long moment, he mastered himself. He took a deep breath, then blew it out. "You're right," he admitted. "It's not you. I apologize. I didn't get any sleep last night, and not much the night before."

Riki moved forward to put one hand on his friend's arm. "I'm sorry. I should have known. I could have the physicians stop by—"

"No, no." Kamose moved away and spoke with his back to Riki. "No," he said again after a pause. "There's nothing wrong . . . physically. I don't know what's the matter. I can't get along with anyone these days." He turned and looked at his old friend, a look of deep hurt in his eyes. "Not even with Mara. Before I left home last time, we quarreled. I . . . I struck her. How could I have done that? But it was as though someone else were in control. I don't know what got into me."

"Domestic quarrels are the worst," Riki sympathized. "To hurt someone you love, or to be hurt by her—"

"But she hadn't done anything! She's everything I wanted her to be—strong, independent." He shrugged. "None of that has changed. It's just that . . ." He let the sentence hang. His broad shoulders drooped; then he shrugged and let out a great sigh, throwing up his hands and letting them fall.

"You could use some time off," Riki suggested. "You've been here on the line for four months without a break. Once we've taken this town, perhaps you could rest for a couple of weeks."

"No! No!" Kamose exclaimed, suddenly agitated again. "When Athribis falls, we've got to pursue Apophis all the way to Avaris! We've already let him get away as it is!" He pounded his hard left fist into his right palm. "Curse the luck! I thought I had him boxed in. But that lot inside there, they outsmarted me! They'll pay for this! When the city falls, I'll turn the troops loose on them—women, children, and old people! I want no one left alive—"

Now Riki spoke harshly and firmly. "That's just the thing you're not going to do. I told you before, and I'm telling you again: We'll respect the white flag. The moment they surrender and are taken prisoner, they'll be treated humanely."

"Humanely? *Humanely?* Those murdering bastards—"

"They're Egyptians, Kamose! They're the people you're going to have to reign over once we've won! If you kill prisoners, everyone will know—"

"Let them know!"

"And as for killing civilians—"

"When did you grow so softhearted? I tell you—"

"*No!*" Riki bellowed, beside himself with rage. "It isn't going to happen! Not while I'm running this army!"

There. Now it was out. Kamose's eyes blazed, and he almost said it. Riki knew that the king was on the brink of dismissing him as commander of the army. Kamose's hand clenched and unclenched; his face was cold and tense.

It was perhaps a time for conciliation, but Riki was in no mood for that. He reached down for his belt, unbuckled it, and laid it on the table between them. "There," he said. "The only thing we lack to make it official is a witness to my resignation and your acceptance of it." His voice was vibrant with feeling. "Pick up my sword, and I go back to Thebes."

His eyes locked with Kamose's. He watched the king's hand open and close not a handspan from the sword belt. "Go ahead," he challenged. "If that's what you want, pick it up. Nibi is just outside, and he can be our witness. If you want someone who'll never say no to you, who'll cut his conscience to fit yours, you'd better pick it up."

"Damn you," Kamose snarled. "You know I won't. You know I need you."

"You don't need me to capture Athribis. And after the surrender, you can do anything you want. But if you allow wholesale slaughter, then you'll be unable to govern because you'll be unfit to govern."

At the word "unfit," Kamose's eyes blazed again but only for a moment. "Pick up the sword," he relented. "We'll have it your way."

Riki's eyes searched his for a long moment; then he slowly reached for the belt on the table and put it on. "I was hoping you'd hold to your position," he said, trying for a light tone but succeeding only in part. "I miss Teti and want to be there when the baby comes."

Kamose clapped him on the shoulder with false heartiness. "I understand, but I can't spare you." There was an insincerity to his voice, which Riki liked even less than the bluster and bad temper that had preceded it, the sort of tone one affected when speaking to a fool. "Come, let's discuss the day's work. I expect to have Athribis in hand by nightfall. Now, look here." The table was a shallow sandbox on tall, thin legs. The order of battle of the besieging army had been set up before the walls of a miniature city in the middle of the sandpile. "Here's the Fourth over here, and here are you and the Third."

The patronizing tone was still there. It had never been there before today. What was wrong? What had gone sour in their long friendship?

The attack was launched at dawn, just as Kamose had ordered. But once Riki had been armed and had gone off to war, the day's work for a noncombatant like Nibi, was largely over. As the war cry went up and the men in the valley stormed the walls of the dying city, Nibi commandeered a skin of wine and a bag of olives and climbed the highest point on the ridge to look down at the fight.

As he did, he was joined by Shu, the king's own batman. True to form, Shu had come well prepared. An experienced old dog robber, he had brought a jug of palm wine and a leather satchel containing bread and cheese. Shu smiled broadly. "Between us, we've a veritable breakfast banquet."

Nibi made a place for Shu on the hard ground beside him. "Here," he offered. "These aren't the best olives of the season, but I'm hungry, so they'll do. Dig in."

Shu gladly did so. "I'll have some of the olives. Lend me your pig sticker, and I'll cut off some of this cheese for you. It's good, strong stuff." He hacked away with the borrowed knife and handed over a wedge of foul-smelling cheese and a handful of flat bread. "Our masters had a bit of a blowup this morning," he said offhandedly.

Nibi, eyes on the scene below, did not respond at first. "Ah," he said, "the king's in a vile mood. What a battler he is when he's out of sorts! Look at him there! He caught the second man with the backswing! One swipe and the recovery, and two men dead! I'll have to tell my master to provoke him whenever we go into battle!"

Shu, looking at him thoughtfully, took this for the answer it was meant to be. "Are they still friends?" he asked.

"They ended friends," Nibi said. He took a bite of the cheese, made a face, and washed it down with wine. "Ugh! Where did you get this stuff? From a goat that died of the plague?"

The word just slipped out. Shu was silent for a long moment. "So you've heard about it, too," he said.

"I thought everybody had," Nibi replied. Now Kamose's troops were storming the main gate of the city. "Six cases in the nearest neighboring town this week, and all of them died within three days."

"Eight cases," Shu corrected. "Two more last night. They're still alive, but no one gives them long."

"Ah, me," Nibi sighed, pulling at his wine bag. "I don't like this at all. Plague, old boy, can strike even at noncombatants like *us*. And here I'd counted on dying in my bed years from now, of old age. I wonder what brought it on? A surgeon from the Fourth Troop told me that he's read every medical scroll he could get his hands on, and not one even mentioned an authenticated case of plague in Egypt."

"Maybe some evil spirit has wished it on us for our sins," Shu ventured. "I wouldn't put it past those Habiru over at Avaris to have that nameless God of theirs put us under some sort of spell."

"Nonsense," Nibi snorted. "You don't believe that, do you? You just don't like the foreigners." He ate a bit more of the cheese. "Really, this isn't too bad. It sort of grows on you. Have some more olives."

"Thank you," Shu said. "Ah! Look! They've breached the wall! They're over the top! Not long now, I'd say. But look you, if the plague hits big here, we're in trouble, aren't we? Nobody has the faintest idea what to do about it. Once the plague decides to come to your town, you might as well choose your shroud."

"Bosh. I have no intention of catching it. Don't tell me you're growing paranoid in your dotage, you old fool."

"I don't know," Shu confessed. Tired of Nibi's censorious tone, he changed the subject back to where it had begun. "I hope our masters can keep their tempers tonight. *Your* master, now, provokes the king beyond endurance sometimes."

He paused expectantly. Nibi turned and stared at him, understanding dawning. "The king would like you to bring back something juicy that I've relayed to you, wouldn't he? He'd like to get something on Riki, something he's said that's seditious. Well, my master simply doesn't talk that way. Let's get off the subject, eh?" He took another stiff swig of wine. "Don't teach an old dog to suck eggs, my friend."

"It was worth a try," Shu said. "No hard feelings, eh?"

In the first moments after the breakthrough, Riki's Third Troop, fanning out into the northern end of the city, had encountered stiff resistance and had lost contact with the Fourth, under Kamose. The defenders had chosen to make a stand in the Market of the Sun, and when Riki's men rushed out of the side streets and into the little square, they were met with a barrage of arrows. Three of his men fell; the advance faltered.

"Here!" Riki bellowed. "Archers to the front! Archers! Archers, to me!"

A squad of bowmen came up from the rear and deployed themselves in various places around the square. Two were sent to the rooftops and immediately began their deadly work, lofting volleys of arrows into the entrenched enemy. Riki looked around, cursed, and motioned to four of his men. "Come with me!" he ordered, and set out quickly through the eastern streets. If he could outflank them now and sneak his men in behind them . . .

He paused at a corner. "Damn!" he said. "I've only been in Athribis once before this. I don't know the town. Do any of you—"

"This way, sir!" a young soldier offered. "There's a way up the back alley."

"Lead the way!" Riki ordered, and set out after him with the other three in tow. The young man did indeed know his way; the path they followed was a tortuous one, through the alleys, over fences, even cutting through a warehouse to emerge onto a new street. But at length the young soldier stopped and faced them.

"Here, sir," he whispered close to Riki's ear. "We're right behind them. If the three of you can go around the building from this direction, the rest of us can slip around the other way."

"Right you are!" Riki said with an appreciative grin. He motioned his men forward, making note of this young soldier's quick and resourceful performance.

But before following them down the narrow path, something caught his eye, something that stopped him in his tracks.

Somehow Kamose's troop had sliced its way through its end of the city almost to meet his unit. The armed Hai defenders had proved little hindrance to them as they battled their way back into the civilian sector of the city.

Down the broad street in which he stood, Riki could see the soldiers of Kamose's command, unopposed now, yanking open doors, pulling civilians out into the street. As he watched, one of Kamose's lieutenants hauled a tall, lean young woman with a child in her arms into the thoroughfare. He threw her roughly to the ground, and the baby flew from her grasp. The soldier's sword rose.

"*No!*" Riki screamed. "*Stop!*"

The sword fell. Again. Again!

Yet another stroke finished the child.

"Stop! Stop, you bastard!" Riki cried. "I'll kill you for that!"

The soldier looked up, saw him, smiled insolently, and turned back to his gory work. Now an old woman cowered before him.

Riki's hand trembled on his sword hilt. It was too far away for him to do anything. He was needed in his own assault. He could not spare the time.

The red rage burned in his heart. He blinked away bitter tears and turned back to his own fight, shaken, nearly vomiting his guts in the street.

The girl who had died, the one with the baby. She had looked like Teti.

And the soldier? The one who had killed her and her child? The one who had grinned at him so insolently? Just following orders, obviously.

III

An hour later it was all over but the surrender of small pockets of resistance that still flared in the southeastern corner of the city. These would be eliminated soon. In the more heavily populated quarters, the Hai army had surrendered one unit at a time, the supreme commander of the defending force having been killed soon after the walls were breached.

Now Kamose's victorious attacking army led long lines of naked, shamed, and miserable prisoners out through the shattered front gate, their hands bound behind their backs, their necks tethered to one another's by leather cords. Once outside the city, they were herded into long files, where the Egyptian sergeant in charge stood before them, awaiting orders concerning their disposition.

Along the long lines strolled Nibi and Shu, Nibi favoring his game leg. Neither was in a hurry; each knew that his services would be needed soon, but neither wished to confront his master while the blood was still up. "Poor bastards," Nibi remarked of the prisoners. "Well, at least the war's over for them."

"The war and everything else, the way I hear it," Shu said.

"What do you mean?" Nibi asked. "My master gave orders that they be given the choice: to fight for us, or—"

"Fight for us?" Shu snorted. "Bunch of Shepherd swine? Not very likely, I'd say. You know what *my* master thinks about the likes of these. Besides, the siege has been long and hard and has cost us a lot of good men."

Nibi, appalled, shot a horrified glance at him. "The king would countermand my master's order after the argument they had?"

"*Particularly* after all the arguing," Shu confirmed. "Good heavens, man. You don't think the argument was over just because they stopped shouting at each other!"

"You mean he'd just line the civilians up and have them killed?" He looked around at the wretched lines of tethered prisoners.

"Don't be an ass. Kamose won't back down." Shu looked up and saw Captain Elset, Riki's right-hand officer, come striding out through the gate, just as Kamose's adjutant, Djoser, came riding around the corner of the city wall on a captured Moabite charger. "Watch," Shu said, pointing at the horseman. "This ought to be interesting." He steered Nibi toward the captain in charge, the better to overhear the anticipated coming exchange.

As expected, the horseman pulled up short, his mount kicking up dust. "You!" Djoser said. "Sergeant! What are these prisoners doing lined up here?"

"Awaiting orders, sir," the sergeant said mildly.

"You have your orders. Carry them out!"

"But, sir. The general said—"

Now, however, Elset caught up with them. He gave Djoser an equal's curt nod. "Sergeant," he said, "Riki says to confine these prisoners down by the river until he can get there. You can move them out now."

"Move them out?" Djoser sneered. "The sergeant has prior orders, which invalidate those. I'm waiting for him to carry them out." His smile was cold and unfriendly. "Well, Sergeant?"

Elset's eyes narrowed. "What orders?" he asked the sergeant. Like Djoser he ignored the two batmen standing nearby.

"Uh, sir, the king ordered them killed."

"Killed? Do that, Sergeant, and you'll decorate a pike above the city wall. Count on it."

"But—"

Djoser barked out a nasty laugh. "It seems our poor sergeant has two sets of orders. The only thing to do is carry out both orders, in order of rank. Kill them first, then move them out."

Standing on the fringe of things, Shu, his eyes still on the confrontation between the two officers, spoke out of the corner of his mouth, keeping his voice down. "Well, now," he said to Nibi, "there's a solution for you."

But as he spoke he chanced to look in the direction of his words. "Nibi?" he said, craning his head around now.

Nibi was nowhere to be found!

"I don't care what he says!" Riki said in a tight voice. "The first Egyptian I catch laying hands on a peaceful civilian who's doing no one any harm, I'll cut his damned heart out myself!"

The under officer before him threw back his shoulders and saluted stiffly. "Yes, sir! It's just that conflicting orders are being circu—"

"Hear me!" Riki said, his voice rising. "The same applies to anyone who wrongly or falsely transmits my orders. Do you understand?"

The officer caught the fire in Riki's eye and further stiffened his brace. "Yes, sir!" With one last salute, he moved away briskly, eager to get out of the general's presence.

Riki looked down and found he was still holding his bloody sword in one trembling hand. "Damn!" he said, sheathing it. He took a deep breath and looked around angrily. The day had not gone as he had wanted it to, and things seemed to be getting worse. Where was Nibi, confound it?

But the thought worked wonders, it appeared. Through the gate came Nibi, hopping along at what might well have been his maximum speed. "Sir!" the orderly called, panting. "There's a situation out front that demands your attention."

"Report!" Riki said, his eyes narrowing.

Nibi, heart pounding, got it all out almost in one breath, his eyes on Riki's fiery face. The batman couldn't remember ever seeing quite this look on his master's face. "Hurry, sir! If we're to stop them—"

"It'll be too late now," Riki said, seething. "Djoser outranks Elset because the king outranks me." His white-knuckled hand clutched the hilt of his sword, and a tremor shook his upper body. "Besides, what good would it do to take Djoser to task? He's just following the king's order."

"But what can you do, sir, in good conscience, but countermand it? And discipline the officers who—"

Nibi caught Riki's eye then and saw the focus had changed to the middle distance. He wheeled. Kamose, his uniform filthy with blood and dirt, strode toward them, trailing two lieutenants walking at heel like dogs.

Riki drew his sword in a trembling hand.

"No, sir!" Nibi begged in a loud whisper.

Riki set out to meet the threesome.

"Please, sir!" Nibi pleaded, limping after him.

Kamose stopped, as did the soldiers flanking him.

"You, you whore's foal!" Riki snarled in a voice throbbing with rage.

It was obvious his words were not aimed at the king. The soldier on Kamose's right stepped back. His hand went to his own sword, but it was already too late.

Riki's sword flashed, and moving forward almost too quickly to be seen, it buried itself to the hilt in the officer's belly!

The soldier was dead before he fell. The light left his eyes, the hand on his sword relaxed, his knees buckled, and he pitched to the sand at Riki's feet.

Kamose's hands clenched, and his eyes blazed. "You drew a sword in my presence," he said in a voice as full of surprise as of anger. "You killed one of my men!"

Riki faced him. His eyes had a terrible look in them. "I caught him killing a civilian woman and her child. They offered no resistance. He knew I was watching, and he laughed at me." His voice was flat and cold. "I would kill a hundred more who tried to stop me."

The king's eyes locked with his general's. Neither said anything for a long, long moment.

"These are your fellow Egyptians!" Riki exploded. "I sent orders regarding the disposition of prisoners. They were countermanded by Djoser." Venom crept into his voice. "He spoke for the king."

He let the accusation hang there, waiting for denial or confirmation.

"He spoke for me," Kamose challenged, hardness creeping back into his tone. "Damn you! Do you think to question orders given by me?" The voice rose in pitch. "By the gods, man, I am your king!"

Riki reached down and harshly yanked the sword from the officer he had killed. "I see no king," he hissed. "I see a pair of butchers before me, butchers who haven't the excuse that they kill for someone's table. Or have you started eating the sort of meat you've ordered killed today? Women? Children? Unarmed prisoners?"

"Don't you talk to me that way!"

"I'll talk to you as I damned well please," Riki shot back. "Who do you think put you on that throne?" Kamose winced. "How high above the crowd do you think you sit, particularly after ordering brave soldiers to cowardly things? Do you have any idea what you're doing to this army we worked so hard to build?"

"Hold your tongue!"

Kamose drew his sword.

Riki's arm went over his head, his still-bloody weapon poised to sweep powerfully down.

Kamose's hand rose to parry.

Riki's sword flashed down and buried itself in the sand between them!

"You—you *dare!*" Kamose gasped.

"I'm done with this war!" Riki exploded. "I warned you, but you wouldn't listen. I'm going back home to my wife. Do your own dirty work."

"You leave now and I'll—"

"You'll what?" he asked with contempt. "Have me killed? The way you have someone kill babies for you? Well, be careful, because *this* baby might fight back!" He let the words

sink in, then spat out more after them. "You've seen me
fight. You must have wondered from time to time if you
could take me. Well, now's the time, Kamose. My sword's
halfway between us. But I'm faster than you, more agile.
Always have been, going all the way back to the bazaars of
Avaris where I saved your life when we were a couple of
beardless urchins with a price on our heads."

"Riki, if—"

"Make your move! Or, by the gods, I'll make mine! And
it'll be right out that open gate!"

Kamose's face was dripping with sweat. His hands flexed
and unflexed. He tried to speak, but his throat was too dry.
"R-riki . . ." he began. His voice broke.

"Good-bye," Riki said, and turned on his heel to march
away.

IV

In the first panicky hours Tchabu had struck out overland, toward the southwest, trusting to the darkness and the
low fog to hide him from the patrols that still roamed the
highroads. Twice he had had to ford shallow branches of the
many streams that crisscrossed the delta, and once he had
had to swim, his tiny limbs churning desperately as he struggled to keep his huge head above water.

Then, in the late morning of the next day, a man driving
an oxcart had offered him a ride southward, which he had
gratefully accepted. The effort of walking and running, given
the stubbiness of his little legs, was more than he knew he
would be able to sustain over the long haul.

The oxcart driver wasn't in a talking mood, for which
Tchabu was grateful. It allowed him to sift out his thoughts
and decide what to do.

His first idea was to try to get through to Kamose directly, to warn him of the impending danger—to tell him
who Amasis and Makare were and what they were up to. The
king's forces must know that they were up against men capable of infiltrating and corrupting any organization—and of
killing anyone who resisted.

Now, however, as he sat curled in the rear of the cart, he was beginning to question the wisdom of this plan. One thing he had learned during the moment he had spent inside their minds still frightened him more than he could say: that Kamose himself was one of them.

This was the extremely unsettling picture he had got. He had taken in none of the details, but he had learned beyond all doubt that there was a link between these evil men and the king. Their association apparently went back a long way, and they thought of him as . . . not a friend, but something more like a puppet, a chattel, a man to be driven and manipulated. This, at least, was the perception he had found in the brutal and contemptuous mind of Makare, the heavy one. Perhaps Makare perceived of all men that way, though: everyone, at least, but his companion Amasis, whom he feared.

Could he, Tchabu, then bring the message to Kamose? "Your friends have returned, sire, and they're evil. Don't listen to them when they come."

No! That was not an option. But there was always General Riki. He was universally said to be a good man of the highest principles. Isesi himself had said so. For a moment back there, Tchabu had found himself inside Isesi's mind, and the thoughts about Riki that he had found there were reassuring in the extreme.

Yes, that was the proper thing to do. He would get through to Riki and warn him. The general would know how to defend himself against these monsters. He could head them off when they came to Athribis and tried to reassert their influence over the man who now was king.

Perhaps Riki could even contrive, somehow, to save Isesi. He shuddered. If no one intervened, Isesi was doomed. Isesi—open, trusting with his friends and with those he thought to be his friends—was no match for the wily Amasis. What a pity there had been no opportunity to warn Isesi before he had fled! But there had been little time to think of saving anyone but himself.

Where were those monsters now? he wondered. That broad road they had passed, running east and west, could be the road from Bach to Phakussa. If this was the case, they were not far from Thmuis! Quickly he wheeled and called up to the driver. "My friend," he said. "Where we go now? We go Thmuis?"

"Why, yes," the driver answered. "I have a load to pick up. I can let you off there if you like."

"No, no," Tchabu replied. "Not want cities. Tchabu not like cities. I get down. I go now."

"Wait," the driver said. "I'll help you down." He turned his lined, kindly face back toward the little man in the rear. "Don't jump; you'll only hurt yourself."

"Is all right," Tchabu said. He poised himself and dropped easily to the ground. He hit the ground rolling and was on his feet again, brushing himself off, before the ox had taken three more steps. "Thanks many," he called after the driver. "Good-bye!"

The driver turned to wave. Tchabu, standing beside the road, watched him for quite a while as the cart made its deliberate way down the dusty thoroughfare. A kind and harmless man, he thought. There were so many such here in Egypt, ruled by such bad men.

Suddenly his eyes went wide. He had had a flash of something important: The river would be nearby! He had to get to the river!

He looked around him. Yes, it would be that way, due west. At Thmuis a deep stream sliced diagonally across the delta before turning southward and paralleling the Damietta branch of the Nile for many leagues. At length it would wend its way all the way to Athribis before joining the Nile farther south.

An ox path cut across a farmer's fields to the west of him. He left the road and hurried along the path, hoping he was not too late. The vision he had had in his mind had been confused and vague; all he knew was that he had to get to the river, and fast.

Sure enough, fifteen minutes' walk down the narrow trail brought him to a place where the stream cut its way through tall banks on both sides, its channel deep and straight. Here a boat bound upriver under sail would need all the wind it could get to make way against the strong current headed northward toward the Great Sea, and perhaps oarsmen to help the wind along.

He stood looking downstream. A stone's throw down the bank a lone fisherman sat lazily regarding his lines. "Good day, my friend," the fisherman said. "Looking for a place to fish?"

"No, no." Tchabu shook his large head. "Look for boat. Boat come this way from Tanis?"

"No," the fisherman said. "Not from Tanis. Although the stream passes nearby. Why? Are you looking for passage?"

"Maybe," Tchabu said. "Maybe want ride." He felt in his tunic for his purse. He still had the money they had given him at Bast for his services, translating during the interrogation of Northern prisoners. "You know when boat come?"

The fisherman looked at the sun and calculated. "An hour, maybe. Wait . . . no. Someone told me it was passing earlier these days. Curse the luck! It'll come through and spoil the fishing." He looked morosely at his lines. "Well, it isn't as if there was much to spoil." He peered downstream. "Speak of a demon, and . . . isn't that a sail?"

Tchabu craned his short neck. "Not stand tall enough. Cannot see. You look for me, yes? Please?"

The fisherman stood. "Why, yes. You're in luck! You want me to hail it as it comes by? It isn't likely they'll see you. No offense," he added courteously.

Tchabu closed his eyes and concentrated, but the flash of premonition did not return. "No, please. Wait and see."

The boat drew nearer. It was a fast packet, and its lateen sail's billowing spread was augmented by six stout rowers: tall, naked, sunburned blond giants with the battered faces of captured mercenaries. Tchabu moved behind a low palm and stared.

Yes! There was the proud pennant of the Brotherhood of Shai, Isesi's flag! In this area Isesi's band had grown bold, flaunting its independence and its allegiance to the Egyptian cause.

He blinked and stared, his mouth hanging open.

At virtually the same moment he saw the figure and recognized it, the dark head also turned his way. The eyes scanned the riverbank, saw him, and knew him.

Amasis!

The eyes blazed, the powerful hands clenched at the rail, and the face grew taut. From this frozen countenance came a terrible smile.

Once more Tchabu suddenly found himself inside that awful mind! His hands covered his ears, but there was no sound. His eyes closed, but shut eyelids could not close out what he saw in his mind.

He screamed. "No! *No!*"

He had no idea how much later it was when he found himself lying on his back in the soft grass, the fisherman bent over him. "Are you all right?" he asked anxiously.

Tchabu sat up, but dizziness forced him down again.

"Please," he begged, grasping the fisherman's arm with his stubby fingers. "Did boat stop? Did man get off?"

"No, no," the fisherman assured him, gently restraining the tiny seer as he tried to rise. "He shouted an order at the boatmen, but they paid him no mind. It would've been a hard place to stop."

"They not come ashore farther upstream?" Tchabu made himself sit up. "They not come back for me?"

"Not as far as I could tell. I watched 'em quite a ways." He sat back on his heels and eyed Tchabu with concern. "You're sure you're all right? You fainted dead away. Look, my name's Bimi. Why don't I take you to my place? My wife could fix you something to eat."

"Thank you, Bimi," Tchabu said. "But must go. Must go upriver, fast as can."

Then he thought about what he had said. Go where? To Athribis? That would be suicide now, for Amasis was obviously heading that way. The monster would be waiting for him when he got there.

If he could reach Riki— But no. He would be taking his life in his hands, going there. What to do? What to do?

"Look friend," Bimi said, "you don't look good at all, and that's a fact. I'd really recommend you come home with me. You look like you could use a good night's sleep."

"Is true. I run all night."

"From that man on the boat?"

"Yes. Bad man. Very dangerous. He kill my friend. He want to kill me."

"He sure looked like it. Well, you better stay out of his way. Where was it you wanted to go? Maybe there's a way there that will allow you to avoid him."

Tchabu thought. If he could get to see Baliniri . . . Yes. Surely Baliniri would have had experience with a cult as widespread as this and would know what to do. From what Isesi and the others told him, Baliniri was resourceful and wise, a man who would not be fooled even by as crafty a man as Amasis. But he was so far away.

Tchabu looked into the fisherman's clear and friendly eyes, and for a moment he also looked into the man's simple and guileless mind. Yes, Bimi was all right. A good man who could be trusted, for a night at least. "I want go to Thebes," he said. "All way upriver to Thebes."

He knew with a certainty that it was the right thing to do—an important journey of many days, but one he had to make, for the fate of Egypt might well depend on it.

"That's a long way," the fisherman remarked. "Tell you what: You come home with me and think it over when you've had a good night's rest and a couple of decent meals." He smiled and helped Tchabu to his feet. "Maybe you'll change your mind. That's quite a trip for a little fellow."

Tchabu smiled back and bowed courteously to his host. "Much thanks," he said. "You lead way. I follow." His mind was racing. If he cut across the river and went overland to where he could pick up the Damietta branch of the Nile and caught a boat from there, he would not be sailing through Athribis, right under Amasis's nose.

"Come along, then," the fisherman said.

Riki's rank was such that he had been able to commandeer a boat and crew for the trip upriver. Still, right up to sailing time he had been braced and ready for a sudden order from Kamose for his arrest. This had not happened. And now he was an hour out of Athribis, with a full sail and ten burly rowers who had settled into a long, powerful cruising stroke under the hortator's steady beat.

When he turned to Nibi, there was still a bitter edge to his voice. "I feel as though I'd escaped from the jaws of a hungry lion."

"I'd say that was an accurate description of things as they stand, sir," the batman replied noncommittally. "Do you think you'll go back, sir?"

"Ask me in a month or so," Riki answered. "And between now and then, if you catch me talking about Kamose, the war, or anything downstream from Thebes, you have my leave to kick me until your foot hurts." He let out a sigh. "You know what, my friend? I've finally figured out what's been eating away at me. I grew up in the streets without owning anything. Now, for the first time in my life, I'm homesick." He smiled. "I wish all my problems in life were as easily cured."

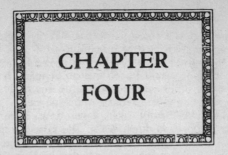

CHAPTER FOUR

Thebes

I

"Hail, Sesa!" the fisherman called when his one-man boat was still some distance from land. "Sesa! It's I!"

Sesa, the boatman, looked up from his work, blinking at the figure far out in the water and trying to place the face. The spokeshave sat idle in his hand. Confound it all, what was the fellow's name, now?

"It's I! Pemu, the fisherman!" the voice called from the Nile. "Stay where you are! I'm coming to shore!"

Now Sesa remembered him—the two had got drunk together one night a year before, over here on the Deir el-Bahari side of the Nile. It was not as if they were friends. Well, that was the way it was with fishermen, who, spending months at a time away from town, made attachments quickly. He shrugged and motioned Pemu to shore. When the little craft had nosed its way to land beside Sesa's own ferryboat and Pemu had jumped ashore, Sesa allowed himself to be embraced as if by a long-lost brother. "Well," he said, extricating himself, "what have you been up to?"

"I've been upriver," Pemu replied. "We've been hearing rumors up that way, and I can't wait to hear the truth."

"Ask away," Sesa urged, taking up his tools again and smoothing out a splintery section of his lee rail.

"All right. Is it true there's plague down here?"

Sesa put the tools down again. "It's true we have a case or two. Nobody's died in Thebes, although two people have over here. Until last week Thebes hadn't had any cases at all. There have been maybe two dozen over here."

"I landed on the wrong side of the river!" Pemu joked.

Sesa sighed. This fellow was stretching his patience. "You can always repair that," he suggested mildly, "but you won't be welcome there either, if you insist upon discussing the plague. You could wind up incurring Baliniri's wrath. His position is that a panic is best averted by not mentioning the plague."

"All right. What's this about there being trouble between Kamose and the army?"

He picked up his spokeshave. "Another subject you'd better not go hollering about over in the city, my friend. I'm amazed such information has made its way upstream. Where have you been this past year?"

"El-Kab, mostly."

"Ah! Then you can settle a rumor or two that float around down *here*. The word is," Sesa said, lowering his voice, "that the upriver nobles are in open revolt against the court. That they refuse to acknowledge Kamose as king. That they aren't paying their taxes." He finished smoothing down the rough spot and tossed his tools into the bottom of his beached boat. "Do we have a revolt brewing or not?"

"The nobles in El-Kab would have gladly seen Baliniri on Sekenenre's throne—the more so as he's now married to Sekenenre's widow," Pemu said. "She was popular with them. There was that story about her having an affair in her youth with one of their countrymen, a soldier."

"Yes, Baba. I remember. But Baliniri isn't king. Kamose is."

"He is as long as he can get a majority of the chief administrators of the districts to endorse him, and as long as the priesthood of Amon goes along with the idea. But the southern nobles don't like having a half-Hai king whose background isn't known. They don't like the fact that they weren't consulted. I mean, one day Sekenenre is killed, and virtually the next moment, we have this fellow—he admits he's a bastard of Apophis's, mind you—coming out of nowhere and taking over, mainly on the strength of some prophecy they never heard of."

Sesa made a moue. "I admit it does sound weak. So they've actually been withholding taxes?"

"Yes, and withholding the draft of their young men for Kamose's war against the Hai. They're actually maintaining a garrison of their own."

"That's illegal!"

"True. But they justify it by saying that they're the buffer between Egypt and Nubia."

Sesa raised one brow. "We weren't at war with Nubia last time I heard."

"No, but the Nubian king, Nehsi, also has reservations about Kamose, way I hear it. Nehsi *and* his mother, Ebana."

"I wouldn't want to be the one to make Ebana angry. She and her women-warriors have settled more than one war, I'd wager. And there's something brewing now, something I'd not want to be in the way of. I've been told to wait here, to transport some women-warriors across the river, and here I'll sit, without complaints or questions. No, it'll take death itself to make old Ebana anything but dangerous." He looked past Pemu now, upriver, and his eyes widened. "Well!" he said. "They've come at last. And aren't they a sight!"

Pemu turned. "Gods!" he sputtered. "Look at them, won't you? One of them's Black Wind, that's for sure. But who is the other one? Some goddess come up from the Netherworld to tantalize us poor mortals?"

Sesa smiled but said nothing as he stood looking at the two women.

They were a striking, exotic sight. Tall and straight like a couple of cranes, they stood side by side looking back at the men. One was as black as coal, her skin so dark that it did not seem even to reflect the sunlight. Her eyes glowed. She wore nothing but a quiver of arrows tossed over one shoulder, from close-cropped hair to bare and hardened soles; her long-fingered hands held bow and spear.

Sesa smiled. "You're right about the Black Wind. The Nubian is a member of Ebana's elite guard, on loan down this way to the warrior-women of the oases. You know, Teti's old unit. And the other is Teti's lieutenant, Weret." He sighed. "Neither has any interest in men. And they could carve us into pieces with five strokes of any weapon known to man."

"You've just broken my heart," Pemu said. "I'm in love with Weret . . . hopelessly, if what you say is true. Gods, what a woman! Look at those thighs! Does she go around naked all the time? They ought to make her wear a tunic, at least, if only to keep people like me from eating their hearts out."

Sesa chuckled. "I'm supposed to take them across the river. I'll tell you what: Meet me at the Inn of the Black Onager at sundown, eh? We can have dinner together." He shoved his beached boat into the water and held it in the shallows, motioning to the two women. As he did, a yellow form, long and low and lithe, moved out of the shadow of a tall palm and rubbed against Weret's naked leg. It was a full-grown cheetah, long muscled and powerful. "Sorry to be so precipitate, but I know of Weret. When she comes out of the desert, she's not someone to keep waiting."

The black warrior-woman's name was Naldamak, Sesa learned halfway across, and she had been a personal guard to Ebana herself. No other information was forthcoming.

Standing in the stern of the boat and pushing the long pole, he looked at Weret's bare back, at her long arms and hard buttocks. *What a pity!* he thought. But all of Thebes knew about Weret's deep, unrequited attachment for her mistress, Teti, and about her refusal to solace her loss with the love of other women. Hard, celibate, as breathtakingly beautiful as a statue, she was a legend in the city.

So what would she be doing here in Thebes? Weret abandoned her beloved desert reluctantly and usually sent her subordinates in her stead when there was business to do with Baliniri's court.

But of course! "I understand that Teti is due to have her child any day now," he said casually.

For a long moment he thought she was not going to answer. As it was, Weret did not bother to turn around when she finally spoke. "It is supposed to be this week. The midwife sent a message to me that Teti's time is close. I will assist in the birth."

"You?" he asked incredulously, before thinking.

Now she did turn, transfixing him with a cold expression. "It's none of your business," she said, "but our women give birth at the oasis at El-Kharga. A girl-child we raise ourselves, after our own rules. A boy-child is given to the villagers at El-Kharga, who find a mother for it. I have delivered many children."

Obviously the subject was closed. As she turned back toward the bow, the cheetah turned and stared at him. He shivered and pulled harder on his pole. "W-well, give Teti my best, will you? She's been a regular customer of mine over the years."

Weret did not answer him but spoke to the Nubian woman, Naldamak, in the language of the southern blacks. Naldamak answered her with a grunt.

Then something occurred to the white warrioress, and she turned back toward him. "Is Queen Mara in the city?" she asked. "I had heard she was planning to go north to join Kamose."

"I don't think she has left yet. Frankly, nobody seems to want to go north. The plague's worse there than it is here, I understand."

"Plague?" she said. "Then it *is* here. The rumors . . . I did not know whether to believe them. I will see to Teti and help with her child; then it will be good to get back to the oasis. The desert is clean—no diseases, no politics. I am always sorry to come to Thebes, except to see my friends. I am always glad to go back."

Her hand stretched out to caress the hard neck of the great cat, which continued to regard Sesa. The boatman shivered again and pushed all the harder on his pole.

On shore, Weret and Naldamak set out through the streets at a brisk pace. The two attracted a great deal of attention, as much because of their great height and flawless fitness and startling nudity as from the huge cheetah that padded along, tense, at Weret's heels, its eyes darting to left and right alertly. They ignored all stares, and crowds parted to let them through.

At one corner the Nubian started to turn left. Weret stopped her. "This way," she said in the Nubian tongue. "Teti shuns the quarter of the rich. Her house is more modest than these." Turning right, she set a smart soldierly pace down the long thoroughfare.

She had not seen her mistress in nearly a year. Teti had had little, in truth, to do with the women of the oases since she had come to the city to live, and the fact had hurt Weret more than she had admitted to anyone. She had resented Riki terribly but realized, after much in the way of tears and pain, that further resentment would only alienate her from the woman she had loved since she was a girl.

Riki had been away for many months at the war. He had not taken a holiday since the fall of Memphis but had pressed on farther and farther into the delta, always hoping for the final victory that would bring him home to Teti for good. And now, with the birth of her first child upon her, she was alone. It would be a good time for her to see an old friend. And perhaps—just perhaps—the friendship could, in the course of the time they spent together, regain something of the closeness that had marked it from the first.

"Look," the Nubian said. "This mark on the door. And that one there. I have seen them ever since we came into this quarter. What do they mean?"

Weret's eyes narrowed. It was true. The sign had been almost totally absent from the first quarter they had come through. Now it decorated perhaps every fourth door. What did it mean? And where were all the people one normally found in the streets of a crowded quarter like this one at this time of day? What was wrong?

At the end of the street an old woman walked slowly along, her back bowed under the weight of a heavy burden. She looked once at the two women, then turned away. "Wait!" Weret called. "Maybe you can tell us. The sign on these doors—what does it mean?"

The old woman stared at them in horror. "For the love of the gods, get away! Get away while you can! Get out of the city!"

"But why?"

"Plague!" the old woman said, backing away from them. "The quarter's full of it! Get away while you can!"

II

A latticed balcony overlooked the great central hall of the lavish apartments where Baliniri, vizier to Kamose of

Egypt, lived with the former queen Ah-Hotep, widow of the martyred king Sekenenre and mother of Riki. When not at work in the great palace of the Theban kings, Baliniri tended to live a withdrawn and private life. For the most part visitors saw him at court and not at home.

Today's visitor was an exception. An old friend—or more than friend, actually, from years before—she sat primly and stiffly in the broad couch before the fountain and looked straight ahead. High above, Baliniri, unseen, stood in shadow and regarded her through the lattice. His thoughts were a jumbled mixture, which he was trying to sort out.

Tuya, he thought. *What is she doing here?*

Suddenly her shoulders slumped, and he could, even at this distance, almost feel her despair. Her little body shook as if with a sob; then she mastered herself and sat up straight again.

Baliniri suddenly found himself looking at her with a new pair of eyes. Or . . . would it be better to say an old pair of eyes, which had, so many years before, regarded her with such undivided love?

She was so tiny, so vulnerable—the very qualities that had so endeared her to him when they first met.

How old would she be now? The late forties, most likely. But from this distance it appeared the years had dealt kindly with her. She wore the elegant black wig of a woman of high caste, and she was made up beautifully, as if she were the hostess of a royal entertainment. There was the old pride in her, as befitted the widow of a prosperous armsmaker and the mother of a brilliant inventor and engineer. The jewelry she wore was simple and tasteful, and below her long robe he could see sandals of expensive untreated buffalo leather on her tiny feet.

How different from the first time he had seen her!

She had been newly married to Ben-Hadad, a man who had taken to drinking to assuage life's disappointments. Tuya, frustrated and neglected, had discarded her rich-girl finery and dressed in old rags, to slip out into the street and see a bit of "real life."

But Lisht, where all this was happening, was full of soldiers made bold by drink. A pair of rowdies had trapped her in an alley behind an inn and stripped her, preparing to have their way with her when he, Baliniri, had wandered onto the scene.

He had easily made short work of them. What problem he had that day was with Tuya herself—her combination of soft vulnerability and fighting spirit was irresistible, and he had fallen hard for her from the first. Desperately in love, he had wooed her ardently, and little by little he had worn her down until she had come to his arms.

At last her conscience drove her back to her husband, leaving Baliniri devastated. He had returned to the delta, taken work with the Hai army, and married the first woman who looked at all like Tuya.

He sighed, looking at her now. The years had passed. After the deaths of his wife and her husband he had found Tuya again, but old love could never be rekindled. Whatever magic had passed between them so long ago was gone forever.

Or was it? There was something about her now that evoked the protective feelings he had felt for her from the first . . . and other feelings he had not felt in a long, long time.

His marriage to ex-Queen Ah-Hotep, contracted between two lonely people hardly looking for a great passion at their ages, had evolved to little more than friendship. Of late he had begun to remember what it had been like to have hot blood flowing in his veins, when he'd been ruled by passion as often as by common sense.

He composed himself and walked over to the stairs, coming out from behind the lattice. Only then did she look up and see him, and stand, hands folded before her. He caught her eye and saw in an instant how difficult it would be for her to open up to him.

"Tuya," he said, coming forward to take her hands. "How good to see you again." His voice was warm and accepting. It was all he could do to keep from embracing her. "What brings you to see me, my dear?"

For all his sympathetic support, it was hard for her to speak. Only after many minutes had passed did she begin to relax, and finally with a great sigh that was almost a sob, she blurted it all out. "Oh, Baliniri, I've been such a cruel and insensitive fool. I've hurt her so. And—and it's worse than that. I've sent her and her child out into the streets at a time when the city is full of plague. Now I can't find her. I can't find any sign of her at all."

Baliniri, seated beside her on the couch, frowned. "Her?" he asked. "Pardon me, but I'm not sure just who—"

"Aset. Isesi's sister, Aset," she said. "She was living with us. We took her in when Seth left. She was a month or two pregnant then, but we didn't know. She said the child was Seth's, that she'd never slept with another man. I didn't believe her. I was *angry* with her. For all his brilliance, Seth had been such a child, and I just couldn't cast him in the role of a man who—"

"I think I understand," Baliniri said gently, taking one of her tiny hands. "I gather this was quite some time ago. Seth's been gone the better part of three years."

"Yes. Well, my husband, Kedar, spoke up for her. He said, what if she was telling the truth? What if the child was Seth's and we were to throw her out with my grandchild? After all, he said, soon enough the child would be born, and either it would have the birthmark of the Children of the Lion or it wouldn't. And there'd be time to act then, if it turned out she was lying."

Baliniri pressed her hand encouragingly. "Wise counsel," he said. "Go on, please."

She looked into his eyes now, and the tension in her grew. "When the child was born, it had a red smudge on its back. But it was on the wrong side and was not the classic paw print. Not the way Ben-Hadad's was. I was full of doubt. The doubt turned to resentment. The resentment grew."

"Tuya," Baliniri ventured softly. "Seth's birthmark. It wasn't a clear one, either. You remember what happened when *he* was born. Ben-Hadad would never believe the child wasn't mine."

"Yes," she admitted. "The thought has haunted me ever since. . . ." She swallowed, and now it was her hand that clutched at his. "But as my resentment grew, I asked myself who was this girl to come into my house and drop a bastard child and claim it was by my son? How did she dare?"

She closed her eyes, and the grip on his hand softened. There was something about her touch, just now, that he found very exciting. "This week I felt unusually bad, contemplating the passage of years, the coming of age, the gray hairs, the wrinkles. . . ."

"You look splendid," Baliniri found himself saying. "I was going to tell you. You look younger, finer than you did ten years ago. There's something about a woman at a certain time of life."

For a moment hope and warmth flickered in her dark eyes. Then reality intruded itself once more. "Oh, Baliniri, I've been such a fool. I was cruel to her in just the way my husband was cruel to me. No, worse. At least Ben-Hadad left me in luxurious circumstances. I didn't have to worry about where to lay my head, or where my next meal—and my child's—would come from. But I threw her out into the street four days ago. With nothing!"

"You've put people on her trail?" he asked softly.

"Yes. I've hired men to scour this city, plus Deir el-Bahari and the hills beyond. I've got others combing the river cities north and south. Nobody has seen her or the child."

"Well, you've come to the right person, my dear," he said with a reassuring smile. "I'll put my best people on this. We'll find her if she can be found. Put your mind at ease."

She took his large hand in her two small ones. "If something happens to her or the child, I'll never forgive myself. Never."

Their eyes engaged, and something passed between them, something that both of them remembered from so long ago, and Baliniri felt his heart pounding wildly. With effort he restrained the impulse to pull her into his arms. Instead, he reached out with a large and gentle hand and softly touched her cheek, briefly, longingly.

"Yes you will," he said. "I'll see to it."

Their eyes held. She slowly brought his other hand up to hug to her heart. Neither of them spoke for a long, long moment. He scarcely dared to breathe. The memories were strong, as if the intervening years apart had never happened, and the two of them were young again, young and lonely and full of desperate need for each other. The years had fallen from both of them, and they were as they had been in the spring of life, in a golden and hopeful time that seemed, now, to have always been with them, if only they had had the eyes to see it and the courage to reach for it.

"Oh, Baliniri," she said in a barely audible voice. "Oh, my dear. My very dear."

"This must be the house," Weret said. "Somehow it doesn't look the same. But it's the third from the corner, so it has to be the right one."

She stood looking up for a moment at the unfinished façade. The cheetah sniffed at the door. Someone had begun a complete restructuring of the front of the house but had abandoned the project halfway through. The result looked like a house half-built.

"How strange," Weret remarked to her Nubian companion. "I wonder if anyone's home. She might have moved. With a plague in the city, that would have been the wise thing to do."

Naldamak stepped forward and rapped sharply on the door with hard black knuckles.

They waited, but there was no sound from within. Then Weret moved forward and knocked soundly on the door herself, and as she did, the door slowly swung open.

The two women exchanged glances. Naldamak's hand went to the sword at her side. Weret drew her own weapon and pushed the door the rest of the way open.

"Teti?" she called. "Teti, are you there?"

Naldamak started to speak, but Weret waved her to silence with one hand. "Listen," she whispered. "What was that sound?"

Then it came again. A tiny woebegone wisp of a sound from the rear of the house.

"Come with me," Weret said. She moved across the polished stone floor on silent bare soles. "Teti?" she ventured again.

Rounding a corner, she tripped and fell over the body of a woman, lying across her path. The body was cold and stiff. The cheetah growled at it.

"Teti's servant," she said, alarmed. She rose and rushed into the bedroom in the rear of the house.

The room was so dark, Weret had to blink a number of times to adjust her vision. The figure on the bed . . . did it move? Or was she imagining—

"Weret," the weakened voice said. "Don't come closer. I'm very sick. I don't want you to—"

"Teti!" Weret cried out, rushing to her friend's side and kneeling by the bed. "Mistress!" She took the thin hand in hers and immediately felt the fever in it.

Plague! she thought. *Am I too late?*

III

"How long have you had it?" Weret looked down sadly at the long body under the coverlet, at the great swelling at Teti's midsection.

"I'm not sure. I have no idea of the passage of time. A day? Two? I don't know. I'm just so glad you're here."

Weret put a hand to her mistress's head and felt the fever there. She looked up at Naldamak. "I have to run for the physicians." She gave Teti's hand a reassuring squeeze and stood up. "You stay with her, Naldamak. Get her wine to drink. She can't be more than a day at the most away from childbirth. We could lose both of them." Weret's habit of using the Nubian tongue as a secret language was strong.

Teti tried to rise from the pillow. "Y-you forget I can understand you," she said. The effort was too great; she fell back onto the bed, panting for a moment. "Don't leave me, Weret. I need you with me more than ever."

"But if I don't bring a doctor, the midwives . . ."

Teti motioned her closer. Weret once again knelt by her side. "No midwife and few physicians will venture into a plague quarter." She was short of breath. "Stay with me. Nothing will alter the outcome of this day." She touched Weret's hand and tried a wan smile. "You forget, dear friend, that I see these things before they happen. I've known for years that I would die the day I was brought to bed."

"But the child—"

"I don't know."

"Oh, mistress! If I'd only known!"

"I could not tell you. Still less could I tell my husband. I fear for him, Weret. He isn't as strong as you. When I'm gone, watch over him. Please. For me."

Weret's mouth hardened, and there was a great hurt in her heart. She had never wanted to share Teti with Riki. "I promise," she said.

Teti closed her eyes, and a tremor shook her. "If only Riki were here! I wanted the two of you with me. The two people in the world that I love most, other than—"

"If I'd known," Weret said in a voice constricted with regret, "I could have brought the boy with me. He wanted to come, but I told him it was too dangerous."

"I'm glad he didn't come. But I want Riki . . . with me. Him and you, my dear friend. Why doesn't he come?"

Weret could only sigh helplessly. She took Teti's weak hand—the hand that had once been a smith's, callused and powerful—and held it to her naked breast. "Let me get you something to drink."

"There's wine on the shelf next to the hearth," Teti whispered.

"I'll find it." Weret stood and went into the front room, where she balled her fists and bit down on the back of one hand to keep from crying out in grief and frustration. *What will I do if I lose her?* she wondered.

From the back room, there came a low, lingering moan of pain and then a muffled scream!

Weret rushed back into the room. Naldamak knelt beside the sick woman and clung to her hand with a powerful grip.

"She's gone into labor!" said the Nubian.

"Is there anything else you'll need?" Meni asked, pulling the cinch tight around the ass's round belly. "You've got food? Clothing? Everything?"

Chetah, Tuya's aging servant, smiled at the young man. "Thank you for your concern, Meni, but I'm sure Sinuhe and I will manage: The guards will be here in a moment or two, and they'll take us to where the caravan is forming."

Meni reached down and picked up Sinuhe, whom he loved as a little brother and would miss terribly. Meni shrugged. "With Tuya off at court and Kedar away at El-Kab, I can't help worrying about you."

Chetah reached out and patted Meni's arm. "We'll be safer in the country with my relatives until the plague has passed." She took Sinuhe from Meni's arms. As she did, the little boy laughed. "Ah! How like Master Ketan he looks when he laughs, Meni! He'll grow up to be the very image of his father, that's sure."

"I didn't know Ketan," Meni reminded her. "Take care of him for me, will you? I don't know what I'll do without the two of you."

"You're sure you won't come along?" she asked. "I'd feel so much better if I knew you were safe."

"I can't leave any more than Tuya can," answered the boy, throwing back his broadening young shoulders. "I have responsibilities now, Chetah."

"Ah! Meaning you've got a girl somewhere! Is that what you've been going across the river to Deir el-Bahari for?"

Meni blushed. "No, no! I haven't got a girl. It's something else altogether." His tone of voice did not invite further discussion. "Well, take care of yourselves."

"And you, you look after my mistress and Kedar, eh? He'll be back in two days. Keep an eye out for both of them."

"I will." And, with a last salute, Meni turned and went away down the street. *Well*, he thought, *there's two fewer to worry about*. Turning a corner, he headed for the river, steering a course well away from the plague quarter.

Too late, he remembered that he should have left a note for Tuya. Then he shrugged, dismissing the thought. After that tantrum she had thrown over Aset, tossing the girl and her child into the street like that, she had not had much thought for him or anyone else. She had been terribly irritable and distraught, and he had not been able to communicate with her at all. Better to stay out of her way for a while.

He had never been able to escape the feeling that he was living in her household on sufferance anyhow. At ten years old, Meni had been brought into the house under false pretenses by a woman who had hoped to blackmail Tuya. The scheme had depended on his own coincidental but very strong resemblance to Tuya's first husband, Ben-Hadad, and the hope that Tuya would believe that Meni was Ben-Hadad's son . . . and be willing to give over generous amounts of Ben-Hadad's estate.

In the end Meni's growing love for Tuya had forced him to expose the plot and even save Tuya's life. In gratitude she and her much older second husband, Kedar, had adopted Meni and taken him to live with them.

Unfortunately, the closeness Meni had hoped for with his adoptive mother had never materialized. He knew it was not due to anything he had done or not done but to problems within Tuya herself that prevented her from a relaxed enjoyment of her loved ones.

Something had been eating away at her for a long time, and for the life of him he could not pinpoint what it was.

There seemed to be some sort of basic inner frustration in her life that even she could not explain. Maybe the problem rested with Kedar, who was growing quite old, his mind usually elsewhere. The loveless, companionate marriage Tuya had contracted with the old man had evolved into something more like the relationship between a woman and her elderly uncle.

Lately she had been venting her frustration on him, Meni, on Kedar, on Chetah, and little Sinuhe . . . and most particularly on Aset and her little boy, right up to the awful moment when she had ordered the two out of the house in a blind rage.

It wasn't fair! he thought, coming to the long quay that ran along the waterfront. That was no way to treat someone who was living with you. At the very least you owed it to her to talk things out.

But now he spied a familiar face down among the boats. "Ho! Sesa!" he shouted. "Wait for me!"

He set out at a trot for the water and watched the boatman, who had already poled his vessel out into the current, slowly turn and come back to shore for him.

"Well, young fellow," Sesa called out. "You're heading across the river to Deir el-Bahari? Despite the plague?"

"The plague's everywhere," Meni replied. "It's as bad on our side as it is on yours. We just lie about it more. How much to cross? An *outnou*?"

"Well, it's usually two, but—"

"One it is," Meni said, and stepped carefully into the boat. "I've got to see a friend."

Sesa poled the boat out from shore again. "The girl I saw you with? The one with the child? Listen here, young fellow, aren't you a bit young to be hanging around with the likes of—"

"It's not like that at all! She's a family friend, and she's in trouble. I found her some folks who took her in."

"There was someone asking about just such a person the other day."

Meni frowned. "What did you tell him?"

"I minded my business, just as I usually do."

Meni smiled. "For that, I pay two *outnou* for the trip. Provided your mouth *stays* shut."

"You're pretty cheeky for a kid. How old are you now? Thirteen?"

"Going on fourteen. But I've always been cheeky."

"So you have." The boatman chuckled fondly. "Well, well, well," he said, looking downstream. "Look at that. When's the last time you saw a boat coming upriver without a lot of soldiers on it?"

"Huh!" Meni said, sitting up and craning his neck. "No, Sesa, there *are* a couple of soldiers on it. And one of them's of high rank. Why, it's General Riki! Isn't that his crest?"

"I think so. I wonder what he's doing here?" Sesa stopped poling for a moment, and the boat began to drift with the current. "Hey, his wife is supposed to have her kid. I took a couple of those desert women of hers across to see her no more than an hour ago. Well, good health to them and to their child!"

"Here," Meni said, standing up. "If you're going to stand there gabbing while the boat turns in circles, give me the pole!"

Weret had disposed of the servant's body. Two hours later, after great pain and suffering on Teti's part, her child was born dead. Weret almost lost Teti as well at least once, and when the frail and feeble heartbeat started again, the warrior-woman almost fainted with relief.

But as Naldamak cleaned up after their time of trial, Weret gently carried Teti into the outer room, where the cheetah slept in the corner, to lay Teti down carefully on a couch. The light in the room was soft and diffused, but even by this limited illumination she could see that Teti was dreadfully pale and weak. Handling her mistress, she had seen the first dreaded sign of the buboes at the armpit, which spelled the horrible truth all too clearly.

She pulled a coverlet over Teti and knelt once again beside her. "Mistress," she said. "The child . . ."

"I know," Teti said. "I think it will not be long before I join him." Teti's voice was hardly more than a hoarse whisper now. "Weret, watch out for him, please."

Weret misinterpreted her words. "My women watch over him right now, mistress," she said. "Back at the oasis they—"

"No. No, dear. *Riki.* I fear for him." The chapped lips opened in a tiny smile. "Poor Weret. I should be worrying about you, shouldn't I? I know how you feel."

"Do you?" Weret said in a strangled voice, and immediately wished her words back.

"Did you think I didn't know?" Teti tried to speak again, but the words would not come at first. "You've been the best, most faithful—"

"Mistress!" Weret laid her tear-dampened face on Teti's breast—only to withdraw in horror as she felt not only the blazing fever, but the wildly fluttering heartbeat as well. "What will I do without you?"

"You'll go on," Teti whispered. "You're strong the way my parents were. I sometimes think you're one of us at heart, the sister I never had."

"Oh, mistress!"

Teti gasped and finally gained the breath to continue. "The more reason I need you to watch over him. Over both of them, my darling."

There was a loud noise, and light suddenly burst into the room! In the pool of bright sunlight a man stood, his body full of tension. "Teti! Where are you? Where—"

"Over here," Weret said softly. "Here she is, Riki." And, her heart ready to break, she stood up slowly and backed away, her eyes abrim with tears and fixed on Teti's wan face.

For a moment she thought he was going to faint. The look on his face was like nothing she had ever seen. She started to move toward him, but then she reined in her emotions and stepped back. He fell on his knees beside his wife. "Teti," he said in a strangled voice. "I came as quickly as I could."

"Riki," Weret said as gently as she could, "she's very weak."

"Leave us," he said. "Please."

An icy hand grabbed at Weret's heart. She looked down at her clenched hands. They were shaking.

But she mastered herself and obeyed. And as she backed out of the room, she knew that she would never see Teti alive again. She took one last lingering glance.

In the adjoining room she finally let herself go. Sobs shook her, and only Naldamak's strong arms around her kept her from collapsing into a heap on the floor.

IV

"Nobody told me," Riki said in a broken voice. "If I had known, I would never have gone to the delta. Oh, Teti . . ."

The sick woman on the couch tried to smile and put a hand, as weak as a child's, on his arm. "It doesn't matter," she replied in a barely audible voice. "You're here now, and that's all that matters." She paused to catch her breath. "Riki, we lost the child. It was a man-child, a Son of the Lion."

"Child?" he echoed, as if the thought had not occurred to him. "Teti, don't leave me. I can't live without you."

"You can. You'll have to," the small voice said. "Riki, I knew about this. But I couldn't tell you." He stared wide-eyed, his face a mask of horror. "I knew the day I met you. I knew we had only just so long." The weak hand tried to tighten on his arm, but there was no strength in it. "I knew we would be happy. That was all that mattered."

"Teti, I've walked out on Kamose. We took Athribis, and then I left. I'm not going back. I'm going to stay here and nurse you through this."

"Riki. I haven't long. Please listen. Please, my dear. Don't give in to grief and despair. Remember, I'll always be with you. Always."

"No, Teti! You can't go! I won't let you!"

The palsied hand reached up and shakily stroked his hair. "I asked Weret to watch over you. Call on her. She's a true friend. And . . . there's someone you don't know. Weret will introduce you. But go to her. Go to her when you need someone."

"Teti!"

"My dear," she said. "You've made me so happy. Please . . . remember that."

"Please, Teti." His voice broke. Like the soldier he was, he tried to fight back the tears, but they came anyway. He took the weak hand on the coverlet and held it to his face. He closed his eyes, kissed the hand, and gave in to his weeping.

He was not sure when the life left the hand he held. After a long moment he wiped his eyes and looked down at her. The warm brown eyes had closed forever, and there was a look of peace and acceptance on her wan face. He kissed her hand, then put it down gently and sat back on his heels. His great shoulders drooped.

When Weret came quietly back into the room, she found him still kneeling there, his face blank, his posture speaking eloquently of his sorrow and loss.

Silently she walked to the far side of the couch, looked down on the placid expression of her dearest love, then pulled the coverlet up to cover Teti's face. She held out her brown hands to Riki. "Here, let me help you up." She waited a moment; he did not respond. "Here," she repeated. "Take my hands. Don't be proud. You need help now. You need a friend."

He looked up. His eyes were devoid of emotion. His face was blank. His mouth worked, but no sound came from it. He let himself be pulled gently but firmly to his feet.

"She's gone," he breathed. "My Teti. She's gone."

Weret kept her face expressionless. It took some effort. *Your Teti,* she thought. There was ice in her heart.

Hidden from view in the hills behind the quarries of Deir el-Bahari, the artisans' village lay. No place could be more unlike either Thebes or Deir el-Bahari. Whereas the fear of the plague had emptied the streets and bazaars in the cities, the artists' village's single market was full of exuberant life. Women argued amiably with the vendors while children played merrily nearby.

Meni strolled up the meandering street, hailing old friends on every side. He had discovered this place shortly after his adoption by Tuya and Kedar and had quickly fallen in love with its carefree way of life. A child of the street himself, he had been quick to notice the subtle differences between street life here and in the city. In Thebes, it seemed that every man's hand was against his neighbor's. In the artisans' village, however, there was a feeling of community. People liked and respected one another.

Besides, Meni liked to watch the artisans at work. The weavers spread their looms right out in the street, where a boy could watch. The sculptors banged happily away at their stone; the woodcarvers let him sit beside them and occasionally allowed him to borrow a tool and hack lustily away at discarded scraps of wood imported from far up the Nile. He had no trace of talent that anyone had been able to discover yet, but he had not let that stop him from aping their motions, and they liked him for that.

He liked them back, all in all—even the gruff ones like the tinker. A huge, black-bearded, immensely powerful man, the tinker had a harsh voice that concealed a sentimental heart. Now Meni called out to the tinker as he passed the forge and got back a growl that fell on his ear like a comrade's caress.

But most of all he was fond of the family of painters who lived at the end of the village's single street, their houses spreading up the hillside. They were a jolly and warm lot who had been painters for centuries—all of them except for the young soldier Netru, a great hero of the Egyptian army who had fallen at the battle of El-Kab.

Meni had heard army talk about Netru, back in Thebes— how in his first battle, Netru had been deserted by his cowardly troops. Faced with an assault by the fierce warriors of the upper Nile, Netru had stood his ground bravely, defending the flag of his unit. At last he had been surrounded and reluctantly cut down by the Nubians, who had forborne to desecrate his body.

His lonely death had been seen by his men, and they had rallied and come back, to fight like lions. Some gave the boy credit for turning the tide of the battle, which had begun with the Egyptians clearly the underdogs and had ended with a glorious Egyptian victory.

Now a whole body of legends about Netru were told around army campfires. One of the best of them portrayed Netru as the lover of Teti the armoress, now the wife of General Riki. According to the stories, a bereft Teti had withdrawn to the desert for ten years, living with women and honing her craft until Riki had come to her oasis and brought her back to the city to be his woman.

For all Meni knew, it could be true. Because Tuya and Teti had never been particularly close, he never heard the actual account of Teti's relationship, if there indeed had been one, with Netru. Meni preferred to believe it, given his knowledge of and affection for Netru's kin. He always looked them up when he came across the river, and when he had problems, he had felt no hesitation in sharing them with his friends of the painter caste.

Now he found himself passing the shop of Netru's second cousin Felot, and he smiled and waved at the heavyset, bowlegged painter as he sat decorating a papyrus with bright inks. "Felot!" he called. "What are you painting today?"

"A sketch for a mural for the apartments of the lady Ah-Hotep," Felot said. "See? Dancers and flute players performing for Her Ladyship. Isn't the curve of the dancer's leg nice? I like it myself. Why wait for a stick-in-the-mud like you to praise it when I can praise it myself? Ah! It's good. Very good. I wish I could get one like that off every day."

"It *is* very nice. Who's the girl? Did the greengrocer's daughter model for the dancer?" He caught a certain look in Felot's eye and pressed on. "No! It's somebody's wife over in Deir el-Bahari! Now who could it—"

"Hush!" Felot warned. "Even the walls have ears!"

"The guardsman's wife! The captain of the town guard!"

"Quiet, you fool!"

"Now when could you have seen her with no more on than that? I'm sure she never comes down to the river to bathe with the other women."

"You young puppy! One of these days—"

"You old bear, nobody who does naked pictures of the wife of the captain of the guard gets to tell *me* what's going to happen to me one of these days if I don't mend my ways."

Felot grinned, then threw back his head and guffawed. "A point well taken. But, my young friend, you don't have to bellow it all over the neighborhood, do you?"

"You're right, you're right. From now on I'm as quiet as a dove."

"Quieter."

"All right. As mute as a lizard. Where is she now? I want to see her."

The painter gestured with his brush. "Try the house of my sister Hat-Nefer."

Meni saluted him with a grin and set off up the slope. At the third house he stopped and rapped smartly on the door. It opened a crack, then wider. "Meni!" Aset welcomed him. "Come in!"

The boy looked around at the modest house. "It looks nice," he said, sitting down. "Where's the boy?"

"Hat-Nefer took him with her when she went into the village to buy food for dinner. I don't dare go in myself."

"They're looking for you here, then?"

Aset nodded. "There was someone asking in the bazaar yesterday."

"You know, Tuya could be sorry she threw you out."

"I don't care if she's had a total change of heart. Until Seth comes back and acknowledges his son, nothing good can come of my being under the same roof with Tuya, much less dependent on her. Something's eating her. I wouldn't put it past her to change her mind, decide that my little Keshu is Seth's son after all, and try to take him away from me. Well, let me tell you, she'll do that over my dead body."

"But, Aset, if she wanted to take Keshu away, well, couldn't she do it? She's rich, and you haven't got an *outnou* to your name. I don't mean to hurt you, but you don't even have a permanent place to stay. My friends can't put you up forever. They're kind and good, but none of them has extra money just now."

"Don't you think I feel bad sponging like this?"

Meni crossed his legs and laced his fingers over one tanned and dirty knee. "Well? What *are* you going to do?"

Aset frowned. "I don't know."

"There's the plague, too. It won't stay away from the village forever." He pondered for a moment, then went on. "Maybe the best thing for you to do would be to get clean away. And stay away until it all blows over—Tuya, the plague, everything."

Aset stared at him, her mouth a tight white line. "B-but where?" she asked at last.

Baliniri came back from the open door. "I'm afraid I've just received some bad news from the guardsman," he said. "Teti has died of the plague." He let this sink in for a moment, watching the stricken look on Tuya's face. "The child died too."

"Oh!" she moaned. "Not Teti. She was so strong."

"Nobody is strong against the plague." He cursed beneath his breath. "I should have been informed as soon as she got it. I see I'm going to have to dismiss some people from my spy network and discipline others."

"You mean . . . you ordinarily have people like her watched over? People like me?"

He shrugged. "I have had your house watched ever since I became vizier."

"Then you . . . cared—all those years."

"There was something very strong between us once." He

smiled now, the same old nice smile she remembered from so long ago. "The fire was never completely extinguished, despite some confusion on my part."

"Oh, Baliniri, if only—"

"And here we are, middle-aged and married to people we don't love, and lonely and in need—"

"Need? You? The mighty vizier Baliniri?"

"Yes, I need you. Now that I've finally admitted it, I confess I've needed you for as long as I can remember." He came to her and embraced her.

She laid her face against his broad chest and felt the powerful beating of his heart. "Oh, Baliniri, I want to stay with you forever."

He stepped back, held her at arm's length, and smiled. "My feelings exactly. But things being the way they are, we'll have to be circumspect for now. Let me have the guards take you home. I have to see Weret; she's in from the oasis. I have appointments. Sitting and waiting around here would bore you terribly. Come to me . . . *hmmm* . . . come to me tomorrow afternoon, eh? It'll take until then to clear my agenda and reschedule everything."

Her heart sank, but she knew he was right to handle things this way. She stifled her feelings of disappointment and put her face up for his kiss.

V

Coming back into the great hall, Baliniri found Weret and the Nubian woman-warrior waiting for him. As he strode down the long avenue of columns, he could see their tall, spare, startlingly nude figures, Weret's skin picking up highlights from the filtered sun overhead. At the Nubian's heels the cheetah sat patiently looking at him through great, glasslike eyes as he approached.

"My lord," Weret said, inclining her head slightly. It was as close as she ever came to deference, even to the man who had trained her and the rest of Teti's women years before. "This is Naldamak, on loan to us from Ebana's personal guard."

"I am honored," Baliniri said haltingly in Naldamak's own tongue, then turned back to Weret, whom he looked on as a daughter . . . who had not turned out quite as he had planned. "I understand Teti is dead," he said sympathetically. "I know what that means to you. You're taking it well, considering."

"You trained me well, my lord. A warrior does not show her emotions publicly. Her grief is a thing to be shared only with the desert, which sees but does not tell."

"Well, my condolences. I wonder when the news will reach Riki."

Weret's eyes widened. "Then you don't know? He was with her. And frankly, I'm worried about him."

"Riki? Here?" Baliniri was genuinely surprised. "But he didn't report in."

"Nevertheless, he was with her when she died. He's taking it badly. He was already in quite a state when he arrived. It appears he squabbled with Kamose and walked out on him."

"Walked out on the war? That isn't like him. He's always been dominated by a sense of duty, of responsibility. And he and Kamose have been close friends since they were boys."

Weret's face hardened. "People change, my lord. And it is noised about in army circles that Kamose has changed more than most."

Now Baliniri narrowed his eyes. "I see. You have your own spy network."

"From time to time we get deserters at El-Kharga oasis, coming through with a caravan. We detain them for questioning. Often they think that, if they inform on their commanders, we will let them pass. They are mistaken. But they only learn this too late."

"I'm glad to hear that discipline remains tight out there," Baliniri said. "Tell me what you've learned about Kamose."

"Well, my lord, his personality seems to be changing very rapidly, and along lines guaranteed to give offense to a man like Riki. They have apparently had several arguments over such matters as the treatment of prisoners. One disagreement came almost to blows."

"Has Kamose been short-tempered? Violent?"

Weret nodded, wondering what Baliniri was getting at. "He came within the blink of an eye of killing one of his own officers in a rage. That caused rumblings among the officer

caste, which Riki quelled. But he had another quarrel with
Kamose over it privately."

"And the one that caused Riki to come back here?"

"I do not know, my lord. And he hasn't said. He arrived
only barely in time to speak to Teti before she died. He
thought he was returning to a tranquil household, to his
woman, and perhaps to a new child. Instead he finds . . ."
Her words trailed off.

"Yes," Baliniri said, rubbing his tired eyes with the heels
of his hands. "You know things haven't been going well
between the king and queen?"

"That rumor has reached us, my lord."

"*Hmmmm.*" Baliniri was silent for a long moment. "I suppose I'll have to see him and see what I can get out of him.
Thank you for the information. My own communications net-
works are breaking down. People I trust to keep me informed—
their messages arrive late or not at all. I've been expecting a
message from Isesi for some time. Oh, incidentally, there's a
problem with Aset. Tuya wants to find her."

Weret studied his face, and written there was his opinion that Aset should not be brought back to Thebes. "I know
a few people I could ask."

"Good. Frankly, I'd like her kept out of the city, away
from the plague area altogether if it's possible. Her son's a
Child of the Lion, after all, and a dwindling resource—as
both of us are reminded today, to our sorrow. I also owe it to
Seth to keep her safe."

"I will do what I can." The young philosopher Seth was
the only man, other than Baliniri, whom she had ever admitted to her circle of friends. "And would you meanwhile keep
a close eye on Riki? He could do something desperate."

Baliniri raised one brow. "I'll see him right now."

Weret stood tall and straight-backed. She nodded to
Naldamak. "There is one more thing. We have someone at
the oasis who has something of Teti's prophetic gift."

"I know of whom you speak. Young Neku-re. Go on."

"Very well. This person speaks of a force of great evil
coming to sink deep roots in the Red Lands, to drain this
kingdom of hope, optimism, and the will to survive. It is
something to be greatly feared."

Baliniri frowned. "I should go to the oasis to speak about
this warning with the source, but I'm not sure when I can get
away. I have so many pressing problems here."

"I know, my lord."

"I've got to deal with a revolt among the upriver nobles, and very quickly. This friend of yours could not come to Thebes, I suppose."

"I would strongly advise against it."

"Very well." He switched dialects. "Naldamak, are you still in regular contact with your mistress, the lady Ebana?"

"Yes, my lord," the Nubian answered. "And she visits from time to time."

"Good. I may need to use you to convey messages for me to your queen."

He was ready to call an end to the interview, but Weret held him up, one hand on the cheetah's sleek head. "My lord."

"Yes?"

"It is the custom here to dishonor the bodies of those dead of unclean diseases. Please, where my mistress is concerned—"

"She will be buried with great honor and all ceremony. You have my word on that."

"And may I leave the problem of Riki to you? I promised Teti that I would look out for him, and I will. If he needs me, he can come to me, and I will do what I can for him. But now, my lord—" Her composure broke, and she let out a great shuddering sob. Then, quickly recovering, she threw back her shoulders and firmed her mouth. "Now," she continued, "I have my own grief to live with, and I think that my shoulders will not bear the sorrows of two."

She looked down at the great cat at her side, and her hand again touched the rough hair of the animal's proud head. "In the desert a cat such as this goes off by itself to heal injuries. I think I could use such a time myself."

"So be it," he said. "Leave Riki to me. I will give him your message. There will perhaps come a time when he will need to speak with you."

"Thank you, my lord. Then I have your leave to go?"

"Yes. And you, Naldamak"—again he switched to the Nubian tongue—"I will send a message to you for the lady Ebana, and very soon."

"I will relay it," the black woman promised. "Good-bye."

Scowling, Baliniri summoned an aide. "General Riki's in the city. Bring him here. Make the order to report to me seem as diplomatic as possible. I don't want his feelings ruffled."

"Yes, sir. Would he be in camp, perhaps?"

"More likely at his home. Come to think of it, I'll have to go with you myself. His wife just died of the plague. The guards will want to take her body out to the garbage dump and burn it. It'll take an order from high up to stop that. Better round up a couple of squads of soldiers for me."

"Yes, sir. Two squads it is. They'll be waiting for you at the side door when you're ready."

"Good man. I'll be right with you."

At the quay Weret waved away two waiting boatmen and hailed Sesa from the far side of the river. She shrugged off the boatmen's angry glares as easily as she had shrugged off their lecherous stares and whispered comments earlier. As Sesa neared the shore, she gestured imperiously to him to make haste.

"Yes, ma'am," the boatman said as he held the vessel for the two women to climb in. He closed his eyes and made a face as the cheetah followed them aboard. "Where to?"

"The far side. But we also want information." Quickly she described Aset and her child. "You've seen her. Don't tell me you haven't."

Sesa, remembering Meni's two-*outnou* payment, frowned. "Ma'am, I promised not to tell."

Weret's mouth was a straight line. "Promised whom?" she demanded. "And for how much?"

Sesa blinked. She was so direct! "Two *outnou*, ma'am."

Weret slipped the golden anklet off her slim leg. She held it up in one brown hand. "Imagine, boatman, how much *this* is worth!"

Sesa's eyes were large and round. "Well, ma'am, that may be another matter. If you're a friend of hers, I could be doing her a disservice by keeping you from finding her, couldn't I?" He looked more closely at the golden anklet she dangled before him. "Heavens, ma'am, that must be worth—"

"The question is what it is worth to you right now. Is it worth the information I ask?"

"Well, now that you put it that way, ma'am . . ."

With an athlete's grace Weret leaped ashore, Naldamak

and the cheetah following. "Thank you, boatman," she said.
"I will not tell anyone that I got the information from you."
This said, she turned on one heel and strode strongly up the
bank, her two companions—one human, one not—close behind.

*Surely the gods and the stars collaborated to make this
meeting come about,* she thought.

Imagine Aset taking refuge with Netru's family!

"You stay here," Baliniri decided. "Let me talk to him
alone." He held the soldiers up at the door and walked slowly
over to the couch where the man sat alone by the covered
body, staring disconsolately at the wall. "Riki," he said softly,
putting a hand on his protégé's shoulder. "It's Baliniri."

Riki did not look up. "She's dead," he whispered. "Gone.
But they won't take her away. I won't let them."

"My men are here to take her to the embalmers." His
voice was gentle. "Riki, you can't do anything for her now.
Come with me. You need to be with friends. I've saved a
room for you at my house. This is a time when a man needs
looking after. I can do that for you better than anyone else
can."

"Go away."

"I can't. Riki, look at me. This is Baliniri speaking.
Baliniri, who raised you, who brought you out of Egypt, who
trained you for the army."

"I just want to be with her a little longer." Riki looked
up at his mentor. The young eyes spoke of horrors beyond all
description—seen and felt and endured. "Before her I never
had anything to lose or fear. She breathed life into me.
Before I met Teti, I'm not sure I was fully alive." He took in
a deep shuddering breath, and it came out in one long
heartbroken sigh. "Without her I won't know who I am."

With a stricken expression on his face he let himself be
helped to his feet.

CHAPTER FIVE

Upper Mesopotamia

I

Abi-sakim reined in his chariot's great white stallion at the top of the rise to look down on the broad marshland below, where the river slowed its already sluggish pace, dividing into many small streams that threaded their way through the palms and marsh grass. "Everything appears to be prepared for us," he said. "Our quarry will be down there. Look, the beaters are fanning out to surround the marsh, and the slaves have brought up the dogs. We'll have good sport today, I think. What a pity your master Seth could not have joined us! He would have found this part of the hunt interesting, to say the least."

Criton pulled up beside him in his borrowed chariot. "I am sure he regrets his inability to join us," he said diplomatically. "Seth finds virtually everything interesting. The aurochs hunt in particular would have pleased him. And they do not have wild boars where he comes from."

"Ah. But you yourself know the animal?" The nobleman,

110

a ranking lord at the court of Mari, removed his headdress to wipe his brow. "Then you know what a feast we're going to have tonight. We took six of the beasts today."

"I'm sure all of us eagerly anticipate the delights of your table, my lord. And I'm sure my comrades as eagerly await the pleasure of hunting down the lion." His tone betrayed a trace of skepticism. "As for myself, I generally prefer to kill beasts I can eat, rather than beasts that eat the likes of me."

Abi-sakim smiled indulgently; he could afford to patronize an Achaean like Criton, whose people were held in low regard in the Land of the Two Rivers. "Well, your friends will have great sport down there today. The runners told me that there's not one lion in there—there are two. The old one has a mate."

"The more reason for a peace-loving man like me to watch it all from up here," Criton said.

He looked down now to where the handlers were bringing up the dogs, a dozen of them: giant mastiffs with reddish fur on the head and black-furred bodies, straining mightily against their leashes. They were formidable-looking animals, with huge, overdeveloped jaws. They gave the impression of immense strength and tenacity. "Magnificent dogs," he remarked.

"Yes. They're from my own kennels. I breed them. Samsi-ditana himself hunts with a pack of my mastiffs. Once that breed fastens those jaws on its prey, you can tear the dog to bits but it won't let go."

"Impressive." Criton looked over the terrain. The spongy marshland lay a bit below the level of the surrounding plain; the river broadened where it entered the area. There were stray pools of stagnant water scattered here and there, clumps of reeds and water plants, and a veritable forest of giant rushes twelve or thirteen feet high. Palms lined the stream and marked the few paths that the fishermen had beaten into the marshy thicket.

Abi-sakim bellowed downhill to his assistants. "Bring up the boats! Cut off their retreat!"

Criton watched as two flat-bottomed vessels full of bowmen immediately deployed in the shallows, ready to block any avenue of escape for the two lions.

"Since you're sure you won't join us," Abi-sakim said, "I'll pick up your two friends and go in after the lions." The hint of contempt in his tone clearly gave his opinion that discretion and cowardice were one and the same thing. He raised his voice again. "Loose the dogs!" he cried out, and rode down the hill toward the marsh.

Set free, the mastiffs plunged into the thicket and straight-away began baying lustily. Abi-sakim, snatching bow and quiver from a lackey, led Criton's companions Khet and Anubis in after the dogs, followed by grooms who carried their master's spare weapons and led his extra horse.

Yes! There was the first of the lions; the dogs had it trapped in a little clearing. Criton, observing everything from safety, winced at the lion's deafening roar, which rose easily above the chorus of yelps from the dogs. Abi-sakim nocked an arrow and fired at the animal; next to him, Khet, unfamiliar with the short bow used in the North, fumbled with his own weapon.

Abi-sakim's arrow struck the lion in the shoulder; then Khet's caught it in the spine, above the loins. The lion fell, then rose again on its forepaws. The dogs advanced cautiously; but Anubis, gigantic, as fearless as always, ran past them and speared the wounded lion.

Suddenly, unexpectedly, out of the rushes charged the second lion! Before Abi-sakim could nock another arrow, the lioness bowled over two of the dogs and made for Anubis. Khet had an arrow nocked but could not shoot because the man and lioness were too close together.

Criton stood watching, his heart in his throat, as Anubis gave ground, keeping his lance at the ready, teasing the lioness with feints to its face. The great forepaw swung and almost knocked the spear out of Anubis's hands. A dog attacked the lioness's flank; then another joined the attack from the other side. Distracted, the lioness took her eyes off Anubis. Swiftly, the giant lunged forward; his lance caught her in the neck just as she reared high to hook a powerful paw at the second dog's head. The lioness stumbled and fell; Anubis quickly recovered and lunged again. He put all his considerable weight behind the thrust, and the lance sank a forearm's length into the lioness's throat. She fell back, mortally wounded, and the dogs rushed in, emboldened by the smell of blood.

Criton winced. With a weary sigh he searched his mind for a series of appropriate compliments. It would pay to have a few handy, even if they were insincere. Until the moment when Anubis had gone in, Criton had been cheering silently for the lions. . . .

* * *

The feast, of course, was everything Abi-sakim had said it would be. The hunting party had brought along not only tents, cooks, and servants, but musicians and dancers as well. As darkness fell, the Mariite noble and his guests—including diplomats from Carchemish and beyond who had arrived too late to join the hunt—sat around a great roaring fire and ate fresh-roasted aurochs meat right off the spit, washing it down with the splendid red wines of the country—tart and rich and satisfying.

Anubis, of course, was the hero of the day. No one could remember the last time anyone on foot had taken on a cornered lion as yet unhurt by the bowmen's shafts, as yet unharmed by the dogs. And Anubis had killed the animal before anyone could get close enough to help him! The giant, with a dancing girl perched on each knobby knee, grinned off Khet's sarcastic gibes and reveled in the attention.

Abi-sakim caught Criton's supercilious smile and let out a low chuckle. "Let him have his hour of glory," he suggested. "After all, he did do something spectacular." He took a swig of wine. "Too bad he won't be around for the next hunt. I'd like to have shown him off before the army bigwigs."

"Won't be around?" Criton echoed. "What do you mean?"

"I assumed he would be going along with you and your master. No? Were you planning to leave him here?"

Criton raised his eyebrows. "So far as I know, we've no plans to go anywhere for the rest of the year. My master hasn't finished his appren—" He stopped, then continued. "My master is studying various arcane disciplines with a wise man of the city. You know: the motions of the stars," he lied. "The hidden powers of numbers. That sort of thing." For a moment he had considered mentioning alchemy; but that was uncomfortably close to the truth. "I can't imagine him leaving until he's learned what he came here to learn."

"Then you haven't heard."

"Heard what, my lord?" Criton asked, remembering his manners. "Is there something I don't know?"

There was a subtly superior smile on the courtier's face as he spoke, wine cup poised before his face. "Why, your master has been summoned to Babylon. By order of no less than the great king Samsi-ditana himself!"

Criton stared. He could not think of anything to say.

Abi-sakim drank, backhanded the wine from his mouth, and smiled. "To Samsi-ditana's court. It's a very great honor. How odd that I and not you should have heard of it. Or does your master perhaps repose less confidence in you than . . ."

He let the sentence hang there, full of quiet malice.

But Seth had not heard, either. Back in Mari, he was alone in his room, poring over a problem in Mesopotamian mathematics, when his teacher, Marduk-nasir, returned from a dinner appointment. Seth looked up and smiled as the older man entered. "Ah, master, every time I think I have the local arithmetic down, I stumble again. It can't seem to make up its mind whether it's decimal or sexagesimal."

"Relax, my son," Marduk-nasir consoled. "It will suddenly lose its strangeness and begin to feel the natural thing."

"But why all this emphasis on six and sixty?"

"It has to do with time, with the passing of the hours. The Mariites have twelve double hours in their day, each divided into thirty parts. From this came a division of the visible bowl of the sky into three hundred sixty degrees, and the division of the ecliptic into segments of twelve double hours." He smiled and put a fatherly hand on Seth's shoulder. "Relax. You're working too hard. What, after all, has this to do with your mission here?"

"Well, it—"

Marduk-nasir sat down across the big table from Seth and acted as though the young man had not spoken at all. "Your mission is—or was—to learn the secrets of ironmongery. Therefore, your mission, at least so much of it as you can know, is complete. What more do you need?"

Seth stared. "Complete? But, master, I've only just begun."

Marduk-nasir reached for the leather wineskin beside him and accurately squirted a long stream into his mouth. Then he smiled benignly. "Take my word for it, my boy. I do hereby bear witness to your mastery of the twenty-ninth degree. That's as far as I am empowered to certify you. For all I know, you may pass me." He belched delicately, covering his mouth. "You may have *already* passed me."

"But I've hardly even worked iron with you yet! You haven't seen what I can do. We've studied the formulae and the principles, to be sure, but—"

"That's it. The rest is applying what I have taught you.

That requires work at the forge, and for that you do not need me. Now it's solely up to you. From a certain point a man must go it alone. And I think you will go very far." He frowned. "Or is there something more than this in your destiny? You do have a restless mind, one that wishes always to encompass all knowledge. Look at you, now: The day is done, and a hard and strenuous day it was, yet you sit here studying mathematical formulae like a schoolboy."

Seth looked perplexed. "I'm not sure I understand what you're getting at."

"I hereby certify that you are a master of the craft: You are not only a Child of the Lion but a Chalybian, you know all of the signs by which you can recognize a fellow member of the order, you have learned the ethical and moral precepts of the craft; and you have learned the seven formulae. I cannot make an artist of you—only the gods can do that, as they did with your grandfather Hadad the Cripple. As they did with Ahuni and Belsunu. Now either the metal will warm to your hand, or it will not. Either the sword you make will sing in a soldier's hand, or it will not. This is not the province of the brotherhood, which can only teach you the wisdom that it alone can pass down."

Seth reached for the wineskin and drank deeply. He put the vessel down and wiped his mouth. "Does this mean that you and I must part?"

"Yes, but the sadness of that is tempered with good news—a great honor, in fact. In two days a caravan will leave promptly at dawn for Babylon. It carries the personal protection of the great Samsi-ditana, king of kings, who requests your presence at his court. Despite the actual wording, a request from such a great king of course carries the weight of an order. You *will* be a member of the caravan. I trust your companions will accompany you."

"They go where I go. But, master, why me? And why can't you come along?"

Marduk-nasir reached across the table and put a hand as powerful and as hard callused as a galley slave's on Seth's arm. "My path lies elsewhere, my son, and after a certain point, a teacher can only get in the way." His voice softened. "I had a son once. He did not turn out half as well as you. In you I have found a second and better son, and now I have to lose you. There is more pain in this than I could have imagined. But a part of me will go with you wherever you go."

Seth's mouth opened, but no words that could express his feelings adequately would come.

Marduk-nasir willed a smile to his lips. "Your friends will be back tomorrow," he said with false enthusiasm. "We will celebrate . . . and then we will part. But I will carry the memory of our brief time together for as long as I live."

"And—and I," Seth said brokenly. Tears rimmed his eyes but did not fall.

II

In the morning Criton was back, looking fit and sunburnt after his three-day hunting expedition. He knocked on Seth's door just as his friend was dressing to go out and, after a moment's hesitation, let himself in. He raised his arms high and grinned. "Behold, esteemed sir, the mighty hunter!" he proclaimed.

Seth laughed. "I was just going out for something to eat. Care to join me?"

Criton grimaced. "You should have been along on our hunting party. We all ate ourselves sick on roasted aurochs." He thought about the matter for a beat, then added, "I mean that literally in Khet's case. Of course, that strong backwoods wine they make around here may have had something to do with it."

"Then you disgraced yourselves before the noble—uh, what was the man's name?"

"Abi-sakim," Criton said. "You're going to have to start remembering names, even these tongue twisters of Mesopotamia if you're going to be a courtier or whatever—" He stopped and looked at Seth, waiting for comment.

"Marduk-nasir just told me yesterday."

"Good." Criton was satisfied that Seth had not withheld that information. "Anyhow, no, we did not disgrace ourselves. Anubis won himself a reputation that will precede him all the way to Babylon, I'll wager. He killed a lion yesterday. Just walked right up to her and rammed a spear down her throat before the bowmen could even get off a shot."

Seth laughed and shook his head. "And you?"

"I did the finest job of watching that anyone had ever seen. I ascended to the very pinnacle of the onlooker's art."

"Come on, you can tell me about it while we walk." Seth moved out into the street. "My master certified me as a full-fledged member of the craft yesterday. Apparently without realizing it I had already walked right up to the brink, so all it took was for him to pass on some precepts and formulae, then kick me over the edge." He sighed. "I'll miss him more than I can say."

"He's not going to the city with us?"

"No. From now on I'm on my own. I tell you, Criton, that's a heavy burden to carry. I've gone around being a child in so many ways, and now someone tells me I'm grown and must act like a man, independent and self-starting."

"You *are* a late bloomer, to be sure."

Seth made a wry face. "Joke about it all you like. All this time I've been studying, and now I have to deliver."

"I ought to say something comforting and encouraging, but I can't think of anything. It is a bit early for my usual brilliance, no doubt. Here, isn't this where Marduk-nasir was staying?"

"Yes. The second door on the right. I'll get him." Seth knocked on the door once, twice. He waited and then knocked a third time. Only then did an adjacent door open and the innkeeper come out, a bucket dangling from his hand. "Pardon me, sir," Seth said. "Is Marduk-nasir here?"

"He checked out yesterday afternoon. Paid in gold, he did. There was something about a caravan headed west this dawn—to Carchemish or Haran, I think."

Seth stared at the closed door. His mind was a hopeless muddle of conflicting emotions.

At the bazaar they found their companions, both nursing various ills contracted during the long night of eating, drinking, and roistering. "Oh-ho!" said Criton. "The mighty lion killer."

"Go away," Anubis moaned. "Unless you brought a fresh boot of palm wine. Nothing else will kill the monsters in my head and guts."

Criton ignored him. "And look here, won't you? This one kills a lion single-handed; his companion, equally unaided, eats a whole aurochs—"

Khet's face sported a slightly greenish hue. "He isn't kidding, master. I know I vomited up at least two of them. Ugh! How could anything so delicious—"

"Spare us," Seth interrupted. "I haven't eaten yet." He sat across from them and motioned to the fruit vendor. "Two plates of figs," he said. "Unless the two of you would like to join us?"

"*Food?*" Khet stuck out his tongue and leaned back against the patio wall. "I can't even watch you. I'll just turn the other way and hope the wind doesn't change."

Seth grinned. "You can spend the day recuperating, but be ready to travel tomorrow. Why don't you lie down under a tree by the river and sober up, both of you? There's a place where the women bathe every afternoon. Or are all your appetites equally impaired now?"

There was a delayed reaction. "Pardon me," Anubis said. "Did you say something about leaving tomorrow? Where are we going?"

"Babylon!" Seth answered. "By special request of the great king himself. I'll bet he's got wind that there's a Child of the Lion in Mari and thinks that having me at his court would be some sort of honor. Actually I'm a little surprised to learn that we're not totally forgotten. The last of us to leave the city was Ahuni, and that was more than a century ago!"

"You know how it is," Criton said. "Your very absence makes you legendary. Come to think of it, Ahuni left Babylon still a slave, if I've got the story right. You might have all kept collars around your necks. Instead, here you are being summoned to the royal presence. We'll travel in some state and be welcomed like visiting dignitaries."

"This is going to take some getting used to," Seth said. "I've enjoyed traveling unknown and unnoticed. There was a lot of freedom about it."

"It's the same thing you were talking about earlier," Criton noted. "You've come into a man's estate. No more carefree youth, with nobody paying much attention to you. On the other hand, I have the feeling you're going to have some fun in Babylon. Samsi-ditana has the reputation of surrounding himself with brilliant people of many nationalities and finding some royal use for their talents and capabilities."

Seth frowned. "He'll have a hard time seeing past my ignorance. There's so much to be learned from these people. For one thing, their astrologers are better than ours. They have an ingenious way of measuring planetary motions along the ecliptic. It's based on units of time that refer to a water clock they use here for working out the time after the sun is down."

"I know," Criton said. "We borrowed the system from them centuries ago. I will agree they're better at it than we are, but their air's clearer. They can see stars here that we can't make out at all on the islands. I do agree that being exposed to new ideas is something to look forward to. Even if they initially see us as a bunch of hayseeds from backward countries, I think Samsi-ditana will be able to detect something out of the ordinary about you . . . if only because you're so damned stubborn and won't let a problem go until you've solved it."

"We run to hard heads in our family," Seth agreed. "Just think of Kirta, who threw away two decades of his life to learn a fraction of what my master has just taught me in a matter of weeks."

Having said this, Seth fell silent for a time, thinking. If it were possible to find a pattern, what characteristics were held in common by members of his clan? What character traits had his father—a frustrated man who felt disappointment from his failure to live up to the high standards set by his own father, Hadad—in common with Hadad's brother, Ben-Hadad's Uncle Shobai. On the surface, it would seem that the two men had had no common ground. After all, Shobai had been one of the most responsible and thoughtful of men. Ben-Hadad, Seth thought bitterly, was neither responsible nor—

But of course! Suddenly Seth sat up straight. Ben-Hadad had had much in common with Shobai, really. They had both made terrible mistakes while young: Shobai had neglected his mother and his younger brother, leaving them to eke out desperate lives on the edge of starvation and want while he lived in great wealth and luxury. And Ben-Hadad had neglected his wife and son, had rejected both of them; he had left his son, Seth, to grow up without a father's love and guidance.

Ah, yes. Where they had differed was only in the fact that Shobai had lived long enough to rectify his mistakes. Ben-Hadad had died quite young, barely thirty. What if he had lived long enough to correct his errors?

A sudden rush of feeling ran through him. He shud-

dered, shaken by the new thought. Now that he thought
about it, he was quite sure this *was* what had happened. He
was *sure* his father had learned better about Tuya and himself, about the legitimacy of his, Seth's, parentage. If he had
only lived, he would have come back to them and made good
all his wrongs. The idea came as a great emotional relief.

Idly his mind inverted his situation, making himself the
father rather than a deserted son, allowing him to view the
mystery of the relationship between fathers and sons through
the eyes of a father.

I wonder, he thought suddenly. *What if that liaison with
Aset, back in Thebes, had produced—*

But he tore the thought from his mind—or tried to. It
stubbornly lingered at the edge of his consciousness. What if
he'd been a fool like his father? What if he had abandoned
her with child and had thoughtlessly gone away, leaving her
to bear his son or daughter alone, unwed and unprotected?
How would he make up for it?

Would he have tremendous strength of character like
Shobai, learning to live down terrible errors? Or would he
sweep away the guilt and refuse to acknowledge his responsibility?

It was a thought that had never occurred to him before.
Am I a good man? Or a bad one, a weak one?

Who was he? He had never really been tested morally or
ethically. How then did he dare to sit in judgment or to think
ill of poor, blundering Ben-Hadad?

Who am I? he wondered frantically. *Well, perhaps I'll
find out now, once and for all.*

Yes! The test lay ahead, in Babylon! It was there that he
would learn what manner of man he was, find his limits, and
learn to live with the knowledge of them.

"You've turned awfully pensive all of a sudden," Criton
commented. "What are you thinking about?"

Seth groped for words. "I don't know. I think I've had an
insight. It's something about my father. I think I may be
learning how to forgive him."

Criton looked at him thoughtfully. "Well, that's a good
sign," he said. "It's good practice for learning how to forgive
yourself, when the time comes that you have to."

Seth stared, impressed. "You've read my mind," he said.
"I'm fortunate to have such a friend. You always tell the truth
as you see it. Please, don't ever stop doing that."

Criton's brow rose. His expression grew even more thoughtful, if anything. "You may come to regret that request," he warned. "But—yes. I promise to speak my mind honestly to you. Even if I am not sure whether this signifies the beginning of something, or the beginning of the end of something." The look in his dark eyes was unreadable.

III

Having left Mari, bound for Haran and Carchemish along the ancient trade route, the westbound caravan was intercepted by a fierce armed patrol of the great Hittite army, which now lay encamped outside Haran. Technically, the caravan was passing through territory not at war with Mari. Technically, the caravan lay under the imperial protection of Samsi-ditana of Babylon. Nevertheless, the Hittite soldiers expropriated all the trade goods carried by the caravan, put to the sword the tiny token guard that had accompanied it, took as slaves all the able-bodied men of the party, and took as whores all the women. At length the captain of the Hittite patrol found himself facing Gudea, leader of the caravan, and the dark-eyed, black-bearded Marduk-nasir, Seth's mentor. The captain was not quite sure what to do with either captive, since both looked like men of standing. The Hittite soldiers had permitted Gudea and Marduk-nasir to retain their robes when being led into the captain's outpost, even though their hands were bound behind their backs.

"All right," the captain said belligerently. "Who are you? Make it quick. Give me some reason why I shouldn't dispose of you. You're too old to make good beasts of burden."

"This is an outrage!" Gudea sputtered. "Caravans have been plying this route for hundreds of years, even in times of war. You have no right—"

"I have such rights as Mursilis, the great king, says I have," the captain retorted. "You are wasting my time. Guard! Kill him."

"No! No!" Gudea exclaimed. "We can work something out. If it's money you want, I have on deposit in Carchemish—"

"All money on deposit in Carchemish is already forfeit,"

the captain said. He nodded to the guards. A noose slipped around Gudea's neck. A jerk on the rope tightened it. A second yank pulled Gudea to his knees, gagging and gasping. Now two men pulled on the rope, dragging the caravan master by his neck out of the tent.

Marduk-nasir frowned; Gudea had been a friend. The captain saw the expression and marched to within a handspan of the bearded man's face to spit out the next words. "Now!" he demanded. "You! Tell me why I should not have you garroted as well!"

"No reason at all. I do not wish to live a great deal longer. The great joke of life is something I no longer find diverting. Having lost the carefree laughter of my youth, I yearn for the oblivion of the next world, if there is one. And from my roost in the Netherworld, perhaps I will find the sport I seek at last when Mursilis learns that in your ignorance you have killed Marduk-nasir the Chalybian, who made the great king his first sword when he was no more than a neglected nephew of the divine Hattusilis and had yet to be adopted as the son of the king."

The captain's eyes widened. "You? You are Marduk-nasir the smith?"

"I am that same man. Not that it matters, since you have suspended all humane and civil laws and allowed a peaceful caravan leader to be strangled on a foolish whim. Oh, it is a wicked and lawless world, and I wish to live in it no longer. Have the man strangle me, and be quick about it." Marduk-nasir sighed wearily, not for so much as a moment taking his dark eyes off the captain's fidgeting, sweating face.

"Guard!" the captain ordered. "Cut this man loose. Call the messengers! Get me an extra horse! This man is to go directly to Mursilis, under heavy guard! And treat him with respect. Do you hear me?"

The guard heard and lost no time in complying.

Back in Hattusas, capital of the great Hittite Empire, Mursilis lived in great state. Opulence, however, did not befit a warrior-king on the march, so the tents of the great king in his encampment outside Haran were hardly to be distinguished from any others except by the number of guards who surrounded them. Mursilis had learned from his adopted father, Hattusilis, that soldiers more readily fought and died for a man who lived as they did, and he had taken the lesson to heart. Even the uniform he wore was that of an ordinary army officer, and he could be taken for any of these any time the royal helmet, with its towering eagle plume, was off the royal head.

He had in fact been born hardly more than a commoner, a nephew of Hattusilis's and illegitimate at that. At birth his expectations had not been great. But Hattusilis had had no blood sons live to adulthood, and the succession was settled on Labarnas, a boy only slightly better blooded and connected than Mursilis.

But Labarnas, ten years older than Mursilis, had been ambitious—and impatient. As prince, he plotted with various nobles of the court, fretting at what appeared to be a long, long wait for the crown. Then Hattusilis had been unexpectedly disabled by an attack of lung disease. Labarnas had lawfully assumed the regency but then had begun immediately to reorganize the state along lines thought up by himself, firing Hattusilis's trusted advisers and appointing his own. This was clearly an act of usurpation.

In the end Labarnas had confined the old king to quarters and ordered the royal physicians to poison him slowly. This had been too much. The king had rallied, called together his friends in the army and among the nobility, and had seized control of the palace and the government in a lightning coup.

Hattusilis magnanimously had not ordered Labarnas put to death. Instead he had publicly censured and exiled him, under heavy guard, to a country villa where he could live the dull life of a pastoralist.

For an heir, then, to replace the disgraced Labarnas, Hattusilis had reached down and elevated the astonished Mursilis. In the same poetically worded proclamation that had announced the fall of Labarnas, the old king had proclaimed Mursilis his successor and son and had called upon all citizens of the empire to honor and obey him as such.

In the days to come the old king had grown ever closer to his new son, teaching him the ways of statecraft and of war—and, little by little, giving him territorial ambitions that now began to extend beyond the boundaries of the Hittite lands.

It had always galled Hattusilis that the Hittite territories did not extend to the kingdom of Yamkhad, whose high-walled, stoutly defended capital, Aleppo, would be a rich prize. Hattusilis's own attempts to take the city had failed. What better way for his young protégé to honor his adopted father's name than by completing the conquest of Yamkhad?

After careful planning, Mursilis launched the attack and after a fierce siege took Aleppo. The love of conquest began to stir in his veins, and in rapid succession Carchemish and Haran fell to his soldiers. The next step was obviously Mari.

But what was all this leading to? the ailing Hattusilis had wondered. It was then that his adopted son had unveiled for the first time the plan he and his advisers had been hatching for many months: Babylon was rich, powerful, and secure—perhaps too secure. According to Mursilis's emissaries and spies, King Samsi-ditana had grown lax and self-satisfied and considered himself to be beyond challenge. Thus Mari, his western outpost, was ill defended.

Mursilis had moved forward stealthily . . . and then had been felled for a time by illness—the same illness that had finally felled Hattusilis and elevated Mursilis to the kingship. Now the fever was gone, and he had gathered his army beside the broken walls of Haran. On the morrow they would march on Mari.

His strategy complete, Mursilis now took practice with the sword, exchanging half-serious cuts and sweeps with Anittas, his favorite general. Mursilis had just scored a point, nicking Anittas's armor with a lunge, when the guards brought in Marduk-nasir, his hands untied, flanked by two stout Hittite warriors.

"Sire," the soldier in charge said. "A prisoner from the outpost on the Mari road. He claims you know him."

Mursilis sheathed his sword, nodded the end of the session to Anittas, and turned to face the black-bearded man before him. "Know him?" he said, his eyes slits. "Nonsense. Take him away."

"The great king has a short memory," Marduk-nasir said. "Let him ask himself whose hand fashioned the sword at his belt."

"You!" he said, remembering. "Marduk-nasir! Why didn't anyone tell me you were here?"

"They were too busy robbing my peaceful caravan and murdering my associates," the bearded man retorted. "All in the name of the king of the Hittites. Things are not as they were. I am glad to be old and near death."

"Are disapproval and disrespect the ways to renew our friendship?" Mursilis asked testily.

"Friendship?" Marduk-nasir echoed mildly. "A strong word to use between one man who robs caravans and his most recent victim. Tell me, O Mursilis, how can friendship survive the death of law? The death of honor? The death of civility between nations not at war?"

"What are you talking about, old man?" Mursilis asked. "We are at war. There is war between Samsi-ditana and me."

"Indeed? You have not declared it."

"I have not wasted my breath shouting insults across half the known world. Instead I have declared war with my actions, by taking Carchemish and Haran."

"Ah." The word was a long sigh. "So you have. The actions of a cringing, two-faced coward do indeed speak with a voice louder than any words."

"What's got into you?" Mursilis demanded, advancing on the older man. "You deliberately provoke me! If you were not still the friend of my youth—"

"The great king should not allow a triviality like loyalty to stand between him and the humoring of his every bestial and idiotic whim. It ill becomes a king to listen to anything but the promptings of his own corrupt and conscienceless heart. If he developed any common virtues, he might be mistaken for a mere human being, and not for some sort of demigod."

"You go too far!" Mursilis exploded, hand on the hilt of the weapon at his side. "Don't test me, old man!"

"There would be no reason to test you. Does a cook test the fire with his finger to make sure it's hot? I saw your hand go to the sword I made you so many years ago. You were but a youth. A man is supposed to grow up, King, not down. He is supposed to advance in wisdom, not folly."

It was too much for the guard beside him. "Sire," he said, "my profuse apologies. This man was brought to you because we thought his services would prove useful. We had no idea he had turned into—"

"*I* have not changed," Marduk-nasir interrupted, his voice taking on added weight and depth. "It is the king who has changed. He and the kingdom, and the honor of the Hittites." His voice rang out lustily. "Hear, O Chalybia! Hear, O brotherhood of the ancient craft and Sons of the Lion! From this day on, let no brother in the craft serve Mursilis, king of the Hittites!"

Mursilis laughed uncomfortably. "Do you think anyone can hear you here in the Hittite camp?"

Marduk-nasir looked him in the eye. "There are brothers of the craft everywhere. You don't know who they are. Many of them don't know each other. But now they will know that a brother member has put the indelible mark beside your name, coward and killer of the innocent! And none will serve you but those who deliberately serve you ill, spying on you for your enemies, poisoning your water and your wine, foiling all your schemes, and giving aid and comfort to those who hate you." His eyes darted to the sword in the king's hand. "A fit weapon for me to die by. I gave this sword life; it shall give me death. Strike! Strike now! I have no further wish to live!"

Mursilis's hand trembled on the sword's handle. He raised it . . . and lowered it again.

"Would you hear more then, King? Hear then a prophecy, the words of Hattusilis, on the day he proclaimed you king: 'My grandfather set his son on the throne, but those close to him deposed him and put another in his place. How many years have passed since then? How many of these have escaped their rightful fate? The houses of the conspirators, where are they? Have they not perished?' He spoke to you, King, 'Never relax, my son! Never turn your back on those close to you! If you do not heed my words, you shall surely perish!' "

Mursilis stared. The sword raised, then wavered.

Marduk-nasir looked up at the weapon and smiled. His voice was quiet now, fearless. "And here you are, far from home on a villain's errand. Who is minding the city? Your sister, who hates you, and her husband, Hantilis, who now finds ambition waking in his heart, now that you are no longer there to defend your back. Conquer, King! Cheat and steal! Murder the unarmed and innocent! Gather great wealth! You will take none of it home with you. It will melt in your hand like ice. You will enter the gates of your home city and find yourself naked and defenseless and alone. No friend's hand will rise in your defense." He smiled, looking up at the sword in the king's quivering hand. "Enjoy the power, the glory, and the riches, Mursilis, for they will not last long." His voice was almost a whisper now. "Strike," he said softly. "I would not voluntarily outlive this day."

Mursilis let out a low roar. "Die, then!" he screamed.
The sword rose and fell.

CHAPTER SIX

The Borderlands

I

Their boat, bobbing ponderously on the Nile's current, passed the tall walls of Memphis on the left. Mara, her ripe beauty concealed by her simple robes and head covering, stood at the port rail watching the activity on the shore: workers staggering to the quays, their backs laden down with burdens nearly their own size and weight; boatmen tying up at the docks; spear-bearing soldiers intently watching their every move.

"There, my lady," said her maid Amenardis. "We've been given the go-ahead to pass. That means they won't be stopping us and searching us. Everything seems to be working as you planned it."

"So far, so good," Mara agreed. "I sent a coded message downriver yesterday, clearing everything. Baliniri still doesn't approve. Only when I allowed him to put a troop of seasoned guardsmen on the boat disguised as sailors did he consent."

"Can you blame him, my lady?" Amenardis asked. "For

the reigning queen of Egypt to travel in disguise to a war zone without her husband's permission—"

Mara snorted. "My husband! He's the problem! When I heard Riki had quit the army in protest against Kamose's policies and actions, I knew there was something terribly wrong. They've been the closest of friends since they were children. If Kamose is now capable of driving him away . . ." She shook her head.

"Pardon me, my lady, but the two of you haven't been getting along, either, in recent months. I mean, I couldn't help noticing—"

"Don't rub it in," Mara said. There was a deep pervading sadness in her tone. "Something's been wrong for a long time, ever since the victory at Thebes, when he assumed the crown. It's as if there were some terrible void in him that nothing can fill. Only killing. Only blood."

"I beg pardon, my lady, but there has been much talk of the fact that there is no royal heir."

"You *are* frank, aren't you?" Mara said, a wry smile on her lips. "Well, that's all right. I'm surrounded by people who never tell me the truth. As long as I have you, I can count on candor, and that's good." She sighed. "No, Kamose seldom comes to my bed. I wonder if he has a girl up here, near the front." She made a face. "I don't know the man at all, really. He's so driven."

The word stopped her. Her gaze scanned the hills behind the city, the long slow rise to the visible forms of the earliest pyramids beyond. *Driven?* she thought. *As I was all those years? By a hatred so strong, so pure, that there was little room in me for anything even remotely resembling love?*

Suddenly she thought of Riki, broken and stricken by his wife's sudden death. *I should have gone to him. I should have helped him, as he helped me so long ago. What a thoughtless, selfish person I must be not to help him now!*

They had met when she was a slave, beaten and despised, and Riki was a half-starved, naked little street urchin. He had comforted her, brought her news of the outside world, and given her hope. In the end he had helped her escape from the horror that Hai-occupied Egypt had become.

Their relationship had been like a brother and sister's from the first, and they had never become romantically involved. In time she had made a marriage that had brought her the crown of Egypt but no happiness. And Riki's wife,

the wonderful, towering goddess Teti, had, right up to the
end, made him happier than he could have ever imagined.
Now Riki had lost everything, and she had had nothing to
lose. But here she was, traveling downriver to see her husband secretly, to find out what had gone wrong and to try to
bring the two of them back together again.

Her thoughts were drawn back to Riki—his pain and loss
and loneliness. She wished that she had not conceived this
impractical plan to go north to see Kamose. What if she had
stayed with Riki and tried to help him during this terrible
time in his life?

What if, in time, he turned his thoughts to her, Mara?
Searching her feelings honestly, she was not sure how she
would react. Riki was not by any means as handsome as a
god, like Kamose. Riki's was a more human appeal; he had
the frank, open, likable face and dancing eyes of an ordinary
man, albeit a man of great gifts. She closed her eyes and saw
Riki's ready smile before her.

"My lady is having second thoughts about this voyage,"
Amenardis said. Mara turned to look at the girl. Her eyes
were large, intelligent, and perceptive.

"How do you know that?" Mara asked. "I'm having
thoughts that surprise even me. Tell me more about what I'm
thinking. I'm curious."

Amenardis's dark eyes searched her face. "For one thing,
you are not much affected by possible danger of infection
from the plague."

"No," Mara affirmed. "That sort of thing is in the hands
of the gods. If they wish me to catch the plague, it will find
me wherever I have hidden."

"Nor the dangers of war—"

"There has been war of one kind of or another in Egypt
all my life. No, that does not worry me, either. What does
worry me, girl? Why do I have vague feelings of disquiet?"

"I am just guessing, my lady, on the basis of what I can
see and hear. A servant who does not have any empathetic
attachment for her mistress is a poor servant, and I pride
myself on being a very good servant indeed. I will answer
your questions, but please do not be offended if my answers
err on the side of excessive candor."

"Speak freely. You can only anger me by lying or
equivocating."

"Then . . . is it possible, my lady, that your relationship

with the king has reached a crossroads? You travel northward in a sort of desperation, hoping against hope that—" She stopped, seeing the terrible look on Mara's face. "But I offend. Please, my lady, forgive me."

Mara mastered herself. "You read the situation correctly," she said in a tight voice. "If I cannot get through to Kamose this time, I do not know what I will do. I do not know what I *can* do."

"But," the girl said, "you have been thinking about precisely this: Can a queen have a lover? It would be very difficult under normal circumstances. Such an arrangement is rarely kept a secret. There are too many tongues at court to wag."

"Go on."

"Yes, my lady. It is also difficult for a queen to choose someone suitable. Baliniri is too old; the other courtiers fall short of what you deserve."

Mara's face reflected her wonderment. "This is amazing. By all means continue."

"Furthermore, my lady, there is the great danger of the wrath of the king when he learns that he no longer commands his queen's undivided attention, as I am sure my lady has considered."

"You are so close to my thoughts it is uncanny. Tell me, then, what sort of notions have begun to find their way into my mind."

"Yes, my lady. The previous queen gave birth to a son fathered by her lover—"

Mara stared.

"—as I am sure my lady already knows. The son thus has some royal blood in his veins, along with the blood of a great hero of the Egyptian people. The son is himself a hero of equal stature." Amenardis paused apprehensively, having said this. "Shall I continue?"

"If you don't, I'll have you flayed."

"Yes, my lady. Such a man might well make a suitable lover. And—who knows?—perhaps a better consort." She paused a moment before continuing. "There are those here and there who whisper, my lady, that he would make a good king someday."

Mara did not answer. *Riki*, she thought. *Riki born Ahmes pen-Nekhbet, natural son of Queen Ah-Hotep by the famous soldier Baba of El-Kab. A man much loved by the people and the soldiery alike.*

And by one other, perhaps? By herself?

She shut her eyes and fought against the thought. *Kamose*, she thought. *I must give him one more chance. I must be fair. He may have been under strain.*

But damn Amenardis! The thought she had planted in her mind would not go away!

II

After the fall of Athribis, the best thing would have been to pursue Apophis's battered and demoralized army all the way to the walls of Avaris, if need be. But Apophis's men managed a better retreat than they had managed a defense of Athribis, and Rasmik, Apophis's best general, succeeded in spiriting the main force of the fleeing army away, leaving behind scattered rearguard outposts, which, fighting bravely and skillfully, delayed Kamose's advance until the army had set up new positions on the far side of Bast.

Besides, Kamose's men, for all their savagery in the first flush of victory, were bone-tired now and needed to catch their breath before a new engagement could be fought successfully. Apophis had abandoned Bast to the fury of Kamose's soldiers. Kamose posted pickets on all sides, left a defense force in place outside the city, and gave his men liberty inside.

Even so, Elset, Riki's favorite officer, hesitated to leave the soldiery free in Bast to do whatever they wished. He had seen back at Athribis what absolute license could do to his army's character, and he had no wish to lead such an army. Strict orders had been issued regarding conduct. A curfew would be rigidly enforced, and military men were restricted to the stews. Anyone caught breaking any of these orders would be dealt with very severely.

Thus Elset had his hands full, and he was glad of it. Dealing directly with Kamose had been difficult even before Riki had left the army; now it was well-nigh impossible. The new man, Amasis, had joined them shortly after Riki's departure and was with Kamose all the time now, as if the two were brothers or—the thought brought a scowl—lovers. Wherever Kamose went, Amasis was with him, and if you talked to the one, you had to do it in the brooding, uncomfortable presence of the other. And Elset had found he could not talk well in front of Amasis. There was something about the man that made him ill at ease.

He had begun to wonder just what sort of hold Amasis had on the king. The explanation they had given—that they had been oarmates on a galley in their younger days—was hardly enough to explain their extraordinary closeness or the impression that they shared some important secret. Even Kamose's batman, Shu, had found himself left out.

Elset, strolling the streets of Bast, wished Riki were here. He was sure none of this would have happened if Riki had been around to put a stop to it. Now, coming into a half-deserted public square in the quarter of the Temple of Amon, he found two drunken soldiers, out of uniform, haggling with a woman of the town over something.

"Here!" Elset said in a voice of command. "You two! Come here!"

The soldiers turned and blinked, trying to get him in focus. Only when they made out the plumes of command on his helmet did they let the woman go.

"Yes, s-sir?" said one, weaving unsteadily. "Begging your pardon, sir, but the girl tried to cheat us. Imagine asking two *outnou* for a bit of—"

"Never mind her price," Elset barked. "I want your names! Rank! Number of your troop! Name of your commander!" He spat the demands at them, fire in his eyes.

The two looked at each other and complied.

"You're out of the prescribed area. You're also out of uniform. Report to your commander immediately and tell him I said to punish you. I'll be by to see him at sundown. If you haven't reported for disciplining by then—and if your account of this meeting between us does not match mine—I'll have you impaled. Do you hear me? Off with you!"

He cursed under his breath, watching them go. That was the hell of it: Everyone knew that the king disapproved of strict enforcement of the troops' behavior—knew, in fact, that his tacit approval of the soldiers' misconduct had precipitated Riki's sudden departure from the army. Thus some of the soldiers had begun to disobey their commanders' orders. It was an absurd situation, which led to bad discipline and poor morale. But try to get that across to Kamose! Try, even, to get the word through to him in the first place, with Amasis filtering out all information he did not wish the king to hear!

Elset now heard a voice hailing him and turned to see his batman, Narmer, hurrying down the street. "Sir! Message from the admiral, on the river! Runner came in just now!"

Elset let himself be led to the far corner of the market. Narmer looked right and left, then said in a low voice, "It's the queen, sir. She's here in disguise to see the king."

"Mara?" Elset said, puzzled. "What is she doing here?"

"Don't know, sir. Admiral says the trip was cleared with Baliniri. He doesn't think the guard she brought is sufficient for traveling overland. I don't either, sir. He suggests the king come to her."

Elset thought about the matter a moment. "She's obviously come for important reasons of her own, or Baliniri wouldn't have allowed it. Very well. Please tell the admiral that I'll bring the king. Tell the admiral to keep her on board, treated, of course, with all possible courtesy.

"Very well, sir."

But it was too late. Mara, ever formidable, had countermanded the admiral's orders and set out to see her husband, accompanied by the guardsmen Baliniri had sent with her and additional troops from the admiral's marine detachment. She had demanded these; the admiral, quickly seeing that he had met his match, threw together a patrol and saw her off, glad to be rid of her.

She arrived at Bast at nightfall, just as the city guard was preparing to close the gates. A guardsman sent messengers inside to inform Kamose of his wife's arrival.

When he came to her, Amasis was at his side. "Mara!" Kamose said with obvious displeasure. "What are you doing here, in a war zone?"

"What are *you* doing, keeping me waiting outside the gates like a vegetable vendor who hasn't paid the proper bribe?" Her eyes flashed, and there was a curious tremor in her voice that made Shu, Kamose's orderly, move back toward the little crowd that had gathered at the gate.

Amasis stepped forward. "A thousand pardons," he said

in the chilling voice feared by the whole garrison. "If my lady will be so kind as to enter now—"

"Who is this man?" Mara demanded of Kamose. "And what gives him the notion that he can address the queen of the Red Lands?"

Kamose looked annoyed with her. "Mara, this is Amasis, an old comrade of mine."

"Someone remove him," Mara ordered coldly. "Well? What are you waiting for? Remove him. Right now!"

No one dared obey. The two commanders of the guard, the one with Mara's party and the one at the gate, both looked helplessly at Kamose for confirmation.

"No one's going to remove anyone," Kamose said with a dark scowl. "Let's go inside. If we're going to have a row, let's do it somewhere where the whole world won't be listening. Captain! Disperse this crowd!" He spoke to the city guard. "Mara, come inside. I'll find a place for you. I've had the offices and apartments of the chief magistrate of the city converted into rooms for the royal party. You can stay—"

"Very well," she said, cutting in on his speech. "Take me someplace where I can wash up. You've servants, I suppose? Here, you." She spoke directly to Amasis for the first time. "Have my baggage taken inside. Get to it, man! I shouldn't have to tell you twice." She clapped her hands, as one might to a menial. "Now!"

"Mara, this is a very important man. You shouldn't—"

She ignored the anger in his tone. "Now," she said, "take me to those apartments." She turned her back on Amasis in a gesture of absolute dismissal, complete and insulting.

Despite the rage growing in him, Kamose kept his temper for the sake of decorum. Once the door was closed to the palatial dwelling of the former magistrate and they were alone, he turned on her. "Don't you *ever* try anything like that again!"

"Who is this Amasis fellow?" she asked, ignoring him. "You act as though I were in the wrong, and not that greasy foreigner with shifty eyes. You've been putting as much distance as possible between us for quite a long time. Is he why you haven't visited my bed? Have you taken up some new habits you haven't been telling me about? Or is he an old habit left over from the past, perhaps? He hangs on your arm as if the two of you were master and catamite."

"Damn you—"

"It's all over Thebes, Kamose! You've driven away Riki, your only hope of winning this war without a long, painful, bloody siege. Did this foreigner have something to do with it? Is he the reason why you drove away the oldest friend you have in the whole world? You've ruined your friendship with Baliniri, and you haven't a friend left at court. The priesthood of Amon hasn't ousted you only out of deference to Baliniri, who's holding your kingdom together. There's a revolt already brewing among the upriver nobles around El-Kab, but all this goes right over your head, while you play house with this new friend of yours—"

"Hold your tongue!"

"—and butcher helpless prisoners as if you were fighting in a foreign country, not the Egypt you hope to reign over. Don't think *that* hasn't got around! No, Riki didn't tell anyone. He's just lost his wife and child"—here, for the first time, Kamose's eyes widened—"and he hasn't the time or inclination to spread rumors about how the king's lost his grasp, throwing away the most valuable friendship he ever had and the finest general his army is ever going to find for the sake of some tramp from up North, some scum from Ebla or Damascus who—"

"Amasis isn't scum! He's a valued friend! I owe him much more than I can ever—"

"More than your life, which you owe to Riki? How many times has Riki saved your life? And yet you leave him for—"

Suddenly her own eyes widened with an insight that was blinding in its clarity. "Gods!" she breathed. "*That's* what they were talking about! The sailors back at the Nile, who unloaded the boats—they were hinting at some odd sort of hold this chap had over you, and like a fool I jumped to the wrong conclusion. But now I think I know what it is!"

"Silence!" he commanded in a voice choked with bile.

"Oh, come now. You can't frighten me. This Amasis fellow—he wouldn't happen to have a brand just under the hairline, where it wouldn't show?"

"How did you—"

"You talk in your sleep when you've had too much to drink."

He stared. The thought had never occurred to him. "You . . . you know about—"

Concern replaced the anger in her expression. "I don't know as much as I want to, now that I can see with my own eyes that something's wrong. Do you want to tell me about this cult of yours, about Amasis, about whatever's got into you this last year or two? Whatever relationship we have left may well depend upon what you tell me, and what you don't."

Kamose's eyes narrowed, and he seemed to tap a new source of strength. "I'll tell you nothing. Thanks for the warning. If I talk in my sleep, I'll sleep alone from now on."

"Kamose!" she said, coming toward him. "I'm sorry. I didn't mean to speak so harshly. But this new thing that has entered your life—"

"Get away from me!" he snarled. She continued to advance, concern in her eyes. But when she tried to touch his arm, he pulled away with a low growl of rage, and almost before he had had time to think about it, his hand swept out and struck her hard in the face. The blow brought tears to her eyes; she stared unbelieving at him through a mist. "Stay away from me!" he shouted.

III

With Riki's departure, two men were elevated to the rank of general: Riki's longtime friend Elset and Kamose's adjutant Djoser. Because an intimate of Riki's could not be permitted to hold, alone, the highest rank below the king's, Elset and Djoser shared rank and held what would at first glance appear to be the same position. But that was a totally political maneuver; Elset actually had the command. Djoser's responsibility was, for all practical purposes, to act as staff adviser to Kamose.

There had been bad blood over this. Djoser resented a position given him mainly for show. He and Elset barely spoke, and even then, relations between them were formal in the extreme.

Amasis, understanding this, took advantage of the opportunity. He sought out Djoser and bought him a lavish dinner at one of the inns, ordering jar after jar of the most expensive Libyan palm wine. As the evening wore on, Djoser's tongue grew looser and looser. A discreet bribe to the innkeeper shooed other guests away from their part of the room, out of earshot.

"Tell me about the queen," Amasis suggested innocently.

"Ah," Djoser said, pursing his lips in a silent belch. "Tough bit of goods, that. For the love of all the gods, keep it to yourself that I said that, eh? But . . . well, you saw that business today? Oh, yes, she tore into you too, didn't she? Embarrassing. Felt bad for you."

"It's all right." Amasis looked down at his companion's bowl and refilled it. "All in the day's work. Think no more of it. Go on, please. What's her background?"

Djoser sipped appreciatively. "Wonderful stuff, this. But . . . yes. Mara. Physician's daughter, as I understand it. Her father apparently botched some sort of operation on a man called Hakoris, to try to remove a brand someone gave him for thievery up in Canaan. You know about Hakoris?"

"Someone told me the story. I gather no one liked him much. Still, I sometimes wish I'd known him. Any enemy of Jacob of Canaan's is a friend of mine."

"Eh? Oh, yes. I forgot you're from the North, too, aren't you? And likewise not too friendly toward the Habiru?"

"We have had our differences." Heavy lids hid Amasis's eyes. His face remained expressionless, his voice noncommittal and conversational. "Go on."

"Yes. Well, when the surgery failed, Hakoris took to wearing a Bedouin headdress to cover it, even at court. He never forgave the physician for his supposed incompetence—or for being still alive, knowing about the brand. I forget the details, but somehow Hakoris got hold of the father's possessions. I suppose he killed him. The daughter—that was Mara— wound up Hakoris's slave. Kept cooped up as naked as a baby and mistreated terribly. The word was that he never touched her—well, I mean in *that* way. Nobody seems to have had any idea what Hakoris did for his, uh, recreation." Djoser hiccuped and drank again. "But he did beat the daylights out of the girl, the way I understand it, and worked her fingers to the bone. She hated him."

"When she probably should have been grateful to have a roof over her head. But do go on."

"She suspected that Hakoris had killed her father, but wasn't sure. Then Riki, who was just a kid at the time, busted her out."

"She and Riki were close when they were young?"

"I suppose so. He ran away and took her with him. There was a price on both their heads. Then she joined Isesi's band, north of here. They raided the Children's Refuge to set the kids free. Hakoris recaptured her but got himself killed shortly thereafter."

"Ah. And how long before she met Kamose, then?"

"They also knew each other as children, but for a short time only. They met again when they were both grown and he'd come back from wherever he had been. Just in time for the victory at Thebes."

"And nothing went on between Riki and Mara in all that time?"

"You know, now you mention it, I always thought that was strange. They say they were just friends, but Riki had a reputation with the girls before he met Teti. And Mara! You should have seen her then! On, she's attractive enough now, but in her teens she was spectacular!"

"And yet nothing happened." The tone implied disbelief.

"If you know any different, I don't even want to hear it. And make sure the king doesn't, either." His tone changed. "Kamose and Mara may not be getting on now, but that wouldn't make him a whit less jealous. If he'd thought that Hakoris had molested her, I don't think he would have touched her himself. It's that way with him."

"And yet here he is at the front, while she's been back in Thebes . . . where Riki sleeps alone—in theory, anyhow." Amasis sat back and raised his eyebrows in question.

"Ah! If that were what was going on—! He's angry enough with Riki as it is, pulling out like that. If insult were to be added to injury . . ."

Amasis shook his head understandingly. "Let's hope the lady has kept her head on her shoulders," he said skeptically. "Changing the subject, Djoser, why were you passed over for Elset's job? I mean, aren't you as much a soldier as he is?"

"Damn right I am! And a lot better too!" Djoser's fist pounded on the table, jolting the wine jar. Djoser barely caught it before it fell. "But the king tended to leave such decisions to Riki—promotions, whatever. Riki left Elset in charge, and Kamose is sticking with that. Why doesn't he see who his real friends are? Everyone knows I'm the better man!"

Amasis let the words hang in the air for a long moment. When he spoke, his voice was confidential. "Perhaps he will, one of these days.

"I sympathize with your position, my friend. I've had my eye on you and have put in a good word for you now and then—not that it's done much good. But when the time comes, Kamose will remember what I've said. I'm one of his oldest friends."

"Oh, any good word you could put in for me, now or in the future, would be—"

"Hear me," Amasis said in a low voice. Their eyes locked. "I know some things you do not. There is a way to get closer to the king. A lot closer."

"Tell me! I've tried everything."

"No," Amasis said with an enigmatic smile. "Not *quite* everything. There is, shall we say, a sort of inner ring to which Kamose and I belong. Its members include warriors, traders, merchant princes, and kings—the great ones of all the lands around the Great Sea."

"Please tell me!"

"It requires commitment, complete commitment, heart and soul, but the blood brothers you will acquire will stand by you in all adversity. In all lands, just saying the word and making the sign will draw them forth." He sipped his drink. "But you understand, their complete and unquestioning loyalty to you will be bought only by your own loyalty to them—and to the cause they, and you, will serve faithfully and for as long as you shall live."

Djoser's eyes stared into his companion's. "I'm your man," he vowed. "Tell me more."

Mara tossed and turned. Try as she might, she could not sleep. Instead she lay tense, eyes staring at the ceiling. The room was half-illuminated with moonlight that streamed through the far window.

She sat up in bed, sighed, and turned to put her bare feet on the cold floor. Savoring the chill feel of the tiles against her soles, she walked to the window. There was a slight breeze, but the feel of it was wonderful against her naked skin.

She stretched, bathed in moonlight, before the window, and looked out over the sleeping city. The wind caressed her breasts and belly and buttocks. She hugged herself in an ecstatic little movement.

If Kamose were to come to her now, from the separate room in which he slept . . .

But no. He would not, and she would not initiate any lovemaking. There had long been a wall between them, one that might never be breached. *Would* never, if the fact depended on her recantation or capitulation!

Her hands softly caressed her body. She closed her eyes. There was something magical about being naked in the moonlight, bathing in the rays of the waxing moon.

Again her thoughts turned to Riki.

He had been a naked urchin in the streets when they met. She had been a naked slave and had seen the first sexual thoughts stir him. They had been like First Man and First Woman together, but of course nothing could happen between them then. If Hakoris had come back unexpectedly and caught them at some mischief—

She shuddered, then stroked herself again, softly, imagining that the hand, gentle and insistent, was his, Riki's.

Imagine now. Imagine if instead of suppressing his feelings, Riki had reached out to her and touched her.

She could feel it, even now.

With a great shuddering sigh she abandoned herself to her fantasy, there in the moonlight. The hands on her body moved faster, faster.

Afterward she felt ugly, soiled, and bitter. She sat on the windowsill, a thin robe now thrown over her shoulders.

What was she going to do?

She could not just go back to Thebes as if she had never come here—not even if it meant getting to see Riki again. She had to do something about this situation first. But what?

She pondered the matter. First she had to find out exactly what was going on here. How widespread was the cult by now? She had gathered from the gossip back at the river that Amasis had been in Egypt awhile, although nobody was certain exactly how long. Had he brought confederates with him?

She sat up suddenly, alarmed.

What if they had already begun to corrupt the army? The leaders? The captains? And how did one go about recognizing cult members before it was too late?

So far all she knew was the business about the brand. There must be signals that they showed to one another to help each one of them recognize his comrades. But what were they? How did you know, when you took someone into your confidence, whether or not he was one of them?

She needed to talk to someone. But whom? These days she knew virtually no one down here in the delta, in the war zone. Many of the old friends she had made in her youth were now dead.

Isesi! Of course! Isesi, and good old Sem and the Brotherhood of Shai, who had saved her from Hakuris! Yes, she would look up Isesi and ask him what was going on. He was sharp-eyed and shrewd and seldom missed much of what was going on around him. He would know about these people, Amasis and whoever. He would be able to tell her what to do.

She frowned. But how could she go to him now? Everyone would recognize the queen, and her very presence would alert the Hai, who still controlled large parts of the delta, and they would have her followed, thus leading them right to Isesi's hideout. That would be the end of all of them!

She would have to travel incognito, and she would have to go it alone.

She stood and threw the robe from her; then she pulled her trunk over to the window and opened it in the cool light of the moon, looking for something plain . . . surely there had to be something plain, something in which she would not be recognized.

But even a queen's everyday clothing was too elegant to travel in: gorgeous cloth, tinted with rich dyes, and expensive sandals made of buffalo leather—all would betray her to even the casual eye. Her maid's clothing might be just the thing, or if not, Amenardis could be sent out to fetch her something suitable to wear.

Filled with a sense of purpose, she tiptoed to her sleeping servants' room.

IV

Isesi stood, arms folded over his chest, watching the big house burn. A grim smile played over his thin lips. "We can go," he said. "It's too late for them to save the place now. The creek's too far to bring that much water. We've done a good night's work."

Makare's harsh voice sounded at his elbow. "I think it a day wasted when I have not killed my man," he said. "No one has died—neither Hai nor Hai sympathizer nor downright traitor."

Isesi and Sem exchanged quick glances by the light of the raging fire. "Look at it this way," Isesi soothed. "As the smoke from those flames climbs the sky, it is a clear signal to other Egyptians who might be tempted to sell out to our enemies. We've destroyed a granary full of hoarded grain and converted a rich traitor into a poor one in one stroke. So what if no one was inside when we did it?" He chuckled. "The son-of-a-dog traitor will lose face with the Hai—make no mistake about it. They have no time for paupers. He won't have a friend left in the world. Could killing him do much worse to him?"

Makare snorted. "Who cares about that? I speak of what it would do for *me*."

Sem looked at Isesi again and shook his head. "Well, we'll try to keep that in mind next time," he said to Makare. "Our job here is done."

The dozen men nodded to each other, then dispersed. As he and Isesi started down the road by the light of the blaze and the moon, Sem caught Makare looking after the two of them. Sem waited until Makare was out of earshot, then spoke in a very low voice. "Ugh! That one gives me the creeps."

"He's a good fighter," Isesi responded. "But I know what you mean. We all have to kill. We don't have to take quite as much pleasure from it as he does. Well, any port in a gale."

"Are you sure?" Sem challenged. "Can we afford one like that? His savagery is beginning to be talked about in the bazaars. He doesn't make us look too good."

"The people who are talking," Isesi said, "where are they when we need them? We need fighters willing to stand up to the Hai. People's opinions will sway me the sooner when they begin to back their words with deeds. At least Makare does that."

"Isesi!"

"I don't care," Isesi replied stubbornly. "When we need him, Makare's there. He even volunteers for the most dangerous assignments. If you were the one who had to raise a raiding party on short notice, you'd begin to appreciate him."

Exasperated, Sem sighed long and loud. "Isesi, I sometimes wonder if, in a long conflict like this one, the heroes and the villains don't slowly begin to take on the same characteristics. Now don't get me wrong; I'm not losing faith in our ideals. Quite the opposite. It's just that our means, Isesi, sometimes begin to resemble those of the enemy."

"Ideals make all the difference."

"I disagree! There are no justifications for barbarous behavior! When we begin to act like the villains, we become them!"

Isesi turned to look at his usually mild-mannered friend, and his steps slowed to a halt. "What a strange thing for you to think. Why, if I got to considering the relative morality of every strategy, whether we're unfair to the enemy or not, I wouldn't be able to act at all."

"I'm not talking about fairness! I'm talking about honor! Self-respect! Human decency!"

"Sem," Isesi said patiently, "there'll be time for all that when we've driven the Hai out of Egypt. There'll be time for all the good things. But for now—"

"Life is nothing but a lot of nows. You can't let your own personal standards down, not for the sake of anything—even victory over the Hai."

Isesi let his shoulders slump. "Old friend, let's argue about this tomorrow, eh? I'm exhausted. It's been a long day. I share some of your concern over Makare. For the time being we need him, though, and I'm willing to put up with his flaws. When the proper time comes, I'll drop him and have done with it."

Sem closed his eyes and exerted all his willpower not to prolong their argument. "I'll see you in the morning, Isesi," he said at last, then turned to trudge dejectedly down the side road to his quarters.

*   *   *

"Father," Amram said, "*you* reason with him. He won't listen to me."

Kohath, sitting cross-legged next to his son, tossed another stick on the guttering coals. "Son," he said, "have you ever considered that he might be the one trying to talk sense to you? Levi is old. He has seen much."

"He is too narrow."

"He is also your grandfather and the head of our clan, plus the chosen leader of all the sons of Jacob now that Joseph is no longer with us. I will thank you to remember that and to honor him. I will not hear harsh words about him."

"But we need all the friends we can get now. . .—and in the future—until we have won our way back to Canaan and regained the land God gave to Jacob."

"Friends among foreigners? Unbelievers? Idolators, for all we know? You are dreaming, Amram."

Amram frowned, frustrated. "Are you saying that a foreigner cannot be a man of honor? That an idolator cannot be courageous and true?"

"Of course not. Our covenant with El-Shaddai does not automatically confer virtue; it must be worked for. And to those outside the covenant, honor costs the same labor, the same diligence, the same commitment it costs us. As Jacob used to say—"

"Please. No hoary homilies. Spare me 'the Sayings of Jacob.' "

"What's got into you, Amram? First you start cozying up to foreigners—murderers, for all I hear—"

"The man I spoke to you about is not a murderer. Killing a Hai is not the act of a murderer. And he killed his man in the service of our people, Father, a man who had insulted your own granddaughter!"

"And for this I am thankful to El-Shaddai that He has sent us a foreigner to do what we could not. But to fraternize, as you suggest, with the unclean—"

"All I know, Father, is that I have met the man and you have not. He seems honorable and decent. I don't know why we can't sit down with him and discuss matters of importance to his faction and to ours."

Kohath stroked his gray beard. "It sounds reasonable on

the face of it, doesn't it? But look around you, my son, at all the foreigners who migrated to Egypt during the great drought. Only we have maintained our cultural integrity. Alone of the foreign immigrants we have maintained our own customs, our own religion, our own bloodlines, and our own language. And all because we wisely held ourselves apart, when all around us were being assimilated. Their children don't know what nationality they are. And even though they have adopted Egyptian ways, the Egyptians call them foreign scum. They intermarry and without exception make bad marriages."

It was hard to argue with this line of thought. Amram frowned. "I understand, Father, but we're talking practicalities now, not high ideals."

"I thought I had raised you on the understanding that it is always germane to every discussion that one introduce precisely those high ideals. I don't know if it was what you heard."

"But, Father—"

Now Kohath leaned forward and put one cautionary hand on his son's knee. "There is more," he said softly. "The other night Levi had a vision. A vision sent by God." He let this sink in, then went on. "He did not share the whole of it with me, but what I heard was enough to frighten me, and I think that even a firebrand like you might find it sobering."

"What?"

Kohath adjusted his legs. They had been sitting before the dying fire for some time. "It has to do with a cult our people drove out of Canaan in Levi's youth," he said. "A diabolical cult devoted to the goddess."

Amram stared. "The so-called Great Mother?"

"Apparently. When our people were allowed to send representatives back to Canaan to bury Jacob, they brought back the melancholy news that the cult is back in all its strength in the land of our fathers."

"That is terrible news! If we ever try to reenter Canaan, we will have to fight our way in."

"Precisely. They are our blood enemies, the accursed of God. Where will we ever find ourselves a leader who combines the skills of a great soldier and a pathfinder, to lead us across the desert with enemies behind us and worse enemies ahead of us? In the history of our clans, only once have we played the warrior."

Amram knew his father was speaking of the time when

Abraham, entering Canaan also from Egypt, had hired a mercenary named Sneferu to train his family and servants to the arts of war, to destroy the armies of the Four Kings from the Land of Two Rivers. "We can do what Abraham did," he said.

"Abraham entered Canaan a rich man. We shall enter Canaan poor and, unless a miracle occurs, unarmed. Where are we going to find ourselves a Sneferu who will show us how to defeat heavy odds? To conquer blood enemies numbering many to our one? And do all this, mind you, without pay?"

Amram scowled, at a loss for an answer.

"The vision was unclear, as messages from God often are. But the burden of it seems to be that the cult is in Egypt, and close. We, the blood enemies of these monsters, are in grave danger."

"Danger? How? Can you imagine what the priesthood of Amon would do to a cult invading their territory?"

"It is here among us already. Since Petephres's death the priesthood of Amon has had little influence in Apophis's court. There is a chance of the cult taking over the delta, as it has southern Canaan while we were away."

Amram's brows rose. "Ah! That's bad news indeed."

"It is. All the more reason to keep ourselves isolated from all others. The cult spreads like the plague, by infection. One man converts another. One day there is one; the next day there are two; the next day four, and so on."

"And you are implying that even my fr—even the man I was talking to you about . . . could be infected by them?"

Kohath nodded solemnly. "It happened that way in Canaan: One day a man was your friend. The next day he was your enemy, professing no allegiance to anything or anyone but the cult. There was no trusting anyone at all."

Amram gaped at him, unable to answer. It sounded so hopeless! If this was the way Levi and Kohath were thinking, he would never persuade them to adopt his point of view.

Well, maybe that was not true. When Miriam had begun to talk with him about Isesi, he had been quite as obdurate as they. Unfortunately, the older a man got, the harder it was to get anything new or different into his mind. It would be a formidable task for him to bring Levi and Kohath around, old as they were.

And now, with this new information—

If information it is, he thought. And it might not be. It could just be the natural tendency of a very old man to dream of the place where he had been young and vigorous. Levi could just be imagining something that had occurred to him in his long-vanished youth. The supposed vision could be a false alarm and no more.

Not that that would make it any easier to talk sense to the two of them! False dreams were as convincing as real visions to the person who had them. Talking Levi out of this vision was going to be very difficult.

Suddenly other thoughts occurred to him: What if the dream were real? A vision of the kind Joseph used to have? The kind that Jacob had had in his young manhood? What if the cult were here? What if it spread quickly through Egypt and won out?

Why, his people were doomed. Doomed!

V

In the night Makare moved from campfire to campfire, passing pleasantries with first this person, then that. The encampment of the Brotherhood of Shai had been moved to one of the marsh islands a month earlier, following Ani's death and Tchabu's disappearance. So far the move appeared to be a good one. There had been no new incidents, and the conspirators felt more secure.

Thus Makare could move safely within the compound. By now he knew every one of the conspirators: what they had done for a living before joining the army of insurgents; who were alone and who had families in the larger community; what were their strengths and weaknesses, their quirks and crotchets. This information gathering had its purpose: He had been looking for a way to convert each one of them.

So far he had six well-placed cult confederates among them, each sworn to the service of the Great Mother, sworn to silence and secrecy, sworn to obey his orders at all costs. There were half a dozen others he thought might prove useful in his campaign of systematic corruption.

Of course there were others who could never be brought

over to his side. These would resist to the last and, as a result, would have to be eliminated.

First among these were Isesi and Sem, Isesi the greatest danger. Makare was not swayed by the fact that Sem distrusted him, while Amasis and Isesi spoke in favor of tolerating newcomers. Makare knew that the smallest misstep on his own part would convert Isesi into a deadly enemy, much more dangerous to the cabal's plans than Sem.

Isesi would have to be murdered, and soon. Makare had been working on the details for days, for any suspicion that his death had been due to betrayal must be avoided at all costs. Ani's death had already caused enough suspicion. No one believed the story Amasis had tried to plant, about Ani's murder at the hands of the suddenly absent Tchabu, and the question of what traitor had penetrated so far into the Brotherhood's defenses remained a pressing one. Besides, Isesi commanded great loyalty not only among the Brotherhood of Shai but in the larger community as well.

Nevertheless, all this forethought was more Amasis's way of doing things than his own, Makare realized. He himself favored slipping Isesi the knife and rowing him to the middle of the Nile in a papyrus boat, then setting the thing on fire with the anchor down at the deepest spot in the river. Yes: Pour pitch over the body first so it would burn faster and hotter. There would be nothing left to identify.

But he had been given the strictest orders by Amasis, in the name of the Great Mother, and the oath he had taken to follow them could not be broken. Thus, Isesi's murder had to look as though perpetrated by the enemy—the Hai, traitors, mercenaries, or someone else.

Now, having paid his respects at every campfire but one, he came to the guttering fire of Ankhu, his most recent recruit. Silently he made the secret sign; Ankhu nodded and followed suit.

"Greetings," Makare said. "Have you given thought to what we were talking about earlier?"

"Yes. It will not be easy, but I will do my best."

Makare kept his grating voice low. "When someone says 'I will do my best,' the possibility that one might fail is implied. This is not what the Goddess wishes from her servants."

"I stand corrected. I will do as you command. It only remains to make sure that I am not caught and that the blame falls upon the proper person."

Makare smiled humorlessly. "Well put," he said. "One's ordinary best is not enough here. For the great plan to come into being, one must reach within himself for resources he may not have known he had."

"I understand," Ankhu said. "When the time comes, Sem will die, and it will look as though he had been caught in the act of committing treason to our cause."

"No one will believe this of Sem," Makare said gruffly. "He is slow-witted and clumsy but straightforward. Treason is not in his character. It must appear as though he had died a hero, saving another, perhaps, from death at the hands of the Hai."

"I shall give the matter careful thought."

Makare nodded, satisfied. "In the meantime, have you found any prospects for recruitment?"

"Yes, one here and one in the city. Both are disaffected."

"Good. Give me their names. I will approach them. How convenient it is that the local beliefs and practices in the religion of Amon have been so eroded by the Hai. And yet the Hai religion has remained the Hai's, with few Egyptians going over to it—and the Hai have shown little interest in guiding their steps in that direction. Leaving us a fertile field to sow in."

Ankhu nodded. "Things are little better in Thebes. There is scarcely a man in Kamose's army command who keeps to the old observances, and attendance at religious functions even at court is perfunctory."

"The Goddess has obviously guided our steps hither with her usual inexhaustible wisdom. Keep up the good work, my friend, and report to me when you have settled upon a plan."

"You *must* go now," Miriam urged, but her actions contradicted her. Her hands gripped his arms all the more tightly, and her breasts, unrestrained under her light garment, pressed against his chest. "Father will be home at any moment."

Isesi pulled her to him tightly and kissed her forehead. "Amram and I are not enemies. You said so yourself."

"No." She pulled back to look up into his eyes. Her face appeared very serious in the moonlight. "He would like to be your friend, but he has promised Levi that he would not have further contact with you, and it would be a grievous sin to lie to the principal priest of our God. Meanwhile he does what he can to reconcile Levi with the idea that you are his friend, the protector of our people."

"But it goes so slowly! I am impatient. You know that about me already. It may be a fault or a virtue, but it is an essential part of me, and I can do little about it. I want it all, and now. I want the Hai out of Egypt, and I want the land united under a king of the old blood. I want justice for your people as well as mine. I want you for my wife."

She laughed softly and snuggled closer to him. "Levi and Amram are talking tonight. Levi has had some sort of prophetic dream. I hope it was a message of hope and reconciliation, one that allows your friends and my people to recognize each other as allies."

"And what are the chances of *that*, I wonder?"

"I have no idea. But I'll get a message to you as soon as I know. Now go, please. He would be unhappy to find you here."

Isesi sighed and held her close. "This is not easy, but I will go." He kissed her and moved toward the door, but then he came back and embraced her once more. "Please. Let me know the moment you hear anything."

"I will," she promised. "Farewell, my darling."

By the light of the moon Makare, standing in deep shadow, watched as the slim figure came down from the far bank and stepped into the water. With as little noise as possible the wader crouched and dived into the water, swimming out into the current with strong and graceful strokes.

I might well do it now, Makare thought. *Isesi will be totally unprotected when he comes out of the water on this side*. His right hand instinctively went to the sharp knife at his side, his heavy fingers curling around the hilt.

It would break his own rule to kill without first thinking things out, but the temptation was strong, and twice he eased the knife out of its sheath only to slip it back again with a curse under his breath.

Suddenly the thought came to him: Was it Isesi? It could, after all, be a spy. One by one he had visited every campfire and accounted for every person who was supposed to be there.

Yes. A spy. The garment on this one did not resemble

the one Isesi had been wearing. It had hung differently, coming down farther on the leg. *A spy!*

He reached back into the darkness and found the bow and quiver he had brought with him when he had taken over the midnight watch. Silently he nocked an arrow, waiting for the figure to come out of the water.

Suddenly he sensed someone behind him. Startled, he turned, peering through the darkness, then saw the moonlight glint on a familiar face. "Isesi! Don't ever sneak up on me like that! I could have—"

"I'm sorry," Isesi said. "I saw the swimmer, too. I have a powerful curiosity to know who has found out about our hideout. Put away the bow for now. Our knives will force the truth from our 'visitor.'"

Makare's eyes narrowed, but he held his temper. "You're right," he said in a changed voice. He put the bow down and replaced the shaft in his quiver. "I wasn't thinking. Here, you go that way. I'll wait here. If he runs when I jump him, you can catch him from the other side."

"Wait," Isesi said. "Where is he? He should have come out of the river by now. I don't see any sign of him at all."

Makare peered forward through the darkness. "Curse it!" he said. "He's disappeared on us. He can't have come out of the water. I'd have heard him."

Isesi put one finger over his lips, motioning for complete silence.

"Hold it right there, my friends," said a new voice.

The two swiveled to look at the business end of a razor-sharp arrow. Behind it, in shadow, they could see a slim, strong hand on a bow drawn to its limit. The arrow was pointed at a spot midway between them, ready to kill the first person who moved. It did not make Makare feel better to realize that the weapon was his own.

"Knives out," the voice commanded. "Drop them on the ground before you nice and slow. Now out into the light, both of you! Put your hands behind your heads! Let me get a look at you."

Makare cursed again below his breath but complied. He felt like a fool. His own bow and arrows, and he was supposed to be on watch! "Who are you?" he croaked.

To his surprise the bow lowered, and the arrow was released slowly as the pressure from the string lessened. He tensed, readying himself for a quick spring forward.

"No!" Isesi ordered, putting a hand out. "It's all right." He managed a baffled chuckle. "It's a friend."

Makare could make out the regular features as the friend came forward. A broad brow, a slim neck . . . "The gods curse me for a coward," he said. "It's a woman."

"Not just a woman," Isesi responded, laughing. "Makare, meet an old friend of mine, one of the first members of the Brotherhood of Shai and as brave a comrade as a man ever had." He bowed low and made a flourish. "Mara, queen of the Red Lands, wife to Kamose of Avaris."

As the woman moved out of shadow into light, her eyes locked with Makare's. He felt something happen. Those dark eyes seemed to stare into his very soul and know him for what he was.

For a moment he was frozen with panic. *She sees! She knows! But how? How could she possibly—*

Witch? Sorceress? What did it matter? It was enough to know she was an enemy, and a supremely dangerous one.

VI

The tension hung in the air like something that could be touched. The two pairs of eyes held until Makare finally blinked. Flustered, angry with himself, he blurted out the first thing that came to mind. "How did Your Majesty know where we—" he began."

"Forget the formalities," she interrupted curtly. "I don't want anyone to know I'm here. Particularly my husband." She looked from one to the other. "As you probably have guessed, this in not an official visit. I have business with you, Isesi—urgent business."

"I am at your command," he said. "But how did you manage to find us? We have not been here long. I would like to think that the few villagers who know of our encampment have not spread the massage far and wide."

"No one has betrayed you," she assured him. "I learned your location from my husband, when I asked how my old friend Isesi was doing." She looked him straight in the eye but found no trace of guile there. "We must talk," she continued. "Now."

Makare cursed under his breath. He had an idea what her urgent business was all about and wanted to prevent her meeting with Isesi.

"Can't it wait until morning?" he said gruffly, the hostility in his tone barely repressed. "Isesi has to go out on a patrol very early and—"

"Never mind," Isesi said. "I'm too keyed up to sleep. You go along to bed, and I'll see what Mara has to say." He turned to watch as Makare moved away through the darkness toward his own long-dead campfire.

"I'll ask you about that one in a few minutes," Mara said. "I'll want to know everything you can tell me about him. But first tell me what's happening here." She sat down and watched as Isesi built a small fire.

He frowned. "It's the usual sort of long, tiring, and frustrating work. I spent most of my day destroying the granary of a traitor who's been dealing with the Hai. When that was done, I wanted to spend some time with Miriam—"

"Miriam?" Mara said. "You've got a woman?" Her smile was affectionate and amused. "Isesi! I'm surprised!"

"Why didn't anyone tell me how much it hurt to be in love with a woman—"

"Or with a man," she said flatly. "I have my own problems. But go on. You obviously need to talk to a friend."

Quickly he described his love for Miriam, her family's opposition, and her father's vow to Levi. "I don't know what to do. I can deal with the enemy but not with the hostility of people I want to be my friends. Even if her father relented, her religion won't let her marry outside her faith."

"You could adopt her religion," Mara suggested.

"That could be managed, I suppose. But first I would have to convince the patriarch, Levi, that I'm not an enemy on the same level as the Shepherds. . . ."

"Poor Isesi. But if the girl really loves you, there's no problem too big for the two of you."

"You don't understand. The Hai oppress these people horribly. They're virtually slaves, and it's all Miriam's family can do to get by, with the heavy labor the Shepherds load on them."

Mara was moved by Isesi's anguish, and she put a friendly hand on his shoulder. "I'm not without resources." Her smile was wry and self-mocking. "Sooner or later I will be able to assert some of my queenly prerogatives with Kamose and get some extra food and supplies to your girl's family. We'll be liberating this area soon anyway, I think. The war's closer than you may have imagined."

"I'll be grateful for anything you can do. I didn't mean to burden you with my troubles. Tell me what you've been up to. What are you doing here? Why aren't you in—"

"In Thebes? I had to find out what was going on. You've heard that Riki's quit the army?"

"I heard he went home to be with his wife when she came to term. Has she had the child yet?"

"Oh, Isesi, she died. She and the child. It's so sad— Riki's totally devastated."

"Gods!"

"But he didn't leave because of that. He left because Kamose has changed, and it was a change that Riki doesn't like." She grunted softly. "Neither do I. This change has been coming over him for quite a while. Lately, however . . ."

She paused for so long a time that Isesi, alarmed, looked at her closely. "Yes?" he encouraged. "Lately?"

"Isesi," she said, "what do you know of the man Amasis? The one who's grown so close to Kamose?"

Isesi's mouth turned down at the corners. "Not much," he admitted. "He appears to have been an old friend of Kamose's. He just turned up suddenly, he and Makare, only a few—"

"Makare? The fellow I just met?"

"Yes. We can use all the reliable men we can get, and both quickly proved their mettle in one engagement after another. Then Amasis went to see Kamose, and that's the last I've heard of him. Makare stayed on with us here. He's a good fighter—if a little on the savage side—and very brave. But I don't think he and I will ever be close."

"Tell me: Has he got a tattoo? But how would you know? He's got that thick hair and beard."

"Tattoo?" Isesi echoed, puzzled.

She pursed her lips in thought. "Maybe I'm overreacting. Makare and I took an instant dislike to each other. It may be no more than that."

"There's something you're not telling me."

"It can wait until morning. Have you a spare tent or a bedroll? I've come a long way in the past two days. I'm dead tired."

"Certainly. We'll both be fresher tomorrow. Just now I probably wouldn't be able to make sense of anything you say. It's good to see you again, though. I've missed you. Oh, by the way, I haven't had any news from my sister in quite some time. How is Aset these days?"

Mara looked at him, trying to think of something to say. "Can it hold until morning?" she asked.

People bustled about in the Habiru compound, suddenly up and around in the middle of the night. Candles, lighted from the last guttering coals of the campfire, were brought to Levi's bedside. Ranking members of his tribe had been summoned, but the first to arrive from the outlying huts was Amram.

"What's the matter?" he said. "Is he all right?"

"He seems to be having some sort of seizure," Levi's neighbor said. "Or it's another prophetic dream. Better go in to him."

"Right." Amram went through the curtains into the room beyond. Candles burned at the head and foot of the old man's bed, and two of his granddaughters hovered nearby anxiously. "It's all right," he told them. "I'll take over."

The women were about to say something, but just then the eyes of the old man on the bed opened. Levi saw Amram at his bedside. "Thank you for coming," he said. "Come and sit next to me."

Amram complied and took the old man's hand. "What happened, Grandfather?"

"A miracle. A miracle, I tell you! The mantle of Joseph has fallen to me at last. I have been given his prophetic gift. El-Shaddai has spoken to me most directly."

"Yes?"

A look of horror suddenly came over Levi's face. "Amram! You must get a message to someone in the camp of the group called the Brotherhood of Shai! They're in terrible danger— and we are as well! This man has to be stopped!"

"What man?"

"The foreigner! His name is Makare! He is of the cult I told you about! If we cannot stop him, he will murder the leaders of the Shai!"

"But, Grandfather, I thought you said they were our enemies, too, and we weren't to mingle with them!"

"True! True! But if their leaders are eliminated by Makare, the Brotherhood will quickly turn on us. And with them *and* the Hai against us, we are doomed!"

"That's what I've been trying to tell you!"

"But now I have heard it from the God of Jacob. You must get a message to the leader of this group!"

"Isesi?"

"Yes. Isesi. It may be too late. He must stop this Makare, or the results for us will be dire indeed!"

He motioned Amram close and spoke quietly, so no other ears could hear what Isesi must be told.

Mara awoke at dawn, drenched with sweat despite the chill of the early hour. The night had been full of frightening, ominous dreams in which she was trying to find her way through a vast thicket of poisonous thornbushes, one prick from which would mean instant death. Time after time as she had peered through the gloom in the dark thicket she had suddenly noticed the same pair of eyes staring at her from the darkness: dark, malevolent, hypnotic.

They had been the eyes of Makare.

Isesi! she thought. *I must get to Isesi before he goes out on the morning patrol with this man!*

She sprang out of her bedroll and looked around. Everything looked different in the dim light than it had last night. *We approached this spot from that side. Or was it this?*

She set out through the low-lying fog. Up ahead she spotted a man. "Hello!" she called. "You over there!"

The man turned, and she looked into the startled eyes of Sem. "Sem!" she said. "Thank heaven it's you!"

"Mara! I can't believe it! What are you doing here?"

"I'll tell you later. Quick! Where is Isesi?"

"He's gone out on patrol with Makare. He'll be back around noon—" But he stopped in midthought, suddenly frightened because of the look on her face. "What's the matter?"

"Where have they gone, Sem? I can go after them—"

"Oh, no! No, that would be a very bad idea. They're going on a very dangerous mission inside the Shepherd lines, intending to get something out. You'd only wind up calling attention to them."

"Sem!" a voice called from his left. "Sem, come here!"

"Wait a moment!" Sem called back, then turned back to Mara. "Come with me. You can tell me what's wrong while I'm looking into whatever's got my men so riled. You over there! What do you want?"

They had come out from behind a thick grove of bushes and could see two of Isesi's irregulars holding a slim, struggling figure. "Sem," one of the two said, "we caught this girl trying to sneak onto the island. We thought you'd like to question her."

"I recognize her," Sem said. "You, girl, you're Isesi's friend, aren't you?"

"Yes! I'm Miriam!" the girl said. "Please! There's not a moment to lose! You have to tell Isesi that he's in great danger!"

Sem and Mara exchanged startled glances. "It appears that more than one person has the same idea," Mara said. She turned to the girl. "What do you want us to tell him?"

The girl quickly told them everything Amram had told her to say. "It must be taken very seriously. Levi distrusts your people and wouldn't have asked my father to get a message to you under any but the most urgent conditions. I told Father the pickets on the island would likely kill him if *he* tried to get over here, but that Isesi wouldn't let anything happen to me. Is he here?"

"He's already left," Mara told her. She looked at Sem again. "Sem! Isn't there any way we can—"

"I'm afraid not," Sem said. Even now there was a skeptical look on his face. "We would only place both of them in mortal danger if we interfered with their mission in any way. And to do that on the strength of a dream? I don't know, Mara."

But now the stunned look on Miriam's white face changed to one of horror. "He won't come back!" she cried hysterically. "I've come too late! It's my fault because I took the wrong road. I was afraid of the low road in the dark. I was afraid of snakes. I took the high road instead."

VII

Isesi cautiously peered through the bushes. "There are five of them," he whispered. "Three of us against five of them. That's good odds."

Ankhu looked nervously at him, then at Makare. "They'll pass us in a moment," he said. "Do we confront them or hit them from behind once they've passed?"

Makare made the decision. "Wait until they're almost even with us; then I'll jump out in front to startle them. You, Isesi, jump them from the flank. Ankhu will simultaneously come at them from the rear. We'll make short work of them."

"Agreed," Isesi said, drawing his sword. Just as Ankhu was about to speak again, Isesi covered his own mouth with his whole hand and shook his head violently, ordering him to silence. To his right Makare moved into position, then looked back at the two of them. He held up his sword, then swept it downward and in the same blink of the eye leapt out into the path with a terrifying bellow of rage.

Isesi did not wait. He jumped through a gap in the bush and lunged. His blade caught his man hard in the side and sank in deep; the Hai soldier staggered to his knees and pitched forward, his fall pulling the sword out of his gushing wound.

Isesi parried a wild stroke from the Shepherd soldier next to him, turned the blade, and very nearly disarmed his man in the process. At the very moment when his opponent's blade was neutralized, he disengaged and hacked expertly at his enemy's neck. The blow opened the carotid artery; blood streamed. Isesi looked right and left. Ankhu had skewered the last man in the file and was pressing forward. One of Makare's victims was down, and the other—

"Look out, Makare!" Isesi shouted. He lunged forward and pinked the second Hai in the upper arm just as the man was about to stab Makare in the back. The soldier dropped his weapon and grabbed at his arm. Isesi hardened his heart, as he had done so many times in the last few years, and ran the man through.

As he did, Makare's first opponent leapt to his feet and engaged Makare again. Whoever the fellow was, he was a hardy chap and a master swordsman.

Ankhu's blow caught Isesi from behind. It was like a powerful blow from a sharp stick in the middle of his back, just to one side of the backbone.

He staggered forward. He looked down. The sword had gone all the way through his body and now protruded from his middle. He tried to pull away, to speak or cry out. But he could not get his breath. His sword fell from his hand, and he clutched at the sharp blade sticking out of his guts. The strength all went out of him at once, and he fell to one knee. "W-why?" he began, but the words would not come.

Behind him Ankhu watched as Isesi fell to his side in a pool of his own blood. He rolled over onto his back.

"M-makare," Ankhu said awkwardly, the horror of what he had done suddenly washing over him. "I . . . I didn't . . ."

With a sneer Makare stood looking down at Isesi. "Get his sword," he commanded. When Ankhu did not respond, he cursed and reached down for the weapon. "Isesi killed three of them himself. I'll claim he saved my life. He's a big hero now." He chuckled sourly, looking down at the dying man. "Hear that, Isesi? You'll have quite a reputation as a swordsman."

"Don't taunt him," Ankhu pleaded. "You don't need to do that." His face was white, and his voice wavered as he spoke. "I think I'm going to be sick."

"Just as long as you don't do it on our friend here," Makare said cynically. "Look, he's still alive. A bit, anyhow. Well, Isesi, your little rebellion is ours now, you know. All that remains is to get rid of Sem, and maybe the queen. No, I'll kill Sem and leave Mara. Killing off Kamose's wife would be a little much. Nobody will believe what she says against us—a queen in rags? A queen who ran away from her husband's bed? They'll think she's crazy, a virago."

Isesi's eyes opened and closed.

"In six months the army will be ours," Makare continued, ignoring the sight and sound of Ankhu vomiting. "In a year we'll have Egypt. Think about it, Isesi. The greatest nation in the world, under the absolute power of the Great Goddess. The Shepherds will seem like errant children when compared to us."

He bent over his fallen enemy and leered insolently into Isesi's face.

"You've lost," he said, "once and for all. Let that be your dying thought. You've been conquered by your worst enemies, people you thought were your friends. You die a pitiful fool, betrayed by your own stupidity and gullibility."

Makare indulged his urge to punish and hurt. "And that girl of yours, and her people? They're old enemies of ours. Their patriarch, Jacob, persecuted us unmercifully up in Canaan. He was the only one sharp enough and shrewd enough to see through us from the first. He killed us by the hundreds and sold to slavers everyone he didn't kill. That's how I wound up on the galleys—and Amasis and Kamose with me. And now I can combine my hatred and contempt for them with the comparable feelings I hold for you and your ragtag band of irregulars. That girl of yours—"

Isesi's eyes fluttered. It was the only sign of life in him. "Don't die on me!" Makare commanded. "Not until I've told you about the plans I have for that girl of yours. Miriam, I think the name is?"

The eyes fluttered even more weakly.

"Can you hear me? Can you hear me, little man?" Makare's voice rose to a fevered pitch. "Before I sell her I'll have her myself. Me, Makare! Shall I tell you how I'll have her? She won't like it, I can tell you that! First I'll—"

But now the eyes closed, once and for all.

"Damn you!" Makare shouted. "Curse you! Don't you dare die on me! Come back! Let me tell you the rest!" He picked up Isesi's limp upper body and shook it violently. There was no response. The body was deadweight. The head lolled.

"You bastard! Come back!"

But there was no sign of life as he dropped the dead body flat on its back. No sound except that of Ankhu behind him, heaving miserably.

Makare's voice rose to a hysterical scream. "You've cheated me!" he shrieked, out of control now. "You've escaped me! Curse you! Curse you, you bastard!"

The shadows grew long, and still the patrol did not return. Mara sat beside Miriam, one arm around the girl's narrow back.

"Don't blame yourself," she said for the fiftieth time. "It wasn't your fault."

"I took too long," Miriam said disconsolately. "If anything happens to Isesi, I won't forgive myself. Oh, why doesn't he come? Please, Isesi! Come back to me safe and sound!"

"He told me a bit about the suffering you and your people have been going through. I intend to do everything I can to help. I may not look it just now, but I *am* queen of Upper Egypt, and when Kamose's army is finally victorious here, I'll be queen of a united Egypt. Kamose wouldn't oppress anyone I chose to take under my wing. In Thebes I have better connections than he has, and Baliniri's arm is a long one."

"But if what Levi says is true . . ."

Mara frowned. "When I go back to Thebes, I'll have a lot to tell Baliniri. I would probably be well advised to sneak some mail back to him in secret long before then, if I can find someone reliable enough to send it back with." Her right eyebrow went up. "Miriam! You'd be perfect! Who would suspect you? Would you carry an urgent message about this back to Thebes for me, under my protection? I'll send another person with a nice and innocuous message, and you'll have the real message."

"But I've never been to Thebes. And I'm sure Levi wouldn't let me—"

"I'll talk to him. As the official protector of your people, my words ought to carry weight."

"Do you think I could?"

"You're a brave girl, full of strength and courage. Isesi's told me." Mara took the girl's hand. "Say you'll do it. You'll be doing your people a great service."

Miriam was about to answer, but just then a sentry called out, "Someone's coming!" and both women sprang to their feet.

"Who is it?" Mara asked. "Is it Sem's party?"

But then the litter-bearers came into view, Sem and Makare and Ankhu with them. And neither woman had any doubt whose body it was that the men were carrying. Miriam's shrill scream broke the near silence and seemed to hang in the air. "No! No, please, no!"

There was general mourning at the camp on the island all through the night and the next day. The tale of Isesi's heroism and his sad end—killed by the treachery of a Shepherd soldier who stabbed him in the back before Makare and Ankhu could get to him—had been retold a dozen times.

Mara escorted Miriam back to her father's house and returned while the funeral feast was still going on. She could not bring herself to eat or drink. Instead she sat, knees up, her chin resting atop them, staring into the great bonfire and thinking.

After a time Makare, emboldened by drink, came to her.

"You seem to take your friend's death hard. He was a brave man. He died in the cause of—"

She shot a glance of cold hatred at him. "I doubt if I'd be able to prove it, but I think you're lying. I don't trust you. Be warned: If anything happens to Sem—anything at all—I'll know. Leave him alone, and my doubts will remain just that. If he sustains even the smallest wound, I will know you for what I think you are. And don't get any ideas about getting rid of me, either. If anything happens to me, certain letters detailing my suspicions will automatically be placed in the powerful hands of men who could crush you." This last was an outright lie; she had not sent the letters off yet. But it was obvious from the look in his eye that Makare did not know this.

She pressed on. "You'll have to work around me," she said. "As long as you do nothing here but kill Shepherds, you're relatively safe. But arouse my suspicions again, and you're a dead man. Understand?"

She stood up now, brushing herself off, and locked eyes with him. He was the first to blink. "I see we have an understanding. Good. You go ahead and kill the Hai, their mercenaries, and their traitors. I'll help the people they've been oppressing. Just remember that if my suspicions are ever confirmed in any way . . ."

Her smile was the deadliest thing he had ever seen. Her voice lowered, and became all the more menacing for its silky softness. ". . . even your Goddess cannot save you." He blanched at the mention of the Goddess. "I see you understand," she said. "A follower of the Goddess will perhaps know of the Death of a Thousand Cuts." His mouth flew open; he cried out involuntarily. "This death will be your reward for displeasing me. See that you do not do so."

Fakery and bluff, she told herself as he backed away, his hands hovering protectively around his waist and groin. But it seemed to be working. That was all that mattered.

Shaken, Makare walked up to a fellow member of the Brotherhood and tore the wineskin from his hands to drink a deep but unsatisfying draught. A sorceress who knew secrets that none outside the cult had ever been allowed to know! A sorceress with the evil eye, who could stare him down! *Great Mother!* he thought desperately. *Protect me against this witch, this she-demon!*

VIII

"I don't know how we can accept this," Kohath said to his son. "Not without knowing where it all comes from. And with the death of your 'friend' "—the word came out with a delicate touch of scorn—"I can't imagine what Egyptian would be giving us food."

"What do you care where it comes from?" Amram asked. "We need food badly. If Isesi hadn't been sneaking food to us all these months, we would have starved. Father, someone has taken great pains to respect our customs. There isn't a thing here in any of these baskets that our religion forbids us to eat."

"Even at that, food grown by heathens—"

"—can be purified according to our laws. Father," Amram said, a little annoyed, "a gift like this, given without strings attached—"

"Hah! Can you say that with such confidence?"

"No one has approached me about terms for acceptance of this!" Amram looked disgustedly at his father, then let his eyes wander to the many baskets of vegetables that had been left at his door. "Look, Father. I have no idea specifically who left this. But it is a gift from El-Shaddai Himself, whomever He may have chosen to carry out his work for him."

"But—"

"But nothing, Father. God has touched the heart of some righteous Egyptian whom He has chosen to become our friend and protector. If He intends for me to refuse this great gift, He will have to tell me Himself. I will take the word of none other in this matter."

"Not even Levi?"

"Has Levi had a vision in which God has spoken to him forbidding the acceptance of His benison?"

"Well, no."

"Well, there you are. That proves what I'm saying, Father. I intend to feed my children. God expects me to feed and shelter my family."

His eyes suddenly had a faraway look in them. "Miriam . . ." he said thoughtfully.

"You're right," Kohath said. "Miriam would know. Have you asked her?"

Amram blew out through pursed lips. "No, I haven't. She was too distraught about our friend Isesi being killed. She blames herself for not getting there in time to warn him."

"Then talk to her. Let me know what you learn." Kohath nodded curtly to his son, ending the conversation, and walked away.

Amram did not stir for a long, long moment. *Miriam,* he thought. *How could I have missed it? How could I not have noticed?* There had been a change in her recently, a sudden shift from the trivial concerns of a child-woman to the outlook of a mature adult. And it had coincided with . . .

"Isesi!" he said to himself. "They were lovers! My daughter and—"

The epithet that sprang to his lips was quickly dismissed. He would not soil the memory of Isesi—the only truly honorable, truly upright Egyptian he had ever known—by calling him an unclean heathen. For all he knew, Isesi's staunch support of the Habiru could have contributed to his untimely death. Did the Habiru turn on their friends? Insult them? No!

He pounded one fist into the other palm. Isesi's memory would be honored in his household—Isesi and the Habiru's new protector, who had secretly and anonymously delivered enough food to his doorstep for his people to live for a month.

But he had to know what Miriam knew of this. He set out across the compound to the river where, he knew, Miriam would be doing the wash at this hour.

Mara, still dressed in the borrowed servant's clothing, dangled her bare feet over the edge of the bank. In the shallow river water Miriam, her skirt hiked up to well above her knees, bent to rinse the last of the robes. "I can't do it," Miriam said. "Father would never allow it."

"Perhaps he would," Mara disagreed. "He's been most reasonable so far. And your God Himself sent us the warning through Levi. If this isn't a portent of some kind, one that links our fates and commands us to cooperate, I don't know how to recognize one."

"Tell that to Amram," the girl suggested, somber-faced, her voice full of despair. She wrung out the robe and carried it to the bank, where the other clean clothing lay in the grass. "I don't feel like arguing with him. I wish I were dead. If Isesi had—".

Mara reached out and touched her hand. "Don't go off in *that* direction. You can't bring him back by blaming yourself."

"Oh, Mara, I'm trying to keep up a good face, but—"

"Miriam! Miriam, are you there?" The voice came into view. "Oh, there you are. I wanted to talk to you—" Then he saw Mara. She stood and brushed herself off. "Who's this?"

"Father, this is—"

Mara broke in. "My name is Mara, Amram. The fewer people who share the knowledge just now, the better. I'm a friend of Miriam's and for many years a close friend of Isesi's. I was one of the original Brotherhood of Shai, which broke into the Children's Refuge in Avaris, took the children to safety years ago, and later killed Hakoris, whom your people called Shamir ben-Hashum."

"Then may El-Shaddai shower blessings upon you!" Amram said warmly. "That was a blow well struck. You have my people's gratitude." Just then his brows went up, and he half smiled. "You wouldn't have had something to do with a certain wildly generous gift of food left behind last night for my people, would you?"

"Miriam," she said, "your father is a man of wisdom and understanding, a fit kinsman to Joseph." She grinned at him. "Make sure your people don't refuse it because of pride. I'm sure you understand that they need every friend they can find just now."

"I think this was the message God sent Levi," Amram said, nodding. "Yes. I thank you in the name of all, even of those too stubborn to thank you themselves. How may I serve you, my friend?"

"I was just going to bring that up," Mara said. She looked at Miriam and winked. "There is a job that needs doing. It is not without a certain peril, and I do not ask this favor lightly. Suffice it to say that Levi's vision was accurate; there is a nest of serpents in our midst, all worshiping the Goddess. So far I have arrived at a standoff with the one who is here in our own camp. I would have your people beware of him as well."

"Go on, please." Amram had blanched at the mention of the Goddess.

"Very well. He is called Makare. And he isn't the only member of the cult in Egypt. There's an even more danger-ous one already in high position in Kamose's army. The cult is spreading fast. It will require more resources to crush them than we in the delta command."

"So where are you going to get reinforcements?"

"Thebes," Mara replied. "Someone has to go upriver in disguise and get through to Baliniri. I'll write the message, but I can't deliver it. My place is here, fighting the cult and looking out for you Habiru."

"For which we are grateful. But who among us would be welcome in Thebes? I'd stick out terribly there. I'd never make it past the first guard post on the river."

"Yes. You'd wind up a galley slave or pressed into army service." Mara's eyes seemed to burn with intensity. "But Miriam wouldn't. Not if they thought she was a slave, sent upriver as a special present to Baliniri."

"Miriam!" he exploded, shocked. "*Miriam?*"

After the first surprise, Amram began little by little to accept the idea. In the end he turned to his daughter and asked, "This is what you want, then?" His voice was warm and full of concern, and his hand rested on her shoulder.

"What I wanted," the girl said, "was to win your permis-sion and Levi's to marry Isesi and bear his children."

"I'm sorry," he said. "I didn't understand how serious you—"

"It's all right, Father. I should have been more open with you. I never gave you a chance to say yes or no, really—I hadn't the courage to ask in the first place."

"My poor dear. He was a fine man. But there are other fine men in the world."

"I will have no other man. I have known one good one. Who could measure up to him? No, that part of my life is over. If I am to bear and rear no child and make a home for no man, what shall I do with my life? Mara has given me a chance to perform a useful service, one that may take my mind off . . . off what might have been."

"That's a good point," Mara agreed. "You'll spend so much time worrying about what will happen next, you won't have time to brood."

Miriam looked with great seriousness at them. "Then it's settled. That's what I will do—if I've your blessing, Father."

Amram hesitated for a moment, then embraced her. "Mara," he said over Miriam's shoulder, "do you have children?"

"No."

He released his daughter to stand at arm's length, looking at her with love and pride. "Imagine a blessing that can break your heart," he said softly. "Yesterday I had a child, a lovely child—or so I thought. But today I look at her and see a woman, strong and brave and beautiful. I am proud, and my heart runs over with love and compassion for her. But at the same time my heart mourns the child I no longer have. Where has she gone?" His voice broke. He tried to speak but could not.

"Father . . . I love you. I'm proud of you too."

He could not look her in the eye. His own eyes were full of tears as yet unshed. "Mara," he implored, "send her back to us safe and sound, please. Don't send her blindly into danger."

Mara put a hand on the shoulder of each of them. "I won't," she promised. "I have the feeling that neither my people nor yours will be able to do without her in years to come. How right Isesi was about her—and about you and your people as well. She gets her courage and compassion in the blood, Amram, from you. May your God bless your every undertaking."

Amram shuddered, still in the grip of strong emotion. "I think He already is," he said.

IX

With great effort Sem had managed to climb to the top of the tall palm. Although Zer had had to give him help up the last stretch, he now had a feeling of great accomplishment as he clung to the trunk and looked down at the river and the great flotilla of boats. A man of his age was not supposed to be able to perform feats of agility like this, even with help from a younger man. For a moment he basked in the thought: *I'm not as old as they all think! If I can still do this* . . .

But then he looked over the river below, and the sight drove all thoughts of personal vanity from his mind. *Gods!* he thought, shuddering. *Just look at them all!*

The river widened here, where the main high road from the border at Sile came closest to its banks. Here moved the mercenaries' many ships—all awash to the gunwales with the heavy burden of imported manpower—flags flying, sails furled, powered by many oarsmen, two abreast, heading for the docks near Avaris. Within sight of them, long lines of soldiers bound for the same destination marched along the road.

"I don't like this at all," Sem said softly. "Look: Greek ships, Cretan ships, ships from Tyre and Byblos and Sidon . . ."

"But the soldiers on the bank aren't foreign," Zer pointed out. "They're ours."

"Quite right," Sem said. "That's the guidon of the Seventh Shairetana. But—" He stopped, and his eyes widened. "But they're garrisoned at the border!"

"Exactly," Zer said with satisfaction. "That's why I brought you all this way. I knew you'd see in a moment what they're doing."

The men exchanged glances. Zer was a trader whose business had been severely curtailed in recent years by the Hai's rigid rules governing foreign commerce. He was rumored to be in sympathy with the rebels' cause, but this was the first evidence he had given of this.

"They're raiding the garrison at Sile for reinforcements," Sem guessed. "Leaving the border undefended."

"Yes. This has been going on for a week. I think the city of Sile could be taken, just now, by fifty hostile Bedouin, if they moved quickly enough and didn't make any stupid mistakes."

Sem estimated the number of soldiers on the bank. "This draft comes to . . .what? Two hundred?"

"Maybe more. And the boats?"

"I'd guess that a thousand or more have passed just since we've been up here."

"I'd estimate sixteen hundred," Zer said confidently. "Oh, don't mind me. That's the bookkeeper in me talking. I was trained as a scribe."

"You are a useful man. I am grateful."

"Then show your gratitude by ridding us of the Hai once

and for all," he shot back with a wry grin. "How does Apophis think he's going to pay all of these mercenaries? That's going to be an enormous payroll. Let's see, at two *outnou* a—"

"Spare me!" Sem said. "Look, I've got to get a message to Kamose. If he were to attack, not knowing the strength of the enemy just now, it would be a disaster for us."

"I'll help you. Getting down will be harder than climbing up was, and a lot more frightening. Take my hand."

Runners, however, had already reached the camp of the Brotherhood of Shai on its island and delivered the information about Apophis's mercenaries to Mara. She hesitated for a long moment, trying to think things out, then called for Ankhu.

When he arrived, breathing hard from having trotted most of the way from his outpost, she looked him hard in the eye. After a brief hesitation, he looked down at her feet.

Ah! He can't meet my gaze, she thought. *Are my suspicions confirmed, then? Is this one entirely too close to Makare?* She gave him a hard smile. "I have a message for you to deliver to Kamose," she said. "As soon as we have spoken, I want you to set off. He must have this information as quickly as you can get it to him."

"I have to report to my superior, Makare, first," he replied.

"No, you don't," Mara said in a voice of command. "I'll tell Makare anything he needs to know." She watched as Ankhu fidgeted, still unwilling to make eye contact. "You doubt my authority to countermand an order, then? Is your loyalty attached primarily at some lower level than the queen of Egypt?"

"No, my lady!"

"Then listen carefully to what I have to say. I want you to memorize the whole thing. I thought of sending a scroll, so there would be no misunderstandings, but scrolls can be lost. Or captured."

"But, my lady, if I were captured—"

"You won't be," she said flatly. "And if you were, you'd die before you said so much as a word. Because if I ever heard that you had betrayed us—"

"No, my lady! I'd never—"

She recognized his vulnerability and pressed on. "Makare

must have told you I was a sorceress. Hasn't he?" She had
said it too suddenly for him to think before he reacted. He
gulped and nodded. Silently she exulted: *I was right! Ankhu
is one of them! Makare would only have told a fellow member
of the cult about this!* "Well," she said, "I'd know, then,
wouldn't I, if you betrayed us, even under torture."

This was a lie, of course, but it sounded good, and it
played on fears already planted in Ankhu by his mentor.
Ankhu swallowed hard. "Never fear, my lady. I'll be silent to
the last drop of blood."

"See that you are. Now, the message I want you to take
to Kamose concerns large troop movements along the river to
Avaris. You must make it very clear to him that before he
makes any movement on the city, a thorough reconnaissance
is necessary to determine the odds against him."

"Yes, my lady. Give it to me one word at a time."

The queen sent Ankhu off less than an hour later. When
Makare finally showed up, Mara enjoyed a feeling of accomplishment. The foreigner nodded to her with minimal courtesy and was about to move past to his own area, but she
called him back.

"Makare," she said, "I sent your man Ankhu to Athribis,
to deliver a message to Kamose about troop movements."
She watched the narrowing of his eyes, the tightness around
his mouth. "Ankhu is one of you, isn't he?"

"I don't know what you—"

"Nonsense. He betrayed you before I'd got ten words
out. He's more afraid of me than he is of you, and it's your
own fault. You shouldn't have told him I was a sorceress."
Her smile was icy and triumphant. "Anyhow, he's on his way
to Kamose with a message that has a coded subtext. No one
but Kamose will understand. It was a signal he and I worked
out years ago, for sending messages by couriers who can't be
trusted."

"What do you mean?"

"The code says, in effect, that the bearer of this message
is a spy for the Shepherds and must be put to death the
moment he finishes passing the message along."

Makare paled. "But—"

"How many people in our camp have you corrupted by
now?" she asked. "It doesn't matter. I'll smell them out,

identify them, and trap them one by one as I have trapped Ankhu. You'll never get a toehold in *my* camp. Your friend Amasis may be able to bamboozle my husband, but you've met more than your match with me, my friend."

"Curse you!" he hissed under his breath. "I ought to kill you right here and now!"

Mara's hand went to the long dagger at her waist. "Men have tried that before," she said. "Ask anyone from the original Brotherhood of Shai. I doubt you could touch me in three passes. I've half a mind to bet you."

It was sheer bravado, but there was a method to her madness. Her very confidence made him falter, and as they locked eyes again, she knew she had conquered him—him, Makare, whom all men feared! She smiled, but her expression was more deadly than any grimace of hatred. "Come," she challenged. "Try me. I'll give you the first pass."

But he did not. In her heart of hearts there exploded a fierce exultation as he turned to go. But although his shoulders drooped with defeat, there was limitless power in the great apelike hands that clenched and unclenched as he stalked away.

Sem arrived just in time to ferry Miriam across the river in a tiny leather-covered coracle. The two of them joined Mara at the newly built fire just as the last rays of the sun were going down in the west.

"You've heard?" he asked. "The enemy—"

"Yes. I sent a message by Ankhu." Her finger made a slow slicing motion across her own throat. "And he carries a second message to my husband that will make fish bait of him five minutes after he's delivered the first message."

Sem's brows rose, and Miriam let out a little gasp of surprised shock. "Ankhu?" Sem asked. "Are you sure?"

"Yes," Mara said. "So shall perish all friends of the cult. The deed's done. On to other things. Miriam, my dear, are you ready to go?"

"Yes. Well, as ready as I'll ever be."

"You'll do fine. I don't even think you'll feel frightened. In some ways I know you better than you know yourself. You forget, I knew Isesi quite a long time. And I know the type of woman he would fall in love with. She would have to be as brave as his sister, Aset—who, incidentally, doesn't think of herself as brave, either."

She could see by the look in the girl's eyes that it was time to change the subject. "Now attend me, my dear. Here's the message I want you to get to Baliniri—and no one but him."

"Yes, Mara. Just tell me what you want me to say."

When Miriam had gone, Mara wearily sat down on a log across from the fire and allowed Sem to send a subordinate to the main campfire for food. But when the roasted meat, flat bread, olives, and wine arrived, she found herself too tired to eat. She stared at the food, then pushed it away.

"Try to have a little something," Sem urged. "You'll need all your strength. We have a full day ahead of us."

She stared into the fire. "Sem," she said disconsolately, "if I'd known how it all was going to come out, I'd have let Hakoris kill me. The golden dreams I had! The high ambitions about what I was going to do, about how I was going to be a force for good."

"But you are! You are!"

"Am I?" She turned her head to look exhaustedly at him. She looked much older than she was. "I just sent Makare's little conspirator friend to his death, with no pangs of conscience!"

"But he was a traitor!"

"He was a pawn, a puppet. No more, surely. And yet my conscience didn't bother me at all."

"It's bothering you now."

"But not a great deal. And the next thing I did was lie to Makare. I seemed to enjoy that, even though I've always hated liars. Then Miriam . . ."

"You've done nothing bad to Miriam."

"I've separated her from her family and sent her into danger. I look at her, and I see something of myself, back in the days of my own innocence. I was much like her once. But I saw too much, heard too much, suffered too much, too early in life—as she has begun to do, poor dear. There's something about the enforced loss of innocence that makes me want to cry. Makes me want to roll in the dirt like a child and weep my eyes out." Sem stared. "For all I know, she and Isesi may never have consummated their love. You know Isesi and his principles. The girl may still be a virgin. If she is, she'll die one. I know her type. And the ideals of her people."

"Now, Mara, you couldn't believe that odd foreign religion of theirs!"

"I don't know. They seem to get something very important from it, something that holds them up under the injustice and pain. Sem, they're *sure* about something. And I'm not sure about anything—not in that way. It's something that has made that little wisp of a girl strong and brave. And here I am removing her from its consolations and its nourishments."

"Ah," Sem said, understanding. "Your conscience bothers you more about this than what you did to Ankhu or lying to Makare."

"Probably," she admitted. Her voice held all the world's weariness. "These people of hers are special. I'm not sure why, but it's very important to me that nothing happens to them. Their destiny and mine are tied together in some way. That doesn't make much sense now that I say it out loud, and I'm probably being a fool, reading importance into things. Maybe it's just that I'm tired and disillusioned."

Sem waited a long moment, then reached over to pat the back of her hand. "Your instincts," he said. "Listen to them. When was the last time they advised you wrongly? And here they are speaking to you again. Heed them, Mara. Heed them."

CHAPTER SEVEN

Thebes

I

At the height of the plague, whole sections of Thebes and the outlying towns were decimated. The disease had even managed to cross the river, so cases had been found all over the Deir el-Bahari waterfront. The only section of the city spared was the artisans' village in the hills, whose inhabitants kept to themselves and thus avoided contagion.

The city had been braced for a long siege, but now the death count began to dwindle little by little. Three weeks passed, and the totals sank to single digits. There were whole days, even two-day periods, when not a single new case was reported. Yet no one dared relax. Attendance at the bazaars on market days remained sparse; neighborhoods drew straws to pick a family who would be asked to venture out and buy in bulk for a whole block. The city's economy stagnated. The streets looked dull and empty. People passing one another in the thoroughfares fearfully avoided each other.

Into this dispirited and virtually unrecognizable version

of Thebes came little Tchabu, sick at heart, half-starved, and frightened of his shadow. Ordinarily the poorer quarters of Thebes would have welcomed him; an old city tradition had it that dwarfs were good luck, good fortune would attend a man who helped one, and better fortune would come to a family who took a dwarf into the house. But now everyone was afraid of contagion, and the old traditions fell victim to fear.

Thus Tchabu stumped the streets for hours without finding a place to lay his head or a charitable inn willing to let him work for his food. As darkness came on, he began to grow desperate. What could he do? How could he get to the court to deliver his message? His name was already quite well known in Theban circles, and Riki and others had told Baliniri about him. He knew that if he could only get someone there to take his name in to Baliniri, the vizier would consent to see him.

But when he applied at the court gates, he was turned away contemptuously. He wasn't surprised; his clothing was ragged and filthy, and he looked ill. He stood in the street, trying to make up his mind. Where was it that they had told him the military officers hung out when they were in the city? Oh, yes, the Inn of the Four Sorrows. But where was it? The city was bigger than he had expected it to be, and his first pass through the lower-class quarters had not turned up anything that would have jogged his memory.

Now, however, a well-dressed merchant came toward him in the street, avoiding his eyes, as expected. "Please, sir," Tchabu asked in his croaking voice, "can tell me where I find Inn of Four Sorrows?"

"Begone!" shouted the man, giving the dwarf a wide berth. "Don't touch me!"

"Please," Tchabu begged, "just want to know where. Please! Not touch. Just tell. Mercy, esteemed sir!"

"Get back!" Emboldened, Tchabu advanced. This set off a burst of rapid speech. "The inn—it's down that street. Now get away! Leave me in peace!"

Tchabu made a tiny bow. "Many thanks," he croaked. He watched the frightened man hurry away. Could this be Thebes, which everyone had always told him was so friendly, so hospitable? He shrugged and, sore-footed, walked crookedly on his miniature legs down the street in the direction indicated.

But as he approached the inn, a vague feeling of disquiet

began to come over him. Might he be getting ill? Everyone had been at pains to warn him of the plague—so much so that he had briefly begun to imagine symptoms before common sense had dismissed his fears.

The closer he got to the door, the worse he felt. Fear grabbed at his guts. More than anything in the world, he wanted to turn and run away as fast as his stunted legs could carry him. Instead he balled his tiny fists and tried to get hold of himself. This was no way to be, now! After all, there was no reason for fearing the place!

He forced himself to the door. He could not reach the high handle and was reduced to banging on the door with his little fist.

After a moment the door opened a handspan, and some-one looked down at him. "What do you want?"

"Is inn?" Tchabu asked. "Is Inn of Four Sorrows?"

"Yes. Go away!"

"Must come inside. Must speak to officer in army."

"What would any of those people want with the likes of you? Begone!"

"Please! Just let in for moment—"

The door slammed. But almost immediately afterward it opened, and two soldiers wearing the uniforms of troop-grade officers spilled out into the street, continuing a conversation begun inside the inn.

"Come now, Thuti," one of them was saying. "You can't tell me that affair went on for so long without her husband ever getting wind of it!"

"I know it sounds unlikely," his neighbor agreed, "but it went on for four months, until she turned up pregnant."

He did not see Tchabu, tiny and easily missed, at his feet. He tripped over the little man, and both of them, soldier and dwarf, rolled to the ground.

"Damn!" said the soldier. "Why don't you watch where you're going? Damned hideous little dwarf!"

"There, now, Thuti. The fellow couldn't help it. Here, let me help both of you up." After he had raised his mate to his feet, he stopped to give a hand to Tchabu. "There now, little man, are you hurt?"

"Not hurt," Tchabu said, pulling at the soldier's gar-ment. "Many thanks. Please. You are soldier from army of Baliniri?"

"Well, yes. I suppose you'd say that. We're all under

Baliniri in a way, for all that he's a civilian now. Why do you ask?"

"Please. Must get to Baliniri. Have message from Isesi, from delta. Very important."

The soldier looked down at him skeptically. "What business would Baliniri have with you?"

"Wait," the other man said. "I've heard of Isesi. He was a leader of the resistance near Avaris, I believe. Is that right, little man?"

Tchabu looked rapidly from face to face. "Yes! Yes! Good friend of Queen Mara. She know Tchabu! She can say!"

It should have been a brilliant inspiration. Of all the people in Thebes who could possibly have known him, she was by far the highest placed. But the soldier called Thuti frowned. "Too bad, old fellow. It almost worked. She's out of town. Try another name."

"Then send to Baliniri. Or Aset. Aset is sister of Isesi. She live with Tuya, widow of Ben-Hadad."

"No longer," Thuti said. "Nobody has any idea where she's gone. There's been a reward posted for information about her for a month or two now, but no takers. You're not doing very well today, my friend."

"Then take to Baliniri! Please! Urgent!"

"What do you think?" Thuti asked his friend. "On the one hand, I'm tempted to ask what business a dwarf would have with Baliniri. On the other hand, Baliniri has more spies than a dog has fleas, and by design quite a number of them don't look any better than this fellow does. If he really does have a message and we don't get it to Baliniri—"

Tchabu took advantage of the opening. "Yes! Yes! I am spy! Have special message for vizier! Secret mission! Must tell now!"

Thuti looked at his comrade. "We could try," he said tentatively.

Weret's conscience had been bothering her ever since her departure from Thebes. Although nothing could be less appealing than the notion of holding Riki's hand and helping him ride out the crisis in his life, her promise to Teti to help him had in the end overridden all objections to helping her much-resented rival. Now she stood in Baliniri's audience hall, gold gleaming at ankles and wrists, her rock-hard body as always bronzed and fit. Behind Weret, Naldamak, her Nubian warrior-companion, inspected the friezes on the walls, with their depictions of the great battle of El-Kab. The cheetah rested by her feet.

"What do you hear from downriver?" Weret asked, avoiding the subject that had brought her to the city.

"Nothing," Baliniri admitted, rising to pace behind his long conference table. "I don't like this. Mara ought to have got word to me by now. I have the feeling that something's wrong—something more than just the bad feelings between Kamose and the world."

"Ah. So now you have developed clairvoyant powers." There was an edge to Weret's voice. She was out of sorts and hardly bothered to hide her abrasive mood.

"No. I'll leave that to you and Neku-re," Baliniri responded testily.

"Please. We agreed not to use his name."

"You're right. I'm sorry. How is the boy? I haven't seen him in some time."

"He shares your belief that something is amiss. He has been having bad-fortune dreams, although he will not describe them to us. Men are perverse creatures, and I do not understand them—not even Neku-re, and he, like Seth, has much about him that is male and much that is female. Like Seth he contains some of the strengths of both sexes." A thought occurred to her. "Any word from Seth?"

"Nothing." Baliniri looked at her. "You liked Seth, didn't you?"

Weret nodded. "Enough to mind his woman for him, and his child, now that he is gone. Aset and the little one are well. I took them to Kharga. Incidentally, if you need to get a message to me quickly, send it by way of Meru the painter and his wife, Hat-Nefer, in Deir el-Bahari. They are trustworthy."

"I know of them already. Imagine, Netru's kin! Teti touched so many lives."

"Please. If you are going to talk about Teti, I will be forced to leave. I would rather deal with Riki than hear you speak of my mistress just now. At least Riki does not talk, being so morose and uncommunicative."

"I'm sorry, Weret. I keep thinking of you as beyond ordinary emotions because you prefer to show your feelings so rarely."

She waved away his apology. "What is Riki doing?"

"Drinking. I've known him since he was ten, and I've never seen him in his cups before."

"I'll look into it." She turned to go but saw Naldamak staring indignantly at the wall. "What's the matter?" she asked in the Nubian tongue.

"Where is Ebana in this picture?" the warrior-woman demanded. "Where is my mistress?"

Weret inspected the mural sourly. "The painter who did this omitted anything that has to do with women. Already the Black Wind is forgotten. Already Ebana is erased from the story of the saving of Thebes. If Meru painted this, I will give him a tongue-lashing he will never forget."

"We have no wish to offend. Perhaps he doesn't know how to draw women bearing arms. Scribes and painters often know little of real life. Sometimes they lack imagination as well," Baliniri soothed.

"This one will lack a head if Ebana visits this room and finds herself missing from this account," Weret replied. "Have it changed."

Baliniri chuckled. "Listen to you," he said. "If any of my army officers were told that you had spoken to me in this manner, they'd never believe it. I have a reputation as a man who brooks no disrespect."

"I mean none. I simply do not waste words. You know me, so you are not offended."

There was an assertive knock on the door. "Come in," Baliniri called.

When the door opened, two men of his own palace guard entered, flanking a misshapen crook-legged dwarf, dirty and wearing ragged clothes. "Pardon me, sir," the one called Thuti said. "This person said he had a message for you. I thought it best to take no chances."

"Yes, yes. You did well. And you, my friend?" he said to the dwarf. "You'd be . . . but of course! Tchabu! I'd know you anywhere from Mara's description! You're up from the delta, then? Have you a message from her, perhaps?"

"No message," the little man said, casting a fearful glance at the cheetah. "Not know she was gone. Please. Must tell. Very important." The dwarf looked suspiciously at the two women. "Very secret."

"So it is," Baliniri agreed. "But not from these." He

turned to the two officers. "Thuti, tell Sothis to come here, will you, please? You may go, gentlemen. You did well." The soldier nodded and went out. "Sothis," Baliniri explained, "is the chief of my intelligence-gathering unit. If you *had* been one of my spies, Tchabu, Sothis would have been your boss."

"Now I remember," Weret said. "This little one has unusual powers—the ability to read the thoughts of others, the ability to see into the future."

"Yes. I'm glad to have him with us. Welcome to Thebes, Tchabu. You will be treated with great respect."

The door had remained open. Now a third soldier appeared in the open doorway.

"Ah! Sothis!" Baliniri said. "Come in and listen to what our friend has to say."

But as he turned back to face Tchabu, he saw the little man's face contort with fear and loathing. *"No! Please! Is one of them!"* he shrieked. "Keep this man away! Not let him near little Tchabu!"

Sothis's hand went to his sword, but before he could even close his fingers around the hilt, Naldamak had picked up her spear and was now holding its razor-sharp tip at his neck. Weret reacted immediately, and her sword's tip pushed hard against Sothis's bared belly, not quite breaking the skin. The cheetah, crouched low, faced Sothis and growled deeply, ready to spring.

Baliniri's eyes narrowed. "Hold him," he directed Weret. "Take his sword. Now, Tchabu. Explain yourself, my friend. One of whom?"

II

In Baliniri's palatial private quarters his wife, the former queen Ah-Hotep, received a guest: Riki's batman, Nibi. "Welcome," she said with a smile, coming to meet him. "No, no bows. Don't stand on ceremony. In the business at hand there is no room for rank. We are merely fellow conspirators at work in the best of causes, the saving of one near and dear to both of us."

"Pardon me, ma'am," the orderly said. "It's just that I've been an orderly for so long, and habits are so hard to break."

"I understand," Ah-Hotep said. She turned to a servant standing by the door. "Bring refreshments," she commanded, and the servant disappeared. The ex-queen showed Nibi to a seat on the long couch beside her. "How is he? Is he getting any better?"

"I'm afraid not, ma'am. I can't seem to get through to him. I can't keep him from the taverns . . . that's the curse of it." He clenched and unclenched his fists impotently.

"No wenching? No fighting?"

Nibi shook his head. "Ma'am, I'd be glad if he started doing either of those things. It'd mean he was beginning to come back into the world. But he's still all locked up inside himself. All he wants is oblivion."

"Could you bring him to see me?"

"That's the last thing in the world he wants, just now. He doesn't look good, and he knows it. Puffy-faced, bleary-eyed. He won't even come to court, much less up here."

Ah-Hotep found herself wringing her hands unconsciously. Her mind was racing rapidly. What to do? How to help her son, Riki?

She understood why he did not want to come to the palace to see her. Since their first meeting just after the battle of Thebes, he had kept his distance. He had never quite assimilated the information that, instead of being the orphaned child of near-indigent parents—a street urchin who had grown up in the back alleys of Avaris—he was in fact the bastard child of Sekenenre's queen and her onetime lover, the legendary soldier Baba of El-Kab.

It was not as though Riki was embarrassed to have his illegitimacy or parentage known. He had in fact been proud to know at last who he was, verifying his long-held belief that he was the offspring of someone special, of distinguished blood and background. But he had also been acutely aware of the scandal this disclosure would have caused for her, his mother. He had deliberately held himself aloof, trying to protect her good name. There was, she had decided, much of the high-minded and gallant Baba in Riki's makeup.

As a result, although she longed to see him, his visits had been furtive and infrequent. This had been a source of sorrow to her. In reality, she did not care in the slightest who knew what had happened long ago in her vanished but vividly remembered youth.

And she needed someone to care about now. Her marriage with Baliniri had become companionable but loveless, its main purpose being to help the two guarantee each other's otherwise precarious position at court. Certain nobles of the upriver nomes had sworn their loyalty to Baliniri; others were hereditary vassals to her own distinguished bloodline. Between her and Baliniri, they had a constituency that far outweighed any loyalty that Kamose, as king of Egypt, commanded this early in his reign. Most of his reign had been spent in the field fighting against the Hai far away in the delta, where the southern peoples could not get to know him.

A loveless marriage. Yes. Even now she was sure that Baliniri was carrying on a clandestine affair with that tiny woman Tuya, whose elderly husband, Kedar, appeared to be beyond caring whether his wife was faithful to him.

Did she herself care that Baliniri was seeing another woman? Not much, so long as they were discreet. It was quite obvious that Tuya's marriage had been the same sort of companionate, sexless convenience that her own to Baliniri had been.

All of it suddenly came into focus: Tuya had had an affair with Baliniri twenty-odd years before, one that had ended when she went back to her first husband, Ben-Hadad. That affair had planted a seed of doubt on the birth of her son, Seth, that—despite the decidedly ambiguous presence of a smudged port-wine stain on the child's back—his father may not have been Ben-Hadad after all.

Well, they were together now, virtually every moment when Baliniri was free. He spent precious little time at home and whenever possible invented excuses to ship her, Ah-Hotep, off to stay with one or another of her wealthy aristocratic family.

Well, let them come together! The gods could affirm that she, Ah-Hotep, was not much interested in the men-women business. She had first lost the great love of her life, then lost the sensitive and gentle husband they had found for her, Sekenenre. Those were quite enough love affairs for her. Such things were behind her.

But her son was another matter. And if he were in trouble now, subject to depressions, drinking heavily, she could not sit by idly. She locked eyes with Nibi. "Bring Riki to see me. Tell him some story about my being ill and wasting away without him."

Nibi frowned. "Perhaps I can convince him that there's an emergency."

"Please, Nibi. Do it tonight, before he starts drinking."

"Evening's usually too late, ma'am. He begins drinking in midafternoon. That's why I'm so worried about him."

"Then you *must* get him to me." She chuckled ruefully. "You don't know how much it has cost me to call him Riki and not Ahmes, his real name. It's been hard getting used to. But wait long enough, and you can get acclimated to almost anything. Anything but the needless pain of others."

The cult-member Sothis lasted the whole afternoon before he finally died of the torture to which he had been subjected. Baliniri had watched, wincing. As an old soldier he did not like torture, but as vizier of Egypt he had had to learn to live with it as the only expedient absolutely guaranteed to get a stubborn prisoner to talk. He had exchanged countless shocked glances with little Tchabu as the thing progressed, and finally the little man, already hypersensitive to the pain of others, had returned to the main floor of the building, three floors above the subterranean dungeons.

Now Tchabu sat, morose and sick at heart, waiting for Baliniri's return. When at last the vizier's footfalls could be heard coming up the steps, his heart began to beat wildly. He did not want to hear what he knew he had to hear, but he sat waiting passively as Baliniri, Thuti, and another guard came into view, followed by the warrior-women and the cheetah.

"We're in your debt," Baliniri commented shortly as he sat down on a bench across from Tchabu. "You've probably saved Thebes."

"Sir," Thuti said, "the prisoner said he was among the first to arrive here. There may be only a handful of—"

"Yes," Baliniri said impatiently. "And then again there may be more than this fellow knows. What do you think, Tchabu? Are there more of them?"

"Many more," Tchabu reported unhappily. "Tchabu feel bad coming all through town. First pain from plague. Many have die, many more are sick in soul. All have lost loved ones. But then come strong feeling that cult is here."

Baliniri exchanged glances with the woman Weret. "That's bad," he said. "On the other hand, if Tchabu is sensitive and can spot these people the way he spotted Sothis—"

"No! Please!" Tchabu cried out, horrified. "Not make Tchabu get close to cult men. Make Tchabu very sick. Mind not work well, after. Maybe die."

Baliniri compassionately put a hand on the little man's twisted shoulder. "I understand, old man. You have my sympathy. After what I learned while putting Sothis to the question—" He shuddered. "But we've got to have a way of sniffing them out. Otherwise they'll take over. You wouldn't want that, I'm sure?"

Tchabu instinctively drew away. "Please not make Tchabu do this," he wept. "I was in mind of Makare once. For moment or two, maybe. Much pain for Tchabu. *Much* pain."

Weret knelt before him. "There's a healer among us, over in the desert where I live, a young man called Neku-re. His mind works something like yours. But his is stronger. It looks not only into the minds of other men, it sometimes heals them—heals their hurts, including the kind you're talking about."

As she said this, though, something occurred to her. "Baliniri!" she said. "What if—Riki and Neku-re? What if—?"

Baliniri stared. "Now there's a brilliant thought. Yes! Do you think you could get Riki to go to the oasis with you? Or what about bringing Neku-re here?"

Weret scowled. "That's out of the question. As for the other . . . I can try. But so far he's wanted as little as possible around him to remind him of my mistress. He says that it all makes him think of her and of what might have been. I confess that I share some of his feelings myself." She stood and squared her shoulders. "There are places I cannot go, activities I cannot indulge in, without thinking of her. Hunting with the cheetahs, for instance, makes me think of her. It's awful."

"I understand," Baliniri consoled, "but we must try. Meanwhile, there's the business of Tchabu."

"Yes." Weret turned back to the dwarf. "Little friend, you've already done more than we have any right to ask. I have some idea of what it will cost you to weed out the cult. Our friend Neku-re interrogated a couple of murderers once, and I saw how it affected him afterward. But the difference is that you will have Neku-re to heal your mind, whereas Neku-re had no one."

"Tchabu afraid."

"But we have to, Tchabu. And when Neku-re heals you, you'll be among friends." She thought a moment. "Aset will be there."

"Aset! Tchabu's dear friend!"

"She'll be there, and so will we." Weret shot a victorious look at Baliniri. "You've never met anyone who has your gift, have you?"

Tchabu looked at her curiously. "Please continue," he requested, beginning to get a hold on himself.

"Very well," Weret said. She turned and moved away, her eyes on Baliniri's. "Neku-re has. He met someone from Nubia whose mind works much as his does, who was sensitive the way you are."

Tchabu seemed to consider the implications. "Continue, please!"

"When the two minds met, curious things happened. Their separate talents became amplified. Both minds became stronger. If the Nubian could see a week into the future, with Neku-re's help the week became a month."

"Enough," Tchabu said. "Tchabu read your mind now. Know what you will say. Say no more. Tchabu will go with you." He sighed heavily. "Even if Tchabu must first do as you ask." He shuddered and closed his eyes.

Baliniri and Weret looked at each other. "What do you think?" Baliniri asked. "Perhaps you can take Riki back to the oasis with you at the same time."

"I'll see what I can do," Weret promised. But her face was hard, and it was obvious that doubts were beginning to enter her mind.

"Sir," Nibi pleaded, pulling at Riki's sleeve. "Please. I have an urgent message for you."

"Go 'way," Riki said roughly, tipping up the wine bowl and drinking deeply. "I don' wanna hear any messages. Not from Kamose, not from Baliniri, not from anyone." His voice was slurred, his words indistinct. "No communications. Don' wanna communica—" The word dissolved in a drunken belch. Heads at adjacent tables turned; he scowled at them. "Min' your own damned business," he said. "Unless you'd argue the matter out—outside?"

Three people at the next table hastily beat a retreat to

the far side of the room. "Hah!" Riki said. "See? No need t'
be rude. T' stare. No need t' do anything. Jus' wanna be
alone. T' be *lef* alone." He turned his head and looked up at
Nibi, trying to get his face in focus. "Don' wanna hear from
anybody, not even . . ." He blinked. "Who is it?"

"Your mother, sir," Nibi said, sotto voce, looking right
and left before he said it. "The lady Ah—"

"*Shhh!*" Riki said, clumsily putting one finger before his
mouth. "Don' say th' name. Secret." He belched again, more
softly this time. "Wants t' see me, eh? Wha' for?"

"Sir, this isn't the time and place to—"

"No, no," Riki agreed. " 'Course. But look. I don' wanna
see her jus' now. Coul'n't it wait a week?"

"She says it's an emergency, sir. She needs you."

Riki weighed the matter, still trying to get the world
around him to stand still. "Wha' tavern is this?" he asked. "I
don' recognize this place. Have I ever been here before?"

"Come along, sir. Please. It's important."

Riki stared up at him and finally got a clear view of him.
"Ah," he said in a voice full of pain and resentment, "tha's
where you're wrong. Nothin's important. Not now. Things
stopped bein' important a while back. How long ago was it?
Wha' month is this?"

III

Crook-backed, stump-legged little Tchabu marched slowly
down the long line of courtiers and palace servants. Occasionally he would pause before one man, look him in the eye, and
after a moment's consideration and evaluation, move on.

Finally, as a third rank was paraded before him, he
stopped, made a move, and pointed to a counselor of the
second-highest caste. "This man," he said. "This man one of
them." Guards immediately took the courtier into custody.
Tchabu shook his head as if to clear it and continued his slow
progress down the line as the vizier and Weret looked on
from their vantage point on a balcony. Naldamak, tall and
aloof, stood to one side and watched the proceedings, her
hand resting on the cheetah's great head.

"It's working marvelously," Baliniri said to the woman-warrior. "I only wish I could keep him here. That's six of them so far, including—I still can't believe it—my body servant."

"Look at his eyes," Weret said, unsmiling. "And the poor thing's dripping sweat. What it must be like to see into the mind of one of these monsters!" Her voice softened. "Perhaps he could be talked into revisiting your court. You'll need your personnel checked periodically. This thing spreads like the plague: Let one cult member get into the palace, and he'll give the disease to half a dozen more during the first month. And if the converts are in crucial positions around here—"

"Enough!" Baliniri said, shaking his head slowly from side to side. "Poor Egypt! No sooner do we begin to gain ground on throwing the Hai and their foreign mercenaries out of the country, than *this* comes on us." A thought suddenly occurred to him. "I wonder if Isesi knows about the cult? Tchabu seemed to think he didn't. And Kamose?"

"This Amasis fellow claimed to have known Kamose. Gods! You don't suppose the king is one of them?"

"I don't know," Baliniri answered frankly. "What Riki tells me of him is not very reassuring. Kamose has changed. When he finally becomes the undisputed king, we may have as much of a problem on our hands as we did under the Hai."

Weret snorted. "It *did* occur to us at the oasis that the Thebans had been precipitate in naming Kamose to the crown. There is more to governing than having a keen eye and a strong sword arm, Baliniri, as indeed you well know."

"Yes," he said grudgingly. "I had a few doubts at first, but like a fool I ignored them. I thought it was enough to find someone who seemed to unify us. We had been divided for so long. Well, I may have been wrong. The question now is what to do about it."

Weret let her gaze rest on Naldamak for a moment. "If I may give you some advice," Weret said, "I think it is time to mend fences with Naldamak's people. With Nehsi and Ebana. Ebana in particular is a source of wise counsel, whom you have neglected to your impoverishment."

"That is true," Baliniri admitted in a surprisingly mild tone. "Go on."

"There is then the matter of the nobility from upriver

and from the Nubian marches. Lords of the cataracts. The priesthood of Amon."

"I have already begun negotiations with some of them. Today's revelations about the cult will help in any new dealings with the priesthood, I think."

"No doubt. Heresy has always been regarded by the peoples of Upper Egypt in particular as little better than treason. If there has ever been dissent in Egypt, it has been in the delta, where foreign influence has always been common."

"Go on."

"If I were you, I would start making secret treaties. If the cult has got to Kamose and he defeats the Hai and drives them out of Egypt, what then happens, my friend?"

"He comes back upriver at the head of a powerful army. Whose leaders are all members of the cult." He shuddered in spite of himself. "A dim prospect indeed. Yes. I will do what you suggest. And what will the women of the oasis do, O wise one?" He smiled to take the sting from his teasing.

"Mind our own business for now," she answered. "Arm. Fortify. Stockpile weapons. Confer with you and with Naldamak's people. Remain alert." She frowned. "I must confess that I have also been lax. Our own spies—and yours—should have caught this cult business some time back. Both of us need to shore up our intelligence-gathering systems."

"You have spies in the delta?" Baliniri asked, surprised.

"I *had* spies there and here," Weret replied coldly. "I will call in the ones in the delta for conference. I will have Tchabu sit near them when they answer my questions. If one of my own has been corrupted—"

"That could be a problem with my own people," Baliniri said. "Damn it, I wish I would hear from Mara. She's certain not to be fooled by anyone. Not for long, anyhow."

"Possibly . . . But let neither of us dare forget that we are dealing with the most dangerous threat we have ever faced."

Baliniri sadly nodded his head. "All too true. You know, the lands where I first served in the army must have been full of this cult, but I was totally unaware of it. Tchabu says it comes from the Valley of the Two Rivers. He says that in some of the northern cities, it's attained the status of a state religion, in spite of the human sacrifice. Gods! And Seth's probably right in the middle of it."

"Yes. I fear for him. For this and other reasons." Weret's

voice grew thoughtful now. "As you know, Seth and I were friends. I have admitted few men to my friendship. But Seth is different. In him is the potential for anything and everything: all good, all evil; all wisdom, all folly. What fate will befall him in lands controlled by such as these? What if that mighty mind of his were to be—"

"Don't say it!" Baliniri implored. "I know! This is his first trip out into the world, late bloomer that he is. He will be facing tests and temptations that he never knew existed." He suddenly thought of something and looked at her. "I hope he's still alive," he said.

"Neku-re says he's alive. That's all he knows. Seth's alive."

An hour more, and Baliniri had had enough. Weret and Naldamak had left with their cheetah some minutes earlier to see if they could find Riki; Baliniri, meanwhile, left the interrogations in the hands of a subordinate and went down a long hallway to a lavishly appointed apartment formerly reserved for visiting emissaries of foreign countries. Its entrance was shielded from the public gaze, so secret meetings could be held. In recent years, though, little such use had been found for it, so Baliniri had recently commandeered it for his own use.

A knock, and the door opened a crack. Then it opened wide, and Tuya rushed into his arms. "Oh! I'm so glad to see you! I waited so long!"

"I came by earlier, hoping to find you," he said, "but no sign. Then when I wanted to get free, I couldn't." He sat down, took her hands, and told her about Tchabu and the cult. "Believe me, nothing but a thing like this could have kept me from you, my dear."

"I understand," she said. "It's just that . . . well, I'm upset. It's Kedar. He's ill. Some sort of fever. He's trembling like a leaf. Hefget is waiting on him hand and foot now. And—and when something like this happens, my conscience works on me. I mean, there he is, sick, needing me, and I am here."

He put a hand over her mouth, gently but insistently. "There, now. No more of that. There's no reason for you to feel guilty. I'll have my personal physician go to visit him as soon as we've had time to talk. Kedar will be in the best of hands." He smiled at her, then held up one of her hands to kiss it playfully. "Same old Tuya. It was this way with us from the first. Remember how long it took you to have anything to do with me, back at the very beginning?"

She allowed herself a wan smile, but it was obvious her heart was not in it. "But this is different. He's ill and no longer young. He can't bounce back from an illness."

"It happens to all of us," Baliniri said. "You can't go blaming yourself. He'll be in better hands than your own by nightfall. Trust me. Besides, if it were to come down to it, old Kedar's had a good life, and you've been a major part of it. Thanks to you his later years have passed in affluence instead of poverty. He's had a chance to teach a genius like Seth. He even wound up a property owner, a respected man in the community."

"I suppose when you put it like that . . ."

"Give it no more thought."

"Well, all right."

"Is that a promise?"

"I promise."

"There's my good girl."

"I'm not your girl. I'm not anybody's girl. I'm a woman, and I'm growing old."

"Not in my eyes."

"You're just saying that."

"Are you accusing an old soldier of throwing empty poetry at you?"

She smiled sadly. "Maybe I'm just on edge. Between Kedar's not feeling well and Seth's being away so long, I can't think straight."

"I have good news for you, then. I talked to Weret. She says Neku-re mentioned Seth. All Neku-re knows—but he's quite positive about it—is that Seth is alive and well."

"Who is Neku-re?" she asked. "And why would he know anything about my son when neither you nor I have had a word from him in years?"

"Easy, now," Baliniri soothed. "I forgot you didn't know about Neku-re. It was a slip of the lip. I'm not supposed to mention him. It's supposed to be a secret between Weret and me."

"Tell me. I have to know."

"Well, Neku-re's something of a seer. Like Joseph of Canaan, who could read dreams and see into the future. Only

Neku-re's powers go beyond the normal even in that least normal of trades."

"Is he a magus, old and wise?"

"Not a magus. And no, he's not old. He's hardly more than a boy. I don't think he's ever had any formal education. Anyway, what could one teach a clairvoyant that would make him better at it? But I'm sending Tchabu to him, and I'm looking forward to learning what the two minds can come up with when they've come together."

"Could you ask him for more about my son?"

"Perhaps. These people leak little things out to us. If they concentrate on a subject, they might pick up more about it."

"Ask him about Seth, please. Ask Weret to ask him. I miss him so—even more so since that foolish, hateful thing I did, throwing out Aset and her child. And Meni—he lives a life of his own. He's basically a street child. If I were to die or go broke tomorrow and repossessors threw him into the alley, it wouldn't matter a jot to him. He likes me well enough, I suppose. But as for being close with me or with anybody else—"

"Tuya! Are you going to talk me to death? Or are you going to come over here and kiss me?"

As always, the two women and their great cat drew startled stares. All the way across the big tavern Weret ignored the stares; Naldamak met glare with glare, saying nothing. All the men who looked at her body had seen the razor-sharp lance at her side and hastily looked away.

Weret stood over Riki for a long moment before speaking. "Riki," she said coldly, "are you too drunk to recognize me?"

He looked up. He did not seem to be drunk, but he was disheveled and pathetic. "Ah!" he said with elaborate hospitality. "The warrior maiden! Sit down. Have a drink. Waiter! More wine!"

"Are you insane? Do you see what you're doing to yourself? To the memory of my mistress?"

"Memory? Do you think I want to remember? Memories hurt too much, my maiden. It is to dull the memory that a man drinks. I never drank before. I used to be poor. I owned nothing. I had no idea I was happy. I had nothing to lose."

"Riki—"

"Then all of a sudden I had something to lose—and sure enough, I lost it." His face turned dark, and his personality seemed suddenly to close in on itself. "Sit down, won't you? Sit down and have a drink, or go away."

"Riki, come to El-Kharga. Better yet, come to El-Dakhla. There's someone I want you to meet. Someone who can help you."

He did not respond. Disgusted, she turned to Naldamak and said in the Nubian tongue, "It's hopeless. If I ever had any interest in doing this, it's gone now. If it weren't for the promise I made to Teti—"

At the mention of Teti's name, Riki's eyes cleared, and he grasped her hand in a grip even stronger than her own. "Teti?" he demanded bitterly. "You speak of Teti?"

"Let go of me! No man lays hands on me like that!" Her free hand was already on her sword hilt. But in a moment his grip relaxed, and he let her go. She left her hand on the sword and glared down at him. "I've discharged my duty," she said in a low, taut voice. "When and if you choose to come to us, we will heal you. The door is open."

With that she turned on one hard bare heel and faced the crowd behind her. "Can't anyone here mind his own business?" she demanded harshly, her hand once again on sword hilt. "Do I have to give lessons in manners?" Eyes flashing, she looked down at the table beside her, at the half-ripe melon lying atop it. "And a lesson in swordsmanship?"

She tossed the melon up. Her other hand was a blur, pulling her sword from its hanger, cutting mightily across. The melon, neatly quartered by the razor-sharp blade, fell in four pieces to the floor. "No takers?" she challenged. "Then I will go. Come, Naldamak!"

IV

In the morning Tchabu, red-eyed and exhausted from lack of sleep, left for the oasis with Weret and Naldamak. Knowing that the little man's short legs could not keep up with their long stride, Weret had rigged a simple sling in which Tchabu was cradled between the two of them from a pair of stout poles. At their heels trotted the cheetah, sleek and lean.

Meni, perched atop a rock in the hills behind Deir el-Bahari, watched them set out along the harsh track. He marveled at their stamina. He had, just once, set out along the narrow pathway across the desert but had turned back when it became obvious that he was being watched, perhaps followed. He had not liked the sensation. Still less, however, had he liked the desert, the fiendish heat, the lack of water, the knowledge that the smallest misstep along the track could lead to a dreadful and lonely death on the rocks below.

Imagine anyone living out there! But it appeared these women preferred it and would choose to live nowhere else. The same was true of the women's army in which they served and of the sizable civilian community, male and female, that inhabited the El-Kharga oasis, the one nearest to Thebes. The El-Kharga community was, by all accounts (few had ever ventured there since the women had taken it over and fortified it against attack), more or less normal, with its own water, farms, and livestock, plus a substantial population to tend these. Of the El-Dakhla community, farther along the desert track, apparently nobody knew anything. Only Riki and Seth had been there and lived to tell about it, and Seth was long vanished and Riki sworn to silence.

When the women were out of sight, Meni shrugged and set off down the hill toward the artisans' town. He hailed his many friends there as he made his way down the main street. In Deir el-Bahari he kept to himself all the way to the river, where he was given a free ride across by one of the boatmen.

Ordinarily he took the simplest path home, but today he chose a roundabout route, pausing in several bazaars in the temple quarter to steal olives here, a fig there.

As he emerged from the last of these Theban markets, his path took him behind the great imposing bulk of the palace just in time for him to see Tuya slip out of the opened rear door. She paused and looked around. Meni ducked behind a wall that flanked the marketplace and peeked out.

Ah! What was this? A large, capable-looking male hand came out from within the doorway and pulled her back inside. Smiling and laughing, she again made her way through the doorway, pulling the man with her. Meni craned his neck and managed to get a glimpse of an imposing and berobed masculine figure holding her close, bending over to embrace her and kiss her. He could not make out the face, but the distinctive pattern of robes alone identified the wearer as a high-ranking member of the imperial cabinet. And there was nobody at court that big and powerful-looking but Baliniri. So this was where Tuya had been going! And hadn't there been some gossip about her having had a love affair with Baliniri some years ago, when she was young?

Meni's eyes blazed. The injustice of it all burned in his heart. Tuya, who had passed judgment on poor Aset and thrown the girl and her baby out of her house, calling her a slut, was cheating on poor old Kedar!

Stealthily he slipped out from behind the wall to get a better look. There was no doubt at all: That was Baliniri, all right! And look at her, hanging onto him.

Fine. If that was the way she was going to be, she would forfeit any right to sit in judgment on him. If she got any thoughts, in the future, of telling him how he should lead his life, she had another thing coming.

Adults! You couldn't trust a one of them!

In the early afternoon, messengers from Kamose's camp arrived upriver. Baliniri heard them out but discounted a great deal of what they had to say. He congratulated them on the army's great victory at Athribis and asked when one might expect the fall of Avaris. The outlook for a quick triumph, the messengers said, was not a particularly good one. Avaris was being fortified and its garrison greatly augmented, with new shipments of troops arriving almost daily. They passed along Kamose's imperious, strongly worded demands that Riki return immediately to his post. Baliniri politely turned the harsh words aside and put the messengers in the hands of his stewards.

With the couriers gone, he secretly summoned the hortator on their galley, a burly, broad-shouldered man named Harsaphes, who had proved his loyalty to Baliniri several times in the past. "Tell me," the vizier said, "is the cult as bad as it looks from upriver? How far has it spread?"

Harsaphes's black brows knitted. "Well, sir, I think it's only a matter of months before they have control of the whole camp, and I'm not sure how long I can stay out of the thing myself—there's pressure on everyone but the footsloggers to join. They don't give a damn about the rank and file. Why should they, when they control the officers and underofficers?"

"Good point. But why should you stay out of the thing, when you can learn so much for me by getting inside it?"

Harsaphes looked incredulous. "Sir, you don't understand. If I were in the cult and found reporting to you, I'd be a dead man."

Baliniri clapped him on the shoulder gently. "My friend, if you stay out of the cult and they take over, do you think either of us will be alive for long?" He let this sink in for a moment, then gave Harsaphes a hard-edged smile. "We are playing for keeps here, young man. Few outsiders have any idea how desperate our situation is. If the Hai are defeated, we will have the cult to deal with. I must organize resistance here in Thebes quickly but quietly. If I can get a good spy like you into the cult—"

"I understand, sir. I'll do it. And, sir, while I was waiting to speak with you, I got to talking to a girl, a foreigner, who's been trying to get through to see you. She's apparently just a slave, but I have a feeling you ought to talk to her."

"She's still there?"

"She was just before I came in. Would you like me to bring her in to you? She's a distant relative of Joseph's, Salitis's old vizier, and no friend to the Hai. Miriam, I think her name is."

Riki's head was swimming when he finally forced himself to dress and come out into the light. He staggered on wobbly legs to the marketplace, bought a fresh skin full of harsh red wine, and quickly assuaged the thirst that had plagued him ever since he awoke.

Only when his hands had begun to stop shaking did he blink, run dirty fingers through his uncombed hair, and look around him. The sun was not yet high, and the light in the marketplace was still relatively soft. That was a blessing. His bloodshot eyes could not stand the full glare of noon.

Around him the parade of faceless humanity came and went, oblivious to his presence, each person intent on his or her own purposes and ends. He let his eyes settle on this face, then that. No one's eyes met his. That, too, was a blessing, perhaps; at present he did not want to be recognized or forced to interact. Since Teti's death he had made no friends, renewed no acquaintanceships. He had avoided human contact to the greatest extent possible.

He moved to one side to let another man pass. What *had* he done since he had come home and buried his wife and infant? Precious little. And what had he even so much as contemplated doing? Nothing at all. Why should he do anything? he wondered, depressed. Why struggle? Why try to exert influence on things, when at any moment everything you had, everything you had ever wanted, could suddenly be snatched away by the random hand of some malevolent god?

Why live?

No! he told himself angrily. *Don't get off into that turn of mind, now.*

But the thought, once planted in his mind, took root and began to grow. It was as if his despair had insidiously begun to sap his strength, willpower, and manhood. He had to fight against it, for he knew that Teti would not have wanted him to be this way. She would have expected him to fight, to hold fast to the ideals they had shared.

Ach! What was the use thinking about her when all it did was bring him pain? *Curse you, Teti!* he thought bitterly. *Why did you have to come along in the first place?*

Why did she have to make herself part of everything he did? Why did she have to move into the exact center of his every thought? Why did she have to destroy his jealously guarded independence?

It had been so easy to be brave and uncaring when he had had nothing to lose. But now he had to come to grips with his own vulnerability.

He buried his face in his hands and turned away from the crowd. There was a great echoing emptiness at the very heart of him, which nothing seemed to be able to fill. The pain! The pain of it all!

Suddenly he became aware again of the great thirst within him. He located his purse in his crumpled robe, shook it, and made a guess as to its contents. Very well, that ought to be enough to buy oblivion . . . for a time, at least—dark and friendly oblivion, with no voices telling him not to give up hope or belief in the essential goodness of humanity and the primacy of conscience, magnanimity, decency, and kindness.

Oblivion! Drink would buy only so many hours of it, but that would have to do, for now!

*　　*　　*

At first Miriam had been all but paralyzed by timidity, but Baliniri had gently led her on by degrees. In the end she had delivered Mara's message and, answering his questions, had added much to his knowledge of the situation.

Thuti and Harsaphes had heard her story in silence; now they moved forward. "Sir," Thuti said, "Mara may need help. Should we send her some?"

"Good idea," Baliniri agreed. "What do you think, Miriam?"

"Oh, yes, sir," she replied. "She's the only friend my people have. And although Makare is frightened of her, he may overcome this. I'd feel better if she had some protection that the cult couldn't penetrate."

"So be it," Baliniri said decisively. He turned to the others. "When Miriam returns to her people, she'll have a dozen handpicked men with her. Mara seems to think our destinies are tied to the destiny of Miriam's people, and I trust her hunches. While I live, the Habiru will have a friend in Thebes."

"Just tell us what to do," Thuti said eagerly.

"We've got a hard few years ahead of us," the vizier said. "Avaris won't fall easily. At least this will keep Kamose busy, so he won't give much thought to us here upriver. That should give us time to shore up our own defenses against him, to consolidate our position against the time when he wins and comes home to take over the Red Lands once more."

"And what will we do then, sir?" Harsaphes asked.

"I don't know," Baliniri admitted. "We'll cross that bridge when we come to it. In the meantime, my friends"—he firmed his jaw and looked each one of them in the eye in turn—"be strong. Be true. And above all, be eternally vigilant! There is so much danger ahead—and so very few of us to deal with it!"

CHAPTER
EIGHT

Mesopotamia

I

After four days on the rocky and dusty track across country to Babylon, Seth and his friends had become thoroughly tired of overland travel. It was the season of hot, dry winds, and tempers flared; there had been grumbling and carping and two outbreaks of violence among the ox drivers. One rash soul had even spoken harshly to Anubis, only to be lifted off the ground and shaken like a rag doll until the fight had gone out of him.

The time was ripe for a change. On the fifth day the track approached the Euphrates, and Seth and his companions had gratefully taken to the river, booking passage on a downriver-based merchant vessel owned and captained by an amiable trader named Nabu.

Halfway between Mari and Babylon, Seth and Nabu had discovered that they had in common a great and universal curiosity about the manners and ways of the world. Unlike most traders, Nabu had indulged himself, exploiting his hobbies both in youth and middle years, and these included searching out the myths, legends, and historical records of all the regions he had visited. Seth spent hour after hour with the merchant, asking him about Babylon, its commerce, folkways, and political peculiarities. Nabu had been the first man he had met who really knew the Valley of Two Rivers well and whose interests went much beyond its stews and fleshpots. Seth lost no opportunity to add to his knowledge or to improve his rapidly growing command of the language of Babylon.

Now, another two days away from Mari, Seth stood in the bow of the squat merchant vessel, looking at a growing concentration of riverside huts, warehouses, and docks. The expedition was approaching a town and, from the look of things, a small but prosperous one. Even the fishermen's huts were well-made and tidy.

"The maps I saw in Mari indicated no city here," Seth said to Nabu with interest. "I think someone sold me out-of-date charts."

Nabu stroked his gray beard thoughtfully. "It's very likely," he said. "For the most part the charts only mention trading ports—unless they're navigational charts for rivermen. Until recently this wasn't a trading port; the old wharves were adequate only for fishing traffic. But expansion and upgrading were overdue, and ten years ago a new tax paid for refurbishing of the quays and docks. Now it's a full-fledged river port. Of course, fishing is still the main enterprise—that and manufacturing."

"Manufacturing? What do the citizens make here?"

"A variety of items for fishermen," Nabu said. "Look here." He reached into his garment and pulled out a curious-looking item, no longer than his thumb, that resembled a spearhead but bent out of shape. "This item alone has made the city rich."

"What is it?" Seth asked, testing its razor-sharp point with a finger.

"A fishhook," Nabu answered, his eyes crinkling at the corners in a jolly smile. "One of the problems with fishhooks has always been how to make one that the fish can't get free of, but that the fisherman has no trouble taking out of its mouth. See how it works?"

"Ingenious," Seth marveled, turning the tiny artifact this way and that. "I wonder who—"

Nabu had anticipated him. "A genius of sorts, I'd say, invented it and gave it to a fisherman to pay him for saving his life. This happened a century or more ago in this very town we're approaching."

Criton, who had been standing at the starboard rail, wandered over to see what the two men were discussing. Seth handed the Achaean the fishhook as the captain continued his story.

"A chap from Babylon made it and gave it to a local fisherman named Binshoumedir in gratitude for saving his life. It made the town prosperous within a single generation, once the villagers learned to make it and get it to market."

"Binshoumedir?" Seth echoed curiously, his eyes alight. "Tell me, Nabu, what was the name of the chap from Babylon? The one who invented the thing?"

"Why, everyone knows that. They named the town after him. He was a one-handed fellow with a price on his head, who'd had a hand cut off at the wrist for some offense committed in the city. He had a half-grown boy with him, the story went: a kid who everybody thought would really grow up to be somebody some day."

"The names," Seth insisted. "Please, the names. The man and the boy."

"Zakir."

Seth and Criton exchanged startled glances. "Zakir?" Seth said. "And the boy?"

"Ahuni of Babylon. He appears to have made quite a name for himself as a smith later on in Mari. Then he and Zakir left Mari, and nobody around these parts ever heard of him again."

"Ahuni!" Seth shouted, grinning at Criton. "My ancestor! And Zakir was the man who trained him!"

Now it was Nabu's turn to stare. "You're sure? After all, this is a long way away from Egypt."

"I'm sure," Seth replied happily. "You see, we're a clan: the Children of the Lion. Ahuni's son was Kirta, who first brought the secret of the smelting of iron from across the Great Sea. *His* sons were Shobai, the blind armorer, and Hadad—"

"Not Hadad, the hero of Haran? Hadad the Cripple? The boy who saved his city?"

"Yes," Seth said with a pride he had not known he felt until this moment. "Hadad. My grandfather." He smiled at the shocked look on Nabu's face. "Look, would you have any objection to stopping here and staying the night? I'll pay for your trouble. I'd like to look around, talk to people."

"Certainly," Nabu agreed. "We have to stop somewhere, and this is as good a place as any. But you'll have to let me tell people who you are. It'd be such a pleasure for everyone to know. They'll probably want to host some sort of feast in your honor."

One of the sailors was passing just then. "Captain," he said, "there's a festival going on in Zakir now anyhow."

"Then it's settled," Nabu said, delighted. "Imagine! A kinsman of Ahuni's!"

Zakir's chief magistrate's name was Ur-Shanabi. As Nabu had predicted, he was delighted to meet a descendant of the legendary Ahuni and to learn the subsequent history of the Children of the Lion at the lavish feast that closed the day. He even made a little speech, wishing Seth and his companions the best of fortune in their quest.

"I can't think Samsi-ditana will not wish to see you immediately," he told Seth. "For all the greatness of Babylon, distinguished visitors of your stripe seldom call there, and a man as remarkable as the king seldom meets his peer."

"You flatter me unduly," Seth said, embarrassed. "Frankly, my head swims from it. With your leave, I would like to take a walk with my friend"—he indicated Criton with a wave of the hand—"and sort out my thoughts. I feel like a man treading on ground sacred to his people."

"You have my leave, of course," Ur-Shanabi said. "Provided you leave the giant and the clown with us. My people have already taken to them. Before dinner the giant was promising the children that he would show them how a man might pick up a bullock and hold it while another man counted to fifty."

Seth chuckled. "Anubis is up to his old tricks again. He'll win a fat prize for doing what he says he will, then will lose it all on some wager. By all means, let them stay with you for now."

Criton and Seth made the proper obeisances and then went into the moonlit streets of the little town. The one straight street stretched down to the water's edge, crossed here and there by gently meandering avenues that followed the soft curve of the land as it sloped down to the riverfront.

"Now," Seth pointed out, "this would be the ropewalk. This, too, Zakir had invented for them, although no one mentioned it tonight. Braiding rope this way is so firmly embedded in the local consciousness, everyone thinks it's always been done after this fashion. But Ahuni told my great-grandfather that Zakir persuaded the fishwives to do it his way. He'd lost his hand and his profession with it, you know—he was a metalworker, but not so much an armsmaker as a jeweler—and until he found something productive to contribute here, he felt he was sponging off Binshoumedir and the villagers. He wanted to pay them back for their kindness."

"It's still a kind town," Criton noted. "Uncommonly generous and hospitable."

"True. I feel very well disposed toward it. Anyhow, Zakir, with Ahuni assisting, set up a stout post and then pounded a nail into it, bending it double so the threads of the rope could be strung through it. That way one woman could braid an entire rope all by herself, backing away from the post and holding the strands taut all the while."

"Curious: We Greeks thought we'd invented the method."

"Probably you did. It's too logical for it not to have occurred to a lot of people about the same time. But here it began with Zakir." He sighed deeply and happily. "And here I am, right where it all began: the whole story of my clan."

"Began? I thought Belsunu came from Ur."

"He did. But Ahuni's apprenticeship began here, with Zakir, not his real father. Belsunu searched all his life for his lost child and died before ever finding him. What an odd stroke of fortune that Ahuni, knowing nothing of his father or his heritage as an armsmaker, should find someone to train him in the trade to which he was born."

"It does seem that a special providence has the future of your clan in hand," Criton agreed. "Imagine your winding up here, for instance."

"I know." Seth sat on a bench and looked down the deserted ropewalk. "I really do feel as though I were working out some sort of preordained destiny."

Criton cleared his throat and looked serious. "Not to intrude upon your happiness, my friend, but there *was* a quest in all this, some years ago. You promised some people in Egypt that you would bring back a certain secret, one that would help them defeat the invaders."

"And you think I have forgotten them."

"Well, I would have put it a little less harshly, you know." But in the clear light of the moon Seth could see Criton's darkly intelligent eyes regarding him intently.

Seth sighed. "I know, I know. And you're right. But can't you see what an opportunity this excursion is for me, Criton? Something strange and wonderful is going to happen to me here—I can feel it! All my dreams and wishes are going to be fulfilled. Here in Babylonia, back in Shinar where my line began."

"Does that mean you intend to stay?"

Seth again paused. "No . . ." he said indecisively. "I don't think so. I obviously have to go back sometime. But . . ."

"Yes?"

Seth's sigh was the longest yet. "I feel as if I were going home," he confessed. The words came rushing out as if he had been holding them in for some time.

II

The morning brought a strange juxtaposition of events. At dawn a messenger arrived by chariot along the overland route from Mari, having driven by moonlight in the clear sky over the upper Euphrates. Ur-Shanabi, seeing the man's exhausted condition, suggested he lay over in the city for a day before proceeding downriver to Babylon.

The messenger, pleading the desperate urgency of his mission, refused. Then a packet arrived from the great city itself, bearing the emissary of King Samsi-ditana, Sardur, who had been sent up the Euphrates to intercept Seth's party and escort them the rest of the way to Babylon.

Sardur's arrival came just as Seth was obeying Ur-Shanabi's early morning summons. The two met in the anteroom before the great hall in which the chief magistrate was interviewing the messenger. Introducing himself, Seth was astonished to learn the nature of Sardur's mission to Zakir and the esteem in which he apparently was already held by the great king.

"Samsi-ditana eagerly anticipates your arrival in the city.

Babylon has become a city of poets and scientists, engineers and philosophers. And of them all, none has a more cultivated or inquiring mind than the great king himself. He was trained as a scribe, you know, and he not only reads voraciously but has assembled a huge library and writes as well. His verse and songs are sung throughout all the lands east of Haran."

"I am *most* impressed. What I have seen of kings to date has seldom inspired admiration in me."

"You will be meeting a man equipped to appreciate your accomplishments."

There was a noise to one side, and an attendant came out of the great hall and bowed to the two of them. "Yes?" Seth said.

"My master will see the esteemed Seth and the distinguished emissary from Babylon," the attendant announced. With an even deeper bow he showed them into the inner hall.

Ur-Shanabi dispensed with the formalities. "Gentlemen," he said, "this is a messenger from Mari. Sardur, I think what he has to say requires immediate action. Perhaps you could take him along to Babylon when you return by boat."

Sardur's brows rose. "Why? What has happened?"

The messenger bowed. "I was told to report that the army of the Hittites is encamped in great strength halfway from Haran to Mari, and that Mursilis has intercepted and slaughtered an entire caravan bound for Haran and Carchemish along the trade route."

"Gods!" Sardur exclaimed. "This is an outrage! He goes too far! A peaceful, law-abiding caravan—"

But now he turned and saw the stricken look on Seth's face. "What's the matter?" he asked.

"The caravan," Seth said to the messenger. "Was it supervised by a man named Gudea?"

"Yes, sir."

"Were there any survivors?"

"None, sir. And one of those killed by Mursilis himself, sir, was—"

Seth's face was suddenly contorted with pain. "Marduk-nasir?" he whispered.

"Why, yes, sir."

His words were interrupted by a cry of anguish from Seth: low, guttural, forced out by shock and horror. "No! *No!*

He was like a second father to me! He was my mentor, my guide!"

"The act has the gravest sort of implications for Mari," the messenger said. "That huge army is encamped little more than a day's march out of the city."

"Has the army been moved up?" Sardur asked. "Have reinforcements been redirected north for the defense of Mari?"

"Yes, sir. But they may be too little too late. The only thing that had spared the city thus far was Mursilis's own sluggishness. He's been ill. If he were at the top of his form, hot-headed and decisive—"

The three men exchanged concerned glances.

"And if Mari were to fall, then surely Zakir will fall," Ur-Shanabi said.

"We'd better get started," Sardur declared, "and get our esteemed guest and his party to court. And this news must reach the king and the generals in charge of the western defenses. We may have enough time to transfer two units to shore up Mari's fortifications and buttress our defense there. May the gods grant that we be so lucky."

Seth, still shocked by the news of Marduk-nasir's death, reached inside his robe and withdrew papyrus, a brush, and ink.

"Excuse me," he said. "Would someone send outside for water? An idea struck me."

Ur-Shanabi gestured to a servant standing silently nearby. "Do as our visitor requests."

"Wait," Seth ordered. "There's a tall Greek fellow outside waiting for me. His name is Criton. Tell him to go to the merchant vessel and bring all of Nabu's maps."

"Yes, sir," the servant said, then turned and went away.

"Please continue your discussion," Seth said.

"Very well," Sardur responded. "The Second and Fifth Infantry are within a day's march along the track toward Mari—"

"The Second and Sixth," Seth corrected. "We passed them yesterday morning. The Sixth is fit and blooded, with a reputation as the finest forced-march unit in the army."

"They could be in place in two days," Sardur agreed. He looked at Seth, impressed; but Seth had closed his eyes, and his mind already seemed to be a thousand leagues away. Sardur turned back to Ur-Shanabi. "Get me a runner, if you please—the fastest you've got."

"Done," the magistrate said, signaling to another servant standing in the shadows.

The men sat down to wait for Criton's return with the maps.

Sardur glanced at Seth again as at last the tall Greek he had mentioned came in bearing rolled charts. "I'm going to send the runner to the generals in charge of the Mari garrison. The generals have a certain autonomy in times of crisis, and I consider this to be one. I suspect they've been waiting for orders from Babylon or for word from someone like me that an emergency exists."

Sardur reached in his pouch and pulled out an imperial seal, with which he intended to stamp the tablet bearing his message. Ur-Shanabi's brows rose; he had not realized just how high Sardur stood in the hierarchy. The great king's representative looked over at Seth again, to see that he had a map unrolled on the floor at his feet and was scribbling wildly away with brush and ink on a separate piece of papyrus.

"Excuse me," Sardur ventured. "Might I inquire? . . ."

"Oh? Oh, yes," Seth muttered. "*Hmmm.* Here. Yes, and here. That was a fine place. Yes. And Mursilis? *Hmmm.* Nothing much you can do. Unless? *Hmmm.* Yes, I think so. Like a game of senet. Give up this in order to get that. Then you have them. But if they . . . No. No, that wouldn't work. They'd spot it in a minute."

"But over there?" the Greek suggested, pointing with a sandaled toe.

"No, no. Too dangerous. Then it'd be all attrition. And they've got the numbers. But if numerical advantage could be nullified? You see? Here and here. This is that narrow defile the track passed through, where we saw the vultures. Remember?"

"Yes, I do."

"Well?" Seth said, his voice taking on a greater urgency. "If the left arm of the pincers were to be decoyed into here, with the defenders waiting . . . you see?"

Sardur looked down, nodding his head. "I do see," he said in a low, astonished voice. "Amazing. Ur-Shanabi, get us a couple of scribes in here immediately. There's not a moment to lose!"

Seth looked up. "You do see that Mari will fall. There's not a thing that can be done about that. But then Mursilis will overrun the city, and the delay created by the siege and fall of Mari will allow you to bring up both the Second and the Sixth. And if I know the ways of a conquering army, the victors at Mari will dawdle for a week, raping and pillaging. That will buy you just enough time to array the augmented defense forces here, here, and here!" He banged on the unrolled map with his reversed brush handle for emphasis.

"I see," Sardur said, awestruck. "And this unit here . . . that'd be the Sixth, I suppose . . ."

"No, no. The Second. The less-experienced Second for decoys, but the Sixth in hiding for the ambush. My caravan-mates told me that the Sixth are experienced soldiers and can be merciless. They can destroy a whole wing of Mursilis's army with a bit of luck. And while Mursilis's main army eats and drinks itself into a stupor, our new units can tie up the other wing right here, where four archers in the right places, with an unlimited supply of arrows and eight good eyes, could hold up a whole army for a week. Don't you see?"

"Indeed I do. And now I know why the great king wishes so much to see you. If I've read this right, you've saved our army, and perhaps Zakir and Babylon as well!" He threw his head back and laughed, giving Seth a friendly punch in the arm. "Here you've put king and city alike permanently in your debt, and you haven't even got there yet!" He bowed deeply, but only for a moment. Then he bellowed out again: "Scribes! Where the devil are those scribes?"

III

The runners went out, armed with a complete battle plan and various contingency strategies, all meticulously based on Seth's recent observations of the terrain east of Mari and his surprisingly certain instincts about the best way to deal with the advancing Hittites. The plans also included Sardur's suggestions to the commanders of the military units. All this material was couched in a tone of sweet reasonableness, incorporating Sardur's notion that his generals would work most effectively with ideas that they thought they had been on the verge of thinking up themselves.

In the morning, Sardur sailed south again, with Seth, Khet, Anubis, and Criton on board. Seth breakfasted privately with Sardur but then joined Criton on deck around noon.

"The word is, we'll be approaching the city by nightfall," he told the Greek. "Don't be surprised if there's a welcoming committee waiting up for us. Our fame precedes us."

"How?" Criton asked. "Does Sardur then send messages by magic?"

"By pigeon," Seth replied. "They've trained the birds to carry messages long distances."

"This is truly a land of wonders. What sort of message? 'Great King Samsi-ditana: Beware of these foreigners'?"

"I think it will have to do with the military moves against the Hittites. If I'm right, we've earned some praise—"

"You have. I'm just along for the trip, remember."

"—but if I'm wrong, we're in the deepest trouble possible."

Criton waved that thought away. "You're never wrong. Well, almost never."

"Good old Criton. Always hedging his wagers, keeping me honest, and preventing me from getting a swelled head."

"I'm glad I have my uses," Criton said. He leaned over the rail and looked down at the dark waters of the Euphrates. "I promise to continue to take issue with you whenever I think you're going astray."

Seth looked startled. "You sound as if you thought I were going astray now."

"Well . . ." Criton kept his eyes on the churning wake as the vessel headed downriver. "There is the danger of forgetting the quest behind all this travel."

Seth did not speak for a long moment, instead looking hard at Criton's profiled form until the Greek, feeling the eyes upon him, turned to look up at him. "This is true," he admitted. "And I may well be betraying my friends and countrymen by coming here instead of taking the information I have learned immediately back to Egypt. You know, I may have been selfish. Self-centered, doing those things it pleases me to do."

"And is this unnatural?"

Seth looked off into the distance. "I was a pretty withdrawn little boy," he revealed. "People thought I was dimwitted or crazy." He turned and looked at his friend now.

"Until I was ten, I had never really communicated with anyone. My father had so completely rejected me that I could not imagine that anyone but my mother would ever love me or even tolerate me."

"Men have lived through worse. But you still have some growing up to do."

"True, and I think I am meant to do some of it here in Babylon. Am I being irresponsible when I give in to this feeling instead of doing what my friends in Egypt have defined as my duty?"

Criton turned to face him. "You're asking me for reassurance? I'm not sure I can give it. Getting the sword to Kamose so he can kill his father may be too vital a mission to be set aside. Egypt's future may depend upon it. And something about this trip to Babylon bothers me."

"You think it's something I shouldn't be doing?"

Criton shook his head slowly. "I don't know. You should do what you feel you must. No one can tell you what to do."

"But?"

"The other night I had a dream. It may mean nothing. But I dreamed I was entering the Great Ishtar Gate of Babylon—the biggest thing of its kind in the world—and just as I was about to enter, a voice spoke to me, saying, 'Make your peace with the gods, Criton the Achaean. You enter the city in which you will die.'"

"And you believed it? Maybe it meant that you will settle down, take a wife, raise children, and pass away in your great age surrounded by your loving descendants."

"Possibly. But then why does the memory of it give me such a sinking feeling?" He sighed, and Seth read the tension in his face. "You haven't stopped the Hittites with that maneuver, brilliant as it was. They'll regroup and come back at the locals again, and—"

"All I have done is slow the advance," Seth acknowledged. "This should buy time for Samsi-ditana to reorganize his defenses, build a stronger army, and plan a campaign to rid Mesopotamia of the Hittites."

"In which, of course, he will have your help."

"If he wishes it. The Hittites murdered my mentor," Seth said bitterly.

"You don't know that for sure. The messenger may have been mistaken."

"No, no, I feel it. He's dead."

"Well, it is just such a feeling that I have about entering Babylon." Criton's voice took on a ruminative tone. "I wonder if it looks as I pictured it!"

"You'll know soon enough," Seth remarked. "Look, the villages along the river are getting closer to each other, a sure sign that the city is not far away. They say you can see the walls and the Ishtar Gate from quite some distance upriver." He stopped, gripped the rail, and leaned forward. "Now isn't that curious! Look at that, will you?"

Criton looked where Seth pointed. All along the waterfront, torches burned at regular intervals. On the banks people had gathered to stand on the shore and look out at the boat as it floated slowly downriver. Many waved; some appeared to be calling out, although their words could not be distinguished. Dimly the sound of drums, shawms, flutes, and horns of various descriptions floated across the water to them.

"Sardur said this was a festival time—" Seth commented.

"Bah!" Criton said. "People at festivals do not waste their time lining the banks of the Euphrates staring at approaching boats. My friend, this outpouring heralds your own arrival."

Seth stared. "But . . . but this would appear to be the entire population of these villages!"

Criton looked at the growing crowds along the riverbank. As he did, a movement in the water caught his eye. A small coracle was being rowed to intercept the ship. In the boat, a soldier held up one arm, a piece of papyrus clutched in his grasp.

"Hold there!" the soldier called out. "I have a message from the great king, intended for Sardur's eyes only!"

In the cabin below decks, Sardur scanned the papyrus. "Wait until you hear this," he said to Seth and Criton. "You have seen the crowds on the banks of the river?"

"Yes. We thought—"

"I can guess what you thought. But as we traveled from Mari, the king's astrologers were at work. It appears that there is a most unusual celestial configuration taking place just now, and the seers have been at great pains to determine what it means."

"And?"

Sardur tapped the papyrus. "The message is this: The alignment of the stars—a thing that occurs only once every millennium, if our mathematicians reckon correctly—portends the arrival of a great seer, a prophet of uncommon power and vision, a man whose arrival heralds the coming of a new era in the long life of Babylon. The king is commanded by the gods to welcome this divinely inspired visitor with feasting and thanksgiving, to open his house to him, and to give him the choice of his goods, of his daughters to wife, of his chattels and movables. The king," he finished with an air of satisfaction, "hastens to obey, with great gladness. Meeting the new prophet will be the finest moment of his life."

Seth exchanged stunned glances with Criton.

"Come on deck, my friend," Sardur said. "Do you hear the music getting louder? That means we've arrived. The people will line the quays to sing your welcome. Doubtless the Great Gate of Ishtar is already visible, and doubtless the great king himself stands before it to bid you welcome to the noblest of cities."

"Does he believe all this?" Seth asked, puzzled.

"I am sure he does," Sardur said. "I am not sure I do not believe it myself! Come, Seth. Meet the people of great Babylon!"

Criton lingered at the bottom of the stairs after they had gone. Why, he wondered, did he himself hesitate? Was it because he did not want to see the Ishtar Gate any sooner than he had to? Was he afraid that if it turned out to look exactly as he had dreamed it, it would portend his death?

He shuddered. *Force yourself!* he ordered himself, and hands trembling, he walked slowly up the stairs.

CHAPTER NINE

Thebes Two Years Later

I

In ordinary times an army returning from victory in the field would have been welcomed back to Thebes with the whole of the city gathered to celebrate the heroism and invincibility of Egyptian arms. There would have been at least three days of feasting and a solemn procession of the priests of Amon to bless the victors.

But these were no ordinary times. Two years had passed, and Thebes was not the place it had been. The king had not been in residence for four years now, and the city had been governed instead by his vizier, Baliniri. In the absence of the king and queen, a number of secular festivals had been canceled, changing the very mood of Thebes. Although the city had weathered the worst of the plague, the morale of the survivors was low. Only the news of a complete victory in the delta over Apophis and the Hai would have inspired any grand celebration.

And the present victory—if that was even the right word—

212

was hardly of such magnitude. Instead of a conquering army led by Kamose, the military force that debarked from the boats at the Theban docks was a small, compact unit at half strength. No matter that at its head was the legendary Baliniri himself, a soldier whose youthful exploits were the talk of every soldier on the eastern banks of the Great Sea. Everyone knew that Baliniri's days of military glory were long over and that the only reason he now commanded this unit was that Riki, Kamose's truant general, had yet to return to the army after two years.

Thus there was no singing, no waving of the palms of peace, no cheers of thanksgiving. The soldiers occasioned hardly a second glance as they stepped down from the gangplanks of the warships onto Theban soil. Even Baliniri himself drew no notice as he stumped wearily down the plank. He was greeted by Sibi, the adjutant he had left in charge of the city's defenses when he had sailed for the upriver nomes.

"Greetings, sir," Sibi said. "I trust you had a good voyage."

"As good as can be expected," Baliniri replied sourly. "We struck a deal. Everything's all right . . . for now. One of the nobles put up a fight; when the others saw what happened to him because of it, they all fell into line. When I explained to them what's been going on here, they didn't believe me at first. Luckily one of them had been getting mail from a kinsman in the delta, and he corroborated my story about"—he lowered his voice— "the cult."

"Very good, sir." Sibi's flat voice did not change in pitch or intensity. "Any orders, sir?"

Baliniri scowled, stretched his great arms, and yawned. "Yes. I'd rather wait until morning—my back aches like I've been tortured; I'm not used to sleeping on the ground or in a hammock—but I suppose I'd better get things done as quickly as possible. Get me Thuti and Bocchoris."

"The high priest of Amon, sir?"

"Yes. And is Harsaphes in town?"

Now Sibi lowered his voice and looked furtively around before answering. "Yes, sir. He came in a day ago, in disguise. He's staying in the apartment below yours, next to—" he hesitated. It was still not clear what Tuya's status was at the palace. Officially she was not there. Unofficially . . .

"Yes. I want to see her, too, but later. This evening. Private dinner for two. Keep the matter quiet."

"Of course, sir. Who else for the big meeting?"

Baliniri frowned. "What shape is Riki in nowadays?"

Sibi shook his head. "You'll be shocked at the change in him. He's out of condition, puffy-faced—"

"All right. Have him brought to the palace. I'll see him right after I've dealt with Bocchoris and the others. That would take it right up to dinnertime, I think." He sighed. "Gods! I'm going to sleep tonight!"

"You'll have earned it, sir."

Baliniri grunted. "I just wish I could have come home with having accomplished more. Get the people I asked for. I'm going to freshen up."

"Yes, sir. Welcome back, sir."

To Baliniri's delight, the servants already had a fire going in his palace apartment and were heating water in bronze pots for his bath. He did not recognize any of them, and although they had the coloring and features of the native populace, they did not seem to be Egyptian. He tried several languages to communicate with them, all to no avail. With a weary sigh he let them undress him.

When at last the tub was full of steaming water, he stood by its side, naked and dusty, while the girls pointed at the crisscrossed scars on his battered and hairy body and chattered incomprehensibly to one another.

He smiled sourly as he stepped carefully down into the pool. "Look your fill, girls. There's a scar here for every year of my age. See this one?" He pointed at the horrid white scar tissue in his right side. "That one comes out the other side. Damned near took my life with it. Caught me in the kidney going out. Gods! Did that ever hurt! Even after it was healed, I walked like an old man for six months. And look at this!" He saw that the giggling girls were not looking at his lower belly at all, but at something else. "Well, *that's* received its quota of wounds too, girls. They have a damned disease up in Tyre that puts a man out of commission for the better part of a year. But then I got taken in tow by a little widow from Nineveh, and the next thing you knew . . ."

He chuckled. Youth! Now that it was gone, he could look back on it with a certain detachment and appreciate the comedy in it. He looked again at the girls. Two had shed their simple tunics—the common costume of house slaves—

and were now as naked as he. Why spoil a clean garment giving a man a bath? They were delicious little morsels, that was sure, wherever they were from. There was a time when he would have had at least one of them backed up against the wall or bent over a table by now. That fresh young skin! That . . .

Now they had filled their bowls and were dousing him, and another was rubbing some sort of soapy oil into his back. He smiled. The other two dipped their hands in the oil and went to work on his chest and arms.

Suddenly they stopped and stepped back, their eyes on something behind him. Irritated, he whirled, blinked, and frowned.

"Good afternoon, Husband," said Ah-Hotep. She stood watching him, thin arms crossed over still-full breasts, an unreadable smile on her face. She spoke to the girls, and they went back to work bathing him. "I took the liberty of arranging for a bath for you," she said. "I knew you'd be tired. I also ordered the wine." She turned and poured him a golden bowl of a favorite rich red wine he recognized. "Here, my darling."

He took it, still not speaking, and drank deeply. The girls' hands roamed freely over his body. "That was thoughtful of you," he said.

"Not at all," Ah-Hotep responded. "I haven't seen you in two months. I haven't seen you naked in a lot longer. You're still a very handsome man, particularly as I find you now." Her smile was wry. "Perhaps I can do something to lure you back to my bed." She looked at the nude girls, now glistening with the same fragrant oil they were rubbing into Baliniri's body. "They're quite charming, aren't they? They're Ionian. I bought them especially for you. I know how innocent youth affects you. Perhaps also *not*-so-innocent youth." Her smile was knowing. "But you know, Husband, youth isn't everything. Experience has its advantages."

"I remember," he said gruffly. "Ah-Hotep, I—"

"It's all right. Enjoy yourself. I know you'll have several appointments lined up for your first day back from a diplomatic mission. That's what it really was, wasn't it? That talk of war was just blather. The upriver nobles don't really want war with us; they just want to satisfy themselves that we're not corrupted the way the garrison at Bast is. And quite obviously you've satisfied them." Her smile was ripely sensual. "You'll satisfy all of us, one by one, I think. First the priests, who need to know what your strategy is against the cult. Then the army. Then, I suppose, the little woman you've been keeping downstairs."

"Please!" he admonished her.

"Oh, they don't understand a word of this language. I know about the woman, this Tuya. Did you think I wouldn't know? But of course you did. Look, my darling, I don't care if you need more consolation than one woman can provide, but couldn't you have sought it from me first, before you looked elsewhere?"

"I—"

"Oh, it's all right. Let me pour you more wine. Ah, look. The girls are beginning to get you aroused. That's very sweet. And here I am watching it. That arouses you all the more, doesn't it? Come on, now, admit it. What arouses you the most? The hands of the girls or my eyes on you while they're doing it? Well, enjoy them. That's why I bought them for you. And enjoy Tuya as well. But when you've done with the girls and Tuya and whomever . . . come home to me, will you?"

He gasped. The girls seemed to have fifty hands among them. Slippery, deft, impudent hands.

His wife padded away on soft bare soles. He watched the round globes of her bottom undulate under the thin, almost transparent cloth.

An hour later Baliniri had just finished explaining the deal he had struck with the upriver nobles who had threatened rebellion. He had been irritated by Bocchoris' trouble grasping the matter—he had had to explain the thing three times before it was clear it had gotten across—and Sibi and the others were equally slow.

"So you see," he said, "as long as the upper nomes, the ones between here and the first cataracts, are satisfied that the cult hasn't infiltrated us, they're on our side. They're even willing to send troops if we need them."

Bocchoris scratched his freshly shaved head. "The priesthood still has some hesitation about taking this 'cult' seriously."

"Oh, it's every bit as dangerous as he says it is, sir," Harsaphes confirmed. "I've been observing it for two years in Kamose's camp. I'm ashamed to say I've been forced to become a member, the better to infiltrate them."

"Horrors!" Bocchoris gasped. "Then you are in direct need of purification. I shall prepare the rituals—"

"As you wish, sir. But I'm an old soldier, and we don't run to piety much. But thank you, sir. I know you mean well. Anyhow, this cult is bad, and their influence is everywhere. Even in your priesthood, sir."

This statement fell like a meteorite. Even Baliniri stared incredulously. "In the temples of Amon?" he asked, shocked.

"Yes sir, since early this year. I thought I'd told you. Three of the key priests at the Bast temple, at least. And if *they* can be corrupted—"

"Is nothing sacred?"

"Apparently not; I was about to add that one of them was the high priest himself!"

"No! I refuse to believe it!"

"You'd better, sir. He was one of the ones who initiated *me* into the cult. You can't get more committed than that."

"Baliniri," Bocchoris said, "we've got to move on these monsters immediately!"

"I don't know how feasible that's going to be," Harsaphes confessed, looking around. "They've got the army too. Well, the commanders, anyhow. All but a very few."

Now Baliniri stood, his hands gripping the top of the table. "I agree with Bocchoris," he said. "Immediate action must be taken." He looked each man in the eye and smiled. "Therefore I'm going to Bast to have a look for myself. I'll leave Sibi here to run things, with Thuti as second in command."

"Sir!" both men said, snapping to attention.

"You two have handled things here very well since I left," he commended. "My spies have kept me well informed." He watched the two sets of brows go up. "Bocchoris, we'll meet again tomorrow, if it's convenient."

"Yes! Action has to be taken at the temple!"

"Of course, but covertly. I have to mend fences with the delta nomes and reassure everyone. And make contact with Mara and the resistance directly, for a change, *and* have a look at Kamose and Amasis myself, up close."

"But sir," Sibi asked, "who will command the army with you gone and us in civilian positions?"

"Don't worry," Baliniri said. "I've thought of that. And I'll tell you in a day or two."

II

After the meeting had adjourned, Sibi lingered on. It was obvious that he wanted to speak in private, so when the meeting hall was finally clear, Baliniri turned to his subordinate and clapped him on the shoulder with a weary but respectful hand. "You did well, assembling them all on such short notice. My thanks."

"Yes, sir," Sibi said a little anxiously. "It's about the rest, sir. I'm afraid I've let you down."

"Riki's not here? He refused a direct order to come to me?" There was fire in Baliniri's eyes.

"Well, sir, you didn't tell me to phrase it as an order. If a direct order has to be issued, rather than a polite but urgent request of a friend—"

"I understand. I did not realize how far apart he and I have grown. I will seek him out myself."

"As you wish, sir."

"And Tuya?"

"I'm afraid I drew a blank there too. I sent a good and trusted messenger. He said she was indisposed and could not come."

"You know more than you are saying. Please."

"It may be nothing. It may be coincidence."

"Tell me. I always want the truth, particularly when it's unpleasant."

"Sir, the messenger said that there are plague signs on the street where she lives."

"I thought we were done with that!"

"Mostly, sir. But it resurfaces here and there. The messenger said that there wasn't any such sign in front of *her* house."

"Quick: how many signs on her block?"

"Three."

"Three? Of the *five* houses on the block?"

"Just so, sir."

"This is serious. She has to be got out of there. Assemble

a party of soldiers with a physician. I'll meet them at her house midafternoon."

"Do you think it wise for you to go, sir?"

"Do you think I could *not* go? There are things you have yet to learn about me, my friend."

"Yes, sir."

"But first I'll be seeking out Riki. It's time for us to mend fences."

"Right you are, sir. There are three taverns. The names are—"

"I know all of them well. Thank you."

There wasn't time for assembling an escort. Baliniri set out through the streets of Thebes alone, his long legs settling quickly into a soldier's tireless stride. For the most part he went unrecognized through the city. This suited him. He had had quite enough fuss and officialdom and wanted straight talk and people who looked him in the eye.

And so it was. From time to time a face in the crowd would brighten, and an eye would blink, and someone would wonder: *Who was that tall man I saw back there? Where have I seen him before?* But by the time the answer came, if it did, Baliniri was gone, long legs churning.

He found Riki sitting in the second of the three taverns, pitching three-*outnou* bronze rings at a dirty wall and wagering with the tavern riffraff over the result. From the look of him, Riki was well advanced toward drunkenness, so much so that Baliniri was not sure his friend could have walked without aid. He sat, splay-legged, his back to a broad table. There was a pile of coins on the table behind him, and several drinking bowls. One was broken; one was spilled and lay in a puddle of dark wine.

"All right," he challenged. "Who'll match me?" There were no takers. "What about two rings for one. Three! Four! Five rings to one? What a lot of cowards!"

"You've taken us for everything we've got," one of the onlookers complained, casting a covetous glance at the pile of rings behind Riki. "Give us a break. Let's play something else."

Maybe it was something in the man's eye, or maybe it

was the way his hand went to the front of his garment, as if to check on a hidden weapon. Whatever the cause, Riki suddenly came alive. He sat up, and his eyes blazed. The indolent smile became a savage grin, one Baliniri had seen many times on fellow soldiers' faces just before a battle.

"And what game would that be, my friend?" Riki asked in a changed voice. "It wouldn't be the one in which you decoy the stranger into the alley and hit him on the head, would it? How about the one in which you spike his wine?"

The sally hit home. "I don't know what you're talking about," the speaker denied.

He tried to edge away, but Riki's hand snaked out and grabbed the man's wrist. "Didn't think I could taste it, did you? My friend, you've brought that game to the wrong tavern and tried it on the wrong man. It might have worked on a man who couldn't hold his drink, but—"

"Let me go! I haven't done anything!"

"—this time you picked a man who *can* drink. I sometimes think that's all I can do really well. I can't lead troops. I can't fight. I can only deal with scum of the earth like you."

"You're hurting my arm!"

Standing in half shadow, Baliniri took note of how the pinned man's two confederates were backing away stealthily, edging around behind Riki's table. He had seen this game played out a thousand times. "It's all right, Riki," he called out. "I've got my eye on the two behind you."

Riki looked up. "Well," he said, "I know *that* voice. So! You're finally getting around to paying me back for the time I took a knife off that fellow who was going to gut you with it, back in Memphis. When was that? Fifteen years ago?"

Baliniri let the question lie for a moment. "You boys," he challenged the two behind the table. "If I were you, I'd find some business elsewhere." He held up hands the size of fat loaves of Syrian bread, which hung from forearms as big around as a strong man's thigh. "On second thought, I haven't had a fight in quite a while now. The two of you together might give me a bit of exercise. Riki! Lend this dog turd your knife, will you?"

Riki gave the arm he held a twist and threw the man heavily to the floor. Then he turned around on his seat and grinned, ignoring the groans of pain from the man whose arm he had just broken. A knife flashed, but Riki saw it. His hand came out of his own garment a blur, went to his shoulder, and flipped his dagger. The would-be thief's knife-wielding hand was pinned to the wall!

Amid howls of pain the troublemakers left, the wounded man holding his bleeding hand. Only then did Riki turn back to Baliniri. "Is this a charity call? Let's see if we can redeem the drunkard?"

Baliniri glowered.

"Well," Riki said angrily, toying with the pile of bronze rings, "the drunkard doesn't want to be redeemed. He only wants to die. Of course the gods remain as perverse as ever and deny him the very thing he wants most."

Baliniri sat down, a sour look on his face. "This is your oldest friend in the world you're talking to. Somebody you can't fool."

"You're not my oldest friend. Mara is."

"Thank the gods *she* can't see you now. Every time I hear from her she asks about you, you know. I have this funny feeling about you and her—"

"Mind your own damned business!"

"As you prefer." He shook his head in disgust. "You're a damned mess."

"Thanks. That sort of unqualified praise is just what I need."

Baliniri's hand shot across the table, grasped Riki by the throat, and squeezed hard. Riki struggled, unable to breathe. He tore with his own strong hands at the huge fingers that gripped his throat, then tried to stand or pull away. He could do none of these things. That powerful hand slowly choked the life out of him. He could not catch his breath.

Suddenly the great hand released him, and he gasped aloud.

"Look, you," Baliniri said angrily. "I came here to talk, and you're going to listen."

Riki tried to speak but could not. He nodded.

"Very well. I've let you fuddle your life away in dumps like this for two years. You lost a loved one, and there's a time for mourning. But there's also a time for being a man and facing up to responsiblities—"

"I d-don't want any responsibilities," Riki croaked. His throat hurt.

"Few of us do. But whether you like them or not, you've got them. I need you. The damned country needs you. And it needs you whole and healthy."

"I won't fight for Kamose!"

"I'm not asking you to."

"I don't even know if I can fight anymore."

"You will when the time comes. For now I want to get you healed and put back together. There's only one way to do that."

"Giving me Teti back again?"

"Don't talk drivel. I can fix it so that you can live without her. So you can be a man again, not a damned drunkard."

Riki stared. "I suppose I deserve that. Go on."

"I want you to go to the oasis. El-Dakhla. I want you to meet someone."

"They don't let men in there."

"It's all arranged. You're to go there. Weret and Naldamak will come for you."

"The Nubian woman?"

"Yes. This is imporant—as much to the rest of us as it is to you, whether you know it or not. Whether you *care* or not."

Riki let out a deep sigh. "What can I say? You know I can't refuse."

"No, you can't. You leave in two days. The women will meet you in Deir el-Bahari at noon of the second day."

"Why there? And where in Deir el-Bahari?"

"At the shop of Meru the painter." He paused a moment, then said, "Meru is of the clan of Netru. Do you know that name? It is the name of the only man in the world your wife ever loved before she met you."

He got up to go. Riki stared openmouthed. "Baliniri—"

"Two days from now. Don't fail me."

III

With the interview ended, Baliniri made his way quickly toward Tuya's house by the most direct route through the back alleys. His mind was elsewhere. Little by little, he was putting together a plan for dealing with the impossible and ungovernable place that Egypt would become the moment Kamose broke his father's lines and drove the embattled Hai out of the country.

There had to be some alternative to civil war. The country had seen nearly a century of this, and he was not sure how much more unrest the people could take.

Kamose, an upstart, would not tolerate a man like Baliniri for long in his kingdom. Baliniri knew he was too independent and likely to speak his mind, saying things Kamose would not want to hear.

It was clearly time to make a move. Baliniri had begun doing this by mending fences first with the upriver nobles—who had never accepted Kamose anyway—and then with the priests of Amon. The next step was to have a look at the delta situation and start making some plans for the end of the game.

These plans included finding, nurturing, and training a successor to Kamose—a successor of Baliniri's own choosing.

His mind had approached the unthinkable thought: finding a successor to Kamose while Kamose yet lived! And what were the unavoidable consequences? Revolution? Assassination?

As he entered Tuya's street, the first thing he noticed was the mark of the plague on the door opposite hers. He shuddered and stepped out into the middle of the street. Yes! There was another. But on Tuya's door there was nothing.

As he was about to step forward, a voice cried out to him. "You! Sir!"

Baliniri wheeled. Standing before him was an adolescent boy. "You're addressing me?"

"Yes. You're Baliniri, aren't you?"

"I am. And who speaks to me?"

The boy stood out from the wall, ready to break and run. "One who has watched Tuya come and go from your place in the palace. One who might know what you've been up to with her."

Baliniri frowned.

"Tuya threw Aset out of her house for doing bad things with a man, but Aset was innocent."

"And of what importance is this to you?"

"Then Tuya seems to have done with you what she said Aset had done. The same thing she'd thrown Aset and her baby out for. Well, everything we do that's bad gets punished sooner or later, Kedar says."

"Ah! Then you're a pupil of Kedar's?"

The boy frowned. "I'm just somebody who doesn't know for sure if you've done anything to be punished for. That's why I'm telling you that coming down this street isn't wise."

Baliniri stared. He remembered that he had told Sibi to have the soldiers and the physician meet him here midafternoon. Where were they? "You, boy. Do I know you?"

"I'm Tuya's son."

Baliniri blinked. Son? Then he remembered that she and Kedar had adopted a boy some years before. What was the name? Oh, yes. "Meni, isn't it?"

"That's right. I don't live with Tuya anymore. But I can tell you you're taking your life into your hands if you come into this street."

"If you don't live here, how do you know?"

"I look in from time to time. I haven't got anything against Kedar. He was like a father to me. Nobody could have been kinder."

His eyes widened. " 'Was'?" he echoed. "You speak of Kedar as if he's dead."

"If he isn't, he will be soon. Yesterday I came by. He met me at the door. He told me to go away. He didn't look good. I think he had the plague."

"And—and Tuya?"

"I don't know. I asked the women in the next block. But nobody has seen Tuya in a week."

Baliniri stepped forward impulsively and grabbed the boy's thin arms.

"A week?" he said. "In five days the fever can—"

"I know."

"Have the physicians been in here?"

"They've been called, but they won't come. Not with three deaths in one week here. The man next door died yesterday."

Baliniri shook the boy. "I've an errand for you."

"That hurts my arms," the boy said.

"I'm sorry," Baliniri said, releasing him. "You can earn a gratitude that I will repay with rich gifts. Go to the palace with a message. Find a man named Sibi in the anteroom. Tell him to get the soldiers and the doctor—"

"He won't listen to me. He'll have me thrown out in a moment."

"Give him this," Baliniri said, handling over the seal ring from his right hand. "Tell him to get the soldiers and the magus here right away."

The boy stared down at the ring. The stone in it alone was worth more money than he had ever imagined.

Baliniri read the nature of his hesitation. "There's no place in the world where you can sell that ring."

"I didn't intend to."

"Just take it to Sibi and tell him what I told you. You might even pass him in the street on his way here, so keep a sharp eye out for a contingent of palace soldiers. Then come to me a week from now for your reward."

Meni looked up at him, still hesitant. "But what if you catch it today? Seven days from now you'll have been two days dead—"

"Be off with you!" Baliniri roared.

With the boy gone Baliniri rushed to Tuya's door and banged on it once, twice. Impatiently he tried the handle. But just as he touched it, the door pulled away from him. Tuya, in a simple dress and barefoot, stood facing him. "Oh, Baliniri! Thank heaven you've come! It's Kedar! We have to get him to the doctor."

He looked her up and down. She seemed all right. "Don't worry. I've got a master magus coming from the palace."

"Come in," Tuya said. "He's very weak."

"How long has he had it?"

She looked at him with those large liquid eyes that had driven him half-mad so many years ago, when they were both young. "The first I noticed was two days ago."

"Two? Then there's a chance. We'll have him purged with aloes if he's strong enough. We'll lance the buboes and bleed him a little—"

"Oh, Baliniri!" she said, rushing into his arms and bursting into tears. "Thank heaven you've come!"

He held her close for a long moment. Then he stepped back, held her at arm's length, and cautiously reached a hand out to touch her cheek.

He stared with horror.

She was burning up with fever!

IV

The tavernkeeper returned to Riki's table. "Do you want some more, sir?" he asked hesitantly. "I see your wine bowl is—"

"No. No, forget it. Just put what I owe you on my account."

"But, uh, sir, you've run up quite a bill today. . . ."

The glare Riki gave him would have eaten the whitewash off a newly painted wall. "Yes, I have. And you've padded it a bit too, I imagine, as you always have. Don't think I'm unaware of your deception. I've been letting you get away with it because your tavern is located conveniently to my home. But I'm not married to this place—any tavern where I can kill time will do."

"Now, sir, don't be hasty—"

"Just write up the bill and send it to me. Well? Why are you still standing there?"

A blink of the eye later, and the offender was nowhere to be seen.

Riki scowled down at the empty bowl. His mind was getting clearer, and the clearer his mind got, the more sour things looked. He blinked angrily and stood, weaving a little. One of the idle dancers came over to him, her skirts flouncing, tiny ankle bells jingling. "A little comfort, sir?"

He pushed her gently away and moved unsteadily toward the door. When he threw it open, blinding light flooded in. He shielded his eyes, cursed under his breath, and moved out into the plaza. Why, he wondered peevishly, did people assume that riding a whore's back would cure anything? That need he could always get serviced; sexual release was cheap. What seemed to be impossible to find was a friend, a woman he could talk to.

Why a woman? Why not a friend like Baliniri, who had gone to the bother of coming down to talk to him? Well, he rationalized, he needed a bit of softness in his life just now, a bit of sympathy, a bit of . . .

No! the other side of his mind insisted. *You don't need someone to snivel with you and pat you on the back. You need someone hard and substantial to lean on. Someone who pushes back.*

But where was he to find that? he wondered, and was appalled to notice how self-pitying and weak the question sounded. *All right, all right. I'll look up Meru. I won't wait two days.* His mind becoming clear at last, he glared at the crowds of people coming and going in the busy marketplace. Which way to the river, now? Oh, yes. All right. He knew where he was.

Firming his jaw and squinting into the sun-washed glare of the street, he set out at a brisk pace through the twisting byways of the city and headed for the quays.

The battery of royal physicians had been closeted with the two plague victims for the better part of an hour. Now Khonsu, the head magus, came out wearing a severe expression. "Sir," he said to Baliniri, "the man Kedar has died. We could do nothing. The disease was too advanced. He was old, and his system could not fight the disease."

"Too few of the elderly can fight the disease," Baliniri said disgustedly. There was a cold and horrible emptiness inside him. "What's your record to date of survivals once the true symptoms of the illness have been diagnosed? Don't give me any pretty blather."

"Well, sir, we're making progress case by case—"

"A flat figure. Number of cases where you saved the patient."

"Uh . . . for the elderly, none, sir. But we're hoping that—"

"And the woman's symptoms?"

Khonsu's forehead began to shine with perspiration. "Uh . . . high fever, of course, which makes her mind disoriented. Her heartbeat is much too fast, too irregular. Her words are slurred."

"She's worse now than when we found her, isn't she? Buboes in the groin, the armpits?"

"Sir, she must possess immense personal strength," Khonsu replied evasively. "She seems to have been holding herself together since the disease came upon her, not admitting to herself that she had it, in order to nurse Kedar through this thing. But while she's been trying to fool herself, the disease has been coming upon her, little by little at first, then very rapidly."

Baliniri lowered himself into a chair. "Yes, she is strong, very strong." He spoke through clenched teeth. "Or was. She had to be. She's had a hard life." He closed his eyes and shook his gray-haired head. "Tell me straight now: How long has she got?"

Khonsu looked up into his employer's eyes, and the look he saw there made him shudder. "Not long, sir. Two days would be a miracle."

"Then she could go soon."

"Perhaps within the hour, sir."

"I have to be with her. I have to talk to her."

Khonsu put up both hands and put his robed back to Tuya's door. "Oh, no, sir! You can't begin to imagine how dangerous that would be, sir. The grand vizier of Egypt, being allowed to take a terrible chance like that? I'd be drummed out of the college of physicians—"

"That," Baliniri said evenly, "would be small stuff indeed, compared to what would happen if you tried to stop me."

Khonsu moved away from the door.

"That's better," Baliniri said. "Now go in and dismiss the other magi so I may be alone with her for a few minutes."

"Y-yes, sir. I'll only be a moment, sir."

Tuya, her mind addled as much by the strong dose of *shepenn* the doctors had given her as by her fever, watched as the magi huddled by the doorway talking. One of them glanced her way, then back at his comrades. What were they saying? Well, perhaps it did not matter. She closed her small hands over the coverlet and stared at the ceiling.

It was all up for her now, wasn't it? She had been trying to fool herself all during the onset of Kedar's illness, but in the end it had proved futile. Poor Kedar was gone. She had heard them say it. At least he did not have to suffer anymore.

And how long did she have? It did not seem to matter. Thanks to the *shepenn*, the pain was gone. All she felt now was weak. She could just slip off when the time came and hardly notice the transition from life to death. No one would be the loser. Whose life would her death impoverish? No one that she could think of. She had left Meni enough to get by on. The rest would go in trust for Seth, for his return, if he ever returned.

Where was Seth? If only . . .

She closed her eyes, and when she reopened them, she had no idea how long they had been closed. Someone was standing over her, someone large and heavily built. It was like being a child again, looking up from her cradle to see her father standing over her. Her father! He had died and left her alone so early in life.

But no. This was not her father. Perhaps it was Ben-

Hadad? But he was dead, she remembered, dead these many years. He had depended on her, and she had let him down, by having an affair with another man. No wonder he had turned sour on life, turning on her and his son and going off to seek a lonely death far away. It had been all her fault.

And look what she had done to Aset and the baby—her own grandchild. She had let them down too, and Seth with them. She had thrown Seth's own son out of her house, with Aset penniless and homeless. *Her* fault!

Whom had she not disappointed? Surely she had disappointed Baliniri most of all. First, she had given him reason to believe she loved him but instead went back to her husband. Second, after Ben-Hadad had died and she was free, Baliniri had taken a new look at her and had seen someone he no longer wanted. She had no idea *how* she had let him down that time—he had just looked at her and decided against rekindling their old flame.

And now? Now when he wanted her again? She was dying, just when he claimed to need her most. *Your fault, Tuya! You've failed all of them—and yourself as well!* Well, under the circumstances perhaps it was time for it all to end. The face above her began very slowly to come into focus. The features took shape, becoming those of a towering, heavy-shouldered giant with large concerned-looking eyes and a great grizzled head and gray beard.

"B-baliniri," she whispered. "Poor Baliniri. I . . . I've been thinking about you." The voice, cracked and unreal, seemed to come from some other place.

"I'll be here," he said, sitting down beside her and taking her small hand in his huge one. She saw him wince as he noted how hot her hand was. "Don't try to talk."

Soon it would all be over: the deceits and disappointments of life; her own guilts and self-denunciations; any troubles she had brought upon him and the many others she had hurt. "I . . . I wanted to ask your forgiveness. For letting you down, for not living up to the picture you once had of me."

His hand gently squeezed hers. "Hush, now. You've let no one down. I love you as I always have."

She knew that was a lie, although a kind one.

"We're going to get you well, now," he added.

Ah, that lie was less than kind. She did not care to live longer. She had made enough of a botch of it already and would only do more of the same. Better to get it over.

What a great pity she did not have them all here, so she could say good-bye to all of them, so she could ask their forgiveness, as she had asked Baliniri's.

But there they were! All clustered around him! Smiling down at her! Ben-Hadad, Kedar, Seth, even poor Anab with his terrible face! And now she could see her father. They were all smiling bravely down at her, reassuringly, just as Baliniri was. And she could see they had all forgiven her, even as he had. "Oh, my darlings," she said in a voice that began to fade from the first syllable. "Thank you, and good-bye. . . ."

The faces also faded until at last there was only the one hovering above her. Strong, gentle, ever protective, ever forgiving. Ever loving despite everything. And when the fear was gone, it was replaced by a marvelous relaxation, then sleep . . . then something more than sleep.

V

"Oh!" The woman stepped back, one plump hand pressed to her breast. "What a pity Meru's not here. He'll be so sorry to have missed you, Captain. It is Captain, isn't it? But no. I heard you'd been promoted to something higher. Forgive me."

Riki's eyes narrowed as he stared at her in the fading afternoon sun. "You know me?"

"Oh, yes, sir. I saw you once at a victory parade. And I once passed you and Teti when you were attending a feast in the city. She waved at me. I had no idea she'd remember me."

Riki stepped back into the shadows and wiped his sweaty brow. "I must ask your pardon," he said. "You'd be . . . Meru's wife, then?"

"Yes. My name is Hat-Nefer. Welcome to our house."

"Thank you. Please call me Riki. I'm not with the army anymore. I'm an ordinary citizen and out of work. You knew Teti?"

"When she was much younger. Could I get you something? A glass of wine, perhaps?"

It was tempting, but he would not give in to the temptation. He wanted a clear head. "Thank you, no," he answered. "But if you've a few minutes, could we sit here under the arbor? I've never run into anyone who knew my wife back then. Please tell me about her."

Hat-Nefer smiled diffidently, not knowing what to say. But as he sat down and looked up at her, the friendly expression on his face reassured her. "Well, sir, I ought to be starting dinner, but seeing it's you, I'm sure Meru wouldn't mind." She joined him on the wide bench, sitting primly at the far end. "Netru was our cousin, the only one in the family who ever went to war. We tried to interest him in one of the arts practiced by our family members, but he never took to it."

"I know about Netru. He was a great hero of the army."

"Oh, yes. A pity he died so young. Did Teti ever tell you what he looked like?"

Riki's eyes opened wide. "Why, no. We never discussed it."

"I was just thinking of what he would have looked like if he'd lived to be our age. He would have looked a lot like you. You're remarkably alike—a certain look in the eyes, a certain set of the head and shoulders, and particularly your smile."

Riki chuckled gently. "If anyone had told me beforehand you'd come up with such revelations, I wouldn't have believed I'd take it this well. So my wife looked at me and saw another man. I always wondered what she saw in me and why she fell for me at first sight."

"Oh, don't sell yourself short. A good man should never undervalue himself! You're a fine-looking man! You and Teti would have had such lovely children."

She realized suddenly that she had gone too far. "Oh, Riki, if I could call back my words . . . I didn't mean to remind you so soon after."

"Never mind," Riki said tightly. "It does seem a shame, though. I'll never know, now, what a child of Teti's would have looked like." He stopped suddenly, seeing the odd look on her face.

"What's the matter? What did I say?"

Hat-Nefer put one hand over her mouth. "Nothing. Nothing." Her eyes darted right and left. "I'd better get dinner started. Please join us. Meru will be along soon. He's just gone into the city to buy twine at the ropewalk. He'll be so pleased to see you."

Riki leaned forward. "I'm supposed to meet two women here tomorrow at Meru's shop. Weret and—"

"And Naldamak. They're great friends of the family."

But now her eyes, lighting on something past him in the shadows, widened.

Riki whirled and looked, startled, into the unblinking eyes of a mature cheetah, standing just behind him on a high shelflike projection on the side of the little house. As the cat coolly regarded him, the tall, spare, unadorned form of Weret slowly walked out of the shadows. Behind her, in deep shadow, he could see bright eyes shining in a black face.

"Weret!" he said.

"Yes," the warrior-woman replied. "We've come early."

"Not necessarily," he said. "If you want to leave right now—"

"There's not enough moon for traveling," Weret said. "The morning will do. Let me get a better look at you." Her strong hands on his biceps, she stood him up as if he were a child. "You've undergone some changes since I saw you last," she said as the last rays of the sun fell on his face. "Apparently for the better. You don't smell like the back stoop of a sailor's brothel, for one thing."

Riki looked her suddenly in the eye. "Baliniri got under my skin," he admitted. "He gave me a talking to."

Weret snorted softly. "It's more than that. Bereavement tends to burn itself out in the end. Grief is a poor friend to make the rounds with. It takes and takes and gives nothing back."

"Wisely observed," Riki said. "I'm ready for a change. As long as it doesn't involve going back to the delta and killing civilians for Kamose. I'm at your disposal. What surprises have you cooked up for me at the oasis?"

Weret looked from him to Hat-Nefer, then back again. "Not much that I can easily discuss here," she said. "Pardon me, Hat-Nefer, I don't mean to snub you."

Hat-Nefer moved back another step, obviously overawed by the towering, statuesque Weret. "Oh, I understand. It's all right, really. No sense discussing things around me that I have no need to know."

"Thank you." Weret turned back to Riki. "You know, I really do think you might be nearly ready. All right. Dawn."

"I'll be up and waiting," Riki agreed. "Ready for what?"

Weret looked at him dispassionately. "For moving on to

the next stage of your life's education," she explained. "If you want to call it growing up, you have my leave to do so."

For a moment Riki almost looked to be on the brink of anger. Then he mastered himself. "Dawn it is." He nodded curtly at the two warrior-women, then bowed gallantly to little Hat-Nefer, standing shyly just beyond them. "My thanks to you for the conversation and the information, dear lady."

There was a chill in the evening air, so one of the servants had lighted a small fire in the brazier beside Baliniri's big worktable. An hour ago he had swept the maps that had been spread atop it onto the floor and since then had sat staring thoughtfully at the dancing flames.

Only gradually did he become aware that he was not alone. He looked away from the fire to take notice of the slender robed figure standing in the doorway.

"I suppose you've heard," Baliniri said.

Ah-Hotep leaned against the wall and looked at him. Her voice was soft when she said, "Yes, an hour after it happened." There was a brief pause; then she went on. "If her death has brought you pain, you have my sympathy."

"I think you actually mean that," he said incredulously, looking directly at her for the first time. "You know, you are really a very thoughtful person. I am grateful for your concern."

"You sound tired. Can I bring you anything? Or would you rather I left you alone?"

Baliniri looked at her for a long, long moment before answering. "No. Sit here beside me. I feel like talking, and I'd prefer having someone with me who makes sense when she speaks."

"That's the nicest compliment anyone has given me in some time," she said, taking the proffered seat. "At my age one learns to settle for whatever compliment happens to come along."

"I've neglected you," Baliniri confessed. "I've been carrying on right under your nose with another woman. I'm sorry, Ah-Hotep. There didn't seem to be anything particularly wrong about it at the time. I haven't been very wise."

"Poor Tuya," his wife sympathized. "The two of you didn't seem to make each other terribly happy. Well, it's a big job, making someone happy."

Baliniri searched her face to see if she was being critical, but he could find no evidence of that. "There's much to what you say."

Ah-Hotep started to speak but let him continue.

"Tuya never learned to value herself. I tried to make her see herself through other eyes, but I failed. She went back to Ben-Hadad and to thinking of herself as a failure."

"Don't blame yourself for that," his wife advised. She sounded truly interested. "That would have made you feel like a man who'd failed—failed to give her a new picture of herself."

Baliniri looked at her. His eyes softened. "I should listen to you more often," he said. "You perceive much. You have thought a great deal about life."

She smiled slightly. "Palace life gives the likes of me little to do, really, but observe and reflect. King's child, young wife, middle-aged wife, middle-aged widow. None is a real sort of job in life. Another woman might have taken a succession of lovers. I had only one, in my youth, with Baba, and I still honor his memory. I wanted no parade of second-rate Babas. Instead I kept my eyes open." She looked directly at him, without guile. "I can be useful to you, Baliniri. We are past the age of passionate perturbations, perfumed giddiness, and coy flirtations."

"Yet there are other relationships than these," he said, completing her thought for her. "And at the proper time of life they can have their own fascinations. If you are amenable to the idea, we might try finding a new relationship, a new way of becoming close to each other."

"Lovers or fellow conspirators?" she asked in a mildly amused voice. "Yes, I'd like that. I'd make a rather good conspirator, you know. I have skills you've never tapped. And"—here she chuckled, low, deep in the throat—"I have spies that you probably know nothing about."

His eyebrows shot up, but he let her continue.

"They tell me you're having trouble with the midriver nobles and with the older Fayum families who don't know how much to trust you in these difficult times."

He nodded appreciatively; she had done her homework.

"I can help you with the worst of these, Husband."

"How?"

"They're my own family, my dear. My bloodlines are very good, you know. A number of those nobles owed my father favors—ones that I can call in."

His hand reached out to hold hers.

"There's more," she offered. "I managed Sekenenre's career for him. He was a sweet man, but he did not understand interpersonal relations well, and he understood court protocol and politics hardly at all. While I, my dear, had been living that sort of life since before he was born. Think of it, Baliniri. Two good minds working in concert. Much better than one."

His hand now caressed her bare forearm.

"You're wondering how to go about finding someone to replace Kamose when the time comes," she said. "That won't be easy. The boys with the good bloodlines are cretins for the most part. We're going to have to create one."

"Create one? How?"

"We have to find a husband for my daughter Thermutis, and I think I may have a candidate or two."

"These are long-range plans," he remarked.

"Yes. We'll both be very old or dead by the time the child comes of age. But if Kamose can be deposed—and if in the meantime Thermutis has produced a child with impeccable bloodlines—we can hope for a peaceful regency while the child matures."

"And to think I've neglected a mind as subtle as this!"

"Well, it's never too late to change," she began. But the next sentence was interrupted by his kiss, and the passion behind it was as much physical as intellectual.

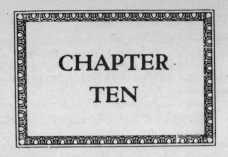

CHAPTER TEN

The Nile Delta

I

The Hai now controlled only a third or so of the delta, having lost the rest little by little either to outright Egyptian assault or to a gradual and unopposed encroachment as the native population reclaimed the land that had been theirs for thousands of years before the arrival of the Shepherd invaders.

Such was the virtually endless wealth of the Black Lands, however, that Apophis could still raise the money to hire an endless stream of foreign mercenaries to fight his war. These had grown and grown in number in the two years since the battle lines had stabilized before Avaris, and now the Hai garrison was the strongest it had been since before the Battle of Thebes, in which Kamose had first made his presence known.

Hai-led, Hai-paid mercenaries now fanned out all around Avaris, protecting the city against flank assaults. With the current lull in the war, the mercenaries had also been pressed into service to control the local population. The foreigners,

236

with their contemptuous ignorance of Hai and Egyptian custom, their bad manners, and their unbridled lust and thirst, had quickly alienated the local people. Around the foreigners no native-born girl was safe; in a community governed by Hellene mercenaries, boy children were no safer than girls were elsewhere.

Unrest had begun to fester in the communities around Avaris as popular reaction against the foreigners became daily more pronounced. After two violent incidents in the nineteenth and twentieth nomes, representatives of those districts with strongly worded demands visited Apophis.

Afterward the king summoned Rasmik, his most capable general. Rasmik had hardly begun the formal salutation when Apophis broke in. "Forget the protocol," he barked. "We've got trouble. I have to do something to distract the locals. The foreign scum have been getting out of hand." He caught the look in Rasmik's eye. "No, no, I'm not criticizing your commanders for lack of discipline. I know you can't do much to control a bunch of outland riffraff when the war's becalmed, as it is now."

Rasmik waited until Apophis had finished.

"It has occurred to me," Rasmik remarked, "that our spies and scouts report that Kamose's troops grow daily more lax and undisciplined. And it cannot have escaped Your Majesty's attention that General Riki continues to ignore Kamose's demands that he return to the army."

Apophis's eyes narrowed. "And you propose—?"

Rasmik replied first with a shrug. "That we control the foreigners by initiating a military offensive. The Lydian unit is idle on our far left flank. If they were to feint a major attack on that front, we could draw troops away from Kamose's main force. This would leave Kamose's center greatly weakened, and at a time when Kamose is much distracted."

Apophis pursed his lips in thought. "What do you mean, distracted?"

"The spy reports, sire. Surely you read them."

"Uh . . . yes. I did. But refresh my memory."

"Well, Kamose and his wife are apparently more thoroughly divided than ever before. This has to do in part with her refusal to share the royal bed. Kamose of course finds this demeaning, particularly since she manages to express her disenchantment so publicly."

"And to this she has added? . . ."

"Her support for the Habiru. She has become their outspoken champion and has staunchly campaigned to secure just treatment for them. This is a particular thorn in Kamose's side, considering the hatred he bears them."

"And would that have anything to do with this cult Kamose has brought into the country?"

"Yes, sire. The queen opposes the cult, and there is great animosity between her and the two cult leaders. This exacerbates the misunderstanding between her and Kamose. It apparently unhinges him altogether now and then."

"But of course! We take advantage of the distraught state of mind in which my son finds himself, and we attack him—"

"Head on—"

"Yes!" Apophis frowned. "But that's where he's strongest."

"So Your Majesty was about to suggest that we precede this with a feinting motion along our flank—"

"The far left flank! Where our Lydians are idle!"

"Exactly, Your Majesty. As always, Your Majesty remains way ahead of me."

Apophis looked down at his knobby-knuckled, battle-scarred hands. He flexed the right one. "What effect would it have on the troops if I were to lead the offensive myself?"

"Splendid, sire. It would be a great morale builder, particularly as Kamose, from all reports, is not himself these days. And there is a rumor within the enemy camp that I *must* bring to your attention." Rasmik's eyes bore into the king's.

"Rumor?" Apophis asked nervously. He flexed his sword hand again. "What kind of rumor?"

"You will no doubt remember the tale of the magical iron sword that Teti is supposed to have made under the supervision of Karkara of Sado? The so-called Sword of Glory."

Apophis looked very uncomfortable. "Remember it? A sword that cleaved right through the best bronze swords—"

"Exactly. But if you remember, it was believed to have magical powers and to have been the sword mentioned in the 'prophecy' that the enemy puts such store in. The one that asserts that with the aid of this sword you will be deposed, and the Hai driven from Egypt, by a son of your own bl—"

"Enough! I remember! I have bad dreams about that thing! I've lain awake nights trying to imagine what to do about it."

"Sire," Rasmik said, "the rumor concerns not just the sword, but its authenticity."

Apophis paused. "Authenticity?" he said at last. "You mean it's a fake? But I've gone up against the thing. It's iron, all right."

"Iron, yes, but *not* the true Sword of Glory. *That* weapon must be made by members of a mystical brotherhood who live far to the north of here. And to this end an emissary has been sent on a quest to find the true weapon. Many years have passed, and the emissary has not returned."

Apophis's eyes were wide. "Then it's just an ordinary iron sword? And I've feared—this? Why, if I'd had just an ordinary iron sword in my own hand when we met, I could have— How did you learn this?"

"From one of their spies. We intercepted one of them and tortured him. It took hours for him to succumb, and this particular bit of information was only divulged moments before he died."

"Why was I not informed of this immediately?"

Rasmik's eyes were hooded. "I did not wish to excite false hopes. Not, at any rate, until I could accompany the passing on of such news with—this."

He clapped his hands, and a servant entered, carrying a long, slender package in his outstretched palms. Rasmik took the cloth-swathed parcel and nodded the servant's dismissal. "I was at some pains to locate one of these, sire," Rasmik said. "I issued an order throughout the entire army, accompanied with the promise of promotions, bonuses, chattels, slaves—not for the man who owned an iron sword, but for the man who turned him in. The man who owned this is now decorating a sharpened stake." He almost smiled. "Open it, sire."

Apophis took the parcel and winced at its unexpected weight. His brows went up, and he slowly began to smile as he unwrapped the package. When the last fold of cloth fell away he held it up. "Gods! Where did this come from?"

"It was in the hands of a captain from Sidon, who apparently took it from one of the soldiers who had sacked Ebla with your ancestors' army, when the Hai marched across Syria and Canaan. It's supposed to have been made around a hundred years ago, by a certain Turios of Tyre, way over in the Greek islands somewhere."

"Turios, eh? I don't know the name," Apophis said, holding the ugly black sword up and turning it this way and that. "Ungainly thing. But the balance isn't bad."

"Turios, sire, taught the secret of the making of iron to Khalkeus of Knossos, the personal armorer of Midas of Knossos."

"It still doesn't mean anything to me." Apophis feinted, parried, jabbed. "You don't fence with these, really. Your arm moves too slowly. You hack away like a butcher." He suited his actions to the word.

"Khalkeus's real name was Kirta of Haran. He was the father of Shobai and Hadad of Haran. All Children of the Lion. All famous men."

"I have heard of them," Apophis said absently. "You know, it's not a bad weapon. Takes some getting used to. The extra weight's remarkable. Puts quite a strain on the wrist, but once one gets used to it—"

"Precisely, sire. That is why I gave it to you now. I implore you to get used to it, sire. Carry it night and day. Do exercises with it in your hand. Practice parries and cuts."

Apophis smiled. "Draw your own weapon," he challenged in a low voice.

Rasmik's brow rose, but he complied.

"On guard!"

"Sire?"

"Have at me! Now! Thrust!"

Rasmik blinked. But he dutifully did so, slowly, clumsily, removing all the risk from the motion.

Apophis parried the thrust easily, then drew back and hacked mightily, catching Rasmik's blade forte to forte.

Rasmik's weapon shivered into six pieces, which fell to the ground with dull clatters.

Apophis, grinning like a man half his age, held up the black sword triumphantly. "*Iron!* How could I have been so superstitious about it? It's just another metal!" He bared his teeth, slashing at the empty air. "I'll smash his blade to pieces, just as I have smashed yours! I'll kill him! I'll crush him! I'll cut off his head!"

II

On the other side of the lines in the vast tent city that Kamose had set up within sight of the walls of Avaris, Amasis received a dawn visit from Djoser, Kamose's adjutant. "Come," Amasis said. "Let us greet the morning out of doors. Is the king awake?"

"No, master," Djoser answered, inclining his head respectfully. "Last night he had a long session after eating the sacred mushrooms. The hallucinations were so frightening that he sought to drown them with palm wine. But that only served to intensify the effects."

"Then he'll be in a vile mood. Well, that may be to the good. He tends to leave all decisions to me when he's out of sorts." Amasis scowled at the soldier. "Avoid calling me your master when we're in public places. Treat me as a civilian official of the court, not as a votary of the Great Mother. We of the faith function best in secret until the moment when we take over entirely."

"A thousand pardons. I'll remember that in the future." The two men strolled easily out of Amasis's tent into the morning air. The sky was already pink, but the sun had yet to appear. "There is a small problem, my lord, one I've been meaning to bring up. Kamose's batman—"

"Ah, yes. The man Shu. I don't trust him either. He has steadfastly refused all our overtures to join the faith."

"What can we do? Think how useful it would be to have at Kamose's side a man of our own persuasion who could report to us everything the king says and does and to plant thoughts in his mind when he is under the influence of drugs or palm wine."

"A good idea, but Shu has been with Kamose for quite some time, and the king would resent any suggestion that the man be dismissed. He might also suspect that he is being manipulated, and we do not want that thought to occur to him, ever."

"Then a knife in the dark . . ."

"Bah. You think like Makare, which is to say you do not think at all. That sort of unprepared action often goes wrong and betrays your purpose. For example, Makare's haste allowed the dwarf Tchabu to get away, and nobody has ever found the damned hideous little homunculus. To have him roaming the country . . . I find that very disturbing. The dwarf not only knows too much about us, he apparently has some powers that can be used against us. If he could have been captured, those powers could have been harnessed in our cause."

"But, my lord, I wasn't advocating precipitate or unprepared action."

"I know, I know." Amasis waved the denial away impatiently. "But if Shu were murdered, there would be unavoidable suspicion of foul play. And that might be traced back to us or our confederates. No, there has to be another way." He frowned and closed his eyes. "Wait, there is a possibility."

"Tell me, my lord."

Amasis looked at him now, sharp-eyed. "No, I'll do this myself. The fewer people in on it, the better. Suffice it to say that the best person to order Shu's death is Kamose himself."

Djoser's eyes widened, and he stepped back. "My lord! How are you going to engineer that? They are as close as near kin."

"Some situation will be improvised in which Shu is seen to let his master down in a matter of supreme importance—preferably in some way that exposes Kamose to danger and impugns his reputation, embarrassing him before his own army, preferably during a military action."

"But, my lord!" Djoser said. "How can that be managed? There's been no action along the line in over a week."

"I don't know," Amasis said slowly, "but something will turn up. Things have been quiet too long. We'll keep an eye out for opportunities."

The now-risen sun illuminated a figure scrambling toward them. It was a messenger from the right wing of the army, the one commanded by Elset.

"I have a message for the king, my lord," the runner said, recognizing Amasis first, then Djoser. He bowed to the one and saluted the other. "The general reports activity on the enemy lines opposite us, sir, the kind that usually precedes a major attack. But the activity seems to be limited to our flank."

"That's curious," Djoser mused, turning to Amasis. "Surely they don't intend to have at us on our right flank alone! Even if the attack were successful, it would only create a dangerous salient, one we'd have little trouble erasing with a counter-attack."

The runner spoke up. "My master put it much the same way, sir. Nevertheless, he said I should report the matter to the king as quickly as possible."

Amasis put a restraining hand on the runner's chest.

"You've informed General Djoser, the king's right arm. The general will inform him. You may go back to your master."

"But, my lord, if there are any messages—"

"If the king has a message for Elset, we'll send it with our own runner. Otherwise Elset will know what to do. There are standing orders with the staff to cover every eventuality. Now be gone."

When the runner was out of sight, Amasis smiled. "We may have just been handed our chance. What if we say that we informed Shu, but he failed to pass the news along to Kamose, thus causing a minor debacle and making it look as though it were Shu's fault?"

"If that were to cause the deaths of any of our men, I would feel very bad about—"

"Don't be squeamish. The will of the Great Mother takes precedence over the lives of a few supernumeraries."

"Well, my lord—"

"Another idea occurred to me. Last week we captured a Canaanite mercenary carrying an iron sword."

"The thing is in my tent. But it's the worst weapon I've ever seen. Quite obviously the bungler who made it had no idea of the proper formula. It's too brittle and has been broken several times and badly mended at that. It'll do against bronze, but against a real iron sword, it'd come apart at the first pass." He stopped, wide-eyed, comprehending. "You don't mean—"

Amasis's smile was that of a predatory beast contemplating its prey. "When the king is not using the heavy iron sword made by Teti, he wears a bronze weapon or none at all. When there's even the smallest chance of personal danger, however, he calls for the iron sword in its special hanger."

Djoser caught his breath. "Which Shu carries and hands to Kamose when he goes into battle. Shu never checks on the sword between times. We could switch Kamose's sword with the brittle one."

"We understand each other. But no real harm must come to the king. When the exchange is made, there must be men of peerless valor and fighting skills at Kamose's side."

"I myself shall be at his side, flanked by a dozen of the king's best. I'll appoint them immediately—a royal body-guard for our gracious master."

"Witnesses of his discomfiture when he finds out he's

carrying not the alleged Sword of Glory but a worthless piece of junk."

"Put there to replace the sword that Shu, in his cups one night, sold to cover his drinking debts."

"Not sold. Gambled away."

"Gambled away, then, my lord. I see I have much to learn where it comes to playing this game."

"But you show natural talent. The Great Mother will smile upon your efforts and your progress in the art."

Someone was shaking him, and shaking him hard. "D-damn you!" he rasped. "Go away!"

But as Shu blinked and tried to get the offender in focus, one horrid fact quickly intruded itself upon his alcohol-addled mind: The sun was already up, and he had not got his master up and ready for the day! He shook his head, cursed, and sat up. But as he did, he noticed the rich trim on the intruder's kilt. An officer, and a high-ranking one at that!

Hastily Shu stood up, braced himself, and saluted.

Djoser scowled. "Why isn't your master up? Haven't you given him the message I gave you an hour ago?"

Shu rubbed his eyes. Message? He could not remember any message! He had been sleeping off the carouse Kamose had importuned him into joining last night and was certain that nobody had awakened him before this. "Beg pardon, sir? Message?"

"Gods preserve us! An urgent message from Elset's flank about an impending attack, and you haven't passed it on!" Djoser loosed a string of choice imprecations under his breath, then mastered himself. "Wake the king now, man! There's no time to waste! Elset contacted us at dawn, saying that the enemy was showing signs of attacking along our right flank!"

"Yes, sir!" Trembling with fear, Shu stumbled into the inner space of the king's great tent, wondering where his mind had been an hour ago. Imagine! Not waking up like that!

Behind Shu's retreating back, Djoser smiled, then quickly hurried to the chest beside Shu's bedroll. Swiftly and deftly he made the switch, returning the king's real sword to his own garment after sheathing the fake in the king's scabbard.

It only remained to have a soldier, picked at random, executed on trumped-up charges; he would claim later to have found the Sword of Glory among the man's possessions after his death. Amasis would be pleased. So, he was assured, would the Great Mother, who knew all and saw all.

Runners reached Apophis, over in the Hai camp. "They're taking the bait, sire!" the lead runner said breathlessly. "Elset has siphoned off half of Kamose's right wing to his own defense, leaving Kamose weak in the center. There seems to be confusion in their ranks. Kamose's center units are unprepared, and there's been no sign of the king at all."

Apophis's eyes gleamed, and his fingers curved eagerly around the hilt of his weapon. Even a day earlier he might have forborn to touch an iron weapon, but now it was as if strength flowed from the weapon into his hand. He smiled. "Splendid! Tell Rasmik to put the second phase of our plan into effect the moment Elset shows signs of counterattacking."

A great shout came from the Egyptian flank, a battle cry learned from the Nubians many years earlier. Apophis wheeled and looked across the plain. "They're doing it!" he squealed jubilantly. "They're going for it! Rasmik will fall back, and they'll be sucked into the trap! And there'll be Kamose, with one whole flank exposed!" He held up the black sword, a look of eager anticipation on his face for the first time in many months. "Now!" he cried. "Now we attack!"

III

Kamose clumsily dipped both hands into the basin and splashed his face. "Damn you!" he shouted again. "Why didn't you wake me sooner? What am I paying you for?" He did not wait for an answer. Instead he picked up the basin and upended its contents over his head. He tossed the bowl aside and stood, naked and weaving, in the cool morning air. "A towel! Quickly!"

Shu hastily handed one to him. "A thousand pardons,

sire," he said, using the formal mode of address he had abandoned years earlier. "I overslept. It'll never happen again, I assure you." He looked around desperately and found the king's loincloth. "Here, sire. And your sandals are right behind you."

But right behind *him*, it appeared, was another of the seemingly endless race of runners and messengers. He failed to recognize the man. "Yes? You have business with the king?"

"Beg to report," the man said, "the queen has arrived on a surprise visit and wishes an audience."

But behind him an imperious contralto voice broke in. "Kamose!" said Queen Mara. "An hour after dawn, and you're just getting up? No wonder we haven't taken Avaris yet."

Kamose wound his loincloth about him. "Mara, what are you doing here? We're in the midst of a crisis. Shu, get her out of here!"

"Put one hand on my arm, and you'll draw back a bloody stump," Mara warned the batman as he timidly approached her. She turned back to her husband. "What crisis? Not that I'm surprised to hear it. With you drinking yourself into a bleary-eyed stupor every night and oversleeping the next day, it's a miracle Apophis hasn't overrun your position a long time ago. Probably the only thing that saves you is his abject cowardice." Her eyes blazed. "Well, so far at least *that* defect doesn't appear to run in the family, I'll give you that. Debauchery, yes, and—"

"Curse it all, Mara, make your point. I'm busy. There's a morning attack going on. We got information that they were planning a move on our right flank, and we decided to hit them first."

" '*We* decided.' " She snorted. "I'd venture a guess that you've done no decision making today. Right flank would be Elset, I think. Well, he's a sound man—unlike Djoser, who was a good soldier before he took up with Amasis."

"Mara! What are you here for?"

She scorched him with a contemptuous look. "All right. It's this latest list of offenses against the Habiru. You've got the children out working on heavy construction projects, just like the parents. They're not up to it, and I countermanded the orders."

"You *what*?"

"And as for this business of parents having to inform authorities every time a woman comes to term—"

"They're not paying enough taxes! They're not reporting births! There's a tax on births. They're getting by with too much because you keep intervening. There are too damned many of them. They breed like rodents. One of these days I'm going to do something about that."

"How do you intend to stop people from having children?"

"Never mind."

"They believe that one of their male children will grow up to lead them back to their ancestral lands, and that bothers you, doesn't it? Because if the prophecy about you can be true, then theirs might be equally valid." Her tone became even more biting. "Your father heard some sort of drivel about how a son of his blood would rise to drive the Hai from Egypt."

"Be still, woman! My head is splitting!"

"Let it split, for all I care." Her beautiful features were like carved stone. "So that's why you're making them report all new births! You're afraid of their promised liberator." But suddenly her eyes narrowed, and her expression grew even harsher. "You *wouldn't* try to kill their children," she said. "Surely there's some shred of human decency left in you."

"For the love of the gods, shut up! With all the other things I have to think about, I don't have to stand here listening to someone bellowing at me like a fishwife!"

But now she stepped forward, and her forefinger stabbed out toward him. "Let me tell you something, Husband. If you try to do to these innocent children the same thing that your bloodthirsty father tried to do to you, I'll see that you regret it. Don't you turn away from me now, because if you let that wretched adviser of yours talk you into taking vengeance on those people now that they're defenseless—"

"Sire! Sire!" Shu cried out, reentering the tent after having slipped out during the argument. "The enemy! They're attacking!"

For a moment Kamose did not seem to understand the serious implications of Shu's report. "Quite likely they have," he said in a calm voice. "Elset has augmented his forces and can handle it."

"No, sire! Not the flank! The center! They're attacking our center! They're broken through the first lines of defense! They've taken us by surprise!"

Kamose stared. His mouth opened wide.

*   *   *

On the far right flank of the Egyptian army, the Lydians retreated repeatedly, putting up only token resistance and drawing Elset's men farther into the salient. Then, by a prearranged signal, all the retreating units stood and held their ground, and Elset's oncoming units suddenly found themselves up against men prepared to fight like demons for every handspan of ground. The first wave of attackers, suddenly encountering resistance, were chopped to bits by the Lydian front line. Then Elset withdrew, regrouped, and prepared to mount a second assault.

Meanwhile, Apophis, at the head of the main assault force in the center, drove forward against Kamose's weakened defenses, which had been raided for manpower by Elset in the dawn maneuver. Apophis's superior forces broke Kamose's front line and thrust heavily into the second rank before encountering units strong enough to hold. These battle-hardened troops fought fiercely and stopped Apophis's advance dead in its tracks. This gave new heart to the raw recruits who had broken, and they came back, whipped into shape with the flat of the sword by their seasoned leaders.

Kamose, having at last sent Mara to the rear in the company of Shu, hastily buckled on the sword belt Shu had handed him, and pushed into the ranks and found his way to the head of his line. On the way he encountered a young soldier whose eyes were glazed with fear. The recruit's face was covered with sweat, and his hands clawed weakly at the battle-ax in his palm. Kamose swore at him, ripped the ax from his hands, and used it to batter the boy to his knees. "Get to the rear!" he spat out with scathing contempt. "And keep on running! Because if I ever catch up to you, I'll have you impaled!"

He did not wait for an answer. He kept the ax, and when he had pushed his way through to the front line he immediately used it to cut a bloody swath as wide as his two arms could swing the weapon. One man fell before him, his face a red mask; he caught another in the temple and felt the skull give way before his powerful swing.

This was more like it! Arguing with a woman took all the strength out of you, and there was nothing to be gained by it. But this was a man's proper work. Here, at least, when a thing was settled, it was settled! With a fierce grin on his face he parried an attacker's sword thrust and, with minimal backswing, brained him with the flat of the ax.

A spearman came at him from the flank. With his free hand Kamose grabbed the spear and yanked it forward; with the other hand he hacked mightily at the spearman's neck and was rewarded by a gout of blood. Grabbing the spear with his empty hand, he pulled it free and hurled it into the crowd, where it caught a Hai soldier in the gut and brought him down.

Gone were his headache and the queasiness in his stomach. He laughed aloud and held his already bloodied borrowed weapon high. "Come and get me, you rabble!" he bellowed. "What? No takers? Is no one among you brave enough to face me?"

But before his words had left his mouth, he saw a bearded, scarred face that made him blanch. The man's angry eyes blazed with hatred. But two ranks of Hai troops separated Kamose from the bearded man. The two locked eyes, and Kamose's face shone with a terrible light. "Out of my way, you foreign scum!" he bellowed. "Do I see Apophis himself? Apophis at last?" He hacked a man's head off with one terrible blow, pushing toward the hated face. "Father! Come to me, dear Father! Come to me and fight, you cowardly swine! Or are you going to run off, as you did the last two times we met?"

That was enough. Apophis loosed a deafening roar and pushed his own men aside. "Clear a space!" he ordered. "Make way for the lord of Two Lands! Make room so that I can rid the world of this misbegotten pup and rectify my mistake in siring him on the scrawny body of a one-*outnou* slut in the streets of Avaris!"

The ranks on both sides miraculously parted, and the fighting slowed. A broad path opened up between father and son so both men could see each other from head to foot. Kamose and Apophis slowly circled each other. "Well, Father," Kamose said in a voice reeking with contempt, "have you come out to entertain my soldiers once more? Are we going to get another spectacle of the cowardly braggart shooting off his mouth only to turn tail and rush from the field the moment I unsheathe my sword?"

Apophis sneered. "What sword?" he asked. "I see no sword! I see only a battle-ax, which looks to be too heavy for your scrawny forearm. Or did you come here to fight with words? Your mother was good at that . . . until I killed her. Perhaps you take after her."

Kamose's eyes narrowed. This was a new, courageous Apophis. He looked to right and left of his father and thought he could see the reason. Close behind stood Rasmik, flanked by a dozen of the toughest soldiers in the Hai army. "Well, Father!" he said. "I understand your strategy now. I come forward to engage you, and your hulking dolts rush me from the side and take me prisoner."

"No!" Apophis shouted. "This is between you and me!" He ordered the flanking guards back, and Rasmik with them. "Now, puppy, draw the paltry Sword of Glory and fight me. Show me what you're made of!"

So insulting was Apophis's tone that Kamose's temper ran high. He tossed the battle-ax to one side contemptuously and unsheathed the heavy sword at his side. His concentration was centered on the hateful smirk on Apophis's bearded face, and the slight unfamiliarity of the weapon in his hand—its heft, its balance—went unnoticed.

"*Have at you, then!*" he screamed and, feinting a thrust, suddenly drew back to level a mighty, slicing cut at his father's face.

Iron engaged iron. The two men stood sword to sword, wrists trembling with the effort, each unable to deflect the other's hand.

Kamose suddenly noticed the color of the sword in his father's hand.

"Iron!" he said, shocked. "You! You carry iron!" He stepped back and disengaged. "But . . . but the Hai fear iron!" he said. "And yet you—"

"The old dog learns new tricks, puppy," Apophis gloated. "Come at me again, iron against iron! Or are you suddenly grown too frightened?"

"*Die, then!*" Kamose screamed, lunging forward and hacking powerfully down at his father's helmetless head.

As iron met iron again, there was a terrible jolt to Kamose's arm. He stepped back and looked at the suddenly lightened weapon in his hand. The blade had broken off a thumb's width from the hilt, and the pieces were scattered at Apophis's feet.

Apophis's smile was deadly triumphant, intolerable. He held his own sword high—black, dull, powerful!

Kamose fell back, stunned. The ranks closed around him. The moment of shocked silence was broken as his own men surged forward to surround him. The battle recommenced.

Kamose, covered with cold sweat, looked helplessly as Apophis, towering over the front ranks, fought valiantly, throwing him a contemptuous glance whenever he could.

"Run, puppy, run!" Apophis bellowed as Kamose watched the battle surge away from him. "But you can't hide! Sooner or later I'll catch up with you! And when I do, you're a dead man, do you hear me? Dead!"

IV

Mara was not there to see Kamose's ignominious personal defeat or the recovery that followed as Djoser's troops quickly and efficiently won back the ground they had lost. Elset, having inflicted great punishment on the retreating left flank of Apophis's army, fell back to erase the huge salient.

She missed all this, commandeering a chariot from her husband's stock and galloping back to the river. Her total understanding of Kamose's prebattle frame of mind had left her panicked. She knew his next step and had to be prepared against it.

At the royal docks the guards moved together as if to halt her progress but fell back when she showed no sign of stopping before reaching the ships. She raced past them and made an expert charioteer's racing dismount, one that would have made her royal tutors proud. "Miriam!" she called out in her strong voice. "Miriam, where are you?"

"Here, my lady," said a voice on board the smallest of the docked vessels.

"I'll come on board," Mara said. "We can talk privately in the cabin." She leapt lightly from the wharf to the pitched deck on the little ship and embraced the girl hastily before they went below.

"Miriam, I came as fast as I could. I want you to get back to your people and spread the word: I think Kamose is going to order something really terrible, and I want you to be ready for it." Mara was visibly tense. "I think he's going to order that all your male children born from now on be put to death."

"Oh, he wouldn't! Please tell me he wouldn't!"

Mara frowned. "I can't. I just saw him. He's on the edge, maybe a little insane. Something's happened to him. My spies say the cult uses the sacred mushroom, which has a permanent effect on a man's ability to think rationally." Miriam was about to say something, but Mara waved it away impatiently. "I'll bet he's heard a garbled version of that vision Levi had a couple of years ago, the one about the sacred child who would grow up to lead your people back to Canaan. He's seized upon that as an excuse to persecute you."

"What can I do?"

"Get back to your people, to Levi directly. He'll know how best to use the information. From now on your women will have to deliver their babies themselves, in secret, and stay away from all midwives. I know Kamose hasn't given the order yet, but I'm sure he will. Keep the pregnant women out of sight as much as possible."

"Yes, ma'am. I'll tell him. What else?"

"Good girl. Since the vision Levi had said only that a male child was going to do it, I suspect Kamose will leave the girl babies alone."

"But what do we do with the boy children?"

"I'll have to give that some thought. Maybe Levi will have some idea how best to hide them."

"Yes, ma'am." Miriam suddenly thought of something, though, and her face showed it. She put one hand over her mouth, and her eyes widened in horror.

"What's the matter?" Mara asked.

"Oh, nothing. Nothing, my lady."

"Miriam, you'd better tell me."

"There are a number of women just now who have recently learned they are pregnant."

"Go on."

Miriam's eyes were large and frightened. "They include my mother. Jochebed."

It was Mara's turn to register shock. "Jochebed? Isn't she too old?"

"Almost, ma'am. It came as a surprise. She thought her time was past."

"Guard her well," Mara said. "Tell Levi to take special care with her. Give her my blessing when you see her next. Now go! I'll clear it with the guards here. Go!"

*   *   *

By midafternoon the battle lines had stabilized, and it was obvious that no further assault by either side was likely to change the disposition of the two armies. Djoser and Elset met just behind the lines. "You heard what happened, I suppose?" Djoser asked.

"They said Kamose broke and ran," Elset said. "Is this true?"

"He did *not* run. If his sword had not been destroyed in the encounter with Apophis, he might well have turned and come again. But there was no facing iron with a borrowed bronze sword."

Elset's face mirrored his shocked surprise. "His sword *broke*? The Sword of Glory we've been hearing about all this time?"

"That's just it," Djoser remarked, looking curiously at him. "It wasn't Kamose's regular sword. Somehow a thoroughly inferior weapon found its way into his scabbard."

"How could that have happened?"

"It seems to have had something to do with his batman. We had him put to the torture, but we still don't know if he's a spy. Things don't look good for him; there was a message he was given for the king, and he didn't deliver it—too drunk to do so, I guess. He swore he'd never received it." He looked significantly at Elset. "It was from your own runner, about the decoying action they pulled on you this morning." Delicately the smallest, most subdued sign of reproach wormed its way into his words.

Elset shrugged. "Oh, you don't have to go easy on me. I got sucked in very badly on that one. It's the kind of thing that happens to all of us sooner or later, I'm afraid. I think I seem to remember it happening to you before the walls of Memphis. Not that anyone else would have handled the matter much better."

Djoser decided to let the matter pass. "Anyhow, the batman claims he doesn't know how the inferior sword found its way into the king's scabbard or, worse, what happened to the real one. You can imagine how angry Kamose is, particularly after having been humiliated in front of both armies. Of course we're having to put out a story for the benefit of the troops. They've believed the Sword of Glory yarn from the first. You can imagine this is quite a terrible disappointment."

"Of course. I'll issue an order threatening anyone caught embroidering the damned story—"

"—or even telling it. We don't even want them gossiping."

"Right. Anyone caught chattering about it will be tied to a wagon wheel and whipped until he passes out."

"I'll issue the same order in my command. Better for us to speak with one voice."

"Agreed. Look, I'm told you fought well today." Elset's smile was open, trusting. "I wanted to say—any differences we may have had over trifles in the past . . . well, as far as I'm concerned—"

"They're dead and buried," Djoser said. They grasped forearms solemnly. "Now let's go back to our commands and see what we can do to mend the damage done today."

Mara was about to approach Kamose's tent, but Amasis stepped out of the late-afternoon shadow and barred her way. "I beg your pardon, my lady," he said smoothly. "I shouldn't see him just now if I were you. He's in a very chancy mood, and the magi are considering giving him a dose of *shepenn* to calm his nerves."

"Don't you dare!" Mara snapped, her eyes flashing. "The person I catch slipping drugs to him now, I'll have him flayed." She looked at Amasis very directly as she spoke. "That means everyone," she said significantly.

"I was only thinking of his own good."

"Don't. That's a direct order from your sovereign's consort."

"I get the message, my lady," Amasis said, his eyes hooded and unreadable. "Still and all, I think I wouldn't visit him just now."

"I'll visit him when I please," she retorted. "Mind your own business. Now, step out of my way, or I will call a guard. Shall we find out once and for all who has more power around here—the queen or the boon companion?"

For answer Amasis, with an elaborate bow, stepped back and waved her ahead with a flourish. "As my lady wishes. Always remembering that I warned her about the king's state of mind."

She pushed past him and hurried up the path, only to stop dead, horrified.

"Oh, *no*," she moaned, closing her eyes and looking away, but not in time to avoid seeing the gory, wide-eyed, staring head, thoroughly recognizable despite the battering it had obviously taken, which now decorated the top of a tall pike at the opening to her husband's tent.

"No, Kamose!" she said hoarsely. "Not Shu, your oldest friend, your most faithful servant, who's waited on you hand and foot ever since the Battle of Thebes."

She shielded her eyes and went inside the tent, thoroughly shaken.

On the rug, Kamose sat cross-legged, looking at the black, unbroken, unblooded sword at his feet. He looked up at her, bleary-eyed. He had been drinking. Or was it the mushroom? The *shepenn* Amasis had mentioned earlier?

"He had gambled it away," he whispered. "Teti's sword. He had gambled it away, and when I had to go into battle, what did he hand me to fight with? A piece of garbage, a sword so badly made that it came apart the first time my father hit it."

"Kamose," she said as gently as she could, "do you really think Shu could have done that to you? Do you think he thought you were too stupid to notice he'd given you the wrong weapon?"

Kamose stared at her.

"I heard all about it. But nobody told me you'd had him killed."

His eyes looked infinitely sad. "He betrayed me. He wanted me to die."

"Nobody's batman wants his master to die. If the master dies, what does the batman live on? You are a destructive, mean-spirited fool!"

"D-don't talk to me like that," he warned. "Damned insolent bitch. Can't keep a civil tongue in her head. Comes from too much hanging around those damned Habiru. Well, I'll show them a thing or two. Think they're fooling me? Think they have me bamboozled? Why, when I was ten years old I knew more tricks for hiding from the authorities than they'll ever learn. Whatever they try, I'll be there waiting for them. Arrogant foreign sluts!"

"Kamose," she pleaded, "don't do it. Don't give the order."

He looked up. "It's too late. Out of my hands now. Order went out an hour ago." He grinned drunkenly. "All of them. Kill every last one of them. That'll show them!"

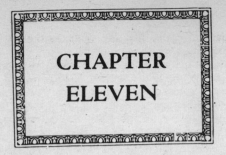

CHAPTER ELEVEN

Babylon

I

The great Hittite advance across northern Mesopotamia had stalled ignominiously a year earlier, when Mursilis had had to leave peace-keeping units of his great army in place and return to Hattusas to put down two minor revolts. Mari, however, remained in Hittite hands, as did Haran and Carchemish—the smaller cities northwest of the northern capital.

Nevertheless, the great parade of caravans across the northern reaches of the Euphrates had resumed, and now the whole trade route was open to any caravans not bearing the banners of Babylon, and it connected both Shinar and Elam with the ports along the Great Sea. From time to time, caravans from exotic places pulled up before the walls of Babylon, caravans whose personnel spoke Greek, Lydian, Canaanite, and the North African tongues. Trade was busy, as if no war, declared or otherwise, had begun two years before.

Today was a day like any other, as the last of the overland processions encamped outside the walls of the great
Shinarian capital an hour before sundown. Criton, having
nothing better to do, mounted to the top of the wall to
converse with his friend Simakura of Ebla, captain of the
guards for this watch, and to look down from the tall battlements at the five or six sprawling tent cities that were beginning to assemble at riverside. "Hail!" he said, saluting the
captain. "What news have we today?"

"Nothing much," Simakura replied, leaning forward, looking down, his elbows atop the wall. "The usual rabble, I
think. If there were anyone worth mentioning, I suspect
Mursilis's thugs back at Ebla wouldn't have let him through.
Tell me, my friend, about the life below the walls. I've been
doing double shifts up here ever since that fever came to
town, and I'm totally out of touch with civilian affairs."

Criton shrugged. "My master's affairs continue to prosper. I suspect that your king is going to adopt him formally
one of these days. Did you hear that Samsi-ditana had proposed to name the Street of the Bridge after Seth, because he
built it."

"Gods! You mean the one that runs from the Esagila
across the bridge into the new city?"

"Yes. There was to have been a great monument erected,
with a small ziggurat and a frieze depicting my master's
accomplishments since his arrival. But Seth would have none
of it. Therefore the street is being named after his grandfather. Officially it will be the Street of Hadad."

Simakura gave him a crooked grin. "Sound thinking.
Hadad was the only person who ever successfully thwarted
the Shepherds when they swept across the country. He's a
folk hero in all of upper Mesopotamia, particularly where the
Hittites hold sway now."

"Oh, yes," Criton agreed. "I'm sure Samsi-ditana knows
very well what he's doing—the more so since it's now the
most important street in the city, connecting both sides of the
river for the first time and running between the tower and
the Temple of Marduk."

Simakura rubbed his nose. "Well, Seth's still being honored, even if it's his grandfather's name they're using. He
deserves any honors he's received. The city will never be the
same. Imagine a workable pontoon bridge across the river!
I'd have sworn the Euphrates would never be bridged."

"Huh," Criton grunted. "You think *that's* something. He showed me plans the other night for a permanent bridge to replace it—one made of stone."

Simakura looked sharply at him. "You're joking." He paused, then continued. "No, I can see you're not."

Criton turned to look at the tent cities below. "The cost will be staggering, and I wouldn't want to bet on the life expectancy of the slaves who are going to have to build it. But Samsi-ditana authorized it yesterday." His eyes narrowed. "Good heavens, look down there. Is that an Egyptian flag over that tent?"

Simakura scowled and squinted in the fading light. "You know," he said, "I think you're right. How many years has it been since an Egyptian caravan called here? I can't remember. The Shepherds have been in the way since before I was born, and you couldn't get a caravan through."

"That's the flag of Shepherd Egypt, or I'm a blind man," Criton said. "Imagine a Hai caravan here! I've got to look into this. There may be news of my master's home country."

"Wait," Simakura said, putting his hand on Criton's hard forearm. "You have a talent for poking your nose into places where it isn't wanted."

"Oh, there won't be any troub—"

"Don't count on that. If you're really set on going down there, let me give you a guard or two."

Criton smiled. "Thank you for your concern. I'll take Khet and Anubis with me if I can find them. Anubis has grown bored, having nobody to brawl with."

"How much good is Khet in a fight? He drinks too much."

"You'd be surprised. He can take care of himself pretty well for someone who loves the grape as much as he does. No, the two of them will do, I think. And you can stop worrying." He clapped the captain familiarly on the arm. "When are you and I going to get drunk together? The girls down at the Inn of the Two Oxen, in the Merkes, have been asking about you. They ask me, 'Where's the fat captain with the big purse and the small—'"

"Damn your eyes! Get out of here! And—take care of yourself."

Criton found his two comrades quite easily. Anubis was in a nearby square arm wrestling a towering black mercenary from the African coast. Khet, already half-inebriated, was going from onlooker to onlooker taking bets.

Criton pushed his way into the center of the gathering. He took Khet's elbow in a firm grasp and bent over Anubis. "Come on, both of you," Criton said. He looked at Anubis, who was locked arm-to-arm with the black giant, his face glistening with sweat. "There's not much time before the gate closes, and I want to pay a visit to one of the caravans that just arrived outside the walls."

Khet made a face. He looked around; there were no new takers anyway. "Oh, all right. Come on, Anubis," he said in a comic whine.

"All right," Anubis agreed. Suddenly the fake strain vanished from his face, to be replaced with a patronizing smile. He looked the black in the eye, towering half a head taller than himself. "Give it your best shot, my friend."

The black strained, and the veins on his arm seemed ready to burst, but Anubis's arm did not budge.

Anubis's smile broadened. "That's your best?" he asked. And with one insultingly easy motion he bent the black man's arm steadily down toward the tabletop. "Come on, make it difficult. I'm not getting any exercise."

The black grunted an unintelligible curse as his forearm slammed into the tabletop.

Anubis smiled and let go. Then he stood and bowed with patronizing courtesy. "Good-bye, sonny. It's a pity to take your money, but there's a fat tavern bill waiting for me across town."

The black's eyes flashed and his hand clenched, but two knives, Khet's and Criton's, were now poised at either side of his neck. He blinked, gulped, and withdrew, leaving his fat purse on the table. Khet grabbed it up.

"All right," the clown said. "Outside the gate, you said?"

"Don't call me sire," the king requested. "Call me Father. It's only a matter of days, weeks at most, then it'll be a legal term."

"Please," Seth said. "In my country, becoming the legal son of another man when I had a father of my own, even if he were dead, would be considered an unforgivable insult to him and to my mother. I appreciate the sentiments, and I'm honored no end, sire." Seeing the hurt in Samsi-ditana's eyes, he hastened to assuage it: "It is no reflection on the affection I feel for you. In the two years since I've been here, you've been more than a father to me. You know what love I bear you, sire. You've made more of my dreams come true than any other man in the world could do. All my life I've dreamed of building things: great buildings, great towers and fortifications, great bridges—"

"Build them you shall. You will create a new Babylon." The gentle mouth curved upward inside the speckled beard, and the warm eyes seemed almost in tears. "Your name will live forever in the annals of this great city."

"I've dreamed of building a great temple of learning—a school and a library where the best of all the world's wisdom could be stored for the use of future generations and taught to the bright youth of our own time."

The king put a pudgy hand on his back, a father's comforting hand. "You will build it. You and I. I will order the stone quarried, and I will bring scholars, philosophers, poets, visionaries, and magi from all corners of the globe."

Seth looked down at the small, rotund man and thought: *If you only knew, you kind and comical little man, how very dear you've become to me. Father? Yes, and more. Could Ben-Hadad ever have meant as much to me? Or wonderful old Kedar? I feel as if I'd known you all my life. But how do I go about telling you that this thing isn't done among my people? How do I say it without hurting you?* "About the adoption," he said. "I . . .I'll think about it."

The king's shoulders rose and fell. "No, you won't," he said, crestfallen. "You've made up your mind. I can see it in your eyes. And I can see that it is not out of lack of love or veneration for me." He sighed deeply. "Well, there is only one thing left to do." He picked up a little bell and rang it; the sound was tiny and sounded far, far away, but Seth could hear sandaled feet scuttling hurriedly about in response to what was evidently a command. Then people had been listening to their conversation!

The king put his two palms together before his chest. "As you will see, my wise Seth, the king is but a mortal and not notable for wisdom or for great deeds."

"Sire! You, whose fame spreads far and wide—"

"Nevertheless, I am not without resources. It is true that I have offered you most of what I have, in my vain scheme of tempting you. But there are one or two things I have not shown you."

"Sire," Seth said, putting an affectionate hand on the smaller man's shoulder. "I doubt if there is a thing in the world that you could possibly show me that would impress me any more than I already—"

"Hush," the king ordered lovingly but firmly. "There is a side of me that no man sees. As well it should be. I have thirty wives. They rank among the most exquisite women in the world. Not only are they beautiful and trained in the arts of love and friendship, but they have been given education far beyond the station of any woman ever born in Shinar. One is a poet of fabled gifts. Her verses are memorized and revered wherever in the world our language is spoken. Another makes delicate sculptures; yet another sings as no nightingale ever sang and plays the kithara as only your grandfather Hadad of Haran could play it. These and many more in my hareem serve to make me the happy man you see before you."

"Sire, if—"

"Yet none of these has given me the man-child I wanted. Three have borne such, and all three died in infancy. Now that I find a son of my own heart, I do not propose to let him escape the destiny the gods have so rightly chosen for him."

There was a noise behind them. Seth would have turned, but the king held him and looked up into his eyes. "There is someone I would have you meet," Samsi-ditana said. "Turn and meet my daughter Shala."

Seth, his arms released, blinked and turned slowly. He felt the king's hand on the middle of his back. The king's voice was gentle and loving as he spoke to the girl before them. "Shala, my dove," he said, "let me present Seth. The man I have chosen to be your husband."

II

His heart pounding with embarrassment, Seth looked at the girl. All he could see at first were large, luminous, meltingly brown eyes regarding him with amused curiosity.

When, overwhelmed, he looked back at the king, he carried away the impression that the girl was smiling at him, perhaps even laughing softly. He forced his eyes to hold to the king's.

"Sire," he sputtered, "really, you shouldn't have. . . .You should have told me beforehand. I don't know what to—"

"Father," the girl said, "he's beautiful. You didn't tell me he was so pleasing to the eye."

Seth turned back to her. She had full red lips, a generous mouth, and high cheekbones. She was almost an Oriental beauty, with almond eyes . . . which, when they opened wide, as they were now, were captivating, mezmerizing. The shade of brown was exquisite: warm, with great depth. Again the enormous brown eyes met his, and this time they held him. "L-look, miss, I mean your royal, uh, I mean your . . ."

"And he's funny," she said, obviously pleased. And now she did smile, and there was no mistaking it. There was the little tinkling sound of laughter in her voice. "What did you say his name was?"

"Seth, my dear," the king replied. "He comes from Egypt, and his family background is a most unusual one. Seth, I hope you'll indulge me for a moment while I tell Shala a bit about you. . . ."

As the king described Seth's illustrious ancestry, the young man tried to collect himself. He tried to speak. He tried to look worldly and, failing that, tried to look away. But her eyes held him. His mouth gaped, and he could not utter so much as a sound.

"He isn't very talkative, Father," she teased. "I think he's bashful." She walked around Seth, looking him up and down.

Seth, eye contact broken at last, gulped and looked back at her. Her figure was slim and delicate, with narrow hips and the breasts of one barely entering into womanhood. Yet she walked with complete assurance, as a mature woman might. Her little hands and feet were tanned and bare and exquisitely made. She wore only a simple shiftlike garment devoid of ornamentation, and the simplest of gold bracelets and anklets. But when she faced him again, all he could look at were her eyes.

"Perhaps he is bashful," the king responded to her assessment. "He's led a pretty detached life. I'm afraid, my dear, that there has been precious little love and friendship in it. In some ways Seth is as innocent as a child." It was apparent from Shala's expression that she was not certain whether to adjudge her intended's innocence as a bonus or a deficit.

"Of course, my dear," Samsi-ditana went on quickly, "Seth is quite possibly the most brilliant man ever to enter our city. He is a master of virtually every discipline our magi can contemplate. In one stroke he can analyze a military problem, find an enemy's weakness, and suggest the precise maneuver to exploit it. He has studied the traffic problems of Babylon and in two days came up with a reordering of our streets that will relieve congestion without sacrificing physical beauty in our processional parkways and thoroughfares. Indeed, in the matter of design, he harks back to his grandfather, perhaps the finest artist ever to bear Shinarian blood. He is so natural an artist, he hasn't any idea he *is* one."

"How can that be?" Shala asked, smiling sweetly at Seth. "You'd think that an artist would have to intend to create a work of art in order to accomplish it."

"Oh, no, my dear. The more functional a thing is, the greater its natural beauty. Seth's mind instantly devises the least cluttered and complicated design a thing can assume, and that always turns out to be the most stunningly beautiful. You should see the civic buildings he's designed! It will take me the rest of my days to build them all, but I've made up my mind that's how I'm going to finish out my life, my darling. I'm going to be remembered as the king who, with Seth's designs, made Babylon into the most breathtakingly beautiful city that ever decorated the world."

"How exciting, Father! You'll have to show me the plans. Or—couldn't Seth show me?" She looked back at her father, and the smile became an impish grin. "He *can* speak intelligibly, can't he?"

Samsi-ditana chuckled. "Oh, he can talk your ear off when he's ready." There was no disrespect intended, only a deep and abiding affection. "Just now we have him badly flustered. His life has not prepared him for social graces, and he has no small talk at all. He always says what he means."

"I think I'll like that," she remarked, "provided he likes me. If he didn't like me, I think I'd die rather than hear him blurt it out."

Seth looked hopelessly from one to the other. He opened his mouth and shut it several times. The girl smiled at him. He knew that, had he accepted Samsi-ditana's offer to adopt him, he would have been this lovely girl's brother and not her intended husband. But was that what he wanted? Did he want to live in Babylon—homeland of his distant ancestors Belsunu and Ahuni—for the rest of his days?

"Seth's life," the king continued, "has been one of gathering immense learning but never being able to put it to total use. Shala, my sweet, I have decided to see that Seth realizes his dreams of designing a new and exquisite architecture, of building a sane and sound and wise society, and of creating a world in which poverty and crime have disappeared. As king of the richest nation in the world, I have the means to make Seth's dreams a reality."

"What a noble goal!" Shala breathed.

"It is, my darling. And you have a part to play in all this too, my dearest. You, with the simple and matchless beauty of form, heart, and spirit, which you inherited from your late mother. You, with your peerless honesty, devotion, and goodness. You, with—if my hopes are answered—your fertile loins, to bear him the sons and daughters who will bring comfort to his heart in his aging years, as you yourself bring it to mine."

"Oh, Father, how can he resist? How unhappy it would make both of us!"

It was more than Seth could take. He gave one last desperate look at both of them and tried one more time to speak but found his throat too dry. He realized that his clenched hands were shaking. He lurched forward and made for the door. Many steps down the long hall, down the long avenue of gorgeous tapestries, he broke into a stumbling run. But even as he escaped from their company, he knew it was no good. This was something he could never run from. There was no place on earth where his destiny, the thing for which he was born, would not follow him and find him. Whatever gods there might be, it was for this that they had made him.

He stopped and made for a wall, to stand leaning, without strength, against a section of tapestry showing a goddess pursuing a mortal man. Her naked limbs were as slim as a deer's. He closed his eyes. But when he did, all he could see were Shala's large, warm brown eyes, looking right into his soul.

Who am I? he wondered helplessly. *What fate has brought me here? And why now?*

He knew with a terrifying certainty that everything Samsi-ditana had said was true. Here, finally all the threads of his life were coming together. Here was the one place in the world where all his dreams could at last be realized. Here was the one place where the funds and the manpower were available to build the ideal city. And the monarch wanted nothing more than to realize his, Seth's, private vision. Here he had found a kindred soul wise enough to find beauty in the pattern that his own mind had formed—a man who not only shared his vision but loved him dearly for having had it in the first place.

He had found a father in the world, the father he had never known. Not Ben-Hadad. Not Kedar. Not Baliniri or even the wise but enigmatic Marduk-nasir. He had found a father, once and for all in this life, in Samsi-ditana, king of Babylon.

He closed his eyes again, saw the great brown eyes, and realized with a start that he had found more: He had found love in a woman so beautiful, in mind and body alike, that the thought of her left him feeling battered and shaken. He would never be the same again.

He had found a home at last, a safe haven after the storm, a place to put down roots. The place to build a house and live in it with her and someday their children.

But what was the tiny voice inside him that said *No*? What was the distant command that said *Beware*? Why, on the brink of a great victory, did a part of him hold back and seek to deny them the acceptance they both wanted to hear?

He balled his fists and leaned his forehead against the tapestry. "*No!*" he said between clenched jaws. "I'll not listen! I want to stay! I want it all! The city, the king, and Shala! I want everything!"

III

Babylon, at first glance, seemed the most well-protected city in the world. The inner city, divided by the great Euphrates, lay within the safe shelter of walls so formidable that they made the sloping fortifications of the Shepherd Kings' fortresses, far to the west, look like child's play for an attacking army.

In actuality there were three walls around the city, plus two artificial bodies of water that encircled the two interior walls. The dual nature of the inner fortification was evident from one look at the fabled Ishtar Gate, actually a double portal separated by a courtyard. This was the first part of the present fortifications to be completed, and upon repeated tests during a war with nearby Elam, the gate had proved very satisfactory. Anyone who managed to breach the outer wall found himself suddenly in an open space between the walls and vulnerable to arrows and pikes and boiling oil from the battlements above. The second, inner, wall was higher and thicker than the first one. The whole system of inner walls came to 150 feet. Above these, ninety-foot towers looked menacingly down, manned by the elite of Shinarian bowmen.

To complicate an invader's approach, one had to negotiate a vast encircling moat fed by the waters of the Euphrates—a moat stocked with crocodiles, which were attracted to the city by the army's habit of tossing garbage over the top of the city wall. Outside the moat lay open land given over to the encampment of the 10,000-man city guard . . . although at the present time this unit had been halved to provide troops to guard the border areas against the Hittites. This open land was in turn encircled first by a canal, then by a much lower outer wall. Finally, beyond this outermost limit a system of warning posts was manned by pickets able to transmit complex information by a series of smoke signals.

It was in the area between the moated inner walls and the surrounding canal that the great caravans had gathered at day's end. In the tent city erected by the caravans, there were the aroma of meat being seared and the grunts and groans of livestock moving sluggishly at hobble.

Khet and Anubis wandered, making friends, in the area around the great campfire set by the Egyptian delegation. Although a Hai-owned caravan in principle, the camp was largely staffed with native Egyptians working for the owner, one Kaloust of Sile, a purebred Hai born and raised in Egypt. Criton had gone to seek audience with Kaloust; Khet and Anubis dallied now with the Hai's servants.

Their commerce with the strangers was made easier by the fat skinful of wine Criton had brought along. It was the finest wine of Nineveh, brought down the Tigris a full year earlier by traders. The Egyptians were not used to finding a common drinking wine this good and had repeatedly said so in the course of their heavy imbibing.

"Ah," said a porter called One Eye. "If this is what you people ordinarily drink here, I'm going to jump ship as soon as our master looks the other way." He winked his one good eye and lustily drank again, passing the bottle to Khet as he wiped his mouth with the other hand.

"Jump ship?" Anubis echoed. "You sound like a sailor who's gone ashore."

The man nodded. "Hai Egypt hardly has a merchant navy anymore. The locals now control so much of the delta that our Hai overlords are hard-pressed to find anything of value to trade to the other countries around the Great Sea in exchange for basic goods. And what we do have is bartered away by Apophis for armaments and the salaries of mercenary soldiers."

"Did you hear that?" Anubis asked Khet. "The war appears to be going Kamose's way."

Khet took another drink and passed the skin around. A towering porter nicknamed Aurochs, half a head taller even than Anubis and with slightly distorted features, drank deeply and smiled lopsidedly at the comrades. "Oh, yes," he rumbled in his deep voice. "Egypt might well be controlled by Egyptians before I'm an old man. I sometimes think that Apophis's stubbornness is the only thing holding the Hai army together. If Kamose could ever get the old man to fight him, I think he'd kill him. And if he did, that'd be pretty near the end of Shepherd resistance." He laughed cavernously. "We'd be out of a job, One Eye."

"I can't wait," One Eye replied, taking a drink. "Mind you, you two, this is treason we're talking."

"Your secret's safe with us," Anubis assured him. "I'm from Bast. The Shepherds took my town when I was a chick barely hatched." A thought struck him suddenly. "Tell me, who holds Bast now?"

"Kamose," One Eye answered. "But don't cheer too loudly just yet. Things aren't very smooth within Kamose's ranks. He's left a foreigner in charge, this Makare—"

"Ugh!" Aurochs broke in. "There's a mean one. *Likes* to kill, he does. Mind you, I'm no sissy. I've killed my share. So have both of you, probably." Khet and Anubis nodded gravely. "But this fellow makes a game out of it. He's very strong—as strong as you, perhaps, Anubis. I'm not sure he's not as strong as me, but I wouldn't care to indulge in a test of strength with him." His words came out slowly and thoughtfully. "Tell them about Makare, One Eye. Remember the time he pulled the head off a kid who'd thrown a rock at him?"

"I don't even like to think about it," One Eye said, cringing. "He's from someplace in Syria, where life's cheaper than it ever gets among civilized people. He and his friend Amasis are thick with Kamose, unfortunately. They all used to be pals out to sea, when they were slaves on the pirate boats. Some time back they just showed up in the delta, bringing this ugly northern religion of theirs. Full of violence—people cutting themselves, going crazy from eating mushrooms, and killing people in some terrible ritual when the moon's right."

Anubis and Khet exchanged significant glances.

"Ever since Makare and Amasis showed up, Kamose has been a different man—and a worse one. I have some serious doubts about what kind of king he'd wind up being if the Hai were driven out of Egypt."

"I thought you were on the Hai side of the lines," Khet commented, all seriousness. "How do you know all this?"

"Oh, I come and go for my master. If he needs something they only have on the other side, he sends me. There are no set borders now. Travel may require a bribe or two, but I always bring back whatever my master wants."

Khet looked Anubis in the eye. "Our own master has to hear this. The war's winding down. I have a feeling Egypt needs us."

Anubis nodded. "There is also the promise Seth made to bring back the Sword of Glory that Apophis was supposed to be so frightened of. Seth did make a commitment, plain and simple, and he's not usually the type to say one thing and do another."

Khet scratched his head, thinking. "Well, when Criton comes out of the tent, we'll ask him what to do. I wonder what he and this Kaloust fellow are up to in there."

"Please," the Hai trader said, "you dishonor my table by eating so little. Have more. Let me call for more wine."

"No, no," Criton protested. The two sat cross-legged on cushions. "I've put on a bit around the middle lately, and my master criticizes me for the fact. It's imperative that I obey *his* orders rather than those of my stomach, which craves further assaults upon your matchless hospitality."

Listen to yourself, Criton thought. *Greasing him up like any born Shinarian. Only two years here, and I am beginning to sound like a man born on the banks of the Euphrates.* A servant approached with ripe figs. "No, no," he repeated. "Please."

"Very well," Kaloust said. "You will at least do me the honor of taking one of my tents, you and your friends, for the night. It's too late to return to the city. The gate will be closed by now. On the morrow perhaps you would introduce me to your master, if you'd be so kind."

"I'll try," Criton agreed. "You must remember, however, that he was the closest of friends with virtually everyone in the Red Lands hierarchy. It would behoove you to keep talk of political matters to the noncontroversial."

"My thoughts precisely," Kaloust said.

His eyes, Criton noticed, were almost black, difficult to read even in broad daylight and impossible now. Kaloust had the hooked nose of the Hai but the manners of an Egyptian. The Hai, after a century in Egypt, were Egyptianized in so many ways, they had lost their national soul. No wonder Kamose was beating them now. "What brings you to Babylon when times are so troubled back home? If you're not sure how things are going back in Egypt, you must have left your affairs in the hands of subordinates."

"A good point. Honestly, my friend, I have no faith in the future of my people among the Egyptians. I am taking steps to remove my chattels and movables to the northern areas. I now own property in various Hai-held cities: Megiddo, Damascus, and some others. I had intended to purchase property in Carchemish, but then the Hittites came."

"Ah, yes," Criton said, nodding. "You did well not to. So you are moving your whole base of operations."

"Yes, probably to Damascus. From there I will continue in commerce. I am here to open new markets. From Egypt to Babylon is a long, long way. But from Damascus . . ." He held up both hands in an expressive gesture.

"Ah, yes. Babylon is a natural market for a merchant based in Damascus. I see you have given serious thought to the future. I commend you."

Kaloust sighed and again gestured, this time expressing

impotence against the whims of the gods. "But this Hittite
business!" he complained. "Surely your king does not approve! Hittites on the march! Hittites in Mari! This in the
land of great Hammurabi! How can this be?"

"I think Samsi-ditana is making a strategic retreat to a
more easily defensible second line of defense. The Hittites'
presence is not quite as serious as you may think."

"But they're in Mari! The great city of Mari, simply
given up to the Hittites almost without resistance! I could
never have imagined it. My ancestors, cutting across Mesopotamia on their way to Egypt, gave Mari a wide berth and
did not attempt to take it as we took Carchemish. Why?
Because we feared Mari? Of course not. We were a million
strong in those days, before the hellish trip across the Sinai,
before the civil wars."

"Then why?"

"We wanted to avoid an all-out war with Babylon. True,
we might have won, but we would have lost more men than
we ever conceivably stood to gain in wealth or power. Instead
we attacked weaker links in the chain of cities along the
upper Euphrates and its tributaries."

"Wise enough," conceded Criton.

"That is exactly why I cannot understand this inaction on
the part of your king. Does he not take the Hittites seriously?"

"I suppose he does—"

"Suppose? These are the Hittites! Men armed with iron
weapons!"

Criton's words came out before he had given thought to
them, and the moment he had said them, he wished them
back. "Babylon will have iron weapons," he said. "We have a
Child of the Lion here. My master, Seth—"

He stopped himself, but the damage had been done.

Kaloust reacted to it immediately. "*Seth?*" he asked. "Seth,
son of Ben-Hadad, here? *He's* your master, the man I'm to
meet tomorrow?"

"Why, yes."

"And his quest is complete? He has learned the secret?"

"Well . . . yes." He cursed his loose tongue. It must be
the wine! He had had too much wine. He had to control
himself now.

"So he was related to poor Teti," Kaloust said. "I'll be
sure to express my condolences." His eyes were narrow now,

watching Criton with renewed interest. "How the Egyptians will miss her. Her death, and Riki's leaving the army . . ."

Criton stared. "Teti? Dead?" he asked incredulously. "How?"

"The plague, dear fellow. Didn't you hear? It swept through all of Egypt as far as the cataracts, killing Hai and Egyptian alike." He stopped, and his expression changed. "But if you haven't learned of this, then you won't have heard."

"Heard what?"

"Seth's mother. She and old Kedar."

Criton stared openmouthed. Tuya? Dead?

IV

"Was I too bold, Father?" the girl asked. She sat, slim hands on narrow knees, on the couch opposite Samsi-ditana. Her eyes, looking up at him, showed her concern. "I know I shouldn't have teased him, but when I kept speaking and he didn't answer—"

"Couldn't answer, more likely," her father pointed out. "Some situations render Seth inarticulate and unable to cope. He had ten years of the most intense loneliness and unhappiness before Kedar, the old teacher, took him in hand. If I remember the story properly, Seth didn't speak to anyone."

"Oh, the poor dear. I feel terrible! But we'll make it up to him, won't we, Father?"

"If he'll let us," Samsi-ditana said gently.

"I just think we should love him and care for him, and if we do that, he'll come around. Unless he was not pleased by me."

"Oh, no. You need have no fear in that regard. His eyes followed you everywhere. You go upstairs, and I'll talk to him. I have no intention of letting him get away."

She rose and embraced him. "I have faith in you. You won't let me down. Oh, Father, I'm going to love him so."

"So you shall. He's a very lovable young man. And if anyone in the world could entice him, it'd be you. You're the image of your mother." He sighed.

She nestled in his arms, patting him on the back. "Mother was very dear to you?"

"Among other things she gave me you, the solace and comfort of my declining years." He kissed her forehead. "Now run along, my dear, and I'll go talk to Seth."

An attendant materialized at his elbow, however. "Sire," he said, "the lord Enzu awaits. He says his message is urgent."

Samsi-ditana frowned. "You run along, Shala." He turned back to the servant. "Take me to him, please."

Criton pulled at Anubis's sleeve. "Come on, we have to talk." He looked around him and frowned. The usual hangers-on had descended upon the camp: whores, jugglers, mountebanks, and purveyors of narcotics and drink. Anubis had had too much wine already, and Khet was dancing drunkenly before the fire with an equally inebriated woman, stout of beam and half-dressed.

"Confound it," the giant complained. "I was beginning to relax. All right. Should I bring him?" He jerked a thumb at Khet.

Criton looked the round-faced clown up and down. Khet was trying to balance his sword on his nose now; thank the gods, this time it was in its scabbard. "No. He'd be of little use to us now."

He led Anubis well away from the revelers, to a bare place from which they could see any eavesdroppers. "This ought to do. Look, I have the unfortunate idea that Seth's beginning to put down roots here, and I don't like it."

"Why not? I could settle here, I think. As a matter of fact, I've been offered a situation. It pays better than any position I ever had. Chief of the guards in a rich fellow's house."

Criton's disapproving glare was visible in the moonlight. "You, too?" he asked. "I thought we all took a vow to stick together."

"I know. But I think the king's going to try to adopt Seth. And where would that leave us? Oh, we'd be all right for now. We'd have a job for a while, as a sort of glorified boon companion, but that's not a thing you can grow old with."

Criton growled with frustration. "You of all people I thought I could rely upon."

"You can," the giant assured him, "while I'm still needed. But if Seth goes into the king's household, who'd need me? There's no dearth of big louts with bulging muscle. And would Seth have time for me? I doubt it."

Criton cursed. "Seth made a vow," he said evenly. "A vow to return to Egypt when his Chalybian quest was done and bring with him the sword that would drive the Hai out of Egypt. Egypt's your country, not mine. Why should I, the foreigner, have to be the one to remind you what your duties are?"

"Your point," the giant said slowly, "would be better made in a less insulting tone, my friend."

"I'm sorry. But I have a theory: Seth chose the three of us as companions for specific reasons. Khet he chose because Khet makes him laugh."

"And I am his bodyguard, more or less. If the king makes Seth his son, he will have as his bodyguard the entire Shinarian army."

Criton nodded impatiently. "I'll grant you that. I've been trying to figure out just where I fit in here, ever since he asked me to come along on this quest. And I think I'm here to act as his conscience—the man who reminds him of the things he doesn't want to be reminded of. Including the fact that he made solemn promises to people who depend upon him."

"Eventually he's got to decide upon matters like that for himself. He's a big boy now."

"True," Criton said. "And if he becomes heir apparent, I may well turn out to be not only expendable but a distinct annoyance."

Anubis scratched his nose. "I must say this for you," he said. "You're a realist."

"Greeks tend to be. We live in a hard country, barely fit for sheep to graze in. Anyway, there are things Seth needs to know—about Egypt, about the direction the war is taking back there, and about his mother. Tuya left him quite a tidy little fortune. There's a bit of it in trust for that urchin she adopted a while back, but the rest is Seth's. He'll be a wealthy and powerful man in Thebes now."

"As wealthy and powerful as a king's son in Babylon?"

Criton scowled. "Of course not. But damn it! There's Aset. Does he know about her? Does he know he's left a bastard by her in Egypt? That she's off wandering with the

child, indigent, without protection? He doesn't even know
he's got a son!"

Anubis gently put a gigantic hand on Criton's shoulder.
"Hold, my friend. Does he absolutely need to know? The
only people he's ever likely to meet who know about it are
you and me. And I won't tell if you won't."

Criton's face was a mask of pain. "Confound it! It's not
your *job* to tell him things like that! But it is mine! Don't you
understand?"

Anubis stepped back. "I begin to understand. You take
things very seriously, don't you? I mean beyond the fact of
being a paid companion of Seth."

"Damn you, I'm his friend. That has nothing to do with
being paid. If he stopped paying me tomorrow, I'd still be his
friend."

The giant squeezed his shoulder gently. "I've misunder-
stood you," he confessed. "Obviously you have to do what
you have to do." He took his hand away and folded those
monstrous arms over his broad chest. "Conscience, eh? You
make a very good one, I see. Me, I can do without one. But
Seth's different."

"Yes, yes," Criton agreed. "He's a bit of an innocent."
He clasped hands in front of his chest. "Until he becomes
totally aware of everything around him, he will need the likes
of me. Even when he's a king's son."

Anubis did not say anything for a long moment. Then he
spoke in that deep, cavernous giant's voice of his. "Yes," he
said. "He'll need them still. But will he *want* them?"

Enzu was Samsi-ditana's most trusted spy. Fluent in
every language that had ever been spoken in the streets of
Babylon, he could, with a slight change of clothing and gesture, pass for virtually any nationality. He had most recently
passed for a Hittite, and his beard was still cut after their
fashion; only his clothing made a credible Babylonian of him.

He stood now before the king, looking up at the raised
dais in the audience room.

"I don't care what the generals say," Enzu said. "Sire, I
was there. I was inside Mari. I was in the army camps. I tell
you Mursilis is planning something big, and soon."

"He's back in Hattusas putting down a rebellion. Everyone knows that."

"Yes, sire, but he did not take his general Anittas with him. He left Anittas behind with specific instructions. Troops are massing along all our southern front. They've been building the garrison for months now. Sire, Anittas is building an impressive instrument there to do Mursilis's bidding the moment he gets back."

Samsi-ditana said, "Well, I'll take it all under advisement. Have you supped? Have you been home to see your family yet? How do you like the new bridge? I'll bet you never thought you'd be able to walk across the Euphrates. Well, you should see the plans Seth has made for the permanent one. All stone! Built to last a thousand years! It'll become one of the wonders of the world!"

"Sire, please don't underestimate the importance of my words. I can't put too much emphasis on—"

"Come now, dear fellow, rest assured I'll give it serious thought. To show you my gratitude, you're invited to stay at the palace tonight. I'll wine and dine you like a conquering hero. You haven't met Seth yet, have you?"

"No, sire, but—"

"Come now. No one says 'but' to the king. It's settled. You're dining here tonight. I'll seat Seth on my right side, and you on my left. We'll have a splendid evening. You'll see."

V

"Seth," Criton implored, "I've got to talk to you."

Seth climbed atop a tall chair, the better to look down on the construction he had built atop the large, low, flat table. "Look," he said, the morning light dappling his head and shoulders through the latticed window. "See this wavy line? It's the Euphrates. And here's Babylon: the outer defenses here, the inner walls there. But *now* look. See this network here? I've devised a system of canals for diverting the spring floods. Imagine being able to farm all through the spring floods. The best part of it is, this can be done in a relatively short time. I can have this whole system in by next year."

"Seth. Please listen."

"In a moment, my friend. I've also been giving some thought to the city's defenses. Some chap—Enzu, I think the name was—came to dinner last night, and he says that the Hittites' advance has only been temporarily stopped and that Mursilis still has designs on Babylon."

"Seth, it's true. The Hittites are going to be a real problem soon."

Criton got no more than this out. Seth's mind was back on its one track again. "The only place we're vulnerable now is by water. Everything else is well defended. If the units south of Mari hold, no one can get through and encircle us. If they attack by land, they'll have a nearly impossible time getting through our multilayered system of defenses. And if I can get the canals in place by winter, that's one more way of controlling them. If, everywhere they turn, they're constantly having to cross water again and again under fire from our bowmen—"

"Seth! They may not wait until winter!"

"That's what Enzu kept saying last night, but the king didn't pay a lot of attention, so I suspect Enzu is a bit of an alarmist. Well, spies are supposed to be alarmists. And then the intelligence they gather is supposed to be analyzed by cooler heads."

"Seth, our world is being threatened even as we stand here! The Hittites won't stand still for your projects to be completed! And meanwhile, back home things have taken a couple of new turns that you haven't heard about. As a matter of fact, that's what I came to talk to you about."

"Back home? Criton, the longer I stay here, the more I think of *this* as my home. For the first time in my life I know what I really want to do. I know what I want to do next year, and the year after that, and so on until I'm an old man." Seth stepped down off the chair and smiled beatifically at his friend. "This place is a dream come true. The king has approved all my projects and is going to build everything. I begin to see how I can create a society without poverty and want and disease. When the Hittites see what we've got here, they won't want to destroy it. They'll ask us how we did it, and I'll tell them. It's going to be too good not to share with the world!"

"But Egypt . . ."

"Egypt too. They'll be the first nation I share it with.

But first I have to build it here, to prove it can be done if only we try, if only we believe. Don't you see?"

"Seth! You made a promise to your friends to return! Have you forgotten?"

For the first time Seth gave clear evidence of having heard. His face suddenly turned sober. "No, my dear friend. I haven't forgotten. But here's a chance to bring back to them something worth far more than anything I have ever promised." He stepped forward, put his hands on his friend's shoulders, and looked Criton in the eye. "This is a chance I can't pass up. What is the one thing—other than the Hai— that keeps Egypt from being six times as rich as it is today?"

"I suppose losing a season to the floods every year. If we could farm four seasons and rotate crops—"

"Exactly. But in Egypt I could never get permission from any king to experiment with changing that. But here I can build the canals to control the water around Babylon and do the same on a larger scale with the delta of the Tigris and Euphrates. And if that works, I can send the concept home to Egypt. I can call the relevant ministers here from Egypt and *show* them a system that already works. They'll be able to see the application of it immediately. They'll never be able to turn it down then."

Criton let out a huge, frustrated sigh. "Seth, what am I going to do with you? These are wonderful ideas, but—"

For the first time Seth grinned—and it was a boy's charming grin. "Criton, what am I going to do with *you*? Don't you know nobody says no to the king's son?"

Criton's eyes opened wide. "King's *son*?" he asked. "Who's a king's son?"

Seth stepped back and jabbed himself proudly in the chest with his thumb. "Why, I am. Or I will be. Samsi-ditana offered to adopt me yesterday, but I refused. Then he made me the sort of offer I could not refuse." He shook his head and beamed. "He's a wise old bird who knows how to find a man's vulnerable spot, I can tell you that. He introduced me to the princess Shala. Ah, Criton, at last I'm in love! And he's going to make me his heir. Me, Seth! King of Shinar! Lord of the Babylonian Empire! Can you imagine it? It's too good to be true."

He paused for a reaction, but Criton did not give him one for a long, long moment. Then the Greek stepped back to the chair Seth had been standing on earlier and sat heavily on it. "Too good to be true," he said in a flat voice. "Perhaps it is, Seth. We live brief, vulnerable little lives, like mayflies. We can be snuffed out in a moment. So when opportunity comes our way, we think the thing to do is seize it." He looked up at his friend with large, serious eyes. His weary voice was low-pitched. "But the trouble with that is that we get involved with people along the way. We fall in love. We make friends. We make covenants with people, formal or implied. And these are not so easily cast aside just for the sake of an ephemeral opportunity. When we try to lay them down, they tend to stick to our fingers, defying all our attempts to dislodge them. Love binds. So do the friendships. The covenants. And up until the moment we break them, we are sure they meant little to us. And when we break them, thinking we do so with impunity, they follow us around as persistently as shadows, and haunt us and tear at our hearts and guts."

"Criton, whatever in the world are you talking about?"

"Are you absolutely sure you don't know?"

Seth stared at him, but behind his blank stare turmoil raged. For one brief, heart-pounding moment Criton was ready to tell Seth about Aset and the son he had abandoned. But then he recovered and clamped his jaw shut. "Your mother's dead," he said between clenched teeth. "So is Teti. They died of the plague. Riki is devastated; he quit the army and has never returned. In the delta Apophis—"

"Mother? Dead?"

"Yes, and Kedar with her. The plague ripped through Black Lands and Red Lands alike. I met a trader from Egypt. He's here in the city now. He says Apophis is fading, that one last assault would finish him. If Kamose had that Sword of Glory you were supposed to bring him, probably the Hai would have been defeated by now. The Thebans control better than half the delta now and are encamped before the walls of Avaris."

"Avaris!" Seth breathed. "Then the end is coming! A free Egypt, after all this time!"

Criton watched the restlessly changing emotions register on his friend's face. *Should I tell him about Kamose?* he thought. *About Amasis and Makare and this foreign cult? Or would it only weaken my argument and strengthen his resolve to stay here?* "There's every possibility that the Hai could collapse in a day now, if Kamose and Apophis were to confront each other and Kamose were to win. Apophis can't get anyone to fight for him, it seems, except foreign mercenaries. And he doesn't have the unlimited funds he once had for hiring them, you know."

"An iron sword," Seth muttered. "Any iron sword would do, really. But a Chalybian one, a real one . . ." But something occurred to him, and he looked at Criton again. "You said Teti was dead?"

"Yes. Quite suddenly. And mind you, Karkara passed on a long time ago. You're the only one who could help them."

Seth's hands clenched. "If it's as close as *that* . . ." he began. And for a long, tense moment Criton was sure he had his man. Seth's mouth worked silently. His fist pounded into the other palm. His eyes stared at the wall unfocused. And then the moment passed. "If I were to make the sword, it wouldn't matter how it got there, would it? I mean, I could send it along with a special mission—even by this Egyptian trader you mentioned."

"I doubt it. He's leaving in a day or two, and he *is* of Hai blood."

"Ah. No good. No, it'd have to be by some other means. But surely I could get the king to send—"

And then Criton knew he had lost him.

The unheralded caravan—an amalgam of various peoples from various cultures—that had brought the lord Enzu back from deep inside the scattered Hittite realm also had brought with it Telepinus, a renowned Hittite spy employed by Mursilis, to slip into the city and report on its state of preparedness. After a day and a half of uninterrupted and highly concentrated work, Telepinus took his ease in a tavern at day's end.

His principle virtue where his profession was concerned was his absolute ordinariness of manner. Speaking under stress to Mursilis or to someone with whom he felt at ease, he could be dynamic, brilliant, even hypnotic. But when he needed anonymity, as he did now, he could disappear without notice into a group as small as five people. All the things that marked a man off as individual would vanish into his unmemorable face; people pressed to describe him afterward could not isolate anything about him.

Now, as the wine poured and the three-piece string

band wailed and identical-twin girl dancers twirled, he sat back and pumped the loose-tongued, moon-faced, alcoholic friend he had picked up on the street a couple of hours before. "Go on," he encouraged. "Tell me more about your master, Khet. He must be quite a fellow. You say he built the pontoon bridge across the Euphrates?"

Khet giggled and tossed one dancer a light brass coin, which she caught without missing an undulation and tucked under her ample right breast, where the weight of her bosom would hold it. "Good girl!" She brushed past him, softly rubbing her bare buttock against his leg, as she spun deftly away. "Damn! What did you say, there, my friend?" He turned back to the table, eyes bleary.

"Oh, nothing. I'm very impressed with the city's defenses. And you say this is all your master's work? This Seth fellow? The one who took lessons from Marduk-nasir?"

"Oh, that. Yes, yes." Khet drained his palm wine and bellowed hoarsely for more. "Designed whole system, he did. Not quite finished, you know. Still a ways to go. Have to do something about the river. Not secure by river. Can't get to us by land. But damned water . . . well, it's the weakness you always find in a city on water. Said Thebes was that way too. Damned true of Tyre, it was, I can tell you that. Attack by water. Place wouldn't last three days."

"Ah. And Seth was going to do—what?"

"Ah, that's a deep dark secret. Not supposed to tell anyone. What a shame. Ought to blow his own horn more. If I'd thought up anything like that, I'd be letting everybody know about it. Everybody." The other girl came dancing past, and he lunged for her. His fingers barely touched one hennaed nipple. The girl smiled. He belched and sat back. "Where's the wine? Steward!"

It was time to go on to the second stage. Telepinus held up a fat purse and jingled it. "Innkeeper!" he called. He jingled the coins again, this time deliberately out of synchronization with the band and the girls' bangles. "More wine! This time bring us your best! Nothing's too good for a friend of mine!

VI

By midmorning of the next day the supplicants lined up to see Seth were many, and despite the orders Seth had left behind to leave him undisturbed, the court functionary in charge of such matters chose at last to interrupt him.

Kabu found Seth alone in the great hall, barefoot and casually dressed, walking the streets of the large-scale model of the proposed New Babylon he had caused to be constructed. It filled the entire room and included the walls and moat and the broad stripe of the river Euphrates, which cut the city in half and marked off the old town from its extension. "Ah, there you are," Seth said. "Get your tablets, will you, please? You could be taking notes. See this quarter over here? See how congested it is? We need to knock out this whole row of buildings. We should put a broad lateral avenue here, sweeping all the way across—"

"Sir," Kabu said. "There are people backed up all the way to the stairs. It's a bit past time for your divan."

"Divan?" Seth said, suddenly looking blank. "Oh. Oh, yes. Can't they come back later?"

"Sir, some of them have been waiting for three or four days. Very patiently too, I might add, which is a token of their respect for you. I can't think of anyone else the chief magus of the Temple of Marduk would show this kind of patience for, unless perhaps it was His Majesty himself."

"Magus?" Seth repeated. It registered slowly. "Temple of Marduk? Oh. Oh, yes. Damn! I did promise to talk to him, didn't I?" He chewed his lip. "Let him in. But the others—"

"They've been waiting even longer, sir."

Seth made a face. Kabu, who knew Seth's background—Kabu made it a point to know everything about everyone at court—stifled a smile. Seth was under pressure to make a decision about a certain matter of great importance, and he was regressing, becoming more childlike, harkening back to a time in his life before human entanglements had begun to encroach upon his intellectual life. "Oh, I suppose I must see them too. But bring the chief magus in first. What's his name again?"

"Fomuzi, my lord. I'll send him in."

Seth did not wait for the visitor to be ushered in. He sat down atop the knee-high city wall and crossed his legs. "But I *can't* knock down out that wretched row of buildings for my transverse street," he complained to himself. "There are holy buildings right in the way. What a pity! Spoil my nice straight line. How much easier to just go bang, bang, and knock down everything in the way. So much more efficient."

"The lord Fomuzi, sir, chief magus of the Temple of Marduk." Seth looked up; Kabu was bowing deeply and backing away. The magus, portly, spade-bearded, Assyrian-looking, made token obeisance befitting his high position.

"Oh, yes. Fomuzi." Seth ran a hand through his hair, leaving it standing out at odd angles. "You had, I believe, a problem. What was it? Refresh my memory, dear fellow."

"My lord, you had a suggestion regarding the treatment of wounds. Some of the lesser magi reported that you treated men injured in battle and that whatever you did, it reduced enormously the incidence of infection." The magus's manner was pompous but not condescending.

"Oh, yes," Seth said. He got up and paced back and forth. "Copper rust is the answer. You, know, verdigris."

"My lord! Copper is toxic!"

"Of course it is! It takes that to kill the thing that causes the infection!"

"Are you sure—"

"*Attend* me. It's wonderful stuff. Very powerful. I've never found anything stronger so far. I tried ground malachite and chrysocolla, but then I stumbled upon copper rust. You can make it yourself. Tell me how it works out. I guarantee the incidence of infection will go down. Now if you'll be so kind as to excuse me? *Kabu!* Kabu, who's next?"

"The head armorer, sir."

"Oh! Gods, I forgot all about him! Send him in immediately! What can I have been thinking of?"

The armorer bustled in, a broad-shouldered, burly fellow who looked the slightly built Seth up and down. "Sir," he said gruffly, "you were going to begin training my men in the working of iron."

Seth scratched his head. His hair was a mess now. So were his clothes. He had just wiped his clay-stained hands, dirty from the model on which he had been sitting, on his tunic. As he turned and paced, the armorer could see the stains on his rump. "Yes, yes," he said. "*Very* remiss of me. *Have* to get down to that. Yes, of course. Look, tomorrow—"

"You promised today, sir. Three days ago. The army is complaining. There's activity on the Hittite front. There are rumors that Mursilis has returned from Hattusas. That he plans an attack, a big one, along our whole front."

"Ah. It can't wait, then." Seth's eyes went out of focus as he thought; he pulled at a loose cuticle; he rumpled his hair again. "Tell them I'll be there midafternoon. Kabu! Did you hear that? Remind me. Midafternoon. Good-bye, uh, yes. Good-bye. I'll see you then. *Kabu!* Who's next?" He climbed atop the Temple of Marduk and looked out over the city model. "Now if I could run that street obliquely, across this way . . ."

He scratched his chest. Everywhere his dirty hands went, they left a smudge. He was growing more disheveled, more disreputable-looking every moment. "Kabu!" he called again. "Who's next?"

"I am," said a soft, sweet voice right behind him. He whirled and looked into the enormous brown eyes of the princess Shala.

Seth was already flustered. He staggered back a step and knocked the temple ziggurat over. He teetered and almost fell from atop the temple. "Oh, damn!" he groaned, stepping down at last. "Now look what I've done!" He brushed himself off, leaving more stains, and when he once more ran his fingers through his hair, he left it caked with dust.

"Don't be upset, please," she said. Her lovely voice was low and husky, but there were bells in it. "I can come back later, but I wanted to see you at work. I see that I am just intruding. Forgive me."

"No, no," Seth said. "It's quite all right. I'm just trying to modify the plan of the city, as I, uh, wanted to rebuild it, but—"

"I'll come back later."

Her eyes. Her beguiling smile, natural grace, and the sweet throaty quality of her voice—all had him rooted to the spot. "No, please, Shala. Stay. I'll show you the new city plan. I think you might like it."

"My lord," Kabu interjected, "the royal engineers have arrived. You told me to let you know the moment they came."

"I did?" Seth asked, his eyes on Shala. "I don't remember."

"Oh, yes, sir. You told me yesterday. They've been quarreling. Only you can referee the quarrel." His voice grew conspiratorial. "Frankly, sir, I think they're all in over their heads. The fortifications beside the Ishtar Gate—"

"Yes, yes, I remember. Well, as soon as I'm done with them . . ."

"When they're gone, you absolutely *must* meet with the delegates from the wharf."

Seth tore his eyes away. "For the love of heaven, Kabu, what wharf? What are you talking about?"

"*The* wharf, sir," Nabu said a little superciliously, "is our money exchange. The men who rule over the money supply for the entire nation of Shinar urgently request your presence, sir. There is a currency crisis, sir, which requires your immediate attention."

Seth looked helplessly at the girl. The Karum was the financial center for a thousand-league empire. The money traders met three days a week at the Merkcs, the great business bazaar of the city, a separate district all its own. This, with the single exception of the palace itself, was the most important single area in all Shinar; it had its own streets and alleys, its own gate, which could be shut at night, and its own inn and hostelries. Under the shade of its awninged alleyways deals were made and bargains struck, and the smallest interruption of its orderly commerce would cause governments two hundred leagues away to fall.

Seth looked helplessly at the princess. "It appears I *have* to see these people," he said.

"Of course you do, dear Seth," she replied. "Father sometimes says he's only a mere appendage of the Karum. He says he owes what little he has done for Babylon and for Shinar to the fact that the merchants of the Karum have so far smiled upon his efforts."

Seth's eyes widened. "So I must be on my best behavior." But now he caught sight of his own reflection in an oval of polished metal in his model. "Is that me? That hapless ragamuffin? Gods preserve me, Kabu, whatever in heaven's name am I going to do? Look at this tunic! Look at my hair! And where have I put my shoes?"

But now Princess Shala came into her own. "Kabu!" she said in a ringing voice, clapping her hands together imperiously. "Bring soap and scented water! Bring towels! Bring appropriate clothing for the lord Seth, fit to be worn at an imperial reception!"

"Yes, Princess."

"Immediately! I shall assist the lord at his toilet. Quickly!" She clapped her hands again.

Kabu went swiftly into action.

And she *did* bathe him, as if she were a maid assigned to the service of a noble traveler newly come to Babylon. Seth blushed, stammered, and submitted. Naked, he covered his vital parts with his hands, blushing furiously. Her little hands were efficient, impersonal, and, however strange it might seem to describe it thus, lovingly attentive. She dressed him, arranged his newly washed hair, stepped back to look him over, and having approved of what she saw, stepped forward to hug him impetuously. "You're adorable," she said. "I love you already. Immoderately! I can't wait until we're married! I'm going to make you so *very* happy!"

And, most astounding of all, she virtually leapt upward to kiss him lightly on the lips. Then, laughing merrily, she scampered to the door, where, smiling fetchingly back at him, she paused to say, "Whatever you do, don't let them devalue the shekel. They're always trying to do that. Father grouses about it constantly. They're always trying to get around him. But don't let them fool you. We're all counting on you!"

She blew him a kiss and was gone. Seth, returning his eyes to his own side of the room, caught sight of his face, washed and shining now, in the same mirror as before. *I look like an idiot*, he thought. *I must be in love. Oh, Gods! Yes, I am! I am!*

Slowly the caravan—fed, rested, its business done—wound its way out across the path on the western bank of the Euphrates, bound for the desert and, ultimately, Damascus. Telepinus, Mursilis's most competent spy, looked back at the great city with its high battlements, its towering ziggurats, and its lofty Ishtar Gate.

He smiled a secret smile.

A day out from the city he would leave the caravan and wend his way northward to Mari. There he would join up with Mursilis, newly returned from Hattusas, where he had won a bloody victory over insurgents, and tell the king the things he had learned from his observations and from his wise investment in strong drink, poured into the hapless, round-faced drunk Khet, whom he had left snoring loudly.

It had been a profitable venture, which would bring him rich reward.

If Mursilis moved swiftly and took his advice, Babylon was doomed.

VII

Seth came out of the meeting looking all elation, enthusiasm, and boisterous self-confidence. As Samsi-ditana came toward him, the king thought: *Gods! He's so young!* There were ways in which even Shala seemed older and more mature. "How did it go?" he asked Seth. "Did you and the august factors of the fabled Karum get along?"

"Famously, sire."

"Not 'sire,' my boy. 'Father.' "

"I'm not used to that yet. As for the bankers, they bought everything! You should have seen their faces when I showed them the planned redesign of the Esagila. When I told them about the canals, they were skeptical at first, but when they began to understand, why, their eyes were popping out of their heads. You know the old one? The one with the long, full beard, like so?" He indicated with his hands.

"Ah, yes. We call him 'the fox.' He may not look like one anymore, but appearances deceive. Whatever he decides, they all conform. Win him, win the council!"

"Exactly, Father! They toppled like bricks lined in a row! And we're to begin immediately! The bond issue—" But something was odd in the king's face. "Excuse me," Seth said. "Is something the matter?"

"You did it," the king said, his eyes wet. "You called me Father. Then it's true—you've agreed to marry Shala."

Seth took a deep breath, squared his shoulders, and said, "Yes." He let the deep breath out and said, "Oh, yes."

And then the two of them said simultaneously, "I'm so very hap—" And stopped, then laughed and embraced.

"The wedding will be soon," the king declared, grasping Seth's forearm. "I don't want any more delay than necessary." Seth nodded, then looked over the king's shoulder. Samsi-ditana wheeled. "Ah, Kabu!" he said. "I have the best sort of news! Master Seth and my daughter Shala—"

"Yes, sire," Kabu said calmly. "The staff have been placing bets. It's the largest pool we've ever done here. I'm proud to say I just won thirty shekels." He bowed at Seth with practiced ease. "My congratulations. Your Majesty, Enzu awaits. He says he must speak with you before he leaves. And you, my lord"—he turned to Seth—"your friend Criton has been waiting for the better part of an hour. It seemed urgent. I have postponed all your appointments until tomorrow, thinking you'd be exhausted after a session with the bankers."

"Well done," commended the king. "Go talk to your friend, Seth. I'll see what Enzu wants." The two embraced once more, both happier than they had been in many months.

The mood of elation carried into the side room where Criton awaited. He rose. Seth, grinning, motioned him to be seated. "Criton! This is the happiest day of my life! Do you know what I just did? I faced down the whole Karum assembled, single-handed! They're going to back us! I'm going to build all of it! And, Criton, the princess Shala—"

"Seth," Criton said in an anguished voice, "oh, Seth. Is there no trace of the man I've followed so unquestioningly all these years? Is there nothing of him left at all?"

Seth stared, openmouthed. "What are you talking about?"

"You're selling out your country, your friends, and your relatives for the approval of a bunch of money-changers," he accused bitterly.

"Criton! What have I done to offend you? I thought you'd be happy for me!"

"You thought wrong. I've never been so disappointed in anyone."

Seth's assured manner began to crumble. "Criton," he pleaded, "don't talk this way to me. Please."

"I have to," Criton retorted, glaring at Seth. "The thing you could always count on me for, from the very first, was that I would be your friend—not your bought-and-paid-for boon companion, but your *friend*—a man who would always tell you the truth, even when it wasn't what you wanted to hear."

Seth's face began to show his pain. "Criton! When have I ever refused to listen to you? I've always listened to you. Always!"

"Until now. I'm telling you that you must keep your promises to your friends back in Egypt!"

Seth turned his back, pacing, gripping his right hand with the left so hard that his knuckles went white. Then he whirled and faced Criton again. "But can't you hear my side of it? I have obligations here."

"Obligations you had no right to take on until you had kept your word, given earlier."

"That's not fair!"

"I didn't sign up to be fair. I signed up to tell the truth. Frankly, the whole thing depresses me. I thought you were one man, and now I find out you're another."

"I'm in love, Criton! I've never been in love before! And the king—it's as if I'd found my father at last!"

"That's your affair. Until now your honor was mine. Well, now I resign. There's no talking to a man who doesn't want to hear what you have to say. Look at you. If I continue much further, you'll be covering your ears with your hands."

"No!"

"Or ordering me out."

"No, Criton! I'd never—"

"Anubis sends his regards. He's quitting, too. He's found work as a bodyguard with one of the great houses here. I suspect Khet will follow if he can sober up long enough to find work. I don't know what I'll do. Perhaps I'll wander down to Ur; a Greek never goes unemployed long in a port city."

"You're leaving Babylon?"

"With the dawn."

"Criton, please!"

"Good-bye, Seth. Let's part on friendly terms. I was your friend. I loved you very much."

But they did not embrace or shake hands. Seth looked Criton in the eye for no more than a heartbeat, then looked away.

Criton bowed formally and went out the open door.

*   *   *

"You're sure that was who it was?" the king asked. "I know Telepinus's reputation. They say he can blend into a crowd and look like anyone he wants to."

"Sire, what can I say to remove the doubt from your mind?" Enzu asked. "I can pick a man out of a crowd by his posture. By gesture. By the shape of his hands. Telepinus I could recognize by the ears. The ears are *extremely* individual. Sire, I got drunk with the man in Mari not three months ago—Telepinus, the Hittite spy."

Samsi-ditana frowned. "Could this be mere coincidence?"

"No. Telepinus was in Babylon as recently as a day ago, drinking with Seth's friend—the one who likes wine too well."

"Khet."

"Yes, sire. I think the situation is grave, sire. Rumors abound about Mursilis being back in Mari already, and if Telepinus is now on the road, bearing state secrets—"

"What secrets would a buffoon like Khet have?"

"Perhaps none. Perhaps some we cannot afford to have Mursilis know."

Samsi-ditana rubbed his temples. "Let me think about this for a day or two, eh?"

"Sire, we may not *have* that much time. The army should be placed on alert from here to the front."

"There's no call for my telling my generals their business! They're fit and ready for any eventuality."

"Very likely they are, sire, but we can't take any chances. Everything I learned behind the lines leads me to the strong feeling that a major offensive is planned—one aimed at our complete destruction and enslavement."

"That isn't possible!"

"They're armed with iron weapons, sire." He knew what the king's response to that would be. "I *know*, sire. But Seth hasn't begun production yet. He hasn't even begun the training of his apprentices."

"But he's getting married and—"

"Later, sire. Please. First he must get the forges going, day and night. I don't know how much time we have before the attack takes place."

The king agonized, hesitated, and then seemed on the brink of going along with it. But then Enzu could see the curtains go down inside Samsi-ditana's eyes. "No," he said at last. "I'm sorry. But first things first. If I don't immediately move on the funding question, the Karum may change their minds and withdraw their backing."

"Sire! Please!"

"My mind's made up. First things first, Enzu. Thank you for your always excellent advice. You are the prince of spies. Go to the Karum tomorrow and draw upon my accounts. I'm trebling your salary."

"But, sire—"

The king misinterpreted the objection. "No sudden attacks of modesty now! You're worth every shekel of it! Invest it wisely. Ask my man on the wharf. I'll instruct him to steer you to an investment that will make you a rich man before you're a year older." He turned and went away. This was dismissal.

Enzu shook his head sadly. *A year older?* he thought. Where would he be a year from now? Not here, certainly. Not knowing what he knew.

Late that night Criton, drunk for the first time in his life, tossed and turned wretchedly in his bed. He had been sick again and again, until the dry heaves had come, and he could be sick no more. Drinking had not brought sound sleep. He had passed out for a while, awakened an hour or so later, and had only occasionally slipped off since then, each time to be awakened by the same horrid dream, the dream he had had coming overland across Mesopotamia to Babylon.

Above his head had towered the great Ishtar Gate of the city. The one that, when he finally saw it, had turned out to look exactly as it had in his dream.

As he had passed through, the voice had come again, telling him the same thing: *Make your peace with the gods, Criton the Achaean. You enter the city in which you will die.*

Four times tonight he had slipped off into drunken half sleep. Four times the voice had said the same thing to him. Four times he had awakened in a cold sweat, feeling sick and frightened.

Now he stared at the ceiling of his room, barely visible in the dim predawn light.

"I don't want to die," he said. "I'll leave. I'll leave tomorrow."

Good-bye, Seth. Good-bye forever.

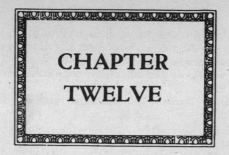

CHAPTER TWELVE

The Nile Delta

I

"Amenardis," the queen said, "this isn't like you. You always give me a straight answer whenever I ask a direct question."

Her maid clasped her hands and straightened her back. "I'm sorry, ma'am. My instructions were to take you to a certain location and say no more. I think you will believe my precautions warranted when you have arrived there."

Mara frowned but could not get angry. Her maid had never failed her before, and there was no reason not to trust Amenardis now. "Whoever could give the order to keep something from the queen herself? Even if I am living on the edge of a slum and keeping company with Habiru slaves?"

"I cannot say, ma'am. Now if you'll be so kind as to come with me, my lady . . ."

Mara's frown slowly became a puzzled smile. "All right," she agreed. "Let me get my head covering. You put one on too. Around this neighborhood we're best thought to be a

291

couple of Habiru women on their way to market for their masters." She covered her head with a drab cloth and tossed another, similar one to the maidservant. "Wait," she said. "I may understand. Is this an errand we could bring Miriam along on?"

Amenardis thought a moment. "I think so. But no one else."

They stopped in the Habiru encampment and added Miriam to their little party. As they did, Makare watched from concealment. Where, he wondered, could they be going?

He had taken to following Mara, watching what she was up to, trying to find some pretext to denounce her to her husband. He knew it was hopeless. Even Amasis, who had called the woman a witch to the king's face, could not get Kamose to condemn her. Should he follow her now? he wondered.

But even as he framed the thought, Mara turned and, keen-eyed, scanned the area. Her eyes slowed and stopped. He suddenly found himself looking directly into them.

Her smile was triumphant. She even waved at him!

He could not meet her gaze. The woman had the evil eye! He was sure of it! He stepped back behind the building and began to walk rapidly away, humiliated, a whipped dog.

Their path led them through an olive grove, then skirted the river for a time. At a certain point they came to a dock. The ancient, silent boatman gave no sign of recognizing Mara as he poled the three women across the shallow creek to the little wooded island beyond.

When they alighted on the far side, four men stepped out of the bushes on the bank's edge and flanked them on two sides. "It's all right," said their leader. "I recognize this one." He nodded to Amenardis, bowed to Miriam and Mara, and said, "This way, please."

As they entered the clearing, Mara beamed, recognizing the newcomers. "Baliniri!" she said. "And *you*, my lady! How glad I am to see you!"

Ah-Hotep smiled warmly. "Please," she said, " 'my lady' is an odd thing for a queen to call an ex-queen. Informality is the right stance among conspirators."

Baliniri chuckled. "You're all looking well," he compli-
mented. "Particularly you, Mara."

"I've found something to live for again," Mara said,
"thanks to my friend Miriam here."

"Miriam is one of our most trusted agents." Baliniri
smiled at the girl. "Her people's battle is our battle. We
share a common, and dangerous, enemy." He gestured to the
tent in the middle of the clearing. "Come inside, please.
There are some very important things we have to discuss." As
Mara followed them inside, she could see soldiers moving in
the shrubbery beyond. Baliniri, traveling downriver on this
secret mission, had not come alone. The soldiers were those of
the palace guard, handpicked and trained by Baliniri himself.

"Our lives are in your hands," Baliniri told her after
explaining his mission, "because what we are planning is
subversive. If you were to tell us right now that Kamose is
worth saving—"

Mara's eyes narrowed. "I think he is, but not as king.
Even if the cult were eliminated, he might have to be deposed. He's too far gone in blood and bad feeling and in guilt.
I would never trust him as a leader again. No. You're quite
right. We must groom a successor." She looked from Baliniri
to Ah-Hotep. "But who?"

Ah-Hotep stepped in. "I have a daughter named Thermutis. She married a courtier of good blood a while back and
is pregnant with their first child. If the child turns out to be a
boy, his bloodlines will be easily accepted by the Red Lands
and Black Lands nobility plus the priesthood. If we win."

"Very good," Mara said. "But what if it's a girl-child?"

Baliniri stepped in. "That's one of the reasons we came
downriver to talk to you. We need to know if you can come
up with an alternate plan."

"Hmmmm," she said. "I'll have to think about that." She
looked at Miriam and Amenardis. "We'll all give it some
thought."

But when her eyes for just a moment locked with
Amenardis's, she could tell that the same thought had occurred to both of them: *Riki*.

She looked away, but the thoughts came crowding in. If
something happened to Kamose . . . if, for instance, he were
to lose the battle with Apophis . . . It could happen, of

course; the startling outcome of their recent duel had proved that. If Kamose's aides had not immediately sprung to his defense and surrounded him, his father would have killed him.

She closed her eyes, and Riki's image came to her immediately. But it was Riki as he had been before Teti's death. His eyes were clear, untroubled, unburdened by grief. His powerful young body was straight-backed, upright, healthy. She thought about his good heart, the basic sweetness of him, his courage, and unswerving loyalty. These loomed very large in her mind now. Suddenly she felt a great, deeply erotic longing for him . . . and then the moment passed. She opened her eyes.

Baliniri was talking. ". . .understand that he suffered a rather humiliating personal defeat at Apophis's hands a while back. That would tend to indicate resistance since then has stiffened. Is there any chance of our taking Avaris soon?"

Mara spoke up: "Frankly, I don't think so unless something happens to strengthen Kamose's hand personally. Mercenaries continue to pour in daily to aid Apophis, so there's a chance that we ourselves could be driven back and lose the ground we've gained."

Baliniri frowned, thinking. "I'm glad we had this meeting. Our plan would have been difficult to discuss through the medium of a courier. I wanted you to know what we're planning and find out where you stood on the matter."

"You can count on me all the way," Mara assured him. "I never wanted to be queen, and in fact I've never felt like one. My marriage with Kamose has been a failure almost from the start. I'd have been much happier as the wife of a lesser man. Kamose is driven; he always has been. And when the cult came on the scene, I lost him altogether. I don't know that I'll ever get him back. But one thing I do know: I'll never again share him with the cult, or the war, or public office."

"I understand, dear," Ah-Hotep said. "I never wanted to be a queen either. I've been much happier since Baliniri and I came together than I have at any time since . . . well, it's been a long time."

Mara took the opportunity. "Your son. How is he? Has Riki recovered from his loss? He must have been devastated."

Ah-Hotep looked at her, and somehow Mara knew that Ah-Hotep knew. She *knew*. "He took it very badly for quite some time, but I believe he'll be back to being himself very soon," she said. "If I see him, I'll tell him you asked after him. I remember what good friends you had been for so long a time."

Knowing Ah-Hotep had seen through her made Mara very uncomfortable. She changed the subject, and for the next hour the five of them talked strategy.

At the end, however, Baliniri drew her aside. "I'm counting on you to keep me informed as soon as anything happens."

"The same with your plans for Thermutis's child. Let me know when she comes to term and if it's a boy."

"Yes. You know, it's a curious thing. The chief astrologer told me of a really extraordinary alignment of the stars that's due right about the time Thermutis ought to be having her child."

"Interesting."

"Yes. All the more so since he says that every indication is that the birth of a great leader, the sort of hero who only comes along every thousand years or so, would take place right about then."

"Oh?"

"Ah, but here's the strange thing: It will not occur in Thebes. It will occur in the delta. I asked him to check his computations again and to compare them with those of other astrologers. He did, but the result came out the same."

"Then there could be no coordination between Thermutis's child and this great hero's birth?"

"No. Unless I have her moved down here before her time comes."

"Then by all means do that." She stopped dead. "Why, what an extraordinary thing!"

"What? What's the matter?" Baliniri asked anxiously.

"Levi, Miriam's great-grandfather and the patriarch of her clan, has been having visions. Some time around the end of the year his own people are supposed to produce a great hero of their own, a liberator, a great man who will lead them out of bondage and back to their own land far to the north, across the desert."

"Perhaps we have *two* important births coming up?"

"Perhaps," she agreed. "While Apophis was here, he got wind of it and put out a rule saying that male issue of the Habiru were to be killed at birth."

"And Kamose's attitude toward the Habiru is just as cruel. Can't you do anything about that? No matter who wins Egypt—Kamose or Apophis—the Habiru lose."

"While Kamose is under the influence of Amasis, there's little I can do. Of course I do what I can to see that they're not mistreated. I make sure they are not needy where food and clothing are concerned. But the overseers do work them very hard. I've come to admire the Habiru. They haven't lost sight of who they are or given up on their religion or lost their sense of purpose." She sighed. "The only real advantage I have is that Makare, Amasis's henchman, is afraid of me. He thinks I'm a sorceress."

Baliniri laughed and gave her hand a fatherly squeeze. "Perhaps you are. There's great power in you—I've always thought that. I feel a lot better knowing you're here, taking care of this end of things." He looked her in the eyes. "You will have noticed that my wife and I have come together of late. I feel a fool for having neglected her. She's a brilliant woman. You two share many qualities." His tone turned serious. "Do your thoughts these days tend to turn toward Riki, now that Teti is gone?"

Mara, to her great surprise, found herself blushing. "Is it that obvious? Yes, I wish I could see him. Where is he now?"

Baliniri's smile was slow and thoughtful. He did not speak for a long moment. Then he said, "He must be at the oasis now. If he is, there are some extraordinary changes taking place in his life. He's like a caterpillar going into the cocoon, with no idea what he will have been changed into when he comes out."

"I don't understand you, Baliniri. What do you mean?"

"I can't tell you just now," he said. "Trust me, it's for the best. You'll like the result. Even if things don't work out quite as you expect them."

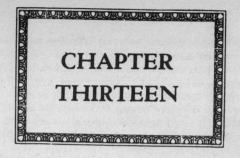

CHAPTER THIRTEEN

The Western Desert

I

Little Tchabu, his eyes closed and his misshapen limbs arranged as casually as relaxation and their natural crookedness would allow, sat cross-legged on a square of carpet. At his feet the guttering coals stirred with every slight resurgence of the evening breeze. Above his bowed head the stars were bright. He was surrounded by three friends: a young man with dark curly hair, and two warrior-women, members of Teti's oasis community.

"Where is Riki?" the deep man's voice asked.

For a long moment Tchabu did not answer. His companions, though, were used to long delays when Tchabu was in a trance; sometimes it was as if he were speaking from far away, his words traveling long distances. Presently he answered. "He is not far away. He is camped atop the pass where the two great rocks come together, one day out from El-Kharga." It was a voice hardly to be recognized as his own, without accent and without faltering, as it always was when he was in deep trance.

"How is his mind?" asked the deep voice. "His heart?"

Again the delay. Then: "He has been in a dark place, but he now travels toward the light. It has not been good for him where he was. He has begun to learn that he was weak in places where he had thought himself strong. He will learn more, that he is strong in places where he thinks himself weak."

"Yes," the deep voice agreed. "Yes."

The same strange, fluid voice came from Tchabu's lips again. His sleeping face held no expression. "He does not know what it is that he seeks by coming here. Still less does he know what he will find."

"Good," the deep voice said. "Here he will find much that will be new to him."

The voice speaking through Tchabu continued: "There is much power in him. He possesses much capacity for good. While he is confused, he cannot use it."

There was a long pause. The wind sighed softly. When the voice began again, there was great sadness in it. "He thinks himself as being alone, as having lost everything. He thinks that this is the natural way of things—that all men are essentially lost and alone and that the years when he and his wife were close were mere illusion. But there is a part of him that knows better, that remembers. Remembrance hurts too much, however, so he struggles to forget—to forget the good as well as the bad."

Although the listeners nearby waited in patient silence, there was no more. At last the deep voice spoke to the silent companions gathered around the little dwarf. "He sleeps. All is well with him, and the news he brings is good. Our friend can and *will* be healed. Initially I had feared Riki too far advanced in his grief, but we will help him."

For the first time a female voice spoke, an older woman's voice, deep and mature. "Whose is the voice that speaks through Tchabu?" she asked. "How can it speak like this? Tchabu has never mastered our tongue."

"This voice is not Tchabu's, but I do not know whose it is. He himself does not know. He never hears himself speak when he's in a trance. When he awakens, he will know nothing we do not tell him."

"How can that be?" inquired a second female voice,

younger, softer, higher-pitched. "And how does this whole process come about? Riki is several days' march from here. Does Tchabu perhaps see into the future when he does this?"

"No," said the deep man's voice. "When Tchabu looks into the future, he speaks with his own tongue, emotionally, with fear, loathing, and all other emotions easily expressed. Whoever this voice is knows nothing of that."

"It's a new voice," the older woman observed. "I don't think he spoke with the voice before he came here."

"This is true," the deep man's voice confirmed.

"It is not you, then, master, speaking through him?"

"No," the calm voice said. "But something does happen to Tchabu when he is near me. His own power is great, but when we're together, it expands in its ability to accomplish new feats. These I cannot teach him because they are beyond any powers of mine. Let me think how best to describe it: At night, in the desert, when the dry wind blows, sometimes a rough cloth will come within a handspan of one's hair, and the hair will fly up to meet it, impelled not by the wind, which may be blowing in another direction, but by some invisible force. One may sometimes feel a spark from this."

"Yes, yes. All who live in the desert know of this."

"Well, no one thing causes it. It requires several factors, which must come together just so or the phenomenon will not happen. The hot wind must blow. There must be the rough cloth and the loose hair. And there must be this mysterious force, which no man can give a name to."

"I see, master. And if one thing is missing, nothing will occur. Perhaps *you* are the thing that must be there for Tchabu."

But now the dwarf stirred. He groaned in his own rough, guttural voice. The younger woman rushed to his side and eased his crooked little body onto the carpet. Tchabu's hands clenched and unclenched. His eyes did not open. "Master," the girl said, "he is not as he was before. Something else is happening."

The man's voice spoke. "Stay by him. Put your hand on his chest. He is not awake, but perhaps the gentle pressure will comfort him. He may have another seizure coming on. The other spirit has left him and so has the tranquillity it brought. Now he is alone with the fear and turmoil in his own disturbed mind. There are dark and evil things in the world today, and when he is unprotected like this, and the spell

comes upon him, he knows great fear. At such times he can
see things that you and I cannot, and hear things to which
our ears are deaf. At such times his mind is a battleground for
great and ominous forces."

"You are fond of him, master," remarked the older woman.

The man's voice was slow and thoughtful. "It is more
than that. I feel that until Tchabu arrived, I was not complete. Now I am happy. I, who have always lived here, who
have never gone into the world, I see the world through his
mind, and he has traveled in many countries. I see the past
through him, I see the future through him. I go into the
minds of men I have never met, men I have never seen.
Tchabu is my brother and more than my brother. Those who
brought him here to me will have me forever in their debt."

He looked down at the fitfully sleeping body of the little
man, who stirred, haunted by bad dreams. Tchabu's mouth
moved, but only grunts came out.

"It is not easy to be as he is," the man said. "He has
been much alone. There are few like him in body, and he has
had to endure hardship and ridicule. Few have condescended
to offer friendship. No woman would have him."

"Pardon, master," the younger woman said, incredulous.
"You mean that he has never—"

"Be honest: Would you want him that way?" Immediately he picked up the shame of her realization. "There, now.
Don't feel bad. It's just the way things have always been for
him. But he is nonetheless a proud man who knows his is a
mighty mind, worthy of anyone's respect. He has an important part to play in our common destiny."

On the carpet, Tchabu writhed and groaned as if in great
anguish. "No, not do this. Please not do this." The thick
accent was back. "Bad men coming," said the harsh voice.
"Come quick. Nobody see. Ambush! Everybody die. All around
him. All around. Nobody save. Must hide! Must run! Must
fight! No good! Fight no good. No help. Help not come. All
die. All ruin. All fire, all around. Men killing, killing . . ."

The little man was drenched with sweat. His eyes remained closed. His body would have thrashed around helplessly, but the women, sitting on either side of him, held him
firmly.

"I wonder what he's talking about," the man said. "The
fall of Avaris, perhaps? The end of the siege?"

Tchabu's slurred speech began again, and they all leaned

forward to hear. "Enemy inside. Enemy walk all around, see where weakness lies. Enemy take secrets out of city."

"Yes," the male voice said, low, thoughtful. "We have spies inside Avaris all right." Even as far away as here in El-Dakhla, he knew their names.

"Enemy give to soldiers. Soldiers first very quiet, then attack. *Attack!*"

The last word was a piercing scream and came so suddenly all three were startled.

"Soldiers attack!" the hoarse voice cried out hysterically. "Soldiers kill old man and woman with baby! Soldiers toss up baby, catch on spear tip coming down! Horrid! Tchabu no watch! Tchabu no see!"

Now, even in the young woman's arms, pressed to her full bosom, the dwarf was beyond comfort.

"There, there, my dear," soothed the older woman, her hand stroking Tchabu's forehead gently. "We're all here with you. Nobody can get you."

She looked up at her male companion. "Master," she said, "isn't it unusual for Tchabu to read the mind of someone he's never even met? Usually it's someone who is close to him, isn't it?"

"True," he answered. "But there are no rules in this. Whatever it is that allows him thus to pick a random voice, a random mind, out of a dying city hundreds of leagues away, it makes up its own standards of what can and cannot be done. We can only observe."

"He's starting again," the older woman said to the younger. "Hold him tightly, now! I'll get his hands. . . ."

But no sooner had Tchabu's deformed body begun to tense up once more than it suddenly relaxed completely. The little man's hands went limp. So did his rock-hard little body. His face softened, and he slept.

When the women had gone, the person they had called the master stood up, painfully, and reached for his crutch. His withered leg dragged behind him as he hobbled over to the dwarf's sleeping body. Unlike the naked women of the El-Dakhla oasis, he and Tchabu, conscious of their bodies' lack of conventional beauty, wore coarse tunics that hung down low, covering most of their legs. He also, this night, wore a shawl over his shoulders that the women had thoughtfully brought along with them. He removed this now and draped it lovingly over Tchabu's twisted, sweat-soaked body.

And just as he did Tchabu stirred in his sleep. And the spell came back over him, just for a moment. "Horrible!" he said in the same voice as before, only quieter this time. "Soldiers come . . . they kill . . . all friends, dear ones. Poor Seth! No one left."

The man leaning on the crutch stared openmouthed. *Seth?* he thought. *Did he really say Seth?*

II

At first they had gone into the desert unaccompanied: just the three of them, plus the ever-present cheetah padding along silently beside them. Weret broke trail for them, marching off the endless leagues with a steady and tireless step; Riki, out of shape after his long layoff, sweating heavily, struggled valiantly to keep up; Naldamak brought up the rear.

But during the first night, when they had encamped near the top of a mountain pass, they had begun to take on additional escorts, presaged by three sets of cold cheetah eyes blinking in the dark just outside the campfire's warm circle of light. Then, when Riki had awakened in the first chill hour of dawn, he had found himself surrounded by six of Weret's women, watching him with an impersonal and detached gaze. As was the custom, all were naked, as slim as reeds, gleaming here and there with gold ornaments, their only adornment other than the iron swords his Teti had made for them.

Now, as the threesome marched ever westward, these six women marched three to the front and three to the rear, like a guard of honor. Riki was surprised to find himself thinking of one of them in particular who had reminded him a bit of Teti. It had been no single feature but her particular way of standing casually, one hip a trifle higher than the other. Since no woman had attracted his attention in the terrible time since Teti's passing, he perked up to realize that perhaps there was hope for him if he was beginning to think of women again, even peripherally.

In fact, he had the feeling that, for the first time in many months, he was not escaping from a situation but going *to* somewhere. And he was looking forward to it. How long had it been since he had looked forward to other than one night's drunken oblivion? How long since he had really cared about anything or anybody? But here he was, beginning to stir, to awaken and look about him, to take note of things. Beginning, little by little, to come alive again.

Their arrival at the El-Kharga oasis was marked by surprise, as it had been the first time he had made this trip, the time he had met Teti. Towering above the small party were posted sentries, each tall, tense, black warrior-woman armed with either spear or bow and quiver. Their bodies gleamed like polished ebony.

"Weret!" he said. "The Black Wind!"

Without breaking stride she responded over her shoulder. "Yes, El-Kharga is now their headquarters. Whoever wins the war, Egyptian or Hai, will get the idea that he does not want the desert trade routes controlled totally by a race of women who do not see themselves as subordinate to any man's authority. The victor and his army will come into the desert and find our numbers much augmented by our Nubian sisters."

"Was this idea yours?" Riki asked, impressed.

"Teti's," Weret answered.

Riki's eyes widened. He wanted to ask how she could have predicted such a situation and made arrangements with Nubia's queen Ebana, but he held his tongue. For now the earth dropped away beneath them, and he found himself looking down into the startling green of the great oasis on the valley floor below them. Green, in the middle of this hellish desert where no life should be able to grow.

He held his peace until they had made their way down the steep, narrow cliffside path. The only access to the oasis was this single track, constantly within range of the sentries' bows—a feature that made an invasion impractical, regardless of who had the audacity to attempt it.

At the bottom the path led them beside a clear lake fed by underground streams draining the Nile many leagues away. At lakeside stood the roofed open gallery he remembered, with the familiar grape arbor at the end of it. Standing before each column of the loggia was a towering black warrior-woman, spear in hand.

Beneath the arbor sat a woman who, unlike the warriors, was clothed. There was little flesh on her old bones but great dignity in her posture as she sat in her many-colored robes of state, head held proudly. Out of her black face her eyes gleamed like precious stones.

Riki advanced to within ten steps and fell formally to one knee, bowing his head in respect. He found he could not keep his face from breaking into the first grin it had worn in many months. "Ebana!" he said. "Queen Mother of Nubia!"

"Welcome," she said, smiling.

Riki rose to his feet. "And what a wonderful sight you are!" he said. "I can hardly imagine anyone I'd rather meet here now. You're well, I trust?"

She shrugged. "If a woman can be well who has outlived her youth, her beauty, her fertility, her vigor, and better than half her dignity. And you? I had heard you were grieving terribly. You look like a shadow of your old self."

Riki smiled ruefully. "There was a time when I could keep pace with Weret or your women on a forced march. But that seems to be in the past."

"Don't be too quick to consign yourself to the scrap heap," Ebana warned. "The world we know may soon have use of you."

"How about you?" he asked. "Are you here on a visit of state?"

"I've been here for some time," she replied. "I don't know how much Baliniri has told you. Apparently not much."

"Perhaps you could complete my education. There's something going on that I don't know about."

"Very well," said Ebana. "Naldamak! Have the women prepare the midday meal. The general and I will eat here, under the arbor."

Everyone sprang to attention and organized into a smoothly functioning unit. Ebana watched her warriors scurry about and smiled as Riki stood, hands on hips. "You've trained them well. I wish we had some of them down in our part of the world. Egypt could use their like."

"Sit down, young man," Ebana said imperiously. "Egypt *has* their like. They—and the rest of my women—are part of the permanent garrison here now. Baliniri has not told you that there has been a secret treaty made with Nubia."

"Secret treaty? But Kamose—"

"—knows nothing about it. It is not a treaty with Kamose. It is a treaty with Baliniri and with your mother, former queen Ah-Hotep. We have come to the decision of whom we shall recognize as the real leaders of the Red Lands, regardless of who the formal king happens to be."

Riki sat down hard now. His eyes were wide. "You'll excuse me, please," he said. "This comes as a bit of a shock."

She put a withered forefinger to her lips. "Listen. There is much you need to learn. First of all, your breach with Kamose has what you might call an intelligible context. Something has happened to him."

"Yes, he's turned into a real bastard."

"Worse than that." Swiftly she explained the coming of the cult and the inroads it had made in Egypt. She told of Mara's breach with Kamose, and the bonds Baliniri had forged with Mara, Nubia, and the upriver nobles who ruled the Red Lands between Thebes and the first cataract, where the Nubian border stood.

Riki's brain reeled. "Then you mean to topple Kamose? When? Are you going to wait until he's driven the Hai out into the desert?"

"He will eventually kill his father and vanquish the Hai. This will likely take him out of Egypt, to pursue the enemy. But when he returns—"

Riki stared. "This is treason!"

Ebana admonished him gently. "You have been asleep under a tree all the time since your wife died, young man. Much has happened here. The Kamose you used to know may not exist anymore. If I am right, he is no more than an abject slave of the cult, mindlessly obeying the goddess." She shook her head. "What a pity! There was much good in him. But now he is a menace to both your country and Nubia. Thus there is no treason in plotting to supplant him."

"And who will replace him as king?"

"I'll get to that later. This is not something that will be done next week. We are making plans. The replacement will restore the *old* throne and reintroduce proper royal bloodlines. There are many nobles in Egypt who have never recognized Kamose, considering him to be a half-Hai bastard of debased blood."

Riki sat back and regarded her. "*Is* there a legitimate pretender anywhere on the horizon? Someone whom all would accept?" He frowned, thinking. "The most pure bloodlines that I know of are my mother's, but she had no sons by the king."

"She has a daughter, Thermutis, who recently married a nobleman. Zer's own blood is not good enough of itself, but united to hers—"

"But Ebana! Even if they have a child, we're two decades from that child's majority."

"Even so," the old woman admitted, smiling sadly. "By then I will be long gone, and Baliniri and Ah-Hotep with me. But in the meantime we shall have saved Egypt."

"So you're thinking about a regency. Who would act as regent?"

"That is one of the details that will have to be worked out. But think on this: We control Thebes and everything above Memphis, including the Fayum. If Kamose were to strike a stalemate with his father and make a coward's peace, he would face an Egypt grown insubordinate, an Egypt that finds itself asked to choose between two unacceptable regimes. Egypt will serve neither one."

Riki nodded, pondering. Impulsively he put a hand on her wrinkled old arm. "There's so much I need to catch up on. I'm so out of touch with the state of affairs."

"Don't worry," she said. "All in good time. We have plans to make. But first there is someplace I want you to go."

"Nubia?"

"No. The oasis at El-Dakhla."

III

After a soldier's simple meal of olives, dates, and flat bread, Ebana curtailed the conversation. "That's enough," she said, sitting back. "These days I tend to tire easily. Weret!"

"Yes, my lady?" Weret responded, stepping forward quickly.

"I'm going to retire for an hour or so. Show the general our encampment, will you? He probably has no idea of our strength here. Show him the defenses along the northern route. At dawn tomorrow, I want you to take him over to the El-Dakhla oasis."

"Very well, my lady." Weret bowed respectfully. "Riki? Come this way, if you will." Her hand on his bicep was as strong as his own; she guided him away almost before he had had time to add his own bow to Ebana.

Silently Weret led him down the long, long row of tents under the olive trees. Not until they had traversed fully half the long axis of the camp did she speak. "As you can see, our numbers are much augmented."

"They certainly are," he agreed. "This is twice the size of the current Thebes garrison. I didn't know the oasis could support a community this size. And there's the civilian population as well."

"Well over ten thousand in all." She pointed to their right. "Look over there. That unit is all Nuer women, from the Sudd far to the south. All of them volunteered to serve Ebana. There's another unit beyond them that came all the way from the Mountains of Fire, where Ebana's late husband, Akhilleus, was born. You have no idea how his name is revered there. And Ebana has the status almost of a goddess."

"Then her son Nehsi's realm is no longer limited to Nubia?"

"All who live in the Sudd and beyond recognize his authority and pay voluntary tribute. He is venerated as Akhilleus's son, but Ebana is held in higher esteem. Imagine, in those southern nations, families send one daughter to serve with Ebana's women. It brings honor to the family."

Riki slowed his pace. "I'm beginning to grasp the implications of all this. If our struggle with Kamose comes to civil war . . . if we cannot stop the cult and Kamose pursues us back to Thebes—"

"There will be the oases—El-Kharga and El-Dakhla—to retreat to. Here he will find us invulnerable: There is provender here to withstand any siege, and the only routes to the oases are controlled by our people. I'm sure you noticed during our travels that there are places along the route from Thebes where six well-armed warriors could stand off a thousand attackers." She looked at him and gave him a confident smile. "It may surprise you to learn that the oasis at El-Dakhla is even better defended than this one is. But of course you will see this when you go there."

Now Riki stopped. "Why *am* I going there?"

Her gaze was steady. "All in good time. Trust us."

In the deep shade of her tent under the trees, Ebana lay on her bed, staring up at the brightly painted cloth overhead. She could not sleep.

The young general . . . he was so *very* young. In his thirties, perhaps, but looking younger because of the hurt in his eyes, the vulnerability. There was a certain innocence of spirit about him, despite his long experience of war.

How he reminded her, in a certain way, of her husband, Akhilleus, when she had first met him! It was not a physical similarity, certainly, for Riki, stocky and well-built, was not above normal height, while Akhilleus had towered above even the storklike Dinka warriors of the Nuer. Furthermore, Riki was sun-bronzed, while Akhilleus had been quite black.

Nevertheless, there was in Akhilleus an underlying dignity, a man of power. He had been special.

And there was the same quality to this young soldier here. There was something more to him than just a leader of troops.

Was there in him, perhaps, the makings of a king?

After a time Naldamak joined her. "I'm glad you've come, my dear," Ebana said, letting the girl help her to a sitting position. "What do you think of Riki? You've known him during the intervening months and have listened to people talk about him while they think you cannot understand their Egyptian language." She smiled lovingly at her daughter. "Tell me about him."

"He was very close with Teti. They were as one," Naldamak said. "When she died, some of him died also."

"Ah. And he thinks this condition incurable. Do you think his grieving period is over? He has come back to himself once more?"

"I am not sure, Mother. Ask me when he returns from El-Dakhla."

Late that night Riki, still sleepless, lingered over the winking coals of the fire, poking them idly with a green stick. He had seen wonders today. The oasis was impregnable, and a force of Nubian infantry—*male* infantry, the cream of Nehsi's army—camped on the border only a couple of days' march away, sworn to the defense of the oasis. It was one of the units that had fought so valiantly beside Akhilleus at the battle of El-Kab—it might even be the unit against which poor Netru, Teti's first love, had made his heroic last stand. There were songs about his legendary valor throughout all the southern country.

He sighed. Everywhere, everywhere he went, Teti had left footprints. Everything served to remind him of what he had lost.

Here now! he chided himself, straightening his back. *No self-pity! No more damned melancholy.*

What had he been thinking about? Oh, yes, the defenses. Was Baliniri planning for an all-out war in which the Nubian army would be brought in to reestablish, once and for all, the ancient throne in the hands of the Egyptian home-born and home-bred?

And what of Baliniri planning to settle the crown on the head of a child by Ah-Hotep's daughter, his own half sister, Thermutis? Why that would make him, Riki, the uncle of a king! Of a true king of Egypt!

"Wait," he said in a low whisper. "If Thermutis has a son, that means a regency, but Baliniri is too old for that. Who, then? . . ."

Across the fire one of the cheetahs suddenly materialized out of the darkness and edged closer to the guttering coals, staring across the small warm patch of light at him, its eyes unblinking.

"Of course," he gasped. "They mean me! Riki, the queen's bastard son!" The thought was unacceptable. "No," he decided, looking the great cat in the eyes. "I can't sit in for the ruler of a nation. I'm just a soldier. I don't feel comfortable in a house of my own, much less in a palace. When Teti and I came together, I could have talked myself into staying here. She was happy here. So was I, although I didn't really know it until I'd already left and headed back to Thebes. It was a good clean out-of-doors life. We could have lived a good life here."

The corollary struck him with shocking swiftness. *And she'd be alive now, here where the plague never came.* And with that one thought, all the pain came back, and the loneliness and confusion. And the tears.

*   *   *

Crossing that last patch of desert there were only the three of them again: Weret, Naldamak, and him, with the great spotted cheetah tagging tirelessly along. An hour out from El-Kharga oasis, the fatigue began to descend upon Riki. He had not slept the night before, as terrible and happy memories had crowded into his mind.

All through the day his strength waned, and when at last they made camp, he threw his bedroll on the ground, fell atop it, and did not wake until dawn. Again, he found himself morose as they marched the endless leagues across the dry wastes toward their oasis destination.

Then, as the sun stood high above, they came at last to El-Dakhla. It was all armed camp, bustling with tall, naked, no-nonsense women soldiers. This camp was dominated by Black Wind warriors, and there were no familiar faces among them as there had been among Weret's soldiers back at the bigger oasis.

Weret led him along a familiar path, though. "You're taking me to the same garden," he said. "The one in which I met Teti."

Weret looked across at him and nodded. Ahead there was the same little spring gushing out of the rock, dancing merrily down the cliff face to feed its cool waters into a little creek. And there, on the dais where he had first met Teti, stood two men. Men! At El-Dakhla, where no men but he and Seth had ever been allowed!

He smiled, recognizing one of them. Who could mistake little Tchabu? "Tchabu!" he called out. "Greetings, my friend!"

The dwarf bowed and stepped to one side to call attention to his companion.

The young man who stood leaning on a stout hand-carved crutch was slim, clear-eyed, curly-haired, and round-faced. His full lips curved in a shy half smile. Riki glanced down at the young man's bad leg; one could hardly not look. Under the long, coarse robe it appeared crooked and unable to support his weight easily.

Riki liked him right away. There was something clean and decent about him, a quality a person could warm to.

The eyes held his.

There was something more than that.

A chill gripped Riki's heart, but it quickly passed.

"Riki," Weret said, "I want you to meet Neku-re." Something about her voice kept him from answering. He waited.

Then she said, "Neku-re is the wisest among us. He is my mistress's son . . . by Netru."

Riki stared. "Son?" he managed, numb with shock. "Teti's son?"

IV

"Thank you, Weret," Neku-re said, still smiling. "Now could you leave the three of us, please? Thank you." He watched, warmth in his eyes, as Weret turned and silently marched away. "She knows to stay within earshot," he said. "If we need her, she'll be here."

Riki shook his head. "Why did Teti never tell me?" he asked. "All these years . . . I thought there were no secrets between us."

"Please, Riki," Tchabu said, sitting down. "Not think bad of us. Not let this offend. We not mean you harm. Better this way. Teti know this."

Riki watched as Neku-re awkwardly settled into a seat beside Tchabu and put his crutch down. "What reason could I have given her not to trust me?" he continued brokenly. "There was complete candor between us."

"Please," Neku-re said. His voice was like the rest of him: mellow, deep, and reassuringly gentle. "You will soon know everything. Sit beside us."

Riki let himself be persuaded into a cross-legged position. He looked from face to face in great hurt and confusion.

"Now," said Neku-re. "Let us join hands, the three of us."

Riki did not like the idea. He withdrew instinctively. Neku-re, however, persisted gently. He reached out and took Tchabu's and Riki's hands. "First," he said, "welcome to El-Dakhla. I saw you once, from afar, when you were here before."

Riki's eyes showed his aggrievement.

"When you left, I was very lonely. You know the tie that exists between Mother and Ketan: a tie beyond that of other brothers and sisters. Well, there is such a bond between Mother and me."

Riki did not miss the special wording. "*Is?*" he asked.

Neku-re nodded, letting the implications sink in.

"But that means you—" Riki blurted out. He sat back and looked from face to face. "I've learned not to be surprised about anything involving Teti," he said flatly. "She knew she was going to die. And how. And when. Didn't she?"

Neku-re nodded. "She was not sad about it. You made her very happy in those few years." He paused. "Would you have been able to live happily if you had known these things beforehand?"

Riki blinked back tears. "I don't think so," he conceded. "She was wise not to tell me."

"She knew you well enough to love you just as you were," Neku-re said. "Think of that as a tribute few men ever receive from another human being."

Riki was finding it hard to keep his eyes open. "But keeping *you* from me," he said. "Didn't she trust me with such a secret?"

"By the time you leave, you will understand why no one can speak of me and why everyone must believe Tchabu is dead. We are weapons—powerful weapons. When you understand this, you will know how I shudder to think how close Tchabu came to being captured by the cult during his long journey here."

Riki tried to speak but was overcome by a sudden, deep fatigue.

"Soon Nehsi and the Nubians will join us here. Soon all will follow who are to play a part in the great plan that involves the future of my clan." His chuckle was low-pitched. "Yes. I'm a Child of the Lion, but I'll never make a sword in my life. Instead, I will make weapons of another kind. I have made one by joining with Tchabu, whose mind can do all the things mine cannot. I will soon make another, with your help."

The voice was a drone now. Riki could hardly hold his head up. His eyes seemed glued shut. "And in the meantime all except the strongest—you, Mara, and Baliniri—will hide here. You will be in great danger. You and Seth. And, yes, the weakest of all."

The weakest? Riki asked, immediately aware that he had not spoken aloud.

"Yes," Neku-re answered, as if the words had been spoken. "The child who will lead the Habiru out of bondage. He has already been conceived. If the cult knew, they would kill him."

But who is he?

"You will know soon enough. Know also that a child-prince of Egypt will be among those who hide here. Aset and her child, and Chetah and Ketan's son, Sinuhe, are already here. But our future depends on the weakest of us all. We are in terrible peril. Each of us has a part to play. You will soon know yours. The Children of the Lion loom large in the tapestry of life. Each has a vital part to play, including those who think they've won and those who think they've failed."

But who am I? Why am I here? What must I do? Who must I become?

There was no answer. The darkness suddenly went from black to gray. Although his eyes were closed, Riki could see Neku-re standing before him. Or was it? The face and the eyes were much the same. So was the ruined leg. But no, it was not Neku-re! It was—

"Hadad," the figure introduced himself. "Teti told you about me. The world requires all to play a part. Mine was to save my brother, then to die at precisely the right moment. If I had instead saved myself at that time, untold horrors would have been unleashed upon the world. The Shepherds might have reigned for centuries. Instead they stand now on the very brink of destruction."

Riki's mind spoke to him. *But what should I do?*

He waited for Hadad's reply, but the form of quite a different man suddenly materialized: a towering, sightless giant with a ruined face and great powerful hands.

"I am Shobai," the blind man said. "I had eyes, but I chose not to see. The part I played demanded I lose my sight in order to see my foolishness. But once I had learned to see things as they were, no Children of the Lion could ever hide the truth about our mission from ourselves. What my blindness taught me to see, all of us now understand in death . . . and Neku-re's is the voice we speak through."

We? Does that include Teti? Please! Let me speak to her! He writhed in anguish.

There was no answer from the presence.

Sudden anxiety gripped Riki's heart. *I'm no Child of the Lion. I'm not wise. I'm just a soldier. Great events do not turn on the doings of the likes of me. How could I be important in the scheme of things?*

The presence still did not reply.

If I could only talk to Teti for a moment. She's the wise one. She'd understand. She'd explain it to me!

Still there was no answer.

In deep despair he held out his hands.

I'm nobody, he said. *My hands are empty, but I offer them for the work at hand. For large things, if you think I am the man to do them. Or for the small things, if that's what I'm needed for.*

No reply.

Do with me what you will. Whatever you ask, I will do. Whatever you wish me to be, that I will become. If I must die . . .

The gray before his eyes slowly became white. The white began to glow, becoming a source of light, blindingly bright.

He could not shut it out!

Stop! I can't take it!

Without warning, he was inside the mind of a presence, invisible before him, looking at him. He saw himself through that person's eyes and knew the person was Teti and knew that she, like him himself, was an infinitesimal mote in a Mind inconceivably larger. In that one instant of total insight he knew what mattered—nothing and everything—and who mattered . . . nobody and everybody. All the moments of his life and Teti's were spread out before them, and for that moment he could almost see and understand it all.

Teti! he screamed.

The moment of intense consciousness seemed to last forever. When complete consciousness became complete unconsciousness, he could not say, but when the light became darkness, he slept deeply.

Riki's inert hand fell from Neku-re's grasp as the body slumped. Neku-re let go of Tchabu's hand also and looked at his companion. "He sleeps," he whispered. "Could you have predicted the form this would take?"

"No tell," Tchabu responded. "No way understand. Much deeper than usual. One moment, Tchabu could see, could hear. Next moment, nothing."

Neku-re nodded. "I think our friend Riki has been given an experience that neither of us could reach. But for a moment I could feel Mother's presence. I'm sure of it. And—I think Hadad spoke to him. That's unusual. He's never spoken to *me* before."

Tchabu stared at him. On his thick lips played a mysterious little smile. "Neku-re very wise," he commended. "What Tchabu not see, Neku-re see. But same true from other side."

"Yes, we're complementary. Where one of us is weak, the other's strong."

"Riki see what you could not. You speak of Hadad, who never speak to you."

"Yes," said Neku-re, looking down sympathetically at the sleeping Riki. "I hope he remembers some of it. Something *that* deep, beyond what even you and I can see . . . I hope he can tell us about it." He turned back to Tchabu. "What were you going to say about Hadad?"

But Tchabu would not answer. And on his broad mouth there remained the same enigmatic smile.

V

Riki slept long and deeply. After a time Tchabu hobbled to his own nearby tent, dragged back a sheepskin coverlet, and gently spread it over the sleeping man.

When he returned, Neku-re looked up quizzically, then shrugged and smiled. "You've locked me out of that part of your mind, haven't you? You know I can't enter unless you let me."

Tchabu eased himself down. "Times hard for Riki. Need something special."

"I take it he *got* something special," Neku-re remarked. "Do you think he'll tell us?"

Tchabu shrugged.

"You think it's none of my business unless he decides different."

This drew a small smile.

"All right," Neku-re said. "Let him sleep. He'll wake when he is ready."

But Riki slept all the way through sundown. The campfire had blazed high, abated, and become flickering red embers before he suddenly sat up, looked around, and made his way toward the warm circle of light, where Neku-re, Tchabu, and Weret sat. Naldamak was nowhere to be seen, but the Black Wind encampment was at some distance, and Riki supposed she was there.

When he approached the fire, Weret made room for him. Her eyes betrayed her curiosity. "If you're hungry, I'll send for food."

Riki smiled. "No, thank you. I'm still somewhat muzzy, having been where the need for food and drink are hardly more than a dim memory. It'll take me some time to get used to being back." He sat down cross-legged and looked into the fire. "How long have I been out?"

"Several hours," Neku-re answered.

"Funny . . . it could have been a moment or several days." He looked at the fire for a long moment, then sought Neku-re's eyes. "Something strange and wonderful has happened to me. Where I was . . . is it a place you can visit at will? How I envy you!" He hesitated. "No, that isn't true. I don't think I'll ever envy anybody again. I know now how Teti felt when she first knew what her last years were going to be like."

"Was there a look into the future for you also?"

"Not that I can remember. But now I can accept whatever happens." He stretched and took a deep breath. "I seem to have some special part to play in the times to come, which does *not* have to do with my military duties, although I will be expected to attend to these also. When the time comes, something will tell me what to do, and I will do it."

Tchabu spoke up. "You not know if live, die?"

Riki took up a green stick he found by his feet and idly poked the fire. "Tchabu," he said gently, "I have no fear of death. For a moment I was inside Teti's mind. I'm a new man for it. For a moment I experienced the enormous peace in which she exists. It made my life feel unbearably tense by comparison."

Neku-re reached over and patted his knee. "I understand," he said softly. "Mother has spoken with me, and although I've not been inside her mind, she's been inside mine. A moment's contact with her, and all my fears are temporarily erased. When I speak with her, I have this feeling that someone else is there."

Riki looked at Tchabu. "*You* understand, too, don't you?" he asked the dwarf. Then he turned back to Neku-re. "Shobai spoke to me," he continued. "And before that I spoke with Hadad."

Neku-re stared. "With Grandfather?" he gasped. "And with Hadad of Haran? The heroes of the two saddest stories ever sung in all the world? How wonderful!"

"They're as happy as Teti is now," Riki said. "Neku-re, tell me something. How did you come by that bad leg of yours?"

"When I was a child, I ran away from the oasis. I took a bad fall and broke the leg very badly. It was two days before anyone found me. I had water with me but no food, and I couldn't move without great pain. The leg never healed properly." He frowned. "Why?"

"The same thing happened to Hadad." Riki let this sink in. "Did you know he looked exactly like you? The same eyes and hair, even posture. Teti told me the family legends about him. He had a beautiful voice for singing. Do you?"

"He sing like bird," Tchabu answered for him. "Make even Weret cry."

Riki, taken aback, glanced at Weret, who nodded reluctantly.

Riki smiled broadly. "This gets better and better. Neku-re, Hadad lives again in you. Do you make jewelry, as Hadad did?"

Weret's back stiffened as her hand involuntarily flew to the golden necklace around her stately neck. "Made by Neku-re's hand. Since his childhood he has made jewelry, not weapons. Teti and the Black Wind wanted him to work iron, but he refused."

Riki beamed. "Better and better," he said. "My mother, Ah-Hotep, has a brooch Hadad made in his twentieth year. You have a touch of his art in you, Neku-re. All you need is advanced training."

Neku-re seemed startled. "Advanced training," he whispered, "or . . ."

Riki bit his lip. "You don't suppose . . ." he began. "If you could open your mind all the way to Hadad . . ."

"It's a thought," Neku-re said. "But although their minds can speak to me, I cannot speak to them."

"But what if your powers and Tchabu's worked together? You might be able to enter Hadad's mind then."

Neku-re closed his eyes and smiled happily. "I *knew* bringing you here was a good thing," he said, "above and beyond what Baliniri asked me to do! I'll try it! And I'll do it, if it takes the rest of my life!"

* * *

When the fire guttered, Riki rose to go, only to feel a slim-fingered hand touch his arm. "Riki, please stay a moment."

"Yes, Weret?"

"Be honest with me. Does Teti think of me now?"

Riki sat again. He knew what Weret would have sacrificed to have shared in his reunion with Teti. "Everything in her life is there. You're there, to be sure; I'm there, and Ketan and Netru, and Neku-re and Karkara, everybody. Inside her mind I could share her love for Netru and not be jealous. I could share her love for *you* and not be jealous." He put a comforting hand on Weret's shoulder, and for once she did not pull away. "I will never be able to look at you, her dearest friend, with the same eyes again, for she showed me what it was like to see you through her eyes."

He heard a stifled sob in the darkness and half expected her to come to him for a comrade's sympathetic embrace, but she moved away.

"Thank you, Riki," she croaked. "I'll not forget what you've given me today—to know she's happy, and that . . ."

The words trailed off, and he heard her soft footfalls as she went away.

In the morning Naldamak had the Black Wind lined up for Riki's inspection, and he walked briskly past the ranks, noting the perfect uniformity of their carriage, the gleaming beauty of the sunlight shining on their razor-sharp swords and spears. He left the last rank to speak with Weret.

"I assume they fight as well as ever," he remarked.

"Better," Weret confirmed. "My mistress trained this group herself, using principles taught her by Baliniri." She translated this exchange into the Nubian tongue for Naldamak's benefit.

"Weret, my friend," Riki said, "she doesn't need that. It's time we stopped fooling one another. After last night you and I are over that, aren't we?"

Weret looked at him with new respect. "How long have you known?" she asked, an uncharacteristic smile threatening to show itself.

"From the start," he admitted. "It's an old trick that I use from time to time. You pretend you don't know someone's language, so that he will speak more freely in front of you." Suddenly he turned and spoke to Naldamak directly. "Isn't that true?"

Naldamak bowed respectfully. "My compliments, my lord," she said good-naturedly.

Riki winked. "Dismiss them," he said. "And give them all an extra ration of wine on me. I can afford it. I keep forgetting I'm a rich man. From now on I don't leave the money rotting in some banker's cellar. I spend it—and on all the right things."

Naldamak smiled and turned on one heel smartly as Riki and Weret marched away.

"Nothing but openness and trust between us," Riki said. "Is it agreed?"

"Yes, my lord!" Weret said.

"Good. What rank do you have here?"

"Captain, my lord."

"Not anymore. You command too large a unit. You're now a general."

"And in what army, my lord?" she asked, a gleam in her eye.

"Good question," Riki replied. "The so-called Army of Egypt is Kamose's—the one I'm going back to now, to win his damned war for him and throw the Hai out of Egypt."

"You are, my lord?"

"Someone has to. Then I'll come back here, and we start figuring out what to do about this king I've been fool enough to put on the throne of Egypt. But *our* army, here. What are we to call it? *Hmmm.* How about the Desert Legion? Do you like that?"

There was a smile in Weret's eyes. "Perfect, my lord." Her manner was full of respect. "I almost begin to believe you speak with my mistress's tongue."

"It may be so." They looked each other in the eye, and there was a moment of complete mutual understanding. "The Desert Legion it is."

She smiled a fierce warrior's smile. "I will inform the troops of your decision tomorrow."

"Make it tonight," Riki said decisively. "I leave for the war at dawn tomorrow."

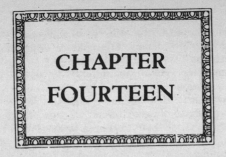

CHAPTER FOURTEEN

Babylon

I

The squad leader kicked angrily, missing the vulture and nearly falling on his back. "Damned thing!" he growled. The vulture half spread its wings but folded them again, backing away unsteadily, eyeing him warily. "I'd like to kill 'em all if I could catch 'em."

That was an impossibility. There were more vultures in the field than there were soldiers walking among them through the carnage. The stench of rotting bodies was overpowering, and the squad leader gagged and drew away. "Come on," he said. "We've seen enough to make the report. Poor bastards! And they almost made it to safety!"

His assistant frowned. "Makes you wonder how they even got this far, doesn't it?" he remarked. "It would have been the first caravan to make it through Hittite-occupied country in months."

"Yes," his leader said. "Hey! You men! Assemble! We're getting out of here!" He lowered his voice. "It also makes you wonder why they started out in the first place. A caravan with only eight travelers, mostly unarmed in times like these."

His assistant was looking down at one body the vultures had not molested. He started. "Gods! I would have sworn I saw this one move! Did you see his hand?"

"Come on," the squad leader urged. "The patrol was due back an hour ago."

"Wait," said his assistant. "I think this one might be alive."

"They've been lying here for a day and a half at least. Nobody could have survived."

The assistant bent over the body and looked close in the fallen man's face. Then he put a hand to the side of the man's neck. "There's a pulse!"

The squad leader came over and looked down at the ravaged face. "I'll get the water bag. See if you can revive him. Perhaps he can tell us what happened." He went back to the horses, hobbled nearby.

The assistant gently shook the fallen stranger. "Help's come. You're saved, friend."

The eyelids fluttered. "Where . . ." he rasped. "Where am I?"

"Six leagues west of the river," the assistant answered. "Well inside Hittite territory. We're a patrol. We found your party."

"They're all dead, aren't they? The Hittites attacked us just when we'd thought we'd got past them."

"You're the only survivor."

"Gods! I have to get to the king. I have to get to Seth of Thebes."

"There, now." The squad leader returned with the goatskin bag. "Have a bit of water. You're in pretty bad shape. What's your name?"

The assistant helped the stranger gulp the water thirstily. "Criton. You've got to help me."

"We'll take you to town," the squad leader said, "if only to get you questioned by the authorities. But you'll have a time getting through to Seth today. It's his wedding day."

The fallen man tried to sit upright. "Then this would be a festival day." His eyes widened. "But of course! That's what they were talking about. They knew you'd be undefended at festival time. Gods! Get me to Seth! Now!"

The assistant frowned. "Sir," he asked his superior, "don't
you think—"

But he never finished the sentence. Atop the far hill,
overlooking the narrow defile in which the caravan had been
trapped, the sentry cried out: "Sir! There's activity to the
west! Hittites! A lot of them."

The squad leader broke his lethargy. "Get to the horses!"
he barked out. "We're getting out of here!"

The assistant stared at Criton. "You're apparently going
to get your audience. That is, if we can make it to Babylon
before we're overrun!"

In an ordinary festival the Great Processional Way, running the whole length of the city from north to south, would
be jammed with people but able to accommodate all the
crowds that lined it. This was, however, no ordinary festival
day: Both the princess Shala and Seth were popular figures
not only with the citizens of Babylon proper, but with all the
river cities as well.

Thus the procession would not begin and end at the two
termini of the Processional Way but wound instead through
the principal avenues of the city in a serpentine pattern. On
all sides the onlookers cheered with joy. The people had gone
for so long without the promise of a male heir for their king; if
the royal couple—Samsi-ditana's daughter and his designated
heir—produced male issue, the succession would be assured
once more and orderly continuity guaranteed at last.

Furthermore, Seth's extraordinary brilliance in all matters of kingcraft, arts, and sciences had become common
knowledge. The people had seen the first signs of what Seth
could do, what with the pontoon bridge across the river and
various short-term projects completed. But it had been his
single-handed conquest of the hard-bitten financial wizards of
the city's banking and trading community that had won everyone over completely in the end. Thus it was that all
turned out today in jubilant celebration of the royal nuptials.

The drums beat, and the flutes played. Scantily clad
dancers capered before the procession, leaping high and tossing flowers. Acrobats leapt and somersaulted; fire-eaters belched
great billowing flames to delighted screams. Magicians, sitting cross-legged atop their mounts, pulled live pigeons out

of their ears and armpits and tossed them skyward. Trumpets blared, and joy reigned.

In the middle of the procession, in a sedan chair borne by four Nubian giants, the young couple sat, waving down at the people around them. Below the level of the chair, where prying eyes could not see, Shala slipped one tiny bare foot out of her slipper and caressed Seth's ankle.

"I'm so happy," she said. "No matter how wonderful our lives are after this, my darling, I'll remember this day the rest of my life. I'll tell our children about it. They'll have to listen to Mother prating on about her happiest day. All the darling little children. All the boys and all the girls."

Seth smiled. "Yes," he said. "You tell the children on the anniversary of this day every year. Their father will tell them on all the other days. I never knew life could be so sweet."

Now the procession was nearing the great Ishtar Gate. Soon they would turn toward all the temple buildings. Up ahead Seth could see Samsi-ditana standing atop the great gate, flanked by priests and soldiers, waving happily at the huge gathering below.

Seth's heart was pounding fast. He was so happy, his hands were shaking. And in the hidden floor of the sedan chair Shala's soft little toes curled sensuously around his bare instep, stroking, stroking.

High above them, on the parapet of the towering gate, the king gazed down at his daughter and his son-to-be, at the cheering crowds, and at the prosperous city behind them.

"Ah, Fomuzi," he said to the head magus next to him, "who would have believed it? When I was young, the courtiers would look at me and roll their eyes heavenward. 'To think that the blood of Hammurabi is so watered down that it inhabits this round little man with the blank face!' they would say. Some were so hateful as to suggest that my father had had no part in siring me. I had to prove them all wrong by leaving my imprint on the greatest city in the world, despite all their contempt. I cleaned the slums, redesigned the canals and the fortifications, and found an even better king to replace me."

"To be sure, sire, the young man is brilliant," the magus agreed.

"Majesty," said a voice behind them. "There's a messenger who wishes to—"

"Later," said the king.

"But, sire, apparently it's quite urgent."

"It can wait. Oh, look! Aren't Seth and Shala a wonderful-looking couple? If they unite their good looks with even a trace of Seth's brains—"

"Sire," the officer behind him persisted. "If you could only take a moment to hear the messenger."

"Please! Am I to have no peace?"

"Sire, a caravan has been attacked six leagues away. By a Hittite body of some substance."

"Can't the army handle this?"

"Sire, the army is upriver. The caravan, apparently one of ours . . ."

But now the roar of the crowd drowned his words, and the king turned back to the rail and looked proudly down. The thousands in the street were screaming as with one throat the names of the royal lovers, and Samsi-ditana, beaming, his eyes brimming with tears, leaned out over the rail as if to embrace them all.

"Seth! Shala!" cried the crowd. "Long life and happiness to Seth and Shala!"

II

Half the city guard had been given the day off to attend the wedding celebration. In the encampment just outside the inner wall, Enlil and Zu, commander and adjutant of the guard, listened to the faraway cheers of the people.

"Why do I feel this sudden itch, as if something were wrong?" Enlil asked. "I feel as though I had forgotten to do something important and was going to be reprimanded by the generals."

"I don't know, sir," Zu replied, watching his commander pace in a tight circle.

"I was in an earthquake once, far to the west of here. My dog felt it before I did and tried to warn me. He started barking and whining."

"It's not too late to send out an order recalling the men, is it, sir?"

"I don't know. But I could be reprimanded for that, too."

"Try to relax, sir. After all, what could go wrong? Seth's realignment of our western defenses, putting the Second and Sixth Infantry in place as he did, was brilliant. The line has been quiet ever since."

"I know, I know."

"Would it make you feel better if I were to seek out General Anu and tell him—"

"And tell him what? That Enlil is getting touchy? That his corns ache so he thinks it's going to rain? I'd look like a fool."

Zu laughed. "Sir, perhaps I can find a less idiotic way of phrasing your concern."

"You'd have to. Yes. Go ahead. Something *is* wrong; I can feel it."

"Yes, sir. I'll get to the general." Zu smiled conspiratorially. "He'll be with the king, you know."

Enlil scowled. "All the more reason to try harder to keep me from sounding like a superstitious old man. Go, and put the best face on it that you can. If you make me look good, there's a week's paid leave for you in it."

"Yes, *sir!*"

The Hittite advance party divided into two groups half a league from the river. Inak and Sarku, commanders of the two forces, lingered for a moment to review their strategy with General Anittas.

Inak, certain that he remembered the plan correctly, recited.

"When Sarku's party hits the walls by land and engages the sentries on the walls, we run the boats downstream and through the gate into the heart of the city—just as Telepinus recommended."

Anittas gave Inak and Sarku a hard-eyed smile. "If this works, let me tell you, *he'll* be a rich man, if I know the king. Mursilis will be grateful indeed." He clapped Sarku on the arm. "He's going to be grateful to you as well, I think."

"We'll try to deserve it, sir," Sarku responded. "Give us half an hour on the walls before you bring the big unit up. If they think they're being attacked by no larger a unit than the one I'm bringing against them—"

"Half an hour it is. It should all be over fairly quickly with our secret weapon: an improved siege machine, one almost impossible to defend against. Telepinus stole the idea devised by their own man, Seth. Telepinus got this fellow's friend drunk, as I hear it, and the fool sat down and sketched the thing out for us."

"Well, sir, I suppose the time has come."

"The favor of the gods go with you." Anittas gravely grasped the forearms of both commanders, then returned the stiff salutes they gave him.

The servants scurried about like so many busy little ants, opening windows, arranging flowers, and turning down the bedclothes; but Seth only had eyes for Shala. Her large brown eyes were full of mischief, and a gay smile brightened her adorable face.

"Tell them to go," he said in a hoarse voice.

She turned and spoke, and the servants filed swiftly through the door. Almost simultaneously there came the soft sounds of flute and kithara, and a lilting voice began to sing a hauntingly beautiful love song.

"Tell the singer and the musicians to stop," he said. "I want no distractions or interruptions. I want nothing but you." Their eyes locked and she smiled; then she spoke three soft orders through the bolted door.

"What else does my lord want?" she teased. "I could close the window and keep out the sounds of the crowd."

"Please," he requested, then watched her step out of her little jeweled slippers and pad barefoot to the window, which she closed. Then, standing with her back to him, she fumbled with something he could not see; but when she turned to face him again, she gracefully swirled her cloak wide and stepped out of that, too.

"Leave me my drums," she asked. "That much I want for myself." And as she spoke the drums outside the door began to beat: various earthen drums with leather heads, with more than one pitch. She pirouetted away to sweep her robe off her graceful little shoulders, and the bells on her toes began to ring. She smiled bewitchingly, and as she turned and spun, the drums beat, and the little bells jingled.

Now she wore no more than a shift of soft cloth, which clung seductively to her every curve. It was held together only by a golden cord around her waist, so as she danced lightly around him, the garment parted here and there, showing him a rosy nipple here, her adorably rounded buttocks there.

His head was swimming.

She laughed as musically as the bells. She reached up and loosened her hair. He had never seen her hair down. It came all the way down to midthigh. She shook it out, so that it surrounded her. The shift fell to the floor. Nothing hid her soft skin but the richness of her dark hair.

She turned and swirled, and her hair flew out, showing him for a heartbeat the whole of her, slim, adorable.

Outside the crowd grew louder as the celebration approached fever pitch.

Shala came within his grasp for a moment. He reached out for her, but she spun away, holding the sash to his own tunic in her hand. His garment gaped open. He tried to close it, but she circled around him and peeled it from his body, leaving him wearing only his loincloth.

The crowd grew louder. There were screams, but he could not focus on them. Her thighs were slim and deliciously rounded; her belly was flat, and her waist a mere handspan. She danced close, her nakedness rubbing past him as the cool softness of her body caressed him through its garment of flowing hair. Then she danced away from him, twirling his loincloth in her teasing hands.

The drums were frenzied now; so were the screams of the crowd in the street below. She tossed the cloth aside and beckoned to him. Her hands and eyes called to him.

She said, "You who cannot sing, I will sing to you. I will sing the song of ecstasy, which the goddess sang to her lover.

Last night, as I, the queen, was shining bright,
Last night, as I, the queen of heaven, was shining
    bright,
As I was shining bright, as I was dancing about,
As I was singing softly of the brightening of the
    oncoming night,
He met me, he met me,
The lord Kuli-Anna met me,
The lord put his hand into my hand,
Ushumgalanna embraced me. . . .

His heart beat faster with every word, his hunger beyond his control. He took her.

He was no longer a man. He was an animal that wanted release. He was a bull, a stallion.

Outside, the crowd roared deafeningly!

In the streets everyone was drunk. Simakura of Ebla, who had gotten leave from his guard duty on the city wall for the day, tried to push his way through the thousands to find his unit commander, who had sent him a summons. "Let me through, damn you!" he bellowed, grown impatient.

There had to be something terribly wrong. The army did not recall troops from leave on a whim. The messenger, from the king himself, had ordered all members of the city guard back and had made it quite clear the message was an urgent one.

Up ahead he spotted another soldier in the crowd. "Nusku!" he called out.

Nusku was drunk. "Do you know what's the matter?" he bawled. "I'm in no shape to go soldiering."

The two of them were just below the wall beside the great Ishtar Gate, which towered high above them. Beyond was the city market, and beyond that were the corner of the wall and the unseen Euphrates.

"I don't know," Simakura yelled back. "But we've got to get to the encampment."

Nusku nodded and continued to push his way through the hundreds of people toward the tall gate. But as Simakura followed, something above caught his eye. Beyond the gate, over the side of the far wall, came a flaming arrow. As he watched, struck dumb, the shaft fell into the crowd and caught a reveler in the breast. The man staggered away, shrieking, his clothing on fire.

"It's an attack!" Simakura shouted, and as quickly wished he could swallow those words. With loud screams the crowd surged forward and trapped him, pinning his arms. He struggled mightily and wished he had come to town armed. "Let me through!" he ordered. "I'm with the city guard!"

Atop the Gate, Samsi-ditana looked down with horror. The boats on the dark Euphrates were a flotilla now, each swarming with armed Hittites. "Gods! Where can they have come from? Where are my upriver armies?"

The officer who had been trying to reach him now spoke, an edge on his voice. "That was what we were trying to tell you," he said from between clenched teeth. "The land arm of the attack apparently came around our southern flank and skirted the Second and the Sixth. So far, sire, it appears to be just these water units and the small land force."

But then both of them happened at the same moment to look across the river to the slopes beyond. A great army began to take shape there. It poured over the top of the rise in a seemingly inexhaustible stream. The Hittites! The main force. As thick as locusts!

III

On the far side of the river the Hittite general Anittas watched the first wave of his force fall upon the walls of New Babylon just as the royal party on handsome Arabian horses pulled up behind him, resplendent in parade uniform. "First wave in place, sire."

"Good work," Mursilis said. "Our advance guard is already inside the city, by water?"

"Yes, sire."

"Splendid. Now split up the reserve force and come around the city by the rear. We want no one escaping."

"Yes, sire." Anittas turned to his adjutant. "Urballa? You hear?"

"Yes, sir!"

"Then pass the order along!"

The adjutant spurred his horse forward, kicking up dust. The general turned back to his king. "We have them outflanked, sire. They've been expecting us by the northern route."

"And by the time the Second Infantry or the Sixth can come to the rescue, we'll have the city burned to the ground and a flotilla heading south to take Ur and the delta of the Two Rivers!" Mursilis's smile was deadly. "Tell the men to show no mercy. I want this to send a message to Assyria, to Elam, to all the Eastern lands! The Hittites have come to stay!"

*   *   *

Atop the wall a pale-faced and distraught Samsi-ditana fussed and worried. "How could it have happened? How could they have surprised us like this?" His eyes were full of tears. "Where are my reserves? Where is the rest of the city garrison?"

"Sire," a staff officer behind him said, "they've been called back. But they were dispersed through the city by your own orders."

"Just look!" the king said in a high, outraged voice. "Did you see that war machine they brought up? It's one of ours! The design was Seth's! The New Babylon gate didn't last five minutes."

The staff officer came up beside him. "How did they get the design? Could Seth have—"

"No!" the king shouted. "Seth would never have betrayed us like that!"

"I wouldn't suggest it sire, but—"

"It has to be a coincidence! Wasn't there some report of a spy being seen here? A Hittite spy?"

"There was some talk of someone having spotted Telepinus—"

But the king was not listening. "Oh, *look!*" he moaned. "They're inside the city, past the city guards! Where are the reserves? Why don't they bring up the reserves?"

In fact most of the reserves had found their way to the Ishtar Gate and, although ill-armed and undermanned, had made a gallant stand. But they had been beaten down and slaughtered. The Hittite besiegers, manning Seth's battering ram, had smashed the gate to flinders and made their way through the inner court. They overpowered the sparse guard in charge of the drawbridge. Now that they were in the city, a flood of Hittite soldiers poured through to fall upon the unarmed citizens.

Simakura of the city guard had been knocked unconscious by Hittite soldiers at the foot of the Ishtar Gate stairs. Now, his head throbbing, he sat up, looked around, and reached for the fallen sword at his feet. As he did, two familiar figures, weapons drawn, rounded a corner and came toward him.

"Anubis! Khet!" he bellowed. "Over here!"

The giant obeyed; the round-faced man followed, weaving on unsteady legs.

"The king's atop the wall!" Simakura said. "We have to hold back the Hittites and keep them off the stairs!"

Anubis frowned. "You're right. Leave the stairs to me. I'll keep everyone out until the king can find his way down the secret passageway. Has anyone sent for Seth and the princess?"

"I don't know," Simakura answered. His eyes scanned the chaos around them and lighted for a moment on the horrid spectacle of a dead mother and baby in the street, trampled underfoot by the Hittites as they fought their way into the city. "I can't leave here."

"No!" Anubis shouted. "Go to Seth and Shala! Save them! You and Khet! I'll stay here. If anyone can hold them off, I can."

Simakura nodded gravely. "The gods be with you. Khet, you come with me."

And with that the two of them set out through the side streets, hoping to avoid combat until they could get Seth and Shala to safety.

The cut on his forehead would not stop bleeding, and blood was in one of his eyes. Criton wiped his face with a filthy hand and blinked through the smoke, trying to determine just where he was. Someone had set the wharfside granaries on fire, and the flames leapt high. He scowled; he had better get away before it was too late! That next building was a warehouse for storing lamp oil!

A Hittite patrol suddenly charged through the smoke. He flattened himself against a wall, ducked inside a niche, and made his way into a narrow passage between two buildings. There was a head-high wall here; behind him he heard footsteps coming closer. He got one leg over the wall, wincing at the sharp pain from his broken rib, and fell heavily on the other side.

He looked around. "That's the tower," he muttered to himself. "Now where would Seth's quarters be?"

As he scrambled painfully to his feet, a Hittite soldier was climbing over the wall behind him. Criton stepped forward, grabbed the soldier by the hair, and took advantage of his off-balance stance as he alighted to ram his head into a wall. The soldier dropped on his face and was immediately unconscious. Criton stole the man's sword and made his way through the smoke-choked alley toward the royal apartments.

The remains of his city guard were fallen about him. Enlil looked around. Only he was left. "Zu!" he called out. "Where are you?"

Three Hittites separated from the attacking force and came toward him. "Just lay down your sword," the first one ordered in a thick accent. "You won't be hurt. You may wind up on an oar, rowing us downriver when we take Ur, but you won't be killed."

"You want my sword? Come and take it from me!" Enlil challenged.

There was a powerful crushing blow in the middle of his back. He staggered forward and looked down. There was a black sword sticking out of the front of his chest, its tip covered with his blood!

The sword fell from his hands. His knees were suddenly weak.

Seth had not armed the city with iron weapons. There had always seemed to be plenty of time for that, so he had procrastinated. Only the beginnings of the system had been set up, with just a few iron swords coming from his apprentices at the forges.

Now his procrastination was reaping a bitter harvest. The iron Hittite swords cleaved through Shinarian bronze on all sides. Iron-headed battle-axes cut through bronze Shinarian body armor and helmets as if they were made of cheese. The many duels seldom lasted more than a couple of moments as the iron-armed foreigners asserted their superiority.

On the stairs of the Ishtar Gate, though, Anubis had somehow bested a Hittite soldier and taken his iron sword from him, and now a dozen Hittites lay dead at his feet, scattered down the steps. "Come on!" he yelled. "One and all! Who'd like to die next?"

For answer two burly Hittites rushed him from either side. Grinning, the giant disarmed one with a single swing of his stolen sword. He caught the other on the backswing and knocked him spinning with the flat of his blade. Then he turned back to the man he had disarmed and ran him through.

It was then that a rain of arrows hit him.

He hardly saw the shafts coming. Seen head-on, they looked like a flight of birds soaring through the air at him. But he did see the archers, a dozen of them, lined up across the street, their bows no longer taut, their forearms quivering, their very posture indicating release.

The bolts hit him almost as one. He staggered but held onto the sword, albeit with a weakening hand. He looked down. The iron-tipped shafts had sunk deep. He raised the sword high and cursed the gods as the archers nocked new arrows.

"Come and fight like m-men!" he rasped. "You cowards!"

The second volley struck home, and suddenly his strength was not a giant's anymore. The world grew dark around him.

"Look! There's Criton!" Khet said to Simakura. "Hey, Criton! Over here!"

The Greek nodded and came toward them. As he did, a Hittite soldier lurched out of the smoke, sword at the ready. With insulting ease Criton knocked the sword away and knifed him in the guts. Only then did he speak. "We've got to get to Seth! Do you know where to find him in the tower?"

Seth, looking with horror out the window, had dressed. Shala wore her shift and held her luxurious robe. She looked down at it and let it drop. "No use wearing this. They'd recognize me, and if they know who I am, it'll go worse for me." A sudden thought struck her. "My father! Do you see him?"

Seth's face was a mask of pain. "He's still standing atop the gate! Poor Anubis died in vain, trying to buy him time to escape, but he didn't even try to get away!" His voice broke. "They've got him! Gods! No! Don't look! Don't look!"

Shala looked and almost fainted, but she recovered. "We've got to get out of here," she said.

One quarter of the city was on fire, and the flames leapt halfway up the great ziggurat whose tall form dominated the skyline. Black smoke choked the streets, and all along the waterfront people were jumping, panic-stricken, into the strong

current of the Euphrates, hoping to be swept out of the city
to safety. A troop of Hittite bowmen, however, flanked the
banks just where the river narrowed, and they fired arrow
after arrow with deadly accuracy into the swimmers in the
water.

Somehow Zu, Enlil's adjutant, had escaped being killed,
although he was marked by many small wounds. He wore
only a bloodstained loincloth and held a gore-spattered sword
in his hand. The fighting had moved into the residential
quarters now that the financial district and marketplace were
ablaze, and he found himself coming out of an unnamed alley
facing the great towering shape of the Ishtar Gate. He sneaked
a peek at the interior; if no one were looking, he could
perhaps escape the city.

He recoiled in horror. His guts churned; his gorge rose.
He vomited into the street, then mastered himself and looked
again.

A figure was grotesquely crucified to the gate, pinned
there by knives through the hands, arms, belly, and groin.
Worst of all, the poor battered head seemed to be moving.
The lips moved too.

Zu staggered closer on unsteady legs. "Sire," he whispered. "L-let me get you down."

The lips moved, but no sound came from the dying
mouth. But for all that there was no sound, the words could
easily be made out.

The dying king said, *"Forgive me,"* silently and expired.

IV

Seth and Shala paused in the doorway before going out
into the street. "You're right," he said. "We'll attract less
attention if we look like commonfolk." He kicked off his
expensive sandals and stopped to pick up a handful of dirt.
This he rubbed on his face, arms, tunic, and legs until he
looked like a man who had slept in the gutter for a week.

As Shala did the same he peered into the street. "They'll
have taken the Ishtar Gate," he muttered. "So that's no
outlet. They'll be very thick in that part of town. Where?"

Where?" He had watched from the window as the bowmen picked off the swimmers in the river; that was no good either. "New Babylon," he decided. "It can't have put up much resistance. Most of the people were on this side of the river for the celebration. We could escape through New Babylon's gate. Or, failing that, get atop the wall there and leap down to the outside. The wall's low over there. Shala! Come on! There's no time to waste!"

But as they stepped into the street, with the smoke of a dozen fires choking the end of the avenue, a Hittite soldier, wearing an iron sword, stepped coughing out of the billows of black smoke and stopped within a dozen paces of them.

Seth froze. He looked down toward the other end of the avenue. Although no activity could be seen, he could hear the sounds of battle. That was no escape. But what to do?

The Hittite looked up and drew his black sword. "You! Stop right there!"

"Stay back," warned Seth, looking frantically right and left for a weapon—a rock, a stick. He could see nothing. He put Shala behind him and backed slowly down the street. "Don't come any closer."

As he spoke he suddenly realized that he had never experienced fear. He had never taken the thought of physical danger seriously. But now he had a wife to protect.

He cursed the icy fingers clutching at his heart. His eyes darted to the right and left of the advancing warrior. He felt so vulnerable, so weak! His fists balled as the blood rushed to his extremities. "That's enough," he commanded. "Stop right there!"

The Hittite laughed. "You unarmed street ragamuffin!" His Shinarian was heavily accented. "Here, *you* move aside. I can't get a clear look at the girl."

Red rage boiled in Seth's heart. "Here I stand," he said firmly, "and from here I shall not move. You'll have to kill me."

"Gladly," the Hittite said, advancing. But at his second step forward, Seth suddenly let out the shrill cry of a hawk—high-pitched, piercing—and feinted a leap at the outstretched sword. The arm rose to parry, and Seth, moving fast, went in under the sword, fists together in a low crouch. Then he uncoiled like a bent bow. His joined fists came up and caught the Hittite squarely in the groin! The Hittite doubled over as Seth spun to one side, knocking the sword clattering from the Hittite's hands.

Shala grabbed at the weapon and tossed it to Seth. "Now!" she screamed. "Finish him!"

Seth had never killed before, but the red rage was still upon him, and he was fighting not for himself but for another. The black sword rose and fell! A severed head rolled at his feet. The body, spurting blood, caved in and sprawled in the street.

Seth looked down at the iron thing in his hand. Such power! Such strength!

"What have I done?" he cried.

"Come, my darling! There's no time to lose! Don't think about him! You had to do it!" She tugged at his arm.

But he stood paralyzed, looking down at the weapon in his hand. "This is what it was all about," he said. "I was sworn to return to Egypt and bring back one of these. The Sword of Glory. It would have done the job." His laugh was bitter and self-mocking. "But I betrayed my friends and forswore myself. I forgot my quest, my honor. It was so good to stay here. I let myself be seduced."

He looked at her now, his eyes abrim with tears, and for a heartbeat he was so moved by the beloved sight of her that he thought his heart would stop. "Oh, gods," he moaned. "You're so lovely. I do love you so much. But I should have armed this place, then gone home. I should have listened to Criton."

"Please, Seth! We have to escape!"

"The sword," he said, rooted to the spot. "Iron. The secret I came so many leagues to learn to make. And then when I had completed my apprenticeship and become a Chalybian, what did I do? *This.*" He gestured with the heavy sword in his hand. "The death of Samsi-ditana, the death of Babylon, and the destruction of all the beauty and sweetness of it . . . it's all *my* doing."

"Seth, darling, *please!*"

There were footfalls to his left. He pivoted. The faces came in focus. "Khet! Simakura! Criton! I can't believe it! You've come back!"

The Greek did not smile. "I had to warn you," he said. "Seth: Anubis—"

"Is dead," Seth said in a hoarse voice. "He died a hero, defending the gate like the lion he was. It took twenty iron-tipped Hittite arrows to kill him."

Criton's face was made of stone. "Quickly. There's no

time. The city is doomed." His eyes bored into Seth's, and Seth flinched.

"You were right, Criton," Seth confessed. "It's all my fault. Forgive me. But we must go. Now."

With that he set off, holding Shala's hand, at a run through the back alleys toward the river. He had never been in these streets but had studied them while planning a re-structuring of this part of the city. It would now never take place. When Shala pulled at his hand at one point, he could say with confidence, "No! That's a dead end! This way!"

Then at last there was the open quay and the Euphrates, and the virtually empty New Babylon on the far bank. "If we can get across the river—"

But there on the near bank, fifty steps away, was a full troop of Hittite iron-armed soldiers.

"Run!" Criton urged. "You and Shala! You're the only hope of saving the blood of Hammurabi! If the Shinarian dynasty is ever to be restored here—"

Seth stared in horror. "You're going to stay?" he said. "And fight them off?"

"I and Simakura and Khet. Simakura is a soldier of Shinar and must not survive the city and the death of his king. Khet must stay because, weakened by wine, he unwit-tingly betrayed the city to a Hittite spy."

Seth's mouth flew open. "Khet! Is this true?"

The drunkard held his head in shame and nodded.

"They have the plans for your siege machines," Criton explained. "They could only have got them from Khet, who was seen drinking with a spy named Telepinus. Khet had no idea who Telepinus was. You know our poor friend has no more control over his tongue in such circumstances than he has over his ability to abstain from the cup."

"Poor Khet," Seth said. "You and I shall carry this guilt until we die."

"Forget that," Criton said. "You *can* live it down. The trust you betrayed, Seth—make it good. Go home. Make the Sword of Glory. Help defeat the Hai. And save Shala, who needs you."

"Criton," he whispered. He made a move to embrace his friend, but Criton pulled back. "I've betrayed you worst of all." He looked down the quay at the Hittites, who were coming at them. "Please forgive me." He suddenly remembered. "Oh, gods! Your dream! The one about dying in Babylon!"

"That's why I'm staying. A man must not fight his destiny. Go, you fool! Take Shala with you! There's no time! We'll hold them off! *Go!*"

"Criton, I loved you. You were the first, the best friend I ever had. If we must part this way—"

"Go!" Criton bellowed in rage. He drew his sword and turned to face the Hittites. Beside him Khet spat on his weapon and gave the enemy an insulting grin as they advanced. Simakura was poised on the balls of his feet, ready to fight his last battle.

Seth's heart was beating faster. He looked at Shala with tear-filled eyes.

"Come!" she said. "Otherwise what they're doing will have been done in vain!"

His whole body shook as if palsied. He turned toward the river. "Stay close behind me," he said, squeezing her hand once before releasing it. Then he dived far out into the roiling Euphrates.

The current at midriver was far stronger than he had expected, and Seth was not the strongest of swimmers. He was pulled under once and came up spitting and coughing. He could not see Shala anywhere when he stuck his head up. An arrow landed in the water not a handspan from his face. He gulped air, dived, swam as far as he could underwater, then resurfaced.

He was being carried too quickly downstream! If he could not make it to the far side, he would find himself near the southern wall, where the troop of archers stood picking off the swimmers! He had to make it!

An arrow grazed his arm.

He dived again and swam as powerfully as he could. The water was numbingly cold, chilled by the snow-fed waters of the far North. When he surfaced once more, he tried to look around. He could see a Hittite soldier on the bank bending over, hacking mercilessly away at something at his feet. Seth dived again and swam until his lungs were bursting. At last he felt his hand touch the stone embankment on the far shore!

He pulled up, surfaced, and greedily gulped air. An arrow passed him and spent itself on the stone.

"Shala!" he cried out. "Shala!"

There was no answer.

He hauled himself slowly, exhaustedly, up onto the bank.

An arrow spun harmlessly past. The current had ripped the tunic and loincloth from his body, and he was naked, shivering, covered with goosebumps.

"Shala!" he sobbed. "*Shala!*"

He shivered, then closed his eyes and besieged no god in particular: *Whoever you are, please! Please send her back to me! Save her! Even if you have to take me instead! I'm willing to die for her!*

But no one emerged from the river near him—no tiny face crowned with dark hair. No slim little body, arms, and legs churning furiously away at the current.

"Shala!" He wept inconsolably, standing miserable, beaten.

The last arrow fell beside him, its iron point scraping on the stone with a dull ring.

He looked at the far bank. None of his three defenders had survived. The Hittites were looting the dead.

Black clouds had drifted in from the west. Soon hard rains would put out the fires that raged out of control. There would be nothing left of the greatest city in all the world but soldiers, moving from house to house, raping and killing and looting. And he, Seth, had allowed it to happen.

On the bank, fighting had taken place some time before, and he noticed a single iron Hittite sword abandoned.

He plodded over to pick it up. He balanced it in his hand, then turned it so the point pricked his belly. He stood, eyes closed tightly, ready to end his own miserable life.

The thoughts came quick and harsh to his disordered mind. He shivered, as much in horror as against the chill, as fat raindrops began to pummel him. Distant thunder drowned out even the noise of the rushing river beside him.

Then he reversed the sword, opened his eyes, and grasped the iron weapon by the handle.

And, his heart as cold as the frigid Euphrates, he marched dejectedly into the bowels of New Babylon, heading for the unseen gate beyond the deserted streets and marketplaces.

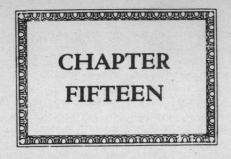

CHAPTER FIFTEEN

The Nile Delta

I

Six grueling months had passed since the terrible day when Kamose was driven from the field by Apophis. The Hai, augmented by new, fresh mercenary troops, had fought back with renewed zeal and viciousness and had taken back much lost ground. By the time Riki had returned to the war, the Shepherds controlled almost everything east of the Damietta branch of the Nile.

Now, however, Riki had brought his leadership skills to the Red Landers, and his first battle had driven the Hai back from the river's shores. The battle line now stood halfway between Avaris and the Nile, and repeated sorties by Riki's skirmishers slowly added new parcels of retaken territory every week.

To Baliniri's chagrin and Mara's horror, though, the Hai now held the lands in which the Habiru—Miriam's people—eked out a grubby existence as little more than slaves. Their treatment under Makare had been bad enough, but now that the Hai had once more become their overlords, Apophis's order went out that all male Habiru babies were to die.

The only defense against this had been for the Habiru women to deliver their own babies, keeping the secret of each new birth sacred within their own tight circle. Stillbirths were falsely and frequently reported, and the infants, who had of course been born healthy, were hidden. No one had any idea how long this precarious deception could be maintained.

Mara, for the most part, remained safe behind her own lines, reluctantly obeying strict directives from Baliniri. In her place Miriam slipped past the Hai guards and swam the river whenever a message had to be carried, delivering it personally to the new court that Baliniri and Ah-Hotep had established at Athribis.

Today Miriam, brought by chariot by couriers from her crossing point at the river, had balked at appearing at court before she had had time to bathe and dress. Mara had intercepted her and taken her to a secluded cove where the women of the court went to bathe in private. The two women tried to relax peacefully in the cool waters of the Nile.

But when they had emerged from the water and lay naked on the shore, letting the warm sun dry the water on their bodies, Mara could avoid mention of the war no longer. "How is it over there?" she asked. "How are your people holding up under the heavy hand of the Hai?"

Miriam stretched her arms high over her head, the motion bringing out the delicate beauty of her little breasts. "We're coping as best we can," she answered. "So far they haven't found any of the boy-children, and if we have anything to say about the matter, they never will. Our God has stood by us." A small breeze stirred the water at their feet; she shivered and pulled on her shift. "Our women have been strong, not missing more than a day of work."

"With any luck," Mara said, standing and hugging herself, "we'll have taken back your part of the country soon. Riki is making a lot of difference on the front." Her lip curled as she added, "My husband is no help at all, unfortunately. That setback some months ago took all the drive out of him. Now he actually believes that business about a Sword of Glory being necessary to his victory." She snorted. "All he really needs is to get rid of Amasis and the cult and get his manhood back. He isn't half the man Riki is."

Miriam looked at her: the ripely athletic, womanly body, with its still-flat belly and full breasts. There had been something different in her tone when she had spoken of Riki. "You and Kamose are still estranged?"

Mara's eyes flashed hotly, and Miriam wondered if she had overstepped propriety. Then Mara's expression softened. "I wish I'd never seen him," she confessed. "If you can keep a secret . . ."

"You know you can trust me."

"I'm not the kind of woman who can do without a man," Mara admitted. "And ever since Riki has returned to the front, my thoughts have gone to him again and again. Sometimes when I'm near him—and I wish that were more often—I get weak in the knees." She chuckled wryly. "Imagine me, tough, independent old Mara, ready to faint for love."

"My lady!" Miriam said, going back to a more formal, and safer, form of address in such dangerous waters.

"Yes," Mara continued as she stepped to the water's edge and looked down at her reflected image. "If he were here now, and you, my dear, were not . . . ah, Miriam! I'd give myself to him in a moment. But the trouble is, I'm not sure he still feels the same about me."

"Ma'am?"

Mara stirred the water with her foot, and the image broke into ripples. "What irony," she said. "We were children together. His first sexual thought was of me. I remember it quite clearly: He was as naked as I am now, and his body could not hide his interest from me. Can it be that, since Teti, he does not look on me with the same eyes? Am I so unattractive?"

"My lady, if I had the good fortune to look as you do now—"

Mara shivered, not from the cold, and bent over for her shift. She slipped it over her head and pulled it down. It hid nothing of her voluptuous beauty. "Queens cannot order men to fall in love with them, or even to feel lust for them." She sighed. "Perhaps he is still in love with his wife. Heaven knows, Teti was a magnificent specimen of a woman, tall and slim, with a neck like a gazelle and marvelous legs. She and her women went around as naked as children, giving the matter not a second thought. That was a provocative sight, let me tell you. They were unbelievably fit and wore nothing but gold jewelry. If I were a man I'd disgrace myself around the likes of them—and probably get my throat cut; better than half of them, as I understand, prefer one another's company to a man's."

Miriam's eyes were wide. She had never heard such talk. "My lady!" she said, shocked.

"No, it's true. I remember getting a hot glance from that assistant of Teti's—Weret, I think the name was—as if she had some designs on my own company. And I tell you, Miriam, the thought did run through my mind for a moment."

"Oh! My lady—"

"Don't be so scandalized. My people don't stifle their thoughts to the same extent yours do." She sighed, and her shoulders sagged. "Don't mind me," she said. "I suppose I'm saying this at least partly to get a reaction from you. But I'm lonely, Miriam. I haven't had a man since—"

"Ma'am, please!"

"All right. But I've tried everything to attract Riki short of throwing myself at him or parading naked around him. I'm almost tempted to try those, but I doubt if I could pry him away from the war! And . . . think how humiliated I would be if he didn't respond *then*."

"My lady, it's getting late. I have to report to Baliniri."

"You're right," Mara said. She stepped into her sandals and took the girl's hand. "I'm sure you'll also want to stop by and see your mother. She's due any day now. I'm so glad we brought her here for safety's sake. I have a feeling about that child of hers. I'm no seer, but I somehow feel it's very important that this child be saved and allowed to grow up in safety. Is Levi sure it'll be a man-child?"

"Yes. His visions are never wrong. God has spoken to him, he says. He agrees with your feelings about Mother's baby. You can imagine what he'd have said otherwise about your asking for Mother to be brought here to be hidden among you 'heathens' as her time approaches."

Mara laughed. "That's Levi. I keep getting the feeling, whenever I talk with him, that the moment I turn my back he makes the sign against the evil eye."

Miriam joined in the laughter. "He may, for all I know. Don't mind him. He's just very strict and old-fashioned. I happen to know he thinks more of you than of any Egyptian."

"That's something, I suppose," Mara said resignedly. The two women, hand in hand, came out of the bulrushes that hid their little beach, then climbed to the high road that led back to the palace. But now Mara stopped and half turned to look back at the little cove nearby. "That's strange," she remarked. "This time of day Thermutis is usually here with her handmaids. She likes to bathe in that sheltered spot around the bend from where we were."

"Isn't she about to come to term, too? You don't suppose—"

"It could be. She spends a lot of time alone since her husband, Zer, died. Poor brave fool that he was! He could have stayed at court, nice and safe, but he insisted on going off to war with Kamose. Zer died the same day that Kamose's sword broke, and he ran from the field." She led Miriam carefully around a depression in the road, where the turgid surface had fallen through. "Well, your people are fortunate to have avoided *that*, at any rate."

Miriam gave her a humorless smile. "Oh, yes," she said. "It isn't necessary to put us on the front lines to kill us. They can do it by working us to death. And killing off our infant sons."

"I'm sorry. I didn't mean . . ."

"Oh, it's all right. At least Mother's child will be safe here, unless the cult gets some ideas."

"Over my dead body. Let's see: This child would be fourth in line for the priesthood after Levi, your grandfather Kohath, your father, and your brother, Aaron."

"Yes."

"I see. And it's traditional for a bit of Joseph's prophetic power to fall upon the high priest?"

"Yes. God will speak through him, as he spoke through Joseph, and speaks through Levi."

"I don't understand the succession," Mara said. "Why not through Joseph's sons? Why Levi's?"

"Jacob was a vessel of God. And before him, Isaac and Abraham, father of *our* line."

Mara chuckled softly. "Oh, yes. Abraham the sorcerer, as our historians call him. The one who struck great Sesostris blind to make him let your people go. Well, I wonder what it will take this time to free the Habiru."

"It will take a Deliverer," Miriam replied in a quiet voice full of emotion. "One of the blood of Levi. Joseph's sons are half-Egyptian."

* * *

Just down the road they picked up a silent squad of soldiers who had been guarding all land approaches to their little beach. Now they escorted the two women from a discreet distance. Mara exchanged glances with their leader and turned back to Miriam with a wicked smile. "That one," she said. "He was watching us. I could see it in his eyes."

"At us?" Miriam said, shocked. "At—me?"

"Come now," Mara said, laughing. "In his place, wouldn't you? But no, I suppose you wouldn't. And maybe I'm imagining things. I've gone without a man too long."

The door to the anteroom to Thermutis's chamber opened a crack. Baliniri quickly rose and walked to the door; fearful that something might go wrong, he had dismissed all the guards and servants from the anteroom, and no one was permitted in this end of the royal apartments but he, Ah-Hotep, and the deaf-mute midwife in charge of delivering Thermutis's child. This had been a troublesome pregnancy, with much weakness and nausea, leaving the princess with little strength for her difficult and lengthy delivery.

Ah-Hotep looked through the door crack. "Is anyone there?" she asked.

"The room's cleared. The whole wing. Why?"

"We have a boy-child."

There was something about her tone. "But?"

"It was a breech birth, but that doesn't explain it."

"What's wrong? Didn't the child survive?"

She let out a deep, deep sigh. "Yes, poor thing. It was born terribly deformed. I don't know how long he will survive."

Baliniri stared at her in horror. This child was their only hope. "What will we do?"

"I don't know. But this can't get out. We have to buy time to think. Poor Thermutis herself doesn't even know. She's all doped up on *shepenn*. The pain of a breech birth was too much for her."

Baliniri grasped her hand. It was sweaty and stained with the blood of childbirth. "You're right. Absolute silence. There has to be a way. There has to be a way!"

The ex-queen looked him in the eye, her face somber and serious. "I have great confidence in you," she said. "You'll think of something. But quickly! Quickly!"

II

Their discreet bodyguards deposited the two women at the palace door and withdrew. A minor functionary whose name Mara could never remember approached them as they entered the great central hall, from which the wings diverged. "My lady," he said, "the lord Baliniri would like to see you in his rooms as soon as possible." Something in his manner subtly conveyed disapproval, but it stopped carefully short of insolence; Mara's sharp tongue was known and feared all through the court and beyond. "Oh, yes. You asked me to let you know when General Riki arrived. He is quartered in one of the guest apartments. He is supposed to see Baliniri, also, so you may run into each other there."

Mara and Miriam exchanged glances. Miriam was about to say something, but the official addressed her now. "And you, my lady." The phrase set oddly on his lips, as if it did not fit a mere non-Egyptian, and a Habiru, at that. "Your mother has gone into labor."

"When?" Miriam asked.

"Moments ago, no more. If you go—"

"Mara, I've got to go to her now."

"Do." Mara pressed her hand warmly. "Call on the staff for anything you need. A midwife will already be in attendance. And good luck!"

Mara watched her go; then she turned back to the court functionary before her. "Just a moment," she said. "How secure do you think your job is, my friend?"

"Why, my lady, I—"

"I can enlighten you with a word. Your buttocks are poised precisely one handspan above an oaken stake so sharp you could clean your fingernails with it. You are being held safe above this formidable weapon by one thing only, and that is my good opinion of you. Do you have any idea how weak and attenuated that opinion has become, watching you tiptoe around insulting me, your queen, and my friend Miriam?"

"A thousand pardons, my lady! If I have in any way—"

"You will treat both of us with *exaggerated* respect in future. You will ooze unctuousness as if it were sweat. Do you understand?"

"Yes, my lady!"

"Very well. You may go. Backward. Bowing and scraping. *Go!*"

Riki, still dusty from the road, met Baliniri in the outer hall. Baliniri looked distracted, his eyes focused on something beyond the middle distance.

"Baliniri!" Riki said. "I have to talk to you. We're going to lose this war if you don't do something about the cult. And I mean now! If I have to deal with those bastards *and* fight—"

"Please," Baliniri said, "can't we discuss that this evening? There are pressing matters—"

"Damn it! People are dying out there! I not only have to fight Shepherds, I have to fight Kamose as well. *And* Amasis. And now you send me a whole new troop of reinforcements led by a cult member. I'm the one who has to deal with him. If I try to discipline him or dismiss him—"

"Shhh!" Baliniri said. "The walls have ears. Come back after dark. We can talk then. Right now I'm very busy." He lowered his voice and pulled Riki close. "I don't even know where that hound Makare is now. He could be hiding behind a tapestry, for all I know."

"Curse him! Can't a knife be slipped into him? Are there no hired assassins left in Egypt? Time was when you had someone around who was that much trouble—"

"I know, I know. We'll talk about it tonight. Just now I've got a problem. Have you seen Mara? No? Well, if you see her, tell her to come to me." He turned and strode away.

Riki scowled. He had come a long way at great speed, hoping for Baliniri's immediate support against his enemies. The inevitable confrontations with Kamose and with Amasis grew more frequent, and worst of all, most of the officer corps were sworn members of the cult. Without firm support from court, Riki and the war effort were doomed.

He stood, closed his eyes, and took a deep breath to calm himself. *No use getting upset. Just do your best. There is a part you must play in all this, and you must save yourself for that.*

Ah! If only he knew what his mysterious role was. But

whatever it was, he would be spared long enough to do it. That much he knew: From that blinding moment of vision, when he had been inside Teti's mind and known that great inner peace, he could remember that whatever his own contribution was to be, he would survive to do it. Beyond that, he could not say.

Nor did he much care. There was strength and comfort to know that he would ultimately be with Teti and that their much-desired reunion was only being postponed long enough for him to accomplish this mysterious and enigmatic deed.

He sighed and opened his eyes. To his surprise, Mara was standing before him. He smiled. "Mara! What a wonderful sight! How glad I am to see you!"

He offered her his arms, thinking to give her the embrace of a brother, only to have her melt against him in his embrace in a most unsisterly fashion! Her body pressed close to his; her arms held him tightly; she drew his lips down. Her kiss was a physical shock—passionate, demanding!

He pulled loose, wide-eyed and startled. "Mara!"

She smiled. It was the smile of a courtesan. He could not pull his eyes away or look down. "Here," she said. She pulled him into an empty room nearby and slammed the door behind them. Then, backing him against the wall, she pressed herself to him once more.

"Riki," she whispered. "Darling Riki."

"Mara, I don't know what to say."

"I've been wanting to do this for so long. Haven't you noticed the way I look at you?"

"Mara, when we were children together—"

"I should never have let you get away from me. What a fool I was to let us drift apart! I've loved you from the first moment I saw you. You came to my rescue and risked your life for me. If it hadn't been for you, I wouldn't be alive now."

"Mara—"

"I know. You're still in love with your wife. But Riki, Teti loved you too much to want you to be lonely after she was gone. I know I can hardly replace her in your heart, but let me try."

Lonely? He was not lonely. After having experienced that moment of complete peace, of complete union, he could never be lonely again.

Then the realization suddenly came through to him—so

sharply defined that his heart almost stopped. She was not really talking about *him* being lonely. She was talking about herself!

Poor dear Mara! Life had let her down so. This damned cult had sucked the guts out of her husband until he was no more a man to her. She was vulnerable, frightened, and lonely. No matter that she pretended to be hard, aggressive, and demanding.

He understood. He relaxed and held her to him, rocking her, rubbing her back affectionately, crooning low into her ear. "Mara, dear Mara. I know. I understand. How hard it is to be on this earth! How painfully lonely we all are! How much we need one another!" He kissed her forehead and pressed her to him. He could feel that she was crying. His hand crept behind her neck and caressed her nape softly. "How brave you are to come to me this way. Proud as you are, I know what that must have cost you."

She tried to speak, but the words were muffled against his chest.

"It's all right. I'm here. I'll be here for you until I have to go back. You're right. We did love each other. My brave, beautiful, lonely friend! I've missed you too. But we had other duties, didn't we? We did them as well as we could, but life disappointed us."

He rocked her in his arms. He felt strangely sad and happy at the same time. He was more at peace than he had been ever since he had come back to the war. This had nothing at all to do with the bond between him and Teti. He knew Teti would not mind. A friend needed him, and he loved Mara too, in a way.

He pulled back and held her at arm's length. "How lovely you are," he said in a soft voice. "Don't think I don't see. There is none like you in all Egypt. You are beyond compare, and yet I would love you if you were ugly, for that great heart of yours. Gods! No wonder Makare fears you!"

Her eyes, red from crying, looked uncomprehendingly up at him.

"Whose room is this?" he asked. "It must have belonged to one of Ah-Hotep's maids. She dismissed a round dozen of them a week ago, and nobody knows why. I'll bolt the door. No one will miss either of us for an hour."

Smiling, he bent to kiss her. Then he moved over to the door and shot the bolt.

* * *

At the end of the long transverse hallway Baliniri spotted a familiar face. "Miriam!" he called out. "Wait! I have to talk to you!"

Miriam paused, a pile of gleaming white towels in her hands, as he bore down on her. "Quickly, please, my lord. My mother's time came." She smiled. "I have a brother, as Levi predicted. But she needs me now."

Baliniri's face changed, and he stopped dead in his tracks. "Quickly! Come into this other room for a moment!"

The two slipped into a room and closed the door. "How many people know about your mother?" he asked.

"I, my mother, and the midwife." She paused. "There was a courtier, a snippy little fellow. I can't remember his name."

"I know who you mean. He knows your mother has delivered? That the child lives?"

"No, only that her time had come. And Mara heard him."

"That's good. I'll talk to Mara, and I'll silence the servant and midwife. Now take me in to see the child. Have you a name for him yet?"

"No. Levi gave us a list to choose from. My father told us before we brought Mother here that he favored one. I can't remember what it was."

"Don't worry. I'll take care of everything. But keep absolutely silent from this moment. I'll bar all entries and exits from this wing. No one comes in, no one comes out."

"Yes, my lord. But why?"

"Wait a moment. I'll explain everything in your mother's room."

"As you wish, my lord."

The guard stopped Makare at the entrance to the suite of apartments in Baliniri's end of the building. "I'm sorry, sir," he ordered stiffly. "Baliniri's personal orders."

Makare stepped so close to him, the guard could feel Makare's breath on his face. "You're not one of us . . . yet," he said in a voice heavy with menace. "But you want to be. You know that without joining us you will never rise. Not in the court guards, not in the army, not anywhere. You understand?"

"Yes, sir. But I have my orders."

"Why cordon the area off?"

"I don't know, sir."

Makare considered. "The queen's daughter, Zer's wife, she was due to come to term, wasn't she?"

"I don't know, sir."

Makare scowled and stepped back. "The child is of royal blood on both sides. Under such circumstances the usual thing is to have officials on hand to certify the birth, not to bar visitors and hide it. Now why would they—?"

"I'm sure I don't know, sir."

Afterward Mara lay in Riki's arms. "I must have been like a clenched fist," she mused, "running around here all full of tension. I don't know how anyone managed to tolerate me."

Riki cradled her breast in one hand, smiled, and bent to kiss it while his hand caressed her naked hip.

"Oh, Riki, I'm so glad I got up my courage and approached you. I've been so alone, so afraid."

"Don't worry. I'm here. While I'm alive, I'm here for you."

After he had gone, she remembered those last words. He had spoken no more; it had been all laughs and caresses. He had kissed her and gone away—to do what, she could not say. She sat on the bed now, still naked, dazzled, trying to think.

The thought had slipped up on her only after he left. Now she could not get it out of her mind.

While I'm alive . . ."

He had said it so oddly, as if he knew he were going to die but were not afraid. As if it did not matter.

III

"Think of it," Baliniri urged, looking from Jochebed to Miriam. "If Apophis wins or if this war continues and we do not win back the land where your people live, his edict will remain in effect. Sooner or later you will no longer be able to hide your son from his butchers."

Jochebed hugged the tiny infant to her bosom. Her face was a mask of shock, and she could not speak.

Baliniri continued. "And if we win but the cult remains strong here, the leaders—Amasis, Makare—will still carry much influence. They hate your people passionately. If the child is among you, will your people be able to suppress the rumors about his special status, about Levi's prophecies concerning his future?" His eyes bored into Jochebed's relentlessly. "And once the truth gets out, how will the cult react to hearing of the birth of a Deliverer, whose destiny is to lead you all back home again, to reign in the land from which Jacob expelled Amasis?"

Miriam shuddered. "You draw a horrible picture. I don't even want to think of it."

"I don't like it either. But consider the alternative. The baby must be saved; we all agree on that. Not just because we want to save every precious life we can in the face of this tyranny but because if he lives, he may be the immeasurably important child of destiny your people dream of."

Miriam looked at her mother, then at the vizier. "But raised as an Egyptian?"

"Egyptians circumcise their sons as you do. No one will know except us." He smiled. "And mark me: raised not just as an Egyptian, but as a favored adopted son of Princess Thermutis. If we manage this correctly, he may even be in succession to the crown of the Two Lands." He let it sink in for a moment. "The choices are two: the child safe and protected or forever a step from violent death. Which will it be?"

Jochebed, sitting up, cradled the tiny figure and rocked it softly. Her eyes were wet with tears, but she did not cry aloud. In a strong voice that startled Baliniri, she said, "We can tell no one. Not Levi, not your father, even if it breaks their hearts. Not for many years can they learn of this—not until the child is grown."

"Oh, Mother!"

"There is no other way," her mother said flatly. "And I thank the brave Egyptian friend of our people."

"I'm originally from Babylon, ma'am."

"That explains your cunning as well as your compassion.

What would you have us do? Do I take the poor defective child home with me and pretend he is mine?"

"That won't be necessary. The princess's child, if he survives, will be smuggled out into the country to be raised by others. The princess will be told that he was stillborn." He blew out a deep breath. "But I doubt if the child will survive the night. As for giving your child to the princess, I haven't decided how to go about that."

"Ah. How can I lie to Levi? And how can I lie to my husband? In some ways this is the bitterest thing of all."

"Mother," Miriam said gently, "we can never tell Great-Grandfather. He's too old and cannot keep a secret. But perhaps as the years go by, we can share the secret with Father."

"What?" her mother asked. "And tell him I gave away his son?"

"When the time comes, Mother, I will take the blame. I will tell him that, fearful for my brother's safety, I put him in a little papyrus basket at the water's edge, making sure that it floated past the place where the princess bathed. I even know the place. Father will be in a towering rage at me." She shrugged. "But in time he will come around."

Jochebed and Baliniri exchanged glances.

"That might just work," the vizier said. "Before her lying-in, the princess made a habit of bathing in the same cove every day at a specific time. . . ."

"I know where that is," Miriam said. "Mara told me."

Jochebed looked at her daughter. "It makes me sad to realize that my little son will grow up not knowing who he is—"

"Mother! *Think*. How else are we to make sure that he grows up at all? He *is* the child of Levi's prophecy, Mother. He *must* be protected."

Baliniri shook his head sadly and could find nothing to say for a long moment. "I wish," he said at last, "that there were something in my life that I was as sure of as you are of this God of yours, and of the rightness of His ways."

Miriam's glance sympathized. "You people of other cultures believe something because it is expedient—that if you make burnt offerings to some god, he will cause the sun to shine, the earth to be fruitful, your crops to grow. You think that the return of spring and seasonal floods in the delta each year are your rewards for propitiating the god."

Baliniri said, not jesting, "I wish you could explain it to me. I really want to know. What is the alternative to believing a thing because it works?"

Miriam's eyes had a triumphant glint in them. "Why, believing a thing because it is true." His eyes showed his surprise. It was evident that he had never for so much as a moment considered this perspective. She went on. "What if your people omitted the ritual, and spring came anyway? Or say they complete the ritual faithfully, but spring is late by a month and a half. Such things have happened. For you there is a crisis of faith. But we do not view the matter in terms of punishment and reward. For us, things are as they are, and God is God. He is not to be doubted or questioned. It is our duty to praise Him, in good times or ill, because this is what we were created to do."

Baliniri was deeply moved. "This," he said huskily, "is a new thing in the world!"

"No," responded Miriam confidently. "It is the oldest thing in the world. It is only your comprehension of it that is new. And it is true, irrefutable, and not contingent upon your belief, mine, Mother's, or Levi's." She looked at her mother, got the confirmation she sought in a silent look of understanding. "We will do as you suggest. We trust you will ensure that my brother will be raised as the adopted son of the princess, under your protection. But there is one condition."

"Name it."

"Mother will be the wet nurse. This way she can be with him all the time, and no one will be suspicious of her love for him or her need to see him daily."

"A stroke of genius," Baliniri said. "I admire the strength of the women of your people."

Miriam smiled. "Just raise my brother well, and you will find out just what kind of hero our tribe can produce. Our men are as strong as our women."

Baliniri smiled. "You make my heart light. I like your idea about the papyrus basket. There are legends common to the delta about children being passed in this way from a poor family to a rich one. Since people have heard these stories, they will be excited by such an event taking place in their own lifetime—and to the princess, who has had such sadness in her young life."

"Wouldn't it be easier just to claim that my son is Thermutis's? Can't we switch the babies without anyone being the wiser?" Jochebed asked. "If we give the child up to the Nile, he would not have the protection of having his enemies think him a prince of the blood."

"It is not his enemies whom I wish to think this," explained Baliniri. "It is his friends. Your people will never accept him as their Deliverer unless the possibility exists that he is *not* of the blood. He *must* be a foundling. And . . . I have a name to suggest for him. I will say that it came from Thermutis's mother, my wife. We shall call him Moses, 'saved from the water.' "

"Moses," said Jochebed. "My little Moses."

"I'm sorry, sir," the servant said. He was backed up against the wall, and Makare's huge hand caressed his throat with a frightening mock gentleness. "I don't know any more than that. The vizier cleared this wing when the princess came to term, and no one has seen her child yet."

"You sniveling hyena," Makare growled. "I ought to twist your head off." The big hand tightened around the man's neck, letting him know how close he was to death.

"Here, what's this?" a contralto voice said behind him. "You, Makare! What are you doing in this wing? You're not allowed or wanted here."

Makare released the man to spin around and confront Mara. The servant scurried away, terrified. "You're up to something," he accused. "I don't know what it is, but I will. And when I find out—"

Mara stood her ground as always. But the edge of hatred, of controlled venom, was gone from her voice and eyes. "Now you get out of here!"

Makare perceived the difference immediately. "Ah! The witch has lost her power! Something's happened to you. You're not the terror you were. The goddess has you in thrall."

"Nothing's changed," Mara retorted stoutly. But even she could tell something was wrong.

"Yes it has!" Makare cried out, triumphant. "There's something gone!" He grinned nastily and stepped forward and put one hand on her shoulder. His grip was intended to give pain, and in fact he could see her wince from it. He increased the pressure, and she cried out. "Aha!" he said, releasing her. "Your power over me has withered away. I will

come and go as I please. The likes of you will not stop me
again. The palace guard is ours already; one or another of
them will tell me what's going on. In the meantime . . . well,
well." His smile was deadly. "My pleasure in destroying you,
a bit at a time, will be intense."

"You dare to speak to me in this way?" she said, indignant. "Just you wait. I'll tell Baliniri about your threats. I'll
tell Riki."

"A dotard and a madman. Ha! I'm trembling with fear."
His voice dripped contempt. "Don't make me laugh. Riki has
concluded his business here, I think, and has left the palace
for the military camp outside. One word from me, and four of
my best assassins will fall upon him."

"You'll do nothing of the sort, not with the delta nom-
archs and the priesthood of Amon on our side," she told him.

"Perhaps not," Makare suggested. "Perhaps I will wait
until he goes back to the war tomorrow, then. Perhaps I will
go to the front myself. All sorts of things can happen during a
war. In the heat of battle, through the dust and confusion,
who sees everything that goes on?"

"You wouldn't!"

"Wouldn't I?" *This* smile was truly frightening. "We
shall see. Meanwhile, my impotent witch, don't sleep too
soundly. If I want to reach you, no walls can keep me away
. . . just as no walls will keep me from finding out what secret
surrounds the lying-in of the princess Thermutis."

With this he turned and walked away slowly, insolently.

She stood, trembling alike with hatred and fear. *If I had
a knife* . . . she thought. But her hands were empty, and her
heart was heavier than it had been in many months.

Baliniri and Ah-Hotep conferred. "I *knew* you'd find a
way," she said, her hand caressing his neck. "And now that
Thermutis's child has died, the way is open for her to accept
a foundling into her empty heart."

"Poor thing," Baliniri said. "I'm sorry for you, too. He
was your grandson." He turned his head to kiss her wrist. "I
can't accept all the praise for formulating the plan. It was the
Habiru women. They're formidable. Now I understand how
their tiny nation, surrounded by enemies, has survived all
this long. This kind of mettle allowed Jacob to challenge the
cult up in Canaan, and to win out. But that doesn't mean I

want you to stop praising me altogether. You can continue that all day and night." Then he scowled. "Except that I have an appointment with Riki. He's going back tomorrow."

Ah-Hotep massaged her husband's shoulders. "Several of the servants told me that Makare was snooping around this wing. One said Makare had threatened him."

"Threatened! That settles it. I have to get him away from court. *Hmmmm.* Why don't I send him to the front as an observer?"

"Not a bad idea," she said. "After all, he's not invulnerable. All sorts of things can happen during a war."

IV

When Ah-Hotep had gone back to Thermutis's quarters, Baliniri rang for an aide. As the fellow's face popped out of a side room, the vizier said, "I'm going to walk in the garden. If General Riki wants me, tell him to look for me there."

Once in the arbor, under the oleanders, he sat on a stone bench and looked out across the shallow pool, where in the dusk hour, a slight breeze stirred the water in long ripples. Suddenly the tension had gone out of him, and he felt relaxed and contemplative.

We're planning a world, Ah-Hotep and I, he thought. *I wonder how much of it either of us will live to see.*

Things were going according to plan so far. There were contingency strategies for quite a number of possible alternative situations that might arise. And with the day's events—the sad but timely death of Thermutis's deformed infant and the acceptance by Miriam and Jochebed of the plans for baby Moses, who could, in the future, be maneuvered into Kamose's place—the network of interlocking possibilities was nearly complete.

Now, thinking the matter out, he remembered the head astrologer's prediction, some months earlier, concerning the great hero who would be born around this time in the delta, during an extraordinary alignment of the stars and planets.

Both he and Ah-Hotep had commented at the time on the odd and perhaps propitious conjunction between this prediction and Levi's vision, which had told of the birth of a promised Deliverer who would free the Habiru and take them back to their ancestral lands. He, Baliniri, had played an important role in bringing the seeming coincidence to pass—he, who had forgotten the chief astrologer's prognostication altogether!

How curious! Innocently he had been the instrument of the fulfilled prediction. What had made him suddenly improvise such an idea?

What if this Habiru God had intervened, using Baliniri as a mere tool of His will, as the Habiru believed He could do? This and the little prince's deformity and death were indeed extraordinary—as was Jochebed's sudden and easy acceptance of the scheme; he had expected vigorous opposition.

Well, events were beginning to take shape. He had the firm support of the upriver and downriver districts and noble families. They were a clear majority, backed by the priesthood of Amon, which hated the cult, feared Amasis, and had never accepted Kamose in the first place. Thanks to the day's doings, he now had a candidate for the crown of the Two Lands. The stage was set for a takeover and a regency, with him at its head until the child reached its majority.

There was also good support building outside the mainstream of Egyptian society. Upriver he had not only the Desert Legion, as Riki had dubbed it, and its shock-troop supplement, the Black Wind; he also, thanks to Ebana's behind-the-scenes maneuvering, had a firm, if secret, treaty between his court—*his* court, not Kamose's—and Nubia. At his call, young King Nehsi and his army would cross the frontier and join with the legion in Thebes to mount a huge offensive to crush Kamose.

With any luck this would happen when Kamose, victorious but battered after the final defeat of the Hai, came straggling home with half an army, bone-tired. Baliniri's legions and Nehsi's, fresh and rested, would meet him.

A long shadow fell across him in the dusk. He turned.

"Riki!" he said. "I'm glad you've come. I shooed everyone away. We can talk without being disturbed or overheard. Sit beside me."

"I can't stay long," Riki said. "Mara ran into Makare. For some reason she doesn't frighten him anymore. He even threatened her. If I can find him tonight, I'll kill him." The thought came out very casually, as if he were talking about cutting down a stalk of grain. "I gather you'd have no objection?"

"None. I'd vote you a medal and a bonus. Only you wouldn't wear the one or spend the other. What am I to do with a soldier who doesn't care about anything that soldiers are supposed to care about?" He chuckled affectionately. "Not even strong drink or wenches."

Riki shrugged. "I've had enough strong drink for a lifetime or two. And as for wenches . . ." He sighed and smiled a very small smile. "Mara declared herself to me today. It appears that her affections have left Kamose and turned themselves to me. She is an extraordinary woman, and in a way I love her as she wishes me to. But not enough. There is a part of me that is not here anymore. It is in a place I cannot describe."

"Please try."

"Before I left the oasis I met Neku-re, as you had intended. Something indescribable happened."

"You were healed. I can tell."

"I was healed of the desire for life—*and* of the desire for death. I feel like a man marking time, waiting for a summons. There is something I was sent among you to do. I do not know what it is, but when it comes, I will recognize it."

"Riki, are you all right?"

"Never better. I'm at peace with myself. I can fight without passion, and I seem to be more efficient for it. I can respond to Mara's needs without feeling a need for her. This is a strangely passive position for me. I do not care which way things go. I will just do my job as it is shown me to do." He looked at Baliniri and smiled, and somehow the smile was the most chilling thing of all. "My time is short," he stated. "It is the way things are. It is not my job to question or to resist."

This was so startlingly close to what Miriam had said earlier about her people's relation to their God that Baliniri blinked, surprised. "You have received a vision of the future, as Teti did?"

"No, but for a moment I was inside Teti's mind. I am neither fearful nor unhappy. Quite the contrary. I think I will never be afraid again. I think I will never be unhappy."

"Riki! I can't let you go to the front thinking like this! A soldier must have the drive to survive."

"I respectfully disagree. There is nothing else you can

do. It is a thing that will happen. Neither of us can stop it. It was preordained a thousand years before either of us was born."

"And you cannot prevent it?"

"I have no wish to. I am surprised to be able to tell you that will is a very heavy burden to bear, and one that feels good when it is at last put down."

"But a *passive* Riki? Can this be the same man?"

"I am a dozen times stronger than before, because I do what I must do without having to carry that terrible burden of free choice. When I go into the field tomorrow, no one will be able to recognize me. While I am allowed to fight, none will be able to stand before me."

There was something new in his tone. He looked off into the distance, then back into Baliniri's eyes. His gaze was clear-eyed, fearless, accepting. "That is curious," he said. "Something has just told me that the day after tomorrow . . ."

"Yes? Go on!"

"That will be the day when it will happen. Just for a moment, I could look into the future and see nothing beyond that day."

"You do not fear this?"

Riki smiled and put a roughly affectionate hand on his old friend and mentor's shoulder. "There is nothing left to fear," he said. He stood up. "I have said good-bye to Mother, and I wanted to say good-bye to you, Baliniri."

"Can I be losing you? The son I never had?" His voice broke.

"Son? Yes, I suppose I am. What a strange life I have had. I spent my childhood thinking myself a bastard with no father. But think of the excellent fathers I have had! You and Baba of El-Kab! The only two men my mother ever really loved!"

Riki took Baliniri's hands and raised him to a standing position. "Ah, Baliniri, you don't get up as quickly as you once did. Age finally comes to the one man in the world I thought was going to stay young and powerful forever!"

"I feel a thousand years old just now. The more so since I am not strong enough to hold you and keep you here with us."

"You are stronger than that, dear friend. You are strong enough to let me go, to wish me well. Nothing can happen to me except the thing that is *supposed* to happen, which neither of us can stop."

"Oh, I wish I'd never sent you to Neku-re! This is my doing!"

"No, no! Because you did, I learned a thing fifty life-times could not have taught me. I have found peace and fulfillment at last." His eyes narrowed. "The child. The child born today. The one the astrologers told you about."

"How did you know about that?"

"I *remembered* it. I knew it before but had forgotten. Baliniri, guard that child! Watch over him day and night! Don't let them near him! This child will change the world!"

Baliniri's heart was pounding so fast he thought it would fail. "Speak. I will do as you say."

"That's all," Riki said. "I can say no more. But you have arranged a great thing today. You have no idea how great. You and I, we mattered to the world for a while. I for a short time, you for a great deal longer. We will be forgotten, and our names will be scattered like the sands. There will come a time when the scrolls bearing your name or mine will rot, when the years will have obliterated our faces on the friezes on the walls at Thebes. All the great buildings of Thebes and Memphis will be rubble, and the Hai will be forgotten. But this child's name, in that unimaginable age, will be a byword on the lips of millions. *Moses . . .*"

Baliniri's heart almost did stop this time. He tried to speak but could not. Riki embraced him, kissed him on both cheeks, then turned and strode away, his step jaunty and military. It was not until he was through the door and out of sight that Baliniri could find breath again.

"M-moses?" he said. "How did you know the name? I didn't tell you! I didn't tell anybody!"

There was no answer but the sighing of the wind in the oleanders as the last rays of sunlight faded. Riki was gone.

Riki took one last turn up and down the halls, looking for Makare, but there was no sign of him.

He stopped at the fountain in the middle of the great entrance hall and closed his eyes, thinking. When he re-opened them, the servants had entered the great room and were lighting the torches before the stone doorways.

No, he decided, he would not see Mara before he left.

His one chance to get away was to go now and not bind her to him more strongly than he had already done. It was a good thing to comfort her, but it would not be advisable or kind to have her make more of the time they had spent together.

He looked up through an aperture in the roof. The stars were clear, and he wondered which were the ones that the astrologers had predicted would foretell the birth of the child, the promised Deliverer of the Habiru.

Well, the moon would be out, large and bright, in a few minutes. If he set out now, without waiting for his escort, he could be at the battle lines by dawn. And he could study the stars along the way and ponder the great thing they were pointing to.

Moses! Where had the name come from? But it had been in his mind, clear and unmistakable.

He smiled and faced the wing where the two women had given birth today—slave and prince's daughter. He saluted them silently. Good fortune to both! Ah, what a gorgeous, exciting future stretched ahead for them!

But not for him. His time had come. His life would be numbered in hours, from this point.

How happy he was!

An hour before midnight Baliniri answered his own door, responding to frantic knocking. When he opened it, a distraught Mara stood in the doorway, her eyes wide with fear and anxiety. "Riki's gone!" she cried. "He left an hour after dark!"

"Here," he said, "come inside, please."

She let herself be ushered inside. He bolted his door. "And Makare left an hour after him, telling no one. I bribed a servant to tell me." She laughed nervously. "Some queen I am, having to bribe people to tell me the truth!"

"Indeed, the cult has most of the staff now . . . on the other end of the building, anyway. So Makare goes to the front. Do you think Riki can't handle him? Anything can happen to Makare at the front. A Hai arrow could rid us of him—"

Mara ran her fingers nervously through her hair. "Makare threatened Riki's life earlier today. I didn't warn him. I didn't want to disturb him. He won't suspect!"

"Yes, he will," Baliniri soothed, putting a comforting hand on her shoulders. "He's not frightened of what's to come. He's happy. It's the most amazing thing I've ever seen."

"Yes!" she said. Her voice was almost a scream. "He knows he's going to die! He won't do anything to stop it! And just when I—"

Baliniri's big arms went around her, strong and comforting. "Mara, what can I say? He loves you. He said so. But he's had a vision of how things must be. Nothing could possibly stop him."

"I'm going to the front," she said.

"No! I forbid it!"

"With your approval or without."

Baliniri sighed and held her at arm's length. "If you go, you go with a handpicked guard. Makare may be lying in wait for *you* on the road."

"Baliniri, wish me luck? Please?"

V

Naked, salt-encrusted, burnt black by the sun, the pirate crew hauled powerfully on the brails until the single sail bunched tightly against the yard. Then they secured the lines and pitched the twin anchors overboard into the shallows at fore and aft.

"Damn your eyes," the captain muttered. "I've half a mind not to let you go. If I kept you aboard, you'd make me rich in a year. I could retire. I could buy land, slaves, and a hundred virgins. I could disport myself with them day and night."

"You *know* I have to go," Seth said.

"Why am I doing this? Why am I favoring you?"

"Because it is your pleasure to do so," Seth said grimly. "Nobody in the world could force you."

"That *is* true," the captain agreed thoughtfully.

"But a great heart alone knows largesse. You can afford to be generous." He shaded his eyes and looked out over the strait. "Egypt is in this direction. All I have to do is march . . . *hmm* . . . north by northeast."

"Right. Ah, Seth! You've made me rich already. That

ram you invented, and the sling that allows me to throw balls of fire long distances in the air . . ."

Seth smiled at the captain, with his big belly and black beard and bulging eyes. "You'll be busy, trying to spend all the plunder I've helped you gather."

"Ach, perhaps you're right," the captain conceded, grinning. "After all, how much palm wine can a man drink? How many women can he deflower? I'd have to hire additional staff just to rape virgins for me." The pirate sighed hugely; he did everything in the same flamboyant style, including admitting defeat. "Very well—go. Leave me at my hour of need."

Seth, as naked and sunburnt as the rest, stepped to the rail. "At some other time," he said, "I would have enjoyed spending another six months with you. There were sailing maneuvers I dreamed up in my sleep and will probably never get to try now. And I had a notion about how to know north from south, even when there's thick fog. A sliver of iron I made from that piece of meteorite . . . but no. Perhaps later. Good-bye, you old reprobate. I'll miss you."

Wearing only the big leather pouch and water bag he had brought aboard, he dived into the clear water of the cove.

When Riki had arrived at dawn, the camp was all but deserted. Far out on the plain the battle was raging; Apophis, determined to win back ground gained by Kamose a week before, had attacked at first light, and while the Egyptian line had held, it had taken every reserve in camp to keep huge salients from being driven into the southerners' defenses.

Riki sought out Nibi, his old batman. "All right, you old scavenger," he said, "what are they up to? Have you been following things?"

Nibi looked skeptically at him. "You look terrible," he said. "You were all night on the road, weren't you?" He scowled and got down the wineskin. "A stiff drink is what you need. Well, you came to the right man."

"No," Riki said with a smile. "Get me some water instead. I'll just splash my face. What is the news from the front?"

"Our runner today reported that Apophis is personally in command and full of hot air as usual, issuing challenges to our illustrious leader."

"And what has Kamose done to respond?"

"Nothing. Our mighty monarch sulks in his command tent like an old dog. Won't come out. Won't respond. Not even when Amasis prods him."

"Amasis? Is he here, too?"

"Right you are, and meddling with everything. The generals hate his guts. Even the cult's generals do, although they don't dare say so. If you ask me, judging from what happened here yesterday in camp, there's a big blowup coming between him and the king."

Riki grinned. "Now *that's* good news."

"Right. They got to bellowing at each other like fishwives. Amasis called him a damn coward. Kamose came within one blink of the eye of putting a knife in Amasis's belly."

"Well," Riki said, "I'm coming back at an interesting time. It ought to prove quite entertaining." He began to change into fresh military clothing.

Nibi stared at him. "There's something different about you, sir," he remarked. "I don't know what it is."

Riki grinned again. "There's something different about you too, you insubordinate old scoundrel. You called me 'sir.' Surely the end of the world is at hand."

"My mistake. It won't happen again. Here's your sword belt, sir. Let me help you."

Amasis and Djoser stood atop a rise looking down on the fighting. Rasmik's Hai soldiers had just driven Kamose's Egyptian flank back to the edge of the palm grove; on the other flank there was fierce fighting down a long line of olive trees. "They need a leader," Amasis said with an angry scowl. "If only that wound in your leg were healed!"

"I'd be no good on the line," Djoser retorted in deep disgust, spitting angrily on the ground at his feet. "You have to be agile, with things moving that quickly."

A runner came up from the rear. "Sir!" he said, stopping, saluting stiffly. "Someone in the rear has spotted General Riki."

"Ah!" Djoser exchanged glances with Amasis. "Two birds with one stone, perhaps! If he can rally them today . . ." He turned to the runner. "Well, what are you standing there for?"

The man's rigid military stance held. "Sir! The same person also spotted Makare in camp. Recently arrived, sir, and suiting up for battle."

Again the exchange of surprised glances. "Suiting up?" Djoser said. "Is this your doing, Amasis? I can't remember the last time Makare—"

"It's the first I've heard of it. But maybe this can work to our advantage." Then he remembered that they were not alone. "That'll be all," he said to the runner, who took off promptly. Amasis watched him go, then said, "I've been thinking. Kamose has become a liability ever since he ran from the field. Perhaps it's time for a change. With Makare here, we can arrange something."

"And ignore that prophecy Apophis sets such store by?" Djoser asked.

"Sheer superstitious blather. The Hai believe it, to be sure, but if we kill Kamose, people will forget about the failed prophecy, and life will go on. People have short memories."

"You think audaciously, I'll say that for you."

"I'm tired of waiting. The time has come."

Only when he was dressed and ready for battle did Riki spot Makare across the camp, belting on his own sword. He winked at Nibi and set out across the camp at an unhurried pace. When he came within earshot of Makare he said, "You! What are you doing here? No civilians allowed in camp!"

Makare glared at him. "I've come to fight. Orders from Amasis."

"Since when does Amasis give military orders? He's getting a bit too full of himself these days, and you can tell him I said so. I'd tell him myself, but I'll be where the fighting is, and that's the last place in the world I'll be likely to find Amasis."

Makare's eyes narrowed. "The general speaks very boastfully today," he said. "His courage and his arrogance seem to come and go. I remember a time when the general himself was not seen on the front lines for quite some time." His smile was insulting. "While the others fought, the general drank himself into oblivion nightly in the stews of Thebes."

This was tantamount to outright challenge, but Riki chose not to take it seriously. "We have all had our ups and downs, it appears. I can remember when a certain assassin, himself the dregs of an inferior race, would back down before a woman half his size, afraid to look her in the eye and so frightened that he could not hold his water."

Satisfied, he waited patiently to see if he had provoked a fight. He had not, so he continued, "All right, we have each had his moment of offensive bluster." He grinned, a man beyond fear or anger. "Now we can go to the ranks. We are both, I take it, here to kill Shepherds and contribute what we can to a victory. Let's not try to get in each other's way."

"Suit yourself," Makare said. But there was something in his glance as he turned away.

Riki thought: *He will not face me down. But the moment my back is turned—*

Makare joined Elset's troop, while Riki joined Kamose's. There was at midmorning a lull in the fighting, and the line had held. Riki took the occasion to visit the command tent.

He barged in without announcing himself. "I'm back," he said, then stopped and stared at the morose figure sitting at the command table.

He thought: *Gods! Kamose looks just like his father, the way Apophis did the day we drove him from Thebes, when his nerve broke, and he ran from the field!*

Shocked, he took a seat beside the king. "Kamose," he said, "what's wrong with you? You ought to be out there on the line! Do you have any idea what impact this has on your army, their knowing they're putting their lives on the line while you cower inside here?"

The word *cower* was designed to provoke. But Kamose just stared off into space. "I cast the bones," he said dully. "The portents for today are bad. Perhaps tomorrow."

Riki thought: *Tomorrow?* Then he vividly remembered his own vision. "Look, man, you don't have to fight if you're convinced it's a bad day for you. But I can remember a time when you scorned casting bones or listening to the astrologers. I can remember a time when you were the bravest man in Egypt. What has happened to the Kamose who drove the Hai out of Thebes?"

"A bad day. All the signs are wrong."

"Gods, man! What have they done to you, these third-rate sorcerers? They've put a spell on you, Kamose! Come out of this hiding place, into the open air where it's healthy!"

Outside, as if by design, there was the sound of commotion. There was a bellow of rage: *"They're attacking! Everyone in place, now!"*

Riki pounded on the table. "Do you hear that?" he asked enthusiastically. "That sort of thing used to be mother's milk to you! Where has he gone, the Kamose who used to leap into battle singing? You could look any man in the eye and match swords with anyone in the world. But these people—they've unmanned you, with their idiotic cult. Get rid of them! They've no real hold on you! Come on, man! Come outside! The day is young! There's a war to be won!"

But now Kamose's eyes met his for the first time. And they were the eyes of Apophis—mad, haunted, frightened. Father and son had changed places!

VI

Riki's return to the army was greeted with cheers from the rank and file and with reserve from their officers. Driven back by the first Hai rush, the Egyptians rallied and held firm, then counterattacked as if new strength had suddenly flowed into their right arms. Riki in particular felt like a new man; he had stopped caring what became of him, knowing that he would survive the day.

There was little time to think as he cut and hacked and parried and stabbed; just once, as he caught a quick breath and looked around him, his thoughts wandered to the morrow: Just what form would the next day's climactic events take? Would the Hai be defeated at last? Would he, Riki, be called upon to face Apophis in Kamose's place? And when he did, what would happen?

Then there was no time for thought. To his right a Hai sortie suddenly drove a wedge into the Egyptian lines, and both his own units and Elset's, to his right flank, converged on the newly created salient to crush the Shepherd-led mercenaries.

To his surprise he got a second wind, and now he battled his way to the center of the fray. Two Hai soldiers struck at him simultaneously from both sides; he disarmed one with a flip of the wrist, sending the enemy's sword flying, and with a graceful continuation of the same motion he hacked mightily at the other man's forearm, drawing blood and sending his enemy's sword clattering to the ground. He turned back to the first man and stabbed him in the throat with great ease and accuracy; finding the second still holding his arm, paralyzed with pain, he sighed, stabbed, and watched his opponent fall.

A growl of rage sounded to his right rear! He spun and found himself facing a blood-spattered, feral-eyed Makare, sword at the ready.

He blinked, then recovered and locked eyes with Makare. "We're supposed to be on the same side," he said, his voice calm but penetrating. "But strike if you will. I'm your man. Now is as good as any time."

Makare glared. His big hand tightened on the grip of his weapon, and he stepped back to salute with it sardonically. "Later," he promised, and turned just in time to parry a Hai guardsman's overhand stroke at his head.

By day's end the Egyptians had driven the Shepherd-led regulars and mercenaries back to the olive grove. Then, at Riki's prompting, Egyptian archers readied flaming arrows and fired volley after volley into the trees themselves, burning down a grove that had stood for centuries.

Both sides watched it burn—the Hai from the heights beyond, where they had withdrawn when the fire broke out. Riki congratulated the bowmen and stood watching the Hai dispiritedly make camp as Nibi came up, bearing a skin bladder.

"There you are," Riki said. "I hope there's fresh water and not wine in that. Not that wine wouldn't be a boon after a hard day's work, but I have the feeling that this is a time when I'll really need my wits about me."

"Water it is, sir," Nibi said, "although I can supply you with the wine if you change your mind. I saw the flare-up with Makare. He came close, didn't he?"

"Yes. I don't know why he hesitated. Well, all in good time. One of these days we will cross swords, once and for all."

Nibi brought out a second skin bag and drank red wine from it. "Well, sir, you'll be doing everyone a favor if you run a sword up his—"

"On second thought, let me have a sip of wine."

"—and preferably the blade is dull and covered with horse dung." Nibi passed over the wineskin.

"I'll see what I can do," Riki said with a grin. He drank; held the wine in his mouth, spat it out, and made a sour face. "Gods! You used to drink better stuff than this. Have you lost your palate, you old scoundrel?"

"You used not to be so picky. Very well, I'll put in better bellywash. Just trying to save an *outnou* here and there against my old age."

Riki laughed and clapped his batman on the shoulder. When he spoke, his voice was more serious. "Old friend, enjoy the time we have together and don't count the cost. I'm a rich man. My wife was very well-to-do, as all the Children of the Lion tend to be, and she had a good business head on her shoulders. She invested my own earnings for me as well, and the investments paid off. On my return from the oasis I stopped in Thebes, spoke to the bankers, and wrote a contract or two. You're provided for on my death, and in a fashion you probably aren't expecting."

"Sir!"

"You can stop worrying about the days after retirement."

"Yes, sir."

"Do you remember that villa I bought in the hills above Thebes? The one where we took the girls from the pleasure boat, the weekend I won them and the boat in a game of senet?"

Nibi laughed. "How could I forget it, sir?"

"And quite right. I daresay the chubby twins with the matching moles on their bottoms won't forget it quickly either. I sold both of them to you. How could you turn right around and lose them to that one-eyed Lydian playing knucklebones?"

"Not my fault, sir," Nibi replied indignantly. "He cheated."

"Well, the more fool you. No matter. The villa's yours. And enough income properties to pay for its upkeep and taxes and keep you in palm wine and fat wenches until they're ready to plant you in the ground."

"Sir!" Nibi grinned, stunned. But then his face fell. "Your *will*, sir? You mean you expect to die?"

Riki thought for a moment. "We all can expect to die, my friend. But I arranged for you to own it all right now. You can retire immediately, if you like, and go live on it. Of course, if you'd like to stick with me until the present work's done, well, I wouldn't object."

Nibi stared, openmouthed; loyalty warred with a newfound

acquisitiveness. "Imagine! Me a lord of the manor! With vassals and whatever! But, no, sir. I'll see this thing through. All the way to the bitter end."

"Good," said Riki. "It won't be long." He caught the guarded glance Nibi threw him. "Oh, it's nothing like that," he lied. "I've been thinking of retiring myself."

Kamose sat alone before the pile of glowing coals. It was late. Far across the glow, Amasis and Makare huddled close together, keeping an eye on him and speaking in low voices. A runner from the pickets manning the far southeastern fringes of the camp had asked for Riki's presence an hour before, and he had not returned.

"Leave it to me," Makare urged, his eyes on the morose and withdrawn figure beyond the coals' warm circle of light. "You're right. It's time. We should have done it long ago. And after that—Riki. I have a score to settle with him."

"Not so fast," Amasis said. "Do as I say. Wait for the proper moment. It must look like an accident. Kamose, I mean. Any suspicion that we've killed the king to advance ourselves has to be avoided. But afterward, any opportunity will do where Riki is concerned, including a duel."

"I came within a heartbeat of killing him today. But everyone was looking."

"That's all right. By tomorrow this time we'll be in undisputed power. I can order his death if I want to. We've got the whole officer corps—except Elset."

"So kill Elset."

"No, not yet. We'll still have to drive the Hai out of Egypt, and we'll need him for that. With Djoser on our left, we won't need Riki. But we've nobody to replace Elset on our right. Wait a while on him. Then, when the Hai are broken and we're all-powerful, kill anyone you want. But be discreet."

"As you prefer. As long as I get to deal with Riki myself."

"Kamose first, then Riki. But wait until I give the signal. We want everything to look like it's on the up and up. All power to the goddess, the Mother of all!"

"You!" Riki said, genuinely surprised.

The figure was almost unrecognizable: skinny and starved,

and sunburnt until he looked like a Nubian. The pickets, they had said, had found him wandering, dazed and incoherent, by the near bank of the last Nile tributary before the great desert began. They had brought him to camp in the chariot, too weak to walk but clutching a leather pouch to his breast with arms that held surprising strength considering his emaciation.

Seth looked up at Riki silently with mad eyes. "Take me to Kamose," he said at last in a voice barely audible.

"Rest. Eat. Drink. There's no hurry. The morning will do."

"That's what I said back in Babylon," Seth retorted bitterly. "There would always be time. There would be time to arm the guard, to reposition the army, to make good Chalybian swords to kill Hittites with."

"*Make* Chalybian swords?" Riki said. "You really mean you went there?"

"I *am* a Chalybian. So was Teti." His face contorted with agony and guilt. "So is my son! Riki! Where is he? Where is Aset? Where is my child?"

"Safe in El-Kharga, with the Black Wind and the Desert Legion. Safe with Ebana and Weret and Tchabu and the army that awaits Kamose when he comes back upriver to pacify the Egypt he's betrayed. Safe with Neku-re—Teti's son." He smiled. There was a look of great calm, of peace, on his face at the mention of the name. "Another Child of the Lion, and a fellow worth meeting."

"Another Chalybian. I have gone halfway around the world to learn I need never have left home." There was such sadness and bitterness in his tone that Riki gave him a sharp look. "How I wish I'd never left! How I wish I'd remained true to myself, my family, my friends! Gods! I thought I was living my wildest dreams! Riches, love, fame, and power, Riki! Power to build! Power to realize my loftiest and most visionary fancies! Power to create!"

"Seth, you need rest."

He began to cry. "Ashes! Ashes and dust! Death and destruction! I killed all the people I loved there. The best friend I've ever had! The woman I loved! The man who was a father! My companions! The people of a city, a nation, who depended on me! And why? Because I forgot who I was— forgot I was a Child of the Lion, an armorer, a maker of weapons to defend liberty!"

"Seth, you're shaking. You're ill."

"Without liberty none of the rest can survive! None of it—not love, or beauty, or art, or architecture, or any of it. If you don't provide for defense first, all of it will die, as it did in Babylon! As it did in all the lands of Shinar! And all because of me!"

"Seth," Riki said gently, "please."

The sick man now fought down his tears. "Get me something to wear," he asked. "It's chilly. I swam the river. I'm cold right down to the bone. I wonder if I'm ever going to be warm again."

"When we're done, I'll take you to see Neku-re. He'll heal your ills as he healed mine." But his mind suddenly broke in: *When? On the morrow it all ends for you. Have you forgotten?* He smiled wryly. How the world did tend to tug at you when you had once accepted taking leave of it. "Now you need sleep."

"No! *No!* If I bed down, I won't be able to get back up for a day and a night. I haven't slept for I don't know how long. I have to see Kamose." The emaciated hands tugged at the leather bag he had steadfastly refused to give up. "Now."

Riki stared. "I'm finally beginning to understand," he said. "Babylon fell months ago. You've been wandering ever since then."

"I worked my way from Ur down the coast, and around the coast that borders the Great Desert, on a pirate vessel. We stopped in Punt to trade stolen booty for supplies. I could not find all the ingredients for good Chalybian iron. But the Great Desert is full of iron fallen from the sky, and I bought some of it. It is strange material. Other items made of lesser iron stick to it. It is almost as though it calls to them and hugs them to its bosom."

"And from this you made—"

Seth's weak hands clawed at the pouch. He reached inside and withdrew a short black dagger. "For one thing I made this for you. May it call your enemies to it as well, and hug them hungrily to its bosom."

Riki held the thing up to the light. "Gods! It's a masterpiece!"

Seth closed the bag and hugged it to his scrawny chest. "No, I'm no Belsunu. But it will do the job. Stick close to Kamose! The prophecy has to be fulfilled!" He lowered his voice, and it was full of weariness and bitterness and a bleak and pitiless self-knowledge. "Well, perhaps it will. Take me to Kamose." His eyes, dark and haunted, sought Riki's. Highlights from the campfire danced crazily in them. "Now!" he said.

VII

When Rasmik, Apophis's ranking Hai general, arrived at dawn at campaign headquarters, his uniform spotless and body armor brightly shining in the pale light of dawn, the king was already dressed, fierce confidence glowing in his eyes.

"Today, Rasmik!" he enthused. "Today's the day! I can feel it! I'll finally crush them and cross swords once and for all with that craven son of mine!" He grinned and drew his iron sword, making passes in the air right and left.

"One may hope, Your Majesty," Rasmik said cautiously. "You know the astrologers did not predict anything so specific, they only said this was a day of major conflict, one in which the fortunes of those of Hai blood would prevail." His eyes were cool, hooded.

Apophis cut, parried an imaginary stroke by an imaginary enemy, and stabbed into space. "I know, I know. One may explain these messages in a variety of ways, of course, but I choose to interpret it as I told you. I feel good, Rasmik! I feel strong! Brave! Powerful!"

"All the better, sire, if we are to fight today. If you fight as you did yesterday, your prediction may well come true. I doubt, however, that Kamose will come out of his tent today. You may be disappointed in that regard, and I'm just trying to prepare you for that contingency."

"I appreciate that," Apophis said expansively, "but mark my words: The day is ours. It's in the air." He strode outside and to the top of the rise on which the command tents stood. "I don't want to fight in the destroyed grove. How can we maneuver things into the open?"

"The best way, sire, would be to give ground at first and lure them out into the clearing this side of the trees."

"Yes, you're quite right. Very sound, Rasmik. Give them

the illusion that they're driving us back, then hit them broadside. With the Third Troop?"

"More likely the First, sire. They're rested and strong. The Third has borne the brunt of every attack this week."

Apophis cut the air impatiently. His constant use of the heavy sword had given him great strength in his arm, and since the pivotal moment when his son had run from the field, fleeing his attack, Apophis had grown steadily more confident. "Very well," he agreed. "The First it is. Deploy them."

"I still haven't found out who the stranger is," Makare complained. "He just turned up late last night. Riki moved him into his own tent. And none of the older hands here have seen him, just the new recruits."

"He's almost as dark as a Nubian," Amasis said, "but his features are Egyptian. Or Shinarian. And he's so emaciated."

"Well, he's in with Kamose now," Makare said. "I'd give a lot to know what they're saying, but I can't get close. The one guarding the doorway now is Riki's batman. They've even shooed Kamose's new batman away."

Seth now wore the uniform of a foot soldier—a simple tunic and sandals, which Riki had borrowed for him, minus all accoutrements of warfare. Over his shoulder he carried a leather bag.

Because Riki and Kamose had been arguing, Seth had stood silently and watched from a dark corner of the tent. Last night it had been too late for seeing Kamose, so he and Riki had waited until the dawn. But as things had turned out, last night might have been more to their advantage: Although Kamose had retired early, he had not been able to sleep. Now, red-eyed, haggard-looking, he stood, weaving slightly, listening to Riki.

"My suspicion is they won't attack," Riki was saying. "They'll let us come through the grove, and while we're weaving our way through the stumps, they'll have the bowmen hit us. Just beyond the grove the spearmen will come at us with pikes."

Kamose was beginning to pay attention. "Pikes. I see. You're saying they want us free of the grove. Then they'll fall on us, eh?"

Riki nodded. "We already know Apophis himself will be leading the attack. But one of their infantry troops is deployed to one side, as if defending a flank we show no intention of attacking. That's strange. What do you make of that, Kamose? Tactical matters were your strongest point. What would you do if you were Apophis just now?"

It was the right technique to draw him out. Kamose closed his eyes. "Let me see now. . . . Yes, I think I'd draw us up the hill a bit at a time, giving ground, and then . . . look, what flank was that other unit on?"

"Their right. That'd be the First Troop." Again the maneuver, drawing him out. "Why?"

Suddenly Seth spoke. "Once up the hill, on the slope, where you're more vulnerable than they are, Apophis will hit you with the First. Depend on it." His voice was hoarse, rasping. "The only way to defend against Apophis is to stop dead just past the grove, deploy your own archers, and force him to move, not you."

Kamose squinted his eyes and scowled. "Who are you to give me advice?" he asked angrily. "I don't even know you. Mind your own business."

Seth ignored the king's command. "There's one way to get Apophis to fight where you're evenly matched. And it has the additional advantage of temporarily immobilizing that First Troop."

Kamose's glare was deadly. "Since when are you suddenly the expert around here?"

"Call him out," Seth asserted.

"Call him—! Who?" Kamose demanded, exasperated.

"Apophis. Issue a challenge. Meet him in no-man's-land, between the armies. You, personally."

"Insolent son of a whore," Kamose growled in a voice filled with danger. "Riki, get him out of my sight, before I—"

"Oh, I'll leave," Seth offered wearily. "I have little genuine interest in whether you face him down or not. I simply came here to complete an obligation that I had shirked and paid dearly for. Now I have to make good on it. Do as you like with what I've brought you. Be brave or cowardly. Fight or run. It matters little. I'm done here. My duties are over, and yours are just beginning."

Kamose stared.

"Riki," Seth said, "work on him. There was some good in him once. Perhaps there can be again. He has to be pried free of the cult, but once that's happened and you have the Hai on the run, see if you can turn him around."

He reached for the bag around his shoulder.

Kamose grabbed for his sword, a gleaming bronze weapon hanging from a tooled belt.

Seth drew a wrapped package out of his bag and tossed it contemptuously at Kamose's feet. "There it is," he said. "It'll kill your man for you—that is, if you've got the mettle to wield it."

Kamose looked quickly at Riki, who nodded, then sheathed his sword, picked up the parcel, and started to unwrap it. "What's going on here?"

Its weight betrayed it, then its shape. He slid the sword out of the wrappings and gaped at the weapon. "Riki, who is this man?" He held up the black sword. "Splendid," he said. "You! What do you want for this?"

"It's yours," Seth said. "Just win us a war with it. Let me caution you, Kamose, about playing with life. It's serious stuff. Take it from me, whose folly destroyed a society far better than any on the shores of the Nile. It's time you grew up! It's never too late to change. Riki, I'm going to Thebes. Be healthy and prosper."

He said this last as he left the tent. Kamose, still preoccupied with inspecting the weapon, did not notice his departure at first. Then he looked up. "Riki! Stop that man! This is wonderful! I've never held anything like it!"

"It ought to be," Riki said. "It's your Sword of Glory. That was my wife's kinsman, Seth. You can't imagine what horrors it has cost him to make that sword and bring it here." His voice took on a harder edge. "All the more reason for me to speak my mind." Kamose looked startled. Riki went on, passion ringing in his voice. "If you have not used it on Apophis before nightfall, I vow I will kill you with it."

He turned on one heel and strode out, his steps heavy and deliberate.

Seth's stride lengthened as he picked up his pace, spurred on by anger and disgust. He was almost running by the time he came to the rear line of pickets, where a woman in a robe and head covering was arguing animatedly with the guards.

Seth paid no attention as he approached, but the woman's voice sounded vaguely familiar. ". . . can't keep me from him! Let go of me!"

Seth stopped. "Let her go," he rasped. "Don't you recognize your queen when you see her, you fools?"

"Queen?" echoed one of the guards, immediately standing aside. The other, however, held her fast from the other side until Mara bit him on the arm.

"Little vix—" The guard held his injured arm, looking up at her. "Queen?" he asked sarcastically. "Dressed like this?"

"Hello, Mara," Seth said. "It's me, Seth. I've come back from the dead. Almost literally."

"Seth?" she said. "Gods! What has happened to you?"

"It's too long a story," he answered tiredly. "I'm going to Thebes. I just learned about my child. I'm going to find Aset. Don't bother Kamose just now. He's busy with Riki, who's trying to prod him out of his lethargy. Kamose!" he said disgustedly. "How did you people ever allow him to degenerate so terribly?"

"*Allow* him? How dare you suggest? . . ."

"Sorry. It's none of my affair. It's in Riki's hands now. And, I suppose, Apophis's. I have responsibilities that I've neglected, and I'm going to go do something about them. Good-bye."

"Seth! Wait!"

Both Amasis and Makare pulled at his arms, but Kamose yanked free. "Step back, curse you!" he demanded. He turned to face them: the two cult leaders, Riki, and Riki's batman, Nibi. "I'll personally kill the first man who tries to stop me!" He turned toward the enemy lines and bellowed out: "*Apophis!* I've come for you! Come face your son in single combat! Father, dear! Stand before me!"

"What's happened?" Amasis asked. "He wasn't like this yesterday."

"The drug," Makare whispered. "It's worn off. He's been sitting in his tent, not taking it. And that sword in his hand is iron. The stranger must have brought it!"

"This isn't what we had planned," Amasis hissed. "This could end disastrously. Stop him. Now!"

Makare's hand edged toward his weapon. Kamose's back was to both of them.

Riki's eyes narrowed. "Better put that away."

Makare ignored him. Riki moved forward. Behind him, Nibi hurriedly limped away toward the armory.

"*Now!*" Amasis shouted.

Makare sprang forward, sword in hand aimed at Kamose's unprotected back!

Riki lunged toward Makare, grabbed him by the tunic, and spun him around. Makare's powerful backswing, fast almost beyond vision, caught Riki broadside in the temple and knocked him to his knees. Dazed, Riki got his hands under him and pushed his way to his feet, but there was something wrong with his balance. He fumbled for his sword, but as he did, Amasis came from the side and hacked at his arm with a dagger he had hidden inside his garment. The cut drew blood. Riki switched his sword to his other hand and parried a furious attack from Makare, giving ground. Amasis fell back as the two fenced, circling behind Riki.

But Riki could not get Makare in focus. The blow seemed to have addled him. Everything was gray before him. He could make out a moving, bulky figure. Riki waved his sword blindly before him, trying to focus on Makare.

Makare attacked.

Riki parried the thrust by instinct, then grabbed Makare's sword arm in a strong grip. He drew back, then lunged at Makare with his sword, but Makare pulled Riki off balance, and the strike went wide.

Makare gave ground, cursed gutturally, then laughed at Riki's clumsy attack. He ripped his arm free and backhanded the sweat from his eyes.

Amasis was in position behind Riki. "Now! Quickly!" he urged.

Riki lunged forward, still somewhat dazed. Makare parried, then turned his own blade down. It caught Riki in the stomach and ran him through!

Riki staggered back, narrowly missing the knife Amasis aimed at him. Makare came on ever more viciously, as, behind Riki, Amasis readied another stroke.

There was a sharp *twang* as a long, powerful, Nubian-made arrow buried itself in Makare's chest. His eyes went blank; then, his face a mask of pain, he pitched forward heavily onto his face.

Amasis rushed forward, only to hear, in acid tones, the voice of Riki's batman, Nibi. "All right! Stop where you are!

Your friend died quickly, and so will you. Just because I'm too old and lame to fight doesn't mean I can't still handle a bow. My arrows are poisoned. Cobra venom guarantees a quick death."

Amasis's eyes shone with horror. He backed away, his eyes on the arrow. "Whatever you say," he agreed. "Only point that thing somewhere else."

Riki staggered forward and fell heavily on his side.

Nibi said, "You! Amasis! Get out of my sight!" And only when Amasis raced away did Nibi drop the bow and rush to Riki's side.

VIII

"Sir!" Nibi said. "Are you all right?" But then he saw clearly the location and extent of the wound. "Oh, gods!" he moaned. "What am I going to do?"

Riki's eyes fluttered open. He tried to raise his head, then fell back. "Nibi," he whispered, "it's all right. You c-can't help. But please, stay with me."

Nibi's eyes were wet. "Stay with you, sir? They'll have to pry me away. Oh, sir, if I'd only gone back for the bow sooner!"

Riki put a palsied hand on his arm. "Kamose," he said. "Did he escape them?"

"Yes, sir. He's out in the field, between the armies, fighting Apophis. He seems his old self, sir. What happened?"

Riki's gasp for breath was like a weak sigh. "The weapon he's using . . . it's the Sword of Glory."

Nibi did not understand at first. Finally it hit him. "Sir! You mean . . . that was what the stranger brought with him from the desert?"

"He's no stranger," Riki said in a voice grown steadily weaker. "He's my wife's kinsman Seth."

Nibi examined the wound and gave up hope. Yet his master looked so peaceful and unafraid. "Well, sir, whatever it was, this isn't the same Kamose who's been sulking in his tent."

"Good. Ah, Nibi, my friend, I'd thought to do great

deeds today. . . . Instead, here I lie, dying." He struggled for breath.

"You stopped him, sir, from killing the king. That'll prove to be a very big accomplishment indeed, sir, if the king kills his father and wins the day." He tried to smile through tears. "As for the rest, sir, well, maybe the gods had a part for *me* to play, too." He did smile now, and the tears came in a rush. "It felt good being a soldier again, sir. Although I wish I'd put an arrow in that Amasis while nobody was looking, sir."

He looked up. "Sir! Here's the queen." He motioned her down beside him and turned away to blow his nose loudly. "Quickly, ma'am; we haven't much time, I think."

Mara leaned far out over Riki's face. "Riki, can you hear me?"

The lips trembled. "Y-yes."

She lifted one of his hands and held it to her cheek. "Riki, did Kamose do this?"

Nibi broke in. "Oh, no, ma'am! It was Makare. My master saved the king! Makare was going to kill him."

Riki spoke. "Mara, he's coming back to himself. Help him. Promise me."

She kissed the unfeeling hand in hers. "Yes, my darling, I promise." And then she found she could not speak and sat looking down at him, holding his hand to her cheek.

"Tell me how the fight goes," Riki asked.

Nibi blinked the tears away and took over. "Well, the king—Kamose—he's on the advance. Very strong, very confident. Apophis is backing off, afraid to strike. The one time I saw him thrust, Kamose almost disarmed him. He looks nervous, sir. Wait, sir! Kamose is attacking, going at him furiously! Sir, it looks like *you* in action! Apophis is falling back! He can't defend himself!"

He looked down, then looked at Mara's stricken face. He looked down again. "Sir?" he ventured in a child's hurt voice. "*Sir!*"

Apophis's knees seemed weak. He stood in a defensive posture, the sword in his hand wavering back and forth. "You're no offspring of mine," he said in a voice full of pain and resentment. "You're evil! I've heard about that cult you belong to. You've sold your soul to that damned goddess."

"You're wrong," Kamose said. "I'm on the verge of getting it back for the first time in quite a while. Come, Father. Let's not dawdle. Show me the man you used to be, back when I was a child, before you started killing innocent boys out of abject fear."

Somehow the calm reasonableness of Kamose's tone struck fear into Apophis's heart. "I . . . I'm not fighting you today," he blustered. "There's some sort of spell on you."

"You have no choice. Fight or die stabbed in the back as you run. I don't care how, but today you die, the last of the Shepherd Kings. Today we begin driving the Hai into the desert to die. Come, Father. End your life like a man."

For answer Apophis drew on hidden reserves. With a roar he charged, stabbing and thrusting. Kamose caught the great hacking blows in glancing parries, turning them away. For a moment he stood his ground; then the sheer fury of Apophis's attack drove him back.

As his retreat moved him ever nearer the charred olive grove, he stumbled over an exposed root and fell to one knee!

Apophis raised his sword high and swept it down, but Kamose held up Seth's sword at right angles to the blow.

Apophis's blade fell with crushing power directly on his son's sword and broke in two!

Apophis fell back. He stared unbelieving at the ruined blade of the weapon in his hand. "Sorcery!" he cried out.

Kamose leapt to his feet. "Yes," he said. "The age-old sorcery of the master armorer. The sorcery of Chalybia, which drove the Hai from Lake Van and the high hills. The sorcery of the Children of the Lion!"

His sword arm rose high. Apophis's broken weapon fell at his feet. His eyes were glazed with horror.

The Sword of Glory slashed down, inspiring a roar from the armies on the two sides of the battleground!

Kamose bent over the fallen body. When he arose, his hand held high a grisly, blood-spattered trophy of the day's fighting: one that stared horribly with eyes that did not see.

"Ma'am!" Nibi said. "Did you see? He's won, ma'am! Oh, if only my master could have seen it!"

Mara had closed Riki's eyes. Now she stood and looked around. "I think that in a way he did," she said in a soft voice. "I thank you for avenging his death—for killing Makare. You'll be rewarded."

"Ma'am!" he said, indignant. "I want no reward. Besides, I know that my master provided for me handsomely." He lowered his voice. "It's all right, ma'am. I know you mean well. You loved him too, didn't you?"

"Yes," she confessed. Her face hardened. "Enough to honor my promise to go back to my husband and help him." She straightened her back and stood proudly. "You know, don't you, that he saw this all coming? All but the details."

"In a way, ma'am. He didn't tell me the whole thing, but I guessed at what he didn't say. He was looking forward to death, I think."

Mara thought about the matter, and a bitter smile played on her full lips. "He's with *her* now, as he knew he'd be." She sighed. "I wish there was someone who felt that way about me." Her words were full of a weary self-knowledge. "I wish there were someone *I* felt that way about. . . ."

Nibi shaded his eyes and peered out over the battlefield. "Look, ma'am! The Shepherds! They're running from the field! And our men are falling on them like lions on a flock of lambs. Ah, it's a great day, ma'am! A great day!"

Mara looked down at the fallen hero. "Is it?" she asked. "Is it really?"

But then she squared her shoulders, took a deep breath, and stood for a moment looking, as once she had done before, as regal as the queen she was. "Yes," she decided. "It is. And if Riki was right, and Kamose is himself again . . . he'll need help. Amasis still lives, and while he does, no man is safe, not even the man who wielded the Sword of Glory and killed the last of the Shepherd Kings and drove the usurpers out of Egypt. I *will* go back to him, and I'll watch his back now that Riki can no longer do it for him."

Nibi's voice held a note of sadness as he said, "He seemed a bit disappointed at the end, my master did. He'd been promised a chance to do a great deed, and he saw what he did as a small one."

"Well, he knows better now," Mara said. "The days of the large single deed done by a solitary man are gone. The cleansing of Egypt will require an enormous number of small deeds, accomplished by ordinary people lacking great pretensions." She smiled and put a hand on Nibi's shoulder. "People like you, my friend." He shook his head self-deprecatingly.

"You think you're no hero, but if we're to prevail at last, it's going to take a lot of people like you."

She gazed out over the field. She could not see her husband; perhaps he was at the head of the army as it tested its new strength, smiting Hai and mercenary alike with renewed fury, driving the enemy into the desert.

Well, *he* would be no hero either. Just another poor flawed mortal who had let his life take a wrong turn but had come to his senses before it was too late. It would have to do. The job was a long one: The Hai had to be eliminated forever from Egyptian soil; then the return would come, and the purging and the purification of the country and the countrymen's hearts. Only then would it be time for a real hero, a great man equal to Egypt's needs.

Suddenly she found herself thinking of the great secret Baliniri had told her, after first swearing her to total silence—a Habiru child would be given to the princess Thermutis, a child who both the court astrologers and the clairvoyant Levi had said would grow up to be one to change the course of history. A child born to fulfill the prophecies of both camps! She had marveled at Baliniri's audacity, tempting the gods so, both those of Egypt and the One God of the Habiru. Was it safe, a meddling layman interfering in their mighty affairs this way?

Baliniri had laughed, and on a sudden impulse hugged her comfortingly, like a father. "I asked Jochebed that," he had said. "She smiled, as weak and exhausted as she was, and took me down a peg. '*You don't suppose you're doing this of your own free will?*' she asked. '*God's hand is upon you, Egyptian. You could not raise your arm now, or turn your head, without His wanting you to.*'"

"What did you say to that?" Mara had asked. But he had only winked at her and smiled. In that enigmatic smile was something of the peace and the happiness she had seen on Riki's face during the last night she had spent with him.

Activity in the field had ended, and all of a sudden there came up from the Egyptian force a great echoing shout of victory, which rang in the air, grew, swelled, and shook her very soul. "Long live Egypt! Long live Kamose—Lord of Two Lands!"

And in Athribis, Ah-Hotep, at her daughter's bedside, looked at Thermutis's sad, pale face and reached for the limp, fine-boned hand on the coverlet.

"My darling," she said in a low, comforting voice, "I know how you must feel. I too have lost a love and a child. But as a princess of the blood, it was my duty—as it is yours now—to carry on."

Thermutis, staring at the wall, did not reply.

"I have arranged for you to go to your little cove for some fresh air. Dangle your feet in the water, if you like. The sooner you return to your daily routine, the better you will feel."

Ah-Hotep clapped her hands, and two sturdy servants came in from the anteroom of the princess's quarters, bearing a litter. She stood aside as Thermutis was carefully transferred from the bed.

After the servants had carried Thermutis from the room, followed by her four handmaids, Ah-Hotep waited several minutes, then walked quickly down the hall to her own apartment, where Baliniri awaited her.

"It is time," she said, her heart thudding. "Tell Miriam to put Moses in the basket."

Epilogue

The wind had died down to a mere whisper overhead.
The dimly glowing coals at the old man's feet left his face
barely visible. Somewhere a baby cried and was silenced by
its mother, who put the child to her breast.

"So perished the last of the Shepherd Kings," intoned the
Teller of Tales. "So died the tyrant Apophis at the hands of a
new king of the Two Lands, who bore the fabled Sword of
Glory. And with no leader, the Hai were driven into the
desert to die forever as a nation.

"And, victorious, bearing the weapon Seth had made for
him, Kamose returned home to face the wrath of the idolators,
the traitors, the servants of the dread goddess, to compete
against them for power in the lands beside the Nile.

"In the South, forewarned of the dangers facing Kamose
as he returned to win back the Egypt he had all but lost, the
free peoples of the Red Lands withdrew into the waterless
vastness west of the Nile, where Teti's women and the Black

Wind joined the emissaries of Nubia and planned resistance, in the event of Kamose's fall.

"The years came and went," he told the gathering, "the old orders passed, and the elderly died away. But the young grew to maturity and fulfilled the promise of their potential. The army of Egypt passed into the able hands of a great leader hardly more than a boy but with unsurpassed cunning and strength . . . a soldier greater than Baliniri or Baka, even in his youth, and fit to lead any army in the world against any enemy."

There was an expectant murmur from the crowd. The old man silenced it with a wave of his bony hand. "But," he added, pausing for a meaningful moment, "a soldier born to move in two worlds and to follow a strange and fateful destiny."

He paused, and the murmur rose again. They knew. They knew the name he had yet to speak. They leaned forward.

"Imagine," he proposed, "a prince who rejects his proper place, exchanging riches for poverty. Imagine a born soldier who lays down arms and never picks them up again, although the might of Egypt rises against him. Imagine a conqueror who refuses a crown, or a strong man throwing in his lot with the weak. I will tell of him tomorrow."

The huddled group cried out as a single voice: "Moses! Prince Moses! Moses the Deliverer!"

The old man bowed, spread his hands, and backed away into the shadows. "Tomorrow," he promised. "Tomorrow."

"FROM THE PRODUCER OF WAGONS WEST COMES YET ANOTHER EXPLOSIVE SAGA OF LEGENDARY COURAGE AND UNFORGETTABLE LOVE"

CHILDREN OF THE LION

☐	26912	Children of the Lion #1	$4.50
☐	26971	The Shepherd Kings #2	$4.50
☐	26769	Vengeance of the Lion #3	$4.50
☐	26594	The Lion In Egypt #4	$4.50
☐	26885	The Golden Pharaoh #5	$4.50
☐	25872	Lord of the Nile #6	$3.95
☐	26325	The Prophecy #7	$4.50
☐	26800	Sword of Glory #8	$4.50

Prices and availability subject to change without notice.

Buy them at your local bookstore or use this convenient coupon for ordering:

Bantam Books, Inc., Dept. LE5, 414 East Golf Road, Des Plaines, Ill. 60016

Please send me the books I have checked above. I am enclosing $_____ (please add $1.50 to cover postage and handling). Send check or money order—no cash or C.O.D.s please.

Mr/Ms _____

Address _____

City/State _____ Zip_____

LE5—10/87

Please allow four to six weeks for delivery. This offer expires 4/88.

★ WAGONS WEST ★

A series of unforgettable books that trace the lives of a dauntless band of pioneering men, women, and children as they brave the hazards of an untamed land in their trek across America. This legendary caravan of people forge a new link in the wilderness. They are Americans from the North and the South, alongside immigrants, Blacks, and Indians, who wage fierce daily battles for survival on this uncompromising journey—each to their private destinies as they fulfill their greatest dreams.

☐ 26822	INDEPENDENCE! #1	$4.50
☐ 26162	NEBRASKA! #2	$4.50
☐ 26242	WYOMING! #3	$4.50
☐ 26072	OREGON! #4	$4.50
☐ 26070	TEXAS! #5	$4.50
☐ 26377	CALIFORNIA! #6	$4.50
☐ 26546	COLORADO! #7	$4.50
☐ 26069	NEVADA! #8	$4.50
☐ 26163	WASHINGTON! #9	$4.50
☐ 26073	MONTANA! #10	$4.50
☐ 26184	DAKOTA! #11	$4.50
☐ 26521	UTAH! #12	$4.50
☐ 26071	IDAHO! #13	$4.50
☐ 26367	MISSOURI! #14	$4.50
☐ 27141	MISSISSIPPI! #15	$4.50
☐ 25247	LOUISIANA! #16	$4.50
☐ 25622	TENNESSEE! #17	$4.50
☐ 26022	ILLINOIS! #18	$4.50

Prices and availability subject to change without notice.

Buy them at your local bookstore or use this convenient coupon for ordering:

Bantam Books, Inc., Dept. LE, 414 East Golf Road, Des Plaines, Ill. 60016

Please send me the books I have checked above. I am enclosing $_____ (please add $1.50 to cover postage and handling). Send check or money order —no cash or C.O.D.s please.

Mr/Mrs/Miss _____

Address _____

City _____ State/Zip _____

LE—10/87

Please allow four to six weeks for delivery. This offer expires 4/88.

**FROM THE PRODUCER OF WAGONS WEST
AND THE KENT FAMILY CHRONICLES—
A SWEEPING SAGA OF WAR AND HEROISM
AT THE BIRTH OF A NATION.**

THE WHITE INDIAN SERIES

Filled with the glory and adventure of the colonization
of America, here is the thrilling saga of the new frontier's
boldest hero and his family. Renno, born to white parents but raised by Seneca Indians, becomes a leader in
both worlds. THE WHITE INDIAN SERIES chronicles the
adventures of Renno, his son Ja-gonh, and his grandson
Ghonkaba, from the colonies to Canada, from the South
to the turbulent West. Through their struggles to tame a
savage continent and their encounters with the powerful men and passionate women in the early battles for
America, we witness the events that shaped our future
and forged our great heritage.

☐	24650	White Indian #1	$3.95
☐	25020	The Renegade #2	$3.95
☐	24751	War Chief #3	$3.95
☐	24476	The Sachem #4	$3.95
☐	25154	Renno #5	$3.95
☐	25039	Tomahawk #6	$3.95
☐	25589	War Cry #7	$3.95
☐	25202	Ambush #8	$3.95
☐	23986	Seneca #9	$3.95
☐	24492	Cherokee #10	$3.95
☐	24950	Choctaw #11	$3.95
☐	25353	Seminole #12	$3.95
☐	25868	War Drums #13	$3.95

Prices and availability subject to change without notice.

Bantam Books, Inc., Dept. LE3, 414 East Golf Road, Des Plaines. Ill. 60016
Please send me the books I have checked above. I am enclosing $_____
(please add $1.50 to cover postage and handling). Send check or money
—no cash or C.O.D.s please.
Mr/Mrs/Miss _____
Address _____
City _____ State/Zip _____

LE3—7/87
Please allow four to six weeks for delivery. This offer expires 1/88.

Special Offer
Buy a Bantam Book
for only 50¢.

Now you can have Bantam's catalog filled with hundreds of titles plus take advantage of our unique and exciting bonus book offer. A special offer which gives you the opportunity to purchase a Bantam book for only 50¢. Here's how!

By ordering any five books at the regular price per order, you can also choose any other single book listed (up to a $5.95 value) for just 50¢. Some restrictions do apply, but for further details why not send for Bantam's catalog of titles today!

Just send us your name and address and we will send you a catalog!

BANTAM BOOKS, INC.
P.O. Box 1006, South Holland, Ill. 60473

Mr./Mrs./Ms. _____
(please print)

Address _____

City _____ State _____ Zip _____
FC(A)—10/87
Please allow four to six weeks for delivery.